HELLFALL

A NOVEL

JAY GOULD

CASTLE BRIDGE MEDIA
DENVER, COLORADO, USA

CASTLE BRIDGE MEDIA
Denver, Colorado

Cover photo by Nima Mohammadi/Unsplash
This photo has been modified.

This book is a work of fiction. Names, characters, business, events, and incidents are the products of the authors' imaginations. Any resemblance to actual persons, living or dead or actual events is purely coincidental.

HELLFALL
© 2024 Jay Gould
All rights reserved.

ISBN: 979-8-9895934-2-2

For Melinda, who gives it all meaning.

One

Northwest Tanzania, Africa

"GRAB THAT CABLE CONTROL AND hit the green button," Toby barked at the kid manning the console on the other side of the rig deck. "We got too much slack in the line. Someone's going to trip over it, or it'll foul up the drill string, goddammit."

He watched with a grimace as the kid scuttled around on the deck, trying to get his hands on everything within reach at the same time. It was clear that the kid didn't know one end of the cable rig from another.

Toby dropped his wrench onto his own console with a clang, "Jesus Christ. Here, let me do it."

He reached out and grabbed the dangling power control box as it swung past. He hit the big green button and heard the whine of the motor as the heavy cable with a length of chain attached at the end started to reel itself in like a snake getting slowly sucked into a vacuum cleaner.

The kid simply stood watching on the opposite side of the massive section of pipe hanging over the middle of the drilling floor and gulped. It was the second time in the shift that he'd failed to manage the most basic of tasks.

Toby shook his head and shot a glance over at the rig mechanic, Floyd, who looked up over the top of the cable motor he was working on and shrugged back at him. Toby gritted his teeth and tried to keep his temper in check.

Goddamn college educated Einsteins and their engineering degrees. Not one of 'em knows how to handle their own dick, let alone guide a forty-foot piece of pipe into a borehole.

All the book learning in the world didn't help you out in the field, was Toby's opinion of higher education, and he'd yet to see one of these jumped-up, paper-toting greenhorns pull his own weight the first season on a rig. In fact, he'd more often than not seen them go back to their offices in the 'States minus a finger or a hand after just a few weeks.

Still, this kid had taken everything that Toby had dished out the past two weeks of denigrating his schooling, his hometown, his family, and him, without so much as batting an eye. He just kept plugging away at it and taking all the abuse. Maybe there was some harder stuff there under that sunburnt skin, he mused.

He cleared his throat and signaled to the kid, speaking over the whine of the machinery, "Here, come over here. Let me show you this again."

The kid scooted over, wiping sweat from his brow, "Yeah, okay. Sorry about that. I didn't know how much had spooled onto the deck…"

Toby nodded, trying to keep the impatience out of his voice, "I know. It's a greenhorn habit. That console over there feels pretty big and important, doesn't it? But the real work happens out here next to the hole."

He pointed at the several metal control boxes hanging down at head-height around the drilling floor, "Use the remote boxes for delicate work."

His finger moved on to the gleaming console against the wall, "If you use the big console and focus on the numbers on that screen, you have to turn your back on the string. Those numbers don't mean shit out here; you have to feel what's going on all the time, listen for the sound the string makes, watch everything that's moving and see that it all works together."

The kid nodded, eyes big, clearly intent on Toby's words. The grizzled old chief engineer smiled to himself, Maybe there's hope for this one; the kid wants to learn.

He grabbed the kid's glove, "Here, put your hand on the rail."

He guided the kid's hand down and set it on the metal bar separating the thrumming mass of cables, wires and piping that was the drill string from the rest of the rig. He looked up at the five-foot diameter pipe hanging above, his eyes following the metal all the way past the dormant top-drive unit that normally turned a drill pipe on shallower drills, up past the one-hundred-foot top of the derrick with its defaced sign and on up to the bronzed African sky above them.

The sign had originally read "Endeavor Engineering", but some smart-ass – and Toby hadn't found out which rig-rat it had been yet – had climbed up one night and spray-painted the ends of the capital "E"s so that it now both words started with "B"s, hence the project's new nickname, "BB", which everyone joked meant, "Big Bore". It wasn't a bad pun, considering they were on the most ambitious drilling project ever undertaken, but Toby was proud of whatever job he was contracted on, and the irreverence rankled.

Out of the corner of his eye, he could see the kid following his gaze upward and he ignored the sign again, "Now, close your eyes."

He pressed the kid's hand harder against the rail, "Feel that? That slow, deep vibration tells you the bit is making steady progress. The slurry pumped through at the bottom dampens it a bit, but it's there, you can feel it."

The kid looked doubtful, but he furrowed his brow in concentration, "How do you know it's not just the vibration from the turning rig up top when you're using it, or just from the motion of the drill string?"

"Well, we're not using the turning rig now anyway, but it wouldn't matter, because they're the same thing, see? Everything that bit is going through down there is reflected in the top-drive and in every foot of the pipe and drill string in the bore. Don't look at all the lengths of pipe, the top-drive, and the string as separate things – they're all parts of one thing. What happens at the top affects the bottom and vice-versa."

He took his hand off and looked at the kid, who was nodding, head still craned upward, and eyes closed, "It's miles down, but it's there and that's all a good driller needs to know. He can tell you what kind of rock the bit is going through by the feel and sound of the pipe and the string, can tell if the bit's getting worn or is out of alignment, you know?"

The kid kept his hand on the rail and opened his eyes, "Yeah. Yeah, I can feel it…I think." He squinted at Toby in the bright sun, "You're not just putting me on?"

Toby clapped him on the arm, "Not on your life, kid. Stick around long enough and you'll get it. We'll make a good rig-rat outta you one day. Now, as for that cable unit…" he trailed off as he thought he felt a subtle change rumble through the rail under his hand.

He cast a quick eye at the drill string cables wriggling in the air in front of them. There was something going on there…

"You two need to get a room together?" The voice came from the interior of the drilling shack, which was one of several concrete and steel buildings mounted around the rig deck.

Cab Nielson stuck his head out the door with a goofy grin on his face, "We're coming up on needing that next section of annular pipe." He pointed at the massive forty-foot length of pipe hanging over the deck.

Toby grunted, "We can see that, boss. We ain't blind," he winked at the kid, who grinned lopsidedly back, "but I'm betting it'll be one of the last we can use. We're getting close."

"Just making sure, Toby," Cab smiled and pointed over at the console to the side, "Also have a look at your readings, kid. I'm getting what looks like some slightly skewed values in here."

He ducked back into the gloom of the drilling shack. Compared to the brightness of the noonday African sun beating down on the deck, the shack doorway looked like a black hole that had swallowed the supervisor up.

"Uh huh, thought so," muttered Toby half to himself as he stalked across the floor to the console, dragging the kid with him, "A bunch of numbers on a screen don't tell you a damn thing…"

They both approached the computer console and stared at the main screen and the numbers scrolling across it. This was where the kid came in and Toby grudgingly gestured for him to take a look, "This is your job, kid. Makes no sense to me."

The kid pushed past him as Toby stood to one side and waved an arm at the two rig hands lounging in the meager shade of the drilling shack's overhanging roof. They both snapped upright and moved to the far side of the deck next to the pipe carrier and its small crane were housed. The shorter of the two, Anderson, stepped up and took a seat in the small cab of the crane.

"Temp just took another spike upwards," the kid called over his shoulder, "and there's a slight shift in angle…just about…point two-five degrees. Maybe we're into a softer area and getting a bit of play in the bit." His voice was firming up now that he was able to use the technical skills he'd been hired for and had a chance again to show off a little of his own knowledge.

Toby ignored him and used several moments to distract himself from what the kid was doing on the computer to direct the rig hands in making sure that next section of pipe was ready.

They had lifted the pipe this morning in preparation for its insertion into the borehole and it had been hanging ready for a couple of hours. Final checks were needed so that the pipe could be added to its brothers below it as smoothly and as quickly as possible.

The annular was the collar of the bore – the outer pipe through which the drill string travelled as it punched its way through the earth on its way down – and the addition of another length was a touchy, nerve-wracking process. Delays meant all sorts of problems onsite, as well as with Head Office.

Toby stared at the hanging pipe and worried. They were now so deep that the ambient temperature in the borehole was well over a hundred degrees centigrade and climbing rapidly, which meant that the pipe would always be slightly expanded from the heating and wouldn't slide downward with the drill assembly, so they had to continue the drilling through phases, changing the materials of the cooling slurry constantly to combat the rising heat.

He knew as well as anyone that it was a losing game. After just over six hundred-fifty pipe-lengths and about eight point five kilometers, or five miles of depth, they were reaching the end of their ability to keep enough of the pipe cool at the bottom. They'd soon have to proceed without using the annular pipe, which brought all sorts of other drilling considerations into play and there was the danger that even the polymers and super-cooled gas mix wouldn't be enough to keep the bit cool and it would overheat, ending their great experiment.

And what an experiment.

Endeavor was punching a hole into the earth in an attempt to go deeper than anyone else ever had. That was it; that was all. It had been a year and a half already and had cost untold millions so far.

And for no reason that he could fathom.

He lowered his eyes from the pipe and looked again at the drill string pulsing in the air before him. To the untrained eye, everything appeared normal, and they'd been making a better than average rate of cutting the last couple of days, though the overall rate of descent was down sharply from even a month ago as the heat increased, and it took longer for each section of pipe to sink into the borehole.

That meant a lot of idle drilling time, as the bit could cut faster than the pipe could cool and sink, and the Endeavor brass were always on them to abandon the piping and just let the bit cut its way down at its own pace. They were eager to make that record mark as soon as possible for some reason he could never fathom.

Endeavor was an extremely wealthy company, but even they had limits and this boondoggle of drilling deeper just for a record didn't make any sense to him. Toby knew they must think they were getting something more out of it than just the pleasure of saying they went deeper than anyone else.

He shook his head finally; didn't matter to him. This had been one of the sweetest jobs he'd ever been on with Endeavor. No pressure to deliver on promises of oil or gas, no regulatory problems with the local government, no worries about them doing any significant environmental damage – all they were doing was digging a deep hole as far as people were concerned.

The only ones suffering were the Endeavor Executive Board; they had to be under a lot of pressure themselves to give up on this expensive hole to nowhere, but he didn't care. It had been almost two years of high-paid bliss for a drilling engineer to do nothing everyday but drill deeper and deeper without people breathing down his neck.

The kid piped up from the console again, interrupting his thoughts, "Temp just took another spike upwards; almost a two-degree jump, and the angle seems to be skewing more. Up to point five-five degrees off-vertical now." He looked over at Toby with an open question on his face, Do we stop pushing?

Toby looked to the open door of the drill shack. Cab stuck his head out with a puzzled look on his face. He was the rig supervisor, but the look said, What do you think, Toby?

Toby kept one hand on the rail, feeling for any sign of a problem, and raised the other in a warding off gesture, just a minute. The supervisor was giving him the call to make; keep going and maybe damage the bit or the string or stop and try to figure out what was causing the discrepancies and fix them before going deeper.

If Toby or Cab did call a halt to things now, though, they'd have to deal with all the mechanical and logistical hassles that would entail, possibly adding days to the project. Still, in Toby's mind, days spent on restart were better than weeks or even months on recovery and repair. Either would cost time and money and would be a disaster for the man who guessed wrong, so Cab was passing the baton to Toby on this one. Perhaps not fair, but Toby was not one to back away from hard decisions.

He opened his mouth to answer Cab when two things happened at once; He saw the drill string assembly jerk to one side like someone had given it a hard yank and he felt an abrupt change in the vibration coming up through the deck rail – not a subtle change either. This felt like a sudden ramping up of the pitch. He felt a deep rumble from below, building from nothing to a shake he could feel in his chest. The rail suddenly felt like an electric razor vibrating under his hand.

He looked down through the grated decking at the degasser assembly next to the wellhead and could see it shudder. That unit alone weighed a half-ton and shouldn't have moved if a small car hit it. He shot a glance at the two-foot-wide flexible pipe leading from the wellhead to the centrifuge that separated the recovered coolant from the sand and cuttings that were brought up out of the well. It was flattening as he watched as if an invisible giant were stepping on it.

"High revolutions on the drill bit!" the kid yelled from the console, "Drastic pressure drop in the pipe!"

Shit! We cut through to somewhere, Toby thought.

He turned from the rail and ran toward the drill shack, "Shut it down! Shut it down! We hit a pocket and we're losing slurry and pressure. It'll create a vacuum and-"

"I hear you!" Cab's voice was heard over the sudden whine of the cable motor as he commanded the drill string to retract a little, hopefully saving

11

the bit from damage.

Toby reached the door of the drill shack at the same time Floyd Anderson ran over sputtering, "What the hell's going on?"

Toby held a hand up to him, "Just a sec."

He turned to Cab, "Good call. I think we cut through to a pocket of some kind."

"Yeah," Cab shook a shock of salt and pepper hair out of his eyes, "but a pocket of what? Could it be high-pressure gas sitting on top of an oilfield? We might blow the lid off the derrick like a champagne cork."

Toby shook his head, "I don't know. We're below most organic levels here. Could be just a primordial air pocket or something."

Cab chewed his lip as he scanned his board. Half the lights on it were red, but the others were still green, "Shit. Could be anything. I'm shutting down all electricals in the meantime, just in case. A spark could blow us all the way back home."

Toby nodded, "Let's hope your retracting the bit might of plugged the hole again if you drew it up far enough."

He turned out the doorway and yelled at the kid, "Go over and have a look at the flexible pipe leading off to the mud pit, kid!" He pointed at the rail where he'd been standing, "See if the coolant is still flowing!"

The kid waved and walked over toward the rail.

Toby waved at the crane and spoke to Floyd, "Better go keep an eye on that pipe up there."

Floyd nodded and headed back across the deck.

Toby turned back to look at Cab, "A couple minutes and we'll know if you plugged it. The vacuum should stop."

"That much liquid should take more than just a few minutes to drain out of the hole," Cab's face was thoughtful as he tried to imagine the scenario that might be happening far below them.

"Yeah, but we don't know how long ago we punched through. At this depth, it could've been a few minutes before we noticed it. It might take that long for the effect to travel back up the string. We had those weird temperature and angle readings for a few minutes…"

"I thought your feel for these things was infallible," Cab grinned at

Toby but there was still a furrow between his eyebrows.

"Never been on a hole this deep before," Toby gave him a warning look, "We're all learning new stuff."

He turned back to the kid and yelled, "What's going on?"

The kid shouted back over his shoulder, not wanting to take his eyes off the degasser below, "The pipe is still flat, but the whole degasser rig is shaking! It's…wait, it's stopped…and the pipe is…fluttering or something."

Toby looked back at Cab, whose face was now grim. The supervisor glanced at his console. There was no change on the board. It was still half red and half green.

That could only mean one thing to him, "The slurry likely bottomed out. Shit, we lost all the coolant."

Toby nodded and yelled back at the kid, "Keep your eyes on that collar where the pipe connects to the rig. Any leaks?" A sudden leak from the slurry pipe could spell disaster, as it would spill contaminated liquids over the ground and release potentially lethal or explosive gases.

The kid called back over his shoulder, "No. Nothing. It looks okay."

"Well, that's something, at least," Toby turned back to Cab again, but his eyes fell on the new red light suddenly flashing furiously on the supervisor's board. His heart thumped up into his throat.

Cab saw the alarm on Toby's face and turned back to the board. He saw the light and frantically began punching buttons, "Shit! Pressure's skyrocketing! It's a blowout on its way up!"

Toby didn't wait; he spun, pushed his way past Floyd and started to run across the deck toward the kid, who was just beginning to turn away from the rail, his eyes wide. The drill string behind him was bucking in the pipe as if a giant was throttling it.

The kid only got his head half-turned away from the borehole when the decking bumped up and everyone's ears popped from a sudden increase in pressure. Toby heard a metallic double whang! from below as the seals from the degasser blew off and the machine jolted to one side, knocking against a support post of the rig.

The whole deck shook, and Toby lost his footing, sliding on his backside halfway to the kid, who was knocked to the deck floor as well, but still holding onto the rail with one hand. There was a rush of hot air as something blew by on its way out of the borehole. Toby heard a crackling and knew it was from his hair crisping in the sudden heat.

Under that, though, was a more ominous sound.

He lay on his back and stared at the huge length of pipe dangling over everyone's head. It was swinging wildly back and forth, either from the jolt caused by the degasser hitting the rig, or from whatever that was that blew out of the well. The cable holding it was making a high-pitched creaking noise.

That cable won't hold with that much strain on it.

Even as he thought it, he saw the clamp holding the pipe to the cable come apart with a ping! and the forty-foot pipe crashed down, end-first, onto the rig deck, shaking it violently again. Toby was bucked up off the deck by the force, landing back down again hard.

Something twinged in his back, but his eyes never left the pipe. It teetered for a second and he jackknifed his body up, forgetting the sharp pain in his spine, ready to scramble away if the pipe fell his way.

For a moment, it looked as if the pipe might actually stay standing, but the severely damaged deck beneath it was no longer level. With a drawn-out, grating groan, the pipe leaned over, falling toward the crane with Floyd Anderson.

He yelled, "Look out!" but his voice was lost under the metallic squeal of the falling pipe.

Floyd had already seen the pipe leaning his way and was scrambling out of the crane. He leapt out just as the pipe hit the crane and Toby saw him land awkwardly and roll right off the side of the deck.

The pipe crushed the crane cab under it, sending pieces of metal and glass across the deck and up into the air. Several smashed through the windows of the drilling shack.

Toby threw his arms over his head to protect himself as pieces of the crane rained down all around him. It felt like a bomb had gone off.

When he was sure the last of the debris had fallen, he opened his eyes and took a breath finally, drawing in the oppressive air. He rolled over onto his back again and looked up at the derrick towering above him, amazed to see it still standing. There was a single cloud directly above and he could see the tip of the derrick slowly sway back and forth slightly across the cloud, accompanied by a slow creaking of straining metal, like the mast of a ship in a swell.

The engineer in him whispered from the back of his mind, *This whole rig is shot now. We're two months on repair at least.*

His face felt tight, and he knew that he'd taken a blast of superhot air full in the face. Likely they all had, but what did that mean for the kid? He'd practically been right over the borehole.

He rolled back over onto his front and pushed himself painfully up. It felt as if his whole body had been pummeled. On the opposite side of the deck, he could see Floyd climbing slowly back up onto the deck. At least he was okay. There was no sign of Pete, the other rig hand, though.

Through the cotton in his ears, he heard Cab clanking around in the drill shack and called out to him, "Cab! You okay?"

Cab's reply was muffled, "Yeah, I'm okay. Jesus Christ! What was that?"

Toby coughed and spat, "I don't know, but we better get under and look at the guts of this thing."

He yelled at the kid, who was slumped against the rail still. Toby could only see his back, "Hey, kid! You okay?"

No reply. And the kid didn't look as if he was moving. Shit.

He scrambled to his feet and called out, "Cab! Get out here! The kid's down!" He waved at Floyd, "Find Pete!"

Floyd nodded and wobbled over to the side of the rig nearest the pipe rack, where Pete had last been seen.

Toby slid over to the still form slumped by the rail, "Kid! Kid!"

The young engineer was slumped on one side, his body facing away toward the drill pipe, his arm still extended upward and his hand gripping the top rail. His head hung down over the lower rail and his long hair draped past his face over the borehole.

Toby shot a glance beyond the kid's form down at the hole. The drill string was still in place, slowly quivering, but the seals around the hole that held the pipe to the degasser assembly had blown off. He was looking directly down the five-mile depth of the borehole.

He put a tentative hand on the boy's back, "Kid? Kid?" For the life of

15

him, he couldn't remember the kid's name now.

No response, but the kid's back felt as if it was on fire. Could've been from the sun beating down on them all, but his shirt felt unusually warm – warmer than it should.

A sudden ripple of movement from the muscles under the shirt startled him and he grabbed the kid's shoulder and hauled his body over toward him just as Cab jogged up beside him and squatted down.

Toby could feel the kid's body tense as he rolled toward him. The head flopped back, and the hair fell away from the closed eyes.

Toby's blood froze and a shock of horror bloomed out from the center of his chest. He heard both Floyd and Cab gasp behind him and stumble backward.

The kid's mouth was locked open in a silent howl that stretched the jaw downward to the point where it must have dislocated. The inside of the mouth was a black maw with a twisting, undulating tongue that looked too large for the mouth.

"W-What the…" Toby stammered.

And then the eyes opened, and black insanity leapt out.

Two

LEE MITCHELL SPRAWLED ACROSS BOTH rear passenger seats of the EC120 Colibri helicopter and watched his boss, Angeline Broussard. She was going through the latest reports and correspondence from Endeavor's corporate headquarters in Houston and seemed oblivious to him and the scenery below.

He leaned his head over to the left and peered down through the tinted window at the brown and green countryside of Africa undulating beneath the helicopter. The tap-tap of Angeline's long fingernails on her tablet could just be heard over the sound of the engine and rotor.

Usually, he found the drone of an airplane or helicopter sleep inducing, but today he couldn't seem to get comfortable. He unspooled his long legs to stretch and shifted in his seat. Angeline caught the movement and raised her eyes from the work she had spread out on the swing-out table in front of her seat.

She caught his eye, and both of her eyebrows went up, "You seem pensive," her nasally twang cut through the rotor sound efficiently.

Lee shrugged, "I guess I got too much sleep last night."

"That's never been a problem for you."

He grinned, "Yeah, I guess not. Just…too much going on in here," he twirled his hand around his head, "Any news, by the way? The assessment crew's been on site for almost a day and a half now," he flipped a hand at her tablet.

Angeline dropped her eyes and scanned the computer screen. It kept her in constant touch with Corporate, no matter how far afield they were – and they were pretty far afield at the moment.

She sighed, "Nothing yet. Duke sent a message a few hours ago saying they'd been at the rig since about four the previous afternoon and were still setting up, but there's been nothing since then. I imagine they're busy."

He nodded absently and returned his gaze to the window, "I'm sure."

He watched the countryside roll under him for a few seconds before looking back at her, "Sure wish we knew what the hell was going on there."

She glanced at her watch, "We'll know in about ten minutes."

"Hmm," he closed his eyes and tried not to think about what they were flying toward.

Lee was Endeavor's Chief Engineer, responsible for supervising all drilling operations the company was undertaking. Though relatively young for the job at only thirty-eight, he'd already clocked two decades on drilling rigs on four continents.

He'd started out as a chain-hauling rig hand at eighteen and had worked his way up through almost every position possible on a rig with various companies, becoming a supervisor of a rig of his own at the age of thirty working for Endeavor. He'd also managed to get a degree in engineering doing summer studies at the same time. His last six years had been first as Assistant Chief and now finally Chief Engineer at Endeavor, where he felt at home for the first time since high school.

Lee loved working for Endeavor and wanted to repay the faith both they and his previous boss, Bill Owen, had in him by accepting the job, but had insisted that he be allowed to be more of a hands-on type of chief, rather than a paper-pusher. He hated sitting at a desk all day and routinely found ways to get back out into the field as a problem-solver, something that he was doing more and more these days with the immense pressure on energy companies to basically get it while the getting was good.

There was less money to be made in the fossil fuel industry these days, with surpluses up, prices down and alternative energy sources now becoming not only politically popular, but economically competitive.

Fearing the coming demise of the industry, companies like Endeavor were exploring, securing leases, and drilling anywhere they could in an effort to forestall collapse. The high-pressure environment called for increasingly creative solutions and made heavy demands of everyone, people in Lee's position in particular, but he thrived on it. He'd had been successful and happy since starting as chief…until this project, that is.

When Endeavor had initially floated the idea of doing this deep drill in Africa, Lee had been opposed. There was no purpose to it, he argued, especially in light of the situation the industry was facing. They were a drilling company, yes, but always drilling for something – oil, natural gas - but just drilling a hole to be able to say you were the guys who drilled deepest? That was for scientists, universities, and governments to do, wasn't it? In his mind, it was a total waste of time, money, materials, and manpower at a time when they could waste none of those resources.

He'd been suspicious of the project from the start, and he'd figured that there was some reason other than the record books for Endeavor to be involved in this, but the CEO and the Board had been resolute to the point of threatening to replace him if he bucked too hard against the project.

In the end, he'd gone along for over two years now, since the initial planning stages. The deep-drill was just one of many projects they had going on, and it was one that rarely caused anything more than routine progress reports to cross his desk, but it was a nettle in his side; one that was made more irritating because his opposition to the project was countered by its approval by the woman currently sitting across from him; Angeline, and on this job her word carried more weight with Corporate.

And now there was a problem at the site, one that he would have to fix.

Angeline was Endeavor's Chief Geologist. It was she who decided where the company drilled and for what. Lee's responsibility was to act on her direction and to figure out ways to drill where he was told to. The arrangement was usually uncomplicated on most drilling jobs, as the responsibilities of geologist and engineer rarely overlapped, and they reported up different chains of command. However, Lee's professional relationship with Angeline was somewhat complicated by their personal relationship.

They'd been sleeping together for over a year.

"...your mind on the job, Lee."

He jerked in his seat, startled, "Huh?" He'd been staring at her legs a remembering the last time they'd been together.

She gave him a sly eye, "I said you'd better keep your mind on the job. I have to send a report to Corporate tonight. They expect this drill to start pushing again within a few days - a week at most," she pointed ahead out the windscreen of the helicopter.

Lee's mouth twisted derisively, "How the hell can we promise that when we haven't even seen what the problem is yet and Duke hasn't said a word to us," he sat up straighter, "And tell me again why this project is so damned important anyway? We've wasted tens of millions already-"

She put up a hand to stop him, "Please. I've heard your complaints about it for over two years. It's an old argument and I'm tired of it."

She sighed and looked out her side window, avoiding looking at him, "It's a drop in Endeavor's bucket and I...I don't know much more about the details than you do."

She relaxed back into her seat and stared out at the smoky landscape of Africa, apparently ending the conversation.

Lee regarded her for a moment. Every time they talked about this project – whether in the office or over their pillows – he had the feeling that she was holding back. She always got pensive and snappish, something neither of them needed at the moment.

He relented, "Okay. Sorry, you're right. I'll put my engineer hat back on," he gave her a small grin and noted her own grateful one in return as she went back to her tablet.

They remained silent for the rest of the trip. Lee looked out his window, but kept casting glances over at Angeline, who seemed completely absorbed in whatever she was doing on the computer. Her fingers never stopped moving over the tablet.

A few minutes later the helicopter banked left suddenly, and the pilot informed them they were in descent. His voice buzzed over Lee's headset, "You guys want to have a look at the site first?"

Angeline's eyes met Lee's and she nodded.

Lee answered, "Yeah, Rich. Give us a lap around."

"Roger that."

The helicopter spiraled down over the rig, about a hundred feet above the top of the derrick. Lee scrutinized the site, his eyes roaming over every part of the rig, the machinery, and the slurry pond.

From here, everything looked a mess, and he imagined it was worse at ground level. A huge section of pipe had crushed the crane cab and there was debris spread all over the rig deck and the ground around it. The derrick seemed to be in good shape, but he noted there was no one on the deck of the rig and the drill clamps were not turning, which meant no pipe was going into the hole, and there was no diesel smoke from the massive generators next to the supervisor's shack.

The rig looked dead.

After they'd circled once, Lee tapped his mic, "Okay, thanks. Take us to camp."

The helicopter immediately straightened to follow the dirt road between the rig and the small cluster of trailers about a quarter mile away. They buzzed over top before settling down in a cleared spot and Lee got a look at the camp.

It was a standard setup for Endeavor; nine twelve-by-forty-foot trailers set up in an "H" pattern, with one across the middle and four attached along their length at each end to make for double-wide areas. One side of the H held the kitchen, eating and recreation areas and the other housed the crew sleeping quarters, showers, and toilet areas. The single unit in the middle was basically a corridor with a couple small offices for the rig's own supervisor and geologist.

The helicopter settled in a cloud of dust and Lee saw the door in the middle of the central trailer open and several men come out, shielding their eyes from the sun and dust. One of them, a head taller than the others, was Duke Milligan, the leader of the assessment team. His dark, bald head gleamed in the sun.

Lee had his door open and jumped out as soon as the pilot hit the kill switch and the rotor started to wind down. Despite the downdraft from the rotor, the heat of the African day hit him like a hammer blow. He turned and held a hand out for Angeline, but she had a grip on the side of the door and stepped down without his help, giving him a nod.

He just shook his head and turned to meet the assessment team, who had moved forward.

Duke was practically bent double out of fear of the still-spinning rotor blades as he extended a hand the size of a baseball glove to Lee, "Chief, good to see you." His British accent always seemed at odds with the deep timber of his voice.

He squeezed the bones in Lee's hand warmly before releasing him and turning to Angeline. Her slim hand was completely swallowed up in Duke's paw, "Angie, how you doing?"

He swept his arm back at the trailers and everyone moved out from under the blades.

Once out from under the effect of the slowing rotor, the heat was a physical weight on their bodies. Lee had worked in every environment from humid jungle to desert to frozen tundra and, though sweat was practically leaping out of his pores, it felt good to be onsite and out in the wild world again.

Duke led them up three wooden steps into the central trailer. It felt almost icy cold inside and they all took a deep breath of the refreshing air. Their skin prickled as sweat cooled and dried.

Angeline was fanning herself, "Whew, it's been a while since I've felt a heat like that."

"Dry season now," Duke said and nodded his head around the group, "You know everyone, right?"

Lee and Angeline shook hands with the other three men, whom they'd met a few times.

Lee asked, "So what can you tell us?"

A strange look briefly flickered over Duke's eyes. Lee caught it, but Angeline didn't.

Duke pointed down the corridor, "Let's head to the rec room. More space in there."

Lee was going to ask him what was wrong. He had the impression that Duke was trying to put off telling him something, but the big man moved away before he could put his impression into a question. Duke's broad back almost filled the narrow corridor ahead of him and seemed to be saying, No questions yet.

They emerged from the corridor into the eating area. The doublewide trailers gave them a space twenty-four feet wide and forty feet long. Six long tables were set up for eating on one side, with the kitchen partially closed off from the room by a counter running along the other.

Lee noted that the entire area seemed deserted.

Beyond the eating area was the recreation room, of equal size and separated from the eating area by a thin wall with two doors. Duke pushed through the door on the right, and everyone followed.

They entered the games room, which held two pool tables, two small tables for cards or board games and several workstations, each with a desk and a computer tablet. There was a dividing wall down the middle and Lee knew that the other side would have a big-screen TV room for movies.

Duke went straight to the back of the room and indicated that everyone should sit. They collapsed gratefully into the chairs around the two tables. Everyone spent a few moments trading cell phone numbers to facilitate communication.

As they finished, Duke glanced around, "Anyone want a coffee?"

The others shook their heads, but Lee nodded, "If it's iced coffee."

"No ice," Duke said.

"I'll take one anyway," Lee turned to Angeline, "You?"

She had her tablet open already. She looked up at him and shook her head.

Duke got up to get the coffees and Lee spoke to his back, "Office area is freezing, but it's sweltering in here." He fanned himself.

"Power's just coming back online as of about an hour ago," Duke swung back with a couple coffees in hand, "The whole system was fried. We're getting it going in stages."

Angeline leaned forward, "So what happened?"

Duke handed Lee his coffee and sat, "We're…not sure yet."

Lee was surprised, "What do you mean? What the hell happened out there? The rig looks like a bomb went off."

Duke turned his cup around and around in his hand, "All we know is that it looks like they had a blowout of some kind. The degasser was knocked off its pins, the flanges torn right off. Looks like a section of pipe was about to be added and that collapsed onto the rig crane. The physical damage you see was likely all the result of those two things."

"Blowouts don't cause that kind of damage," Lee shot a thumb over his shoulder.

Duke shrugged, "Well, there's no indication of an actual explosion. The physical damage all seems to be from the fallen pipe. However, there are signs of intense heat on the walls and decking of the rig; bubbled paint, scorching, that sort of thing."

Angeline's brow was furrowed, "What does the console data show?"

Duke turned to her, "Most of the data is gone and what remains is largely corrupted, just like all the systems here, but what we got so far seems to back up the idea of a blowout of some kind."

"What do the guys say about it?" Lee waved his hand around, pulling the names from memory, "Cab and Toby, where are they? Where the hell is anyone?"

Now Duke looked really uncomfortable, "We...uh, we don't know where they are."

Three

"THIS IS A HELL OF mess," Lee kicked a piece of angle iron, and it skittered across the deck. He turned to Duke, "You tell me, ever see a blowout cause something like this?"

Duke shook his head, "Nope."

Lee walked across the creaking deck to the railing around the wellhead. He peered down, mildly surprised to find that he could see straight down the hole. The degasser and its hoses were in a pile on the ground directly under the deck below him and the enormous well was open to the sky.

He pulled back slightly as a moment of vertigo washed over him. Hovering over a hole so big was unnerving and he was aware that the only thing between him and a five-mile-deep fall was a narrow railing. He focused on the equipment dangling down the hole.

The drill string was still intact, the twisting cables and wires disappearing down the side of the wide hole, hanging almost perfectly straight. That told him nothing, however. Five miles of cable would hang straight as an arrow from its own weight, even without the drill assembly hanging off the bottom.

He looked closely at the top of the well. The sides of the pipe were scorched as far down as he could see. He ran his hand over the railing and wasn't surprised to find that the paint was bubbled.

It would take a lot of heat to do that.

He backed away from the rail, trying to imagine what must have happened on the rig. A dark spot next to his boot caught his eye and he bent to examine it.

Blood.

Not just a drop of blood, either; a small splash of it about the size of his palm. It was maroon colored, dry and flaking at the edges. Lee's brow creased; it could be from something like a cut hand, but he doubted that.

What the hell happened out here?

He stood and looked at the giant spool to the side that held the coiled string cables. One of Duke's men was working on the control unit.

Lee turned to Duke, "How long until we can pull up the string?"

Duke wiped sweat from the dome of his head, "Could be half a day yet. Everything is controlled by the computer and rebooting it has been the trouble. Jimmy has had to rebuild the recovery program from scratch. Plus, the deck crane is toast. We'd have to use the smaller unit we brought, but I don't think it has the power to haul up eight kilometers of string and the drill platform."

Lee pointed down the hole, "Then we have to get a look down there. How long would it take to get set up?"

Duke flashed a grin, the first one Lee had seen since they arrived, "I have the fishing equipment already broken out. We can send a camera down within an hour, tops."

"Excellent. Let's get going on that."

"Righto," Duke flipped him a two-fingered scout salute and headed toward the stairs.

Lee sighed and walked over to the rail at the side of the deck. He leaned on it and stared out at the baked, dusty green and brown of the African countryside.

The Endeavor site was in the far west of Tanzania, south of Lake Victoria and the country of Burundi, between the great expanse of the Moyowosi Game Reserve to the east and the long, deep ribbon of Lake Tanganyika to the west. It was literally in the middle of nowhere and looked like it. All around lay low, dry hills, shallow green valleys spotted with tiny farms, dried riverbeds, and occasional clusters of gnarled trees.

It was a stark and corrugated countryside, the kind of place that Lee actually enjoyed working in, as it felt – and really was – as far from corporate life as he could get. In any other situation, he would be relishing his time here, but not now.

Nine men gone, disappeared. Nine men stationed at this rig and not one of them to be found after an incident like this. Both trucks still here, beds unmade at the camp, dirty dishes in the kitchen sinks – all evidence of recent occupation – but the only sign of the men is a splash of blood on the rig deck.

He'd checked his own telemetry data again from the site while on the way here. Data from all active drilling sites came through to his computer constantly and this one showed routine numbers right up to three fifty-two p.m. local time two days ago. Then the numbers went crazy, and telemetry stopped.

He scuffed his boot on the deck and watched the tiny moving black dot of an animal far off in the haze; a cow or some other domestic animal he figured. Wild animals were a rarity around here these days, even this close to the game reserve. It wavered in the heat-shimmer, seeming to appear and disappear, and he tracked it as he wondered again what the hell they all thought they were doing out here.

Endeavor Engineering was attempting to do what a few others had tried in the past, and they were on their way to setting a record for the deepest artificial penetration of the earth's crust. The current record was held by the Kola Superdeep Borehole, undertaken by the Russians in the '70s and '80s. That project had stopped at just over twelve kilometers, or seven point five miles, because of the heat encountered at that depth. The Kola group, however, had not had the benefit of twenty-first century polymer and nitrogen gas cooling technology, nor did they have the level of artificial diamond hardness achieved these days, and Lee knew that Endeavor would easily break that depth record.

He just didn't know why Endeavor apparently wanted this so badly.

It wasn't just the unnecessary waste of valuable resources that he objected to; it was also that Corporate seemed to want to do it the hardest way possible, by drilling a hole wide enough to practically drop a small car into.

The Kola group didn't try to punch a five-foot wide hole into the Earth. They'd settled for a hole width less than a third of that, which was what everyone had expected Endeavor would try to do as well. Why they felt they needed to go almost triple diameter on this hole of all things was beyond Lee and he'd fought them on it at every step, to no avail.

Still, despite the difficulties of working an outsized hole with outsized equipment, Endeavor was expecting to break Kola's record by the middle of next year. They'd been at it for only a year and a half and were already at a depth that had taken Kola a decade to reach. When Endeavor achieved their record, it would be one of both speed and depth that would likely stand for a generation, if not longer.

Even if it made absolutely no sense to their chief engineer.

Lee chewed his lip and continued to watch the wavering dot of the animal amble around the countryside, feeling as lost as it seemed to be.

He was chief engineer, yes, but sometimes he still felt like he was outside of the loop, more like a glorified rig hand than a senior level administrator. It was partially his own fault, he knew. By insisting that he be so hands-on and involved with the sites, he was away from Head Office most of the time and therefore not part of the inner circle that decided the direction the company went.

Not that he wanted that anyway. That was the sort of stuff Angeline thrived on, not him. He was happiest being out in the field, getting his hands dirty, feeling the grit under his nails and the snow or sand under his boots.

He took a deep breath of the stifling air. As hot and far-flung this site was, and how wasteful the whole enterprise appeared to be, he knew he was happier here than he would be in his office. If he could only find out what had happened and where the men had disappeared to.

He squinted again at that far-off animal, trying to guess what it was. It looked too thin to be a domestic cow. An antelope? A gnu?

Its figure was distorted because of the heat-shimmer and impossible to make out at this distance. It looked to be approaching the rig site, though, moving in almost a straight line toward it.

The hairs on his neck stood up despite the heat. Something about the animal was off. It didn't look right and didn't seem to be moving like it should. Perhaps it was wounded, maybe having survived an attack by a predator.

It slowly resolved into a solid figure as it neared, and the shimmering effect lessened.

The animal turned briefly to the side and Lee jerked erect as a shock of realization went through him suddenly.

It wasn't an animal.

It was a man.

Four

THE JEEP BOUNCED AND BUCKED over the choppy terrain and the men clung to their safety straps as if they were in a rough sea. Duke drove, keeping his attention on the ground in front of the jeep, while Lee kept his eyes on the lone figure walking through the landscape like a dark wraith, appearing and disappearing from view as the jeep rose and fell over the ground.

They crested a small incline coming out of a shallow dry streambed and were suddenly within twenty yards of the figure.

Lee tapped Duke's arm, "Good enough."

Duke slammed on the brakes and the jeep slid to a halt in the dry, sandy soil.

They climbed out and watched the figure stumble toward them.

It was a man wearing the blue coveralls of an Endeavor rig hand. Dark hair flopped down over a pale face and loose arms dangled at his sides. He walked with a strange jolting stride, as if he was slightly off-balance, or not paying any attention to the uneven ground he was walking over. There was a long, dark stain down one leg of the coveralls.

He walked straight toward the jeep, but didn't seem to notice Lee and Duke, who were standing directly in his path.

Lee called out, "Hey, are you all right? Who are you? We're from Endeavor."

The man didn't reply. He drew up to them, and Duke had to step aside so the man didn't walk right into him. The man didn't seem to notice him at all.

"Look at his face," Duke said and walked to keep up to the guy as he went past.

The man's face was very pale, his eyes dull and milky. His mouth hung open and his lower lip wiggled loosely, though Lee thought he could see the guy's jaw working, like he was speaking to himself.

Duke reached out and grabbed the man's bare forearm, "Hey, buddy, hold up there – Jesus!" he yanked his hand back quickly.

Lee was reaching out to put a hand on the guy's chest to stop him, "What is it?"

Duke was looking at his hand, "The guy's burning up!"

The man didn't try to avoid Lee and walked right into Lee's hand.

Lee's palm hit the guy square in the chest, and it felt like he'd put his hand on a warm stove. Even through heavy denim fabric and likely an undershirt, the guy's body heat was immediately obvious.

The guy was still walking forward, pushing Lee backward. Lee dug in to hold his ground and the guy finally stopped moving and stood still. Lee was about to speak to him when the guy's head dropped down to his chest, as if he were suddenly exhausted, and his legs buckled. He collapsed at Lee's feet like a broken doll.

They both knelt beside him, and Duke turned him over. The man's cloudy eyes stared up past them at the endless blue sky.

Duke put his fingers at the man's neck, "Heat stroke, or…what the hell?" He took his fingers off the man's neck and put his hand on the chest.

Lee was staring at the man's eyes, confused, "What is it?"

Duke was incredulous, "The guy's dead!"

"What?"

Duke put his ear to the man's chest, "No pulse, no breathing. He's dead."

"Jesus Christ," Lee grabbed the man's chin and tilted the head back, "Give me some compressions."

Duke started CPR, placing both palms down on the man's chest and giving him thirty rapid compressions in a row. He leaned back and Lee fastened his mouth over the man's, blowing in hard. He felt incredible heat from the lips and almost gagged at the whiff of a terrible odor coming from the man's mouth. It was the unmistakable smell of rotting meat.

He pulled back as Duke applied more compressions and the smell worsened, becoming an invisible cloud in the air between them.

Lee put out a hand to stop Duke, "Hold on, hold on."

Duke stopped and looked at him, "What? We have to-"

Lee shook his head, "I...don't understand, but...this guy is dead."

"I know! We-"

"No, I mean, this guy is *dead* dead. Really dead. You smell that?" Lee waved his hand around.

Duke wrinkled his nose, "Yeah...but..."

"And look at him," Lee pointed at the man's face.

They both leaned over the body, wincing against the odor. The man's face was almost white, the lips blue in the corners, splotches of yellow and purple, like bruising, were on the cheeks. The face looked sunken and dry, the skin flaky and almost desiccated.

"The eyes," Duke whispered.

The man's eyes were cloudy, but not from cataracts or some other internal occlusions.

They were covered in a film of dust.

#   #   #

The medic looked up at Duke, "Tell me again where you dug this guy up?"

Lee paced at the end of the table, his arms folded in impatience, "We didn't dig him up. I told you-"

Duke cut in, "Bobby, like I said, this guy was walking around out there, basically heading this way. Lee saw him and we went out-"

"Bullshit," the medic shook his head and flashed an apologetic look at Lee, "Uh... sorry, boss, but this guy hasn't done any walking for a couple days, I can tell you that."

Duke tapped the table with a sausage-thick finger, "He was *walking* I tell you. He came right up to us, walked past me, right into Lee and then just fell down in front of us."

Bobby pointed at the corpse, "This guy has been dead and in the sun drying out for at least two days, Duke."

He drew his finger down the length of the torso, over the opened coveralls. The flesh underneath was as pale as that of the face, the skin of the abdomen stretched taut, "He's as ripe as the last plum on the tree. If I stick so much as a needle in there, he's going to explode all over this table."

Lee grimaced at the image, "Then how do you explain it?"

"I can't, so I won't. What you guys are telling me simply can't happen."

"Not only was he walking," Duke protested, "this guy was boiling hot at the time. The heat was radiating off him."

Bobby patted the pale arm, "Well he's definitely cold now."

Duke sighed, "Bobby…"

The medic put up a hand, "I'm not calling you liars. I'm just saying that what you're describing simply is not possible. It's unbelievable in fact. Dead guys don't walk all over the African countryside and this," he waved a hand at the corpse, "is definitely a dead guy."

They all stared at each other over the body for a few seconds.

Duke looked at Lee, "So where does this leave us?"

Lee looked at the corpse without really seeing it, "This is only one of nine men stationed here. We have to find out where the others are."

Duke pointed at the ceiling, "I've got Rich up in the chopper right now doing a spiral search out from here. If anyone else is walking around out there," he shot a glance at Bobby, "he'll spot them and let us know."

Lee nodded, "Okay. Beyond that, we have to find out what the hell happened at the rig. Any progress on that?"

"Before we went out on this," Duke pointed at the corpse, "Jimmy told me he was almost finished with the recovery program rebuild. That was over an hour ago, so he should be done, or close to it."

"And you said we were ready to go fishing?"

"Should be by now. We can't set up on the main deck as it's still too unstable, but the guys ran the fishing cables up from the ground and over the end of the collapsed deck crane. It should be good enough just for lowering the camera rig, but I wouldn't put too much weight on it by trying to haul anything up."

Lee nodded approval, "Noted. Let's get a look down there first and then see what we need to do." He turned to the medic, "Bobby, can you try to figure out what killed this guy?"

"I'm not a pathologist, Lee. I can't-"

"Please, Bobby. We need to find out what happened to the guys here and it'd be a week to wait if we have to ship him out."

Bobby looked at the body with distaste and nodded slowly, "All right. I really don't want to, but I can go over him, cut into him a bit and maybe figure out anything that's obvious, but no promises. And you'll have to take the heat if there's any flak from the company or his family."

Lee nodded, "It's all on me. Thanks, Bobby, it's that important."

They both headed out. Just outside the door, Lee almost ran into Angeline, who was about to enter.

"Oh there you are," she blurted. She looked as impatient as Lee had ever seen her.

He tried to go around her, but she stepped in front of him, "I heard you found someone out there. How is he?"

Duke raised his eyebrows at Lee and just kept going.

Lee didn't even know how to respond to her, so he just shot a thumb over his shoulder, "He's…in there. Go see for yourself."

He made to go around her again, but she put a hand up, "Wait. You look weird. What's going on? I've got Corporate breathing down my neck about a restart, and no one can give me an answer. Brent-"

Lee didn't want to hear anything about Corporate or the company's CEO, Brent Copeland, "Ang, I can't tell you much right now, but maybe in a couple hours. We're about to drop a camera down the shaft and the computers should be up and running soon. Can you and Brent just wait a bit?"

His tone was sharp, and he saw her reaction immediately. Her eyes darkened and a furrow appeared between them.

She opened her mouth, but he flashed her a fake smile, "I'm sorry, but I really should be on the deck. Bobby will talk to you all you want about walking corpses," he stepped around her and headed away.

She watched him go with one hand on the door to the medical room, completely perplexed, *Walking corpses?*

It was one of the few times in their professional or personal relationship that she didn't get the last word in.

#   #   #

Lee, Duke and Jimmy, the tech guy, clustered around the monitors in the drilling shack. Jimmy had connected a tablet directly into the console and was running it remotely.

Outside on the deck, the recovery crew was making final checks on their jury-rigged setup to lower the camera. Their murmurs and clanking equipment made the afternoon sound almost normal.

Jimmy was hunched over his tablet, tapping its screen. The monitor in front of him showed a blue screen with white numbers showing time in the bottom right. A few of the console's lights were on, but most were still dark.

Jimmy craned his neck at Duke, "Okay. Should be ready to go. I set it up to show us the last couple of minutes before we lost the data stream."

Lee angled his head at the screen, "Punch it."

Jimmy hit the track pad to turn it on and the screen flickered, remaining blue for a few more seconds. It jumped and the numbers in the corner changed to show the time as the recording started to play.

Lee noted that the numbers read three-fifty p.m. two days ago.

The scene was shot from the camera mounted over the door to the drilling shed. It showed the whole of the rig deck but didn't track or zoom at all.

They watched as the rig hands moved about the deck, an older guy, a young guy with long blond hair and two others off to the side by the deck crane. The older guy, probably Toby, was obviously trying to show the younger guy the ropes, leading him back and forth from the deck console to the rail around the wellhead. There was sound on the recording, but all they could hear was the grinding and whirring of the equipment, no voices.

At three fifty-one on the counter, they split up. Toby headed directly toward the camera, obviously heading into the shack, while the young guy stayed out at the wellhead, looking down over the rail.

"Obviously became aware of a problem there," Duke murmured.

Lee nodded slowly, "Yeah. No progress on the actual data yet, Jimmy?"

"No sir, but it should be soon."

"Fine," Lee squinted at the screen, "Can't see what the hell the blond guy is looking at, but it had to be the degasser assembly. Maybe they knew something was up."

At three fifty-two on the counter, all hell suddenly broke loose on the video.

The camera shook violently, and lines of interference shot across the screen. Toby ran back out onto the deck, directly below the camera. At the same time, the young guy at the rail reared back and it looked like a strong wind or blast of force blew past him up into the air. His hair waved wildly about his head.

The picture broke into fragments and darkened slightly, but still showed Toby sliding across the deck, the young guy collapsing as if someone knocked his legs out from under him and the suspended length of annular pipe starting to swing.

Then it all went black, and the counter froze at three fifty-two and seven seconds.

The three men leaned back from the monitor.

"Jesus Christ," Duke's eyes were wide, "What the hell was that?"

Lee leaned back in, "Run it back to the three-fifty-two mark, Jimmy."

Jimmy tapped his screen and the counter on the monitor went back seven seconds.

"Can you slow it down a bit?" Lee asked.

"You bet. Quarter speed okay?"

"Sounds good."

"Here we go," Jimmy tapped the screen.

The image pixelated slightly and the figures on the screen seemed to be surrounded by auras as they moved.

Duke leaned closer, "What you looking for Lee?"

Lee stared at the screen, "Damned if I know." He focused on the guy at the rail. There was something strange there...

The vibration of the camera and the interference made things even harder to follow slowed down, but still showed enough; Toby emerging from the shack below the camera and losing his footing, the blond guy's hair blowing up over his head as a dark cloud or maybe just a distortion effect from interference went past him, but then...

Lee's finger shot at the screen, "Freeze it!"

Jimmy hit the tablet reflexively and the image froze.

The screen was split diagonally by a line of interference. At the bottom, Toby was on his back, looking up, his face twisted in a grimace.

At the top, the young guy was bent over, one hand still holding the rail, his body, which had been forced upright by whatever had blown by him, was now bent double, his legs collapsing as if under a great weight.

Duke drew his finger across the screen, "What the hell is that?"

He pointed at the man's narrow back, where a smear of black, like a column of wispy smoke, looked like it was penetrating his shirt between the shoulder blades.

Lee frowned and chewed his lip, "I don't know. Distortion maybe? Interference?"

Duke shook his head, "Beats me too, but it must be something like that."

The door to the shack opened and one of Duke's men stuck his head in, "Boss? We're ready to go."

Duke turned away from the screen, "Okay. Be right there." He patted Lee's shoulder, "Time to go fishing."

"Yeah, all right," Lee answered absently as Duke went out. He stared at the screen, at that black smudge sticking out of the young guy's back.

It sure as hell looked like something came up out of the hole, blew past the man, then came back down right on top of him.

The image was very blurry and shot through with interference, though. Impossible to say just what it was, or if it even was anything at all.

He put a hand on Jimmy's shoulder, "Can you try to clean up those last few seconds for us?"

"Might take some time, Lee."

"That's okay. It's still going to be a couple hours getting the camera down the hole anyway."

Jimmy turned back to his tablet, "I'm on it."

"Thanks."

Lee left the shack, his mind now trying to focus on the difficult job ahead but clinging to that weird image of a black cloud seeming to attack the young guy.

Walking dead people and now clouds that attack men.

He strode across the deck under a crystal African sky, *What the hell else is coming today?*

Five

"GETTING GOOD PICKUP STILL," DUKE muttered. He took his eyes off the monitor screen and squinted up at the wheel at the end of the deck crane, "Good turnings as well."

The camera's miles of slim cable were unspooling from the reels on the ground below, being fed up and over the wheel at the end of the crane and down into the well, held steady by two pieces of angle iron that served as guides and kept the cable in the middle of the hole as it descended. The whine of the motor controlling the cable was the only sound in the still afternoon.

Even at the fast speed of a meter, or just over three feet per second, the descent into the well was taking forever. They'd been at it for almost two hours. The afternoon sky above was sliding toward dusk and the air was cooling off quickly.

Lee sipped what felt like his tenth cup of bitter coffee and kept his eyes on the screen, "Uh-huh."

Duke checked the depth counter on the screen, "Nearing the four-mile mark."

Lee rubbed the bridge of his nose. They'd been watching the sides of the well pipe sweep steadily past the cameras for the whole descent, and he started to get dizzy now every time he looked at the image.

The cable carried a payload at its end that had three cameras, lights and several sensors perched on a small platform. One camera was angled down to peer into the hole, another was aimed straight up, and a third focused across the small platform itself. This was the image they were looking at and it showed the same thing it had for two hours; the sides of the pipe and the thick, black mass of cables and slurry tubes that fed down to the drill itself, somewhere still a mile or so below the cameras.

Duke brought his eyes back to the screen, "What was the last reported depth of the drill before the data cut off again?"

"Just shy of eight point three kilometers, five point one miles. What's the temp now?"

Duke tapped his tablet, "Still falling. Ninety-eight degrees Celsius."

Lee drummed his fingers on the blistered rail around the hole, "That doesn't make any sense. It should be closer to one-fifty, almost hot enough to cook a turkey."

"I know. It rose quickly and steadily from sixty degrees at three klicks deep all the way to a peak of one twenty-five at five and a half klicks. Been falling just as fast since then, though. Damndest thing."

"Problem with the sensor?"

"Doubt it. There are two onboard and they both show the same numbers."

Lee shook his head, *Well, I asked what the hell else was coming our way today.*

He walked away from the screen, unable to stare at it for a moment longer. So much about all this didn't make any sense and he was rapidly getting tired of it.

The sound of an approaching engine drew his attention and he saw the other jeep pulling up to the side of the rig. It stopped in front of the stairs to the rig deck and Angeline got out.

Oh great. Lee knew why she was here.

She managed to mount the stairs with elegance despite her boots, using one hand to pull herself up while the other held her ubiquitous tablet.

Lee leaned forward and she allowed him to hand her up the final step to the deck, flashing him a quick smile, "Thanks, Lee. Been trying to call you. How's it going out here?"

He knew she wasn't really asking for herself, "Well, it's going. That's about all I can say right now. We're about two-thirds the way down to max depth and so far, everything looks normal, but I expected it to be anyway."

She eyed the cable running over the wheel of the crane, "Any idea as to how much longer?"

He couldn't help it, "You asking? Or Brent?"

She didn't even miss a beat, "Both."

Fair enough. He relented, "I'm thinking at least another half an hour if we can maintain this rate of descent."

He read the impatience in her face and said, "We may start to know something sooner than that, though."

An arched eyebrow, "How so?"

"Before everything went to shit, we started getting anomalous readings in the data not much farther down than we are now."

"I looked at the data file myself. You mean the temperature changes and the drill misalignments?"

"Yeah, not misalignments per se; drill shafts rarely end up being perfectly straight anyway. You know that."

"Yes."

"Well, you saw the geology reports yourself. The drill was cutting steadily through fairly uniform granulitic rock. Densities were constant, yet the drill was starting to wander like it was encountering much harder strata here and there. Toward the end, they were having to adjust it almost constantly just to keep it basically on track."

"Not totally unexpected on a hole this deep."

"No, but a little unexpected given the nature of the schist they were penetrating. Anyway, it's still an incredibly straight hole for all that, but then there's the temperature anomaly."

Her tablet screen came to life, and she glanced at it. Lee surmised it was another incoming message from Corporate.

She scanned whatever it was for a second and then asked, "Are your readings now showing the same?"

He nodded, "Still falling, though the curve seems to be bottoming out."

She nodded absently and glanced at her tablet again. It was angled away from him, so he couldn't see it. Her constantly dividing her attention between that screen and the real world was irritating at the best of times, but now he was losing patience.

He was also bothered by the fact that she didn't seem to be disturbed by any of this. She, more than anyone else, should be more worked up about drilling delays and the weird readings on this dig, not to mention the loss of men and the damage to the equipment, but she seemed to be taking it like it was no more frustrating than a meeting that didn't go her way.

"Anything else?" he asked archly.

She looked up at him innocently, "No. Just wanting to see where we're at and wanting to get out of that office for a bit."

As usual, he decided it wasn't worth getting into his own concerns, "We're making good time. You going to hang around?"

She turned and waved over her shoulder, "No, I think I've had enough of the great outdoors already."

"I'll keep you posted."

She disappeared down the stairs, "I know you will."

He watched her stride confidently across the uneven ground to the jeep, get in and drive off. Her slim hand flicked him a wave out the open window.

There was a scrape behind him, and he turned to see Duke approaching, a twisted grin on his face as he asked, "She's a cool one, that lady. Everything okay?"

Lee sighed, "You tell me. How we doing?"

"Still getting strange fluctuations in temp, but the general trend is downward. There's something else, though," he hooked a finger at Lee.

They walked back to the monitor together and Duke pointed at it, "Have a look at that. I took a couple stills from the video feed."

Lee squinted at the screen. The image was from the camera mounted to look across the platform at the side of the pipe. It showed black streaks across the metal of the pipe and a characteristic rainbow effect on the metal from the onboard light, like spots of gas or oil on water.

He touched the image with his finger, "Hmm…scorching on the side, but do those spots look like it experienced real extreme heat down there?"

"Yep. And have a look at this," Duke tapped a key, and a string of numbers came up. He pointed at one set of digits, "The sensor picked up a huge increase in electrical conductivity."

Lee leaned back, his mind churning over the information, "It's like it's been annealed or something."

"Yeah. Heated for a short time and then cooled slowly, which shouldn't happen at that depth. The heating, yes, but not the cooling."

"Where are we now?" Lee meant the temperature.

Duke shrugged, "Cooling is slowing but temp is still falling. Now at… around seventy-eight Celsius."

"Not even hot enough to boil water. I'd sure like to know what the hell is going on down there."

Jimmy stuck his head out of the shack and called, "Hey Lee!"

"Yeah?"

Jimmy pointed in the direction of the camp, "Bobby wants you to call!"

Lee instinctively pulled his smartphone out and checked the screen. There were two notifications in messages, one from Angeline, which is maybe why she came out here to talk to him, and the other from Bobby. He'd had the sound and vibration off in order to avoid talking to Head Office in case they called. Even in this part of Tanzania they had reception, though it was spotty.

He hit the reply for Bobby and the medic picked up immediately, "Lee?"

"Yeah Bobby? Got something?"

"You bet I do, and you aren't going to believe it. You got time to head over here?"

"No, not really. We're almost at max depth. What is it?"

There was a slight pause, "I know what killed your guy."

"And?"

"There was nothing I could find on the outside of the body, aside from the expected degradation from two days decomposing in the hot sun."

"Yeah, okay. So what was it?"

Again a pause, "Your guy was cooked."

"He was *what*?"

"He was cooked at high heat…and on the inside only."

Lee was confused, "How the hell-"

"Don't ask me how. All I know is that he looks like he was microwaved or something. His internal organs and muscles are actually cooked…like a roast. There's absolutely no way this guy could have been walking around like you said."

"But…could the sun…"

"No way. The heat required for this would be like an oven…and a microwave oven at that. There's no sign of heating on the outside. This guy was fried internally."

Lee was stunned. He swallowed, "Okay, Bobby, thanks. Uh…don't tell anyone about this right now, okay?"

"Are you kidding? All I want to do right now is take a shower. What do you want done with him?"

Another bizarre mystery, but one that might have to wait a bit, "Uh, can you seal him up and get him into one of the kitchen coolers? It's all we have to work with."

"Right. I'll get one of the guys to help me after I get him packaged up."

Bobby rung off, leaving Lee with a head full of questions. He slowly walked back to the wellhead.

"What's up?" Duke asked.

Lee gave him a grimace, "Later. Let's focus on this right now."

"Righto."

They bent their heads to the monitors again and watched the inside of the pipe blur past the camera.

Lee's attention wasn't fully on the image, though. His mind kept going around the same thing; the dead guy had been definitely walking yet was apparently already long deceased. Not only dead, but actually *cooked* from the inside.

He glanced down at his hand at the memory. The guy's body had been blistering hot when they first touched him.

Lee shook his head. He'd started this morning with what he thought would be a troublesome, but fixable, problem in engineering. Now he was saddled with a human body that was literally cooked and walking around while still hot, and a deep well that was a hundred degrees cooler than it should be.

Maybe I should be spending more time at the office.

#   #   #

Fifteen minutes later, Duke interrupted Lee's thoughts, "We're coming up on it."

Despite the inexplicable temperature readings and other anomalous data, the drop had gone smoothly.

Lee nosed up to the monitor, "Slow to one-third."

The speed of the passing pipe slowed considerably and now they could clearly see the marks of high heat on the inner wall of the pipe.

"Temp?" Lee asked.

Duke checked the number, "Settled at…fifty-five Centigrade."

Barely hotter than Death Valley in summer, "What do you think, gas or water or something keeping the temp down?"

Duke snorted. They both knew that wouldn't likely be it. Any gas or liquid at that depth and pressure should be superheated and blowing out the top of the well like a steam geyser.

Lee patted Duke's shoulder, "Give us a look down."

Duke hit a button and the view shifted from the side of the pipe to a shot of the borehole below. The sides of the pipe were glossy but showed black streaks as they slowly rose past the camera. The drill string cables and tubes still twisted their way down one side, though now they looked kinked and coiled, no longer hanging straight.

"That ain't good," Duke remarked, pointing at them.

"Uh-huh," Lee agreed. Kinked and coiled string could mean that it no longer bore the weight of the drilling platform.

The view ahead dwindled to a black circle where the lights faded. They continued watching the sides roll past the camera for another couple minutes, eyes focused on that black circle, looking for a sign of the platform or the bottom.

The end of the string finally came into view and Lee's heart sank.

Duke voiced their disappointment, "Just as we feared. No platform."

The cables all terminated in a spray like a frayed rope.

"Hold it for a sec," Lee said.

Duke hit a button and the camera cable ground to a halt. The camera had moved past the end of the string, so he shifted to the side view again. They stared at the screen until the image stabilized.

Lee pointed, "Look at the ends there."

Duke was nodding, "Yeah. That's…unusual."

Every length of flex-pipe and cable ended at the exact same spot. It was as if the entire string had been cut cleanly across by a huge knife.

"What the hell could do that?" Lee asked, half to himself.

"Nothing I know of. Do we go on?"

"Yeah, let's see what we have at the bottom. Can't be much farther."

Duke switched the camera, and they were looking straight down again.

He punched a button, "Starting down again at…one-third."

The sides of the pipe started to flow past the camera again. They peered at the screen, straining their eyes to see anything that might indicate what had happened to the drilling platform.

A few seconds later, Lee tapped Duke's shoulder, "Slow it down to one-quarter."

"Roger. What is it?"

Lee pointed at the screen, right in the center of the image where the light faded, "You see that?"

Duke squinted as the camera moved closer. There was a shimmer coming into view, not a reflection of the lights, but something else. It looked like a wavering spot in the middle of the pipe, a spot that got larger as the camera descended, like the rippling of water.

"Is that…is that a liquid of some kind?" Duke mused, "The coolant?"

Lee shook his head, "I don't think that's a liquid. Too diffuse. Looks more like a heat shimmer, like you see out here."

"Coming up on it. Do we stop?"

"No, not after coming this far. The equipment can take a lot more heat than we're getting here. Leave it at one-quarter."

"Righto."

They watched as the shimmer slowly drew closer, filling up the view. One moment, the camera was right on top of it, the shimmer covering the whole screen like they were looking through a rain-streaked window. The next instant it pushed through.

The image wavered and distorted. Lines of static cut it up into pieces. The effect was disorienting, and both men felt a moment of dizziness. The speakers emitted the first sound they'd heard the entire drop – a low, vibrating hum that rose rapidly in pitch for a second then disappeared.

Lights started blinking all over Duke's board and numbers flashed up on the screen. Alerts of all kinds were coming in.

He tapped them each to minimize them, "What was that all about?"

Lee blinked and stared at the screen, "I don't know, but maybe that thing?"

Instead of the remains of the drill assembly at the bottom of the pipe, or a bottom of solid rock, they were looking at a bright reddish-orange circle of light that looked to be about thirty feet below the camera.

Lee's first thought was that it was magma and that the camera rig would be destroyed the moment it touched it. His hand jerked reflexively toward the button to stop the descent, but his eye fell on the sensor readings, and he stopped.

Impossibly, the temperature still showed fifty-five degrees.

Duke was staring at the image, mouth agape, "Fuck me…it's a hole of some kind and it looks like there's something beyond it. Maybe we punched through to an old magma chamber." He also glanced at the temperature, "But it's a cool one, if that's what it is."

The camera kept slowly descending up to and then past the lip of the hole. The feeling was of penetrating through an aperture of some kind to another space.

Duke hit buttons to show all three camera images on the screen.

Lee whistled, "If that's a magma chamber, it's the biggest one I've ever heard of."

The image showed them descending into an enormous cavern with an orange-tinted atmosphere, the sides of which were beyond the focus of the platform camera. The view faded from reddish orange to murky gray at what must have been over several kilometers' distance. There was no obvious light source, but they could see details easily.

Lee looked at the image showing the top view. He expected to see the black circle of the hole they'd come through shrinking as they continued to drop, but all he saw was what looked like an endless white expanse, tinged with orange, like clouds at sunset.

The platform cable looked like it simply disappeared up into it, the cable appearing to end at a clean break, yet Lee could still see the cable feeding down slowly. Whatever the white was, it looked pretty dense.

"Hold it," Lee said.

Duke hit the button, stopping the descent. The platform swung slowly back and forth for a few seconds while they stared at the images.

Duke checked his readings and threw up his hands, "Temp is still at fifty-five, depth is showing eighty-two hundred sixty meters, but I know we went at least a twenty past that, pressure is only slightly higher than sea level and the electronics are buzzing like bees, like there's enormous static electricity all around. What the hell is going on?"

Lee pointed at the screen showing the downward view and spoke softly, "We maybe have bigger questions than that to answer."

Duke shifted his eyes from the diagnostics data to the camera view, "This beats anything I've…" his voice faded to a whisper, "What the…is that a *person* down there?"

Lee's finger tapped the screen lightly, his finger shaking. Just beyond his fingertip was the clear image of a person, or something that looked like a person, far below, skittering over the orange-tinted rocks on all fours, like a lizard.

Only this person wasn't wearing clothes, was colored completely black, and seemed to have a long, sinewy tail that curled around the rocks as it went, looking like it aided in balance or climbing.

Duke shook his head and scanned around the screen, "Oh my God. Look."

He pointed at one after another, tiny black dots receding into the hazy distance.

There were a lot of them.

Six

LEE STOOD ON THE REFURBISHED deck of the rig and watched the huge, twin-rotor helicopter approach. Its massive blades beat the air so hard he could feel it in his chest.

The aircraft blew by overhead, its shiny Endeavor logo winking in the sun. It circled once and settled on a flat spot next to the rig, throwing a cloud of dust over his nearby jeep. At the same time, the other company jeep pulled up, bringing Angeline from the camp.

He descended from the rig and struck out for the helicopter as its rotors wound down. Its wide rear door lowered to the ground with a whine as he and Angeline converged halfway there.

She walked up right next to him, allowing their arms to brush against each other as they neared the helicopter. It was the most physical contact they'd had with each other since they'd arrived.

She nudged him, "Everything ready?"

"It's all ready to go, if they're still thinking this mad scheme is something to 'go' with. I'm all for capping the hole and moving on at this point."

She sighed, "You, more than most, should be able to see the value in doing this. It's possibly the most – no, it is the most important thing humans have ever undertaken and we are the ones who get to be front and center…as long as we stick with the program."

It was a promise as much as a threat; stay on board with Endeavor on this and reap the benefits or be cut out of the project completely.

Lee hadn't seen much of Angeline at all lately. In the two days since they'd sent photos and videos of their well discovery to Head Office, she had spent most of her time in the office at camp, her wireless earphones sticking out and her face buried in her tablet. The entire site had been put on lockdown, with all communications restricted, and Lee had been tasked with getting the rig repaired and ready for what he was told would be the "next phase of the project".

Next phase of the project? What the hell did that mean? Lee's inquiries to Endeavor had all been rebuffed and he'd been told to simply cap the well temporarily, keeping the video and sensor data from the camera platform going and fed straight to Corporate, which they'd done.

A tight seal had been put on the project and its incredible discovery, and so far, only Lee, Duke and Angeline knew about what lay at the bottom of the hole. The rest of Duke's team were simply told that the project was locked down until the missing men could be found and a decision was made about continuing or abandoning the project. It was hard on morale, but they'd managed to keep a lid on things so far.

Lee looked ahead and saw that several people, three wearing Endeavor uniforms and three in casual khaki wear, had emerged from the rear of the helicopter. The three uniformed figures and one of the others started hauling crates out, while the other two headed for Lee and Angeline.

One of the men had a shock of white hair and a wide grin that Lee recognized. It was Bill Owen, his predecessor in his job. The other guy was a head taller than Bill, about the same height and build as Duke. Lee didn't know him, but it was apparent that Angeline did.

The two men came up to them and Angeline leaned in to peck Bill on both cheeks and shook hands with the other man, "Bill, Dan, good to see you both out here."

She swung a hand at Lee, "Lee, this is Dan Crowley. Dan, this is Lee."

The big guy leaned in, a plastic smile on his face, "I know who you are, Mr. Mitchell."

"Call me Lee," Lee extended his hand and Crowley shook it in a crushing grip. Lee took the moment to size Crowley up; mid-forties, no fat to be seen on his frame, wide eyes in a lined, expressive face. Something about the name Dan Crowley was familiar, but he was certain he'd never met the man.

Bill clapped Lee's shoulder and squeezed his hand, "Lee, you son of a gun. Been a while. How you been out here?"

Lee turned away from Dan and basked in his old boss's familiar warmth, "Bill, it's great to see you, but I admit I'm a little…uh, confused as to why you're here. I thought an elevation to the Board meant you were spending your time smoking cigars around a pool now."

Bill's smile had an edge to it and wasn't mirrored in his eyes, "Let's just say I'm basically the low man on the Board totem pole. They need a gofer and I'm the lucky guy."

The implication in his tone and eyes told Lee that Bill was here to report to Corporate on the situation. His eyes also said, *We'll talk about it later.*

Lee nodded and put on what he hoped was a welcoming smile, "Well, let's get you guys squared away first, shall we?" he indicated the jeeps, "We'll get you set up at camp-"

"Actually," Dan interrupted, speaking directly to Bill, "I should stay with Frank and see to the disposition of our equipment," he shot a thumb over his shoulder at the helicopter, "We need to get set up at the rig."

Lee looked beyond Crowley's shoulder at the aircraft, where the crates were still being off-loaded, "Equipment? Sure, but-"

"Thanks," he nodded at Lee, "Time is of the essence."

Lee narrowed his eyes and was about to ask further, but Bill cut him off, "Dan has some work to do out here. Why don't we get set up at camp in the meantime, okay?"

Dan turned away without another word and started back toward the helicopter. Lee looked at Angeline, but she seemed unsurprised by all of this.

He looked at Bill, "Who the hell is he?"

Bill put an arm through Angeline's and Lee's arms, giving them both no choice but to walk with him toward the jeeps, "At camp, okay? In the meantime, fill me in on doings here. I've been in the air for twenty hours and

I could sure use some decent coffee."

Lee spoke in a low voice, "Well, among other things, I got a dead guy here who was walking around in the sun apparently two days after he died."

"I saw your report, as well as the medic's."

"He figures the guy died at about the time the drilling rig went down."

"Yep, I saw that."

Angeline interrupted, "I imagine we'll tackle some of these things in our first meeting, won't we?" She seemed anxious to change the topic.

Lee swung his head around and saw Dan heading for the rig.

He discreetly disengaged his arm, "Excuse me for a sec," grabbed his phone out and tapped a message to Duke, who was currently at the rig, *Incoming buddy. Be nice but be careful.*

He didn't know what was going on and he didn't like it. It was great to see Bill, but Dan Crowley rubbed him the wrong way. Angeline seemed to know the guy well enough, but something was definitely off here.

He trailed Angeline and Bill and felt a twinge of foreboding. He'd been waiting for the hammer to fall since they'd notified Corporate of their discovery and now it seemed it had.

And he was beginning to feel more like a nail every minute.

*

Thirty minutes later, the group convened in the small rig supervisor's room in the central office trailer. Lee, Angeline, and Bill sipped coffee around the circular meeting table and caught up while they waited for Duke and Dan to come in from the rig.

Bill had put off answering any questions until everyone who knew about the discovery was present, insisting that he wanted everyone to be in the loop. A few minutes in the easy, chatty atmosphere Bill usually created had Lee feeling more relaxed, despite his many questions.

Duke finally ducked his head through the doorway, fixing Lee with a serious look. He brightened, though, when he saw Bill, and the two exchanged hearty greetings.

A few seconds later Dan entered with another man, one of the guys who'd been unloading the helicopter. Bill indicated that the newcomers should take chairs, and everyone squeezed close together around the table in the middle of the room.

Once they settled, Bill began by introducing everyone again to Dan and the other man, whose name was Frank Arden. He was tall and slim, with a slightly distracted air about him. Handshakes went around and it was apparent to Lee that neither Duke, nor Angeline, knew who Frank was.

"Okay, now to business," Bill pulled his tablet out of his bag and set it on the table.

"Hold on a sec, Bill," Lee put up a hand. He nodded at Dan and Frank, "It's nice to meet you both, but I'm at a bit of a loss as to what you guys actually do."

They both sat quietly while Bill explained, "Dan is actually Endeavor's new Head of Security."

Lee was surprised, "New? What about Glen-"

"Retired," Bill said, "Told Corporate he'd had enough of the running around and that he couldn't keep up with the switch to digital security. He hated that corporate espionage was now done by kids in bedrooms instead of beefy guys skulking around outside fences."

Dan shrugged, his shoulder muscles bunching up around his thick neck, "I was a bit of a computer geek in school. I'm happy spending most of my time in a nest of computers fending off hackers and the like."

Lee didn't think Dan spent much time behind a computer, given his size and the way he carried himself. He looked like he'd be more comfortable with a gun in his hand than a tablet.

Lee flicked a glance at Angeline, though, and she gave him a tiny nod of confirmation. *Oh well, I guess I.T. guys can spend time at the gym too.*

Bill pointed at Arden, "Frank here is our...uh, what do we call you, Frank?"

Frank looked uncomfortable and his Adam's apple bobbed, "Well, I'm basically a physicist, but I specialize in Quantum Field Theory and, more specifically, Brane Theory."

"Excuse me, brain theory?" Lee tapped his head.

"No. I mean B.R.A.N.E. theory."

"What the hell is that?" Duke asked before Lee could.

Bill interrupted, "I think what we will be discussing will make all of this clear."

He pulled a support bracket out of the back of the tablet and stood it on the table so everyone could see the screen, "Can we continue?"

Lee crossed his arms, "Yeah, by all means." He looked at Angeline, but she was focusing on the tablet, her expression unreadable.

Bill tapped the screen, bringing it to life, and they were presented with a split-screen. One side showed the video feed from the bottom of the hole and the other the streams of data coming in from the sensors.

Bill pointed at the side with the video feed, "What you guys have discovered here is nothing short of astounding, if not even miraculous."

The group could see a black figure in the image. It looked different than the first one they'd seen, it's body bulkier. It moved over the rocks carefully, alternating between a crawling motion and walking erect. They had no idea if it was the same one they'd originally seen, but it appeared unlikely. There were many of the creatures and even now it looked as if there might be another coming into the camera's range at the top of the image.

The action didn't appear to happen smoothly. Since their first sight of the creatures, they seemed to move smoothly at some times and jerkily at others. They even occasionally disappeared or appeared instantly. It was like watching a poorly restored old movie with gaps.

Bill double-tapped the screen and the picture zoomed in a bit, "Unfortunately, the platform cameras have no zoom capabilities and using software to digitally zoom the images on the computers only gets us so far before detail is lost in pixilation."

He double-tapped again and the picture zoomed in more. The black figure became blurry, its form even harder to make out against the shadows of nearby rocks.

He sighed, "This is about as good as it gets right now. We've cleaned up a few still pics and have had people poring over the images for a few days, but we don't know much more now than we did the moment you guys penetrated the barrier."

"Barrier?" Lee asked.

Frank broke in, "For lack of a better word, that's what we call that shimmer the camera went through at the bottom."

Bill continued, "The sensors aren't much more help either. They were designed to only pick up certain kinds of information and they can't be reconfigured, so we only now about what we did that first day."

Duke interjected, "Any ideas, though, as to what that thing is and how it could possibly be living down there, because I sure don't see how any of this adds up."

Bill said cryptically, "We'll get into that in a moment." He turned to Angeline, "You have anything for us on the environment down there?"

She pointed a finger at the data stream, "Those creatures aside for the moment, none of the readings have made any sense to me. I've been going over it all for two days and have rechecked the data from the entire last week, as well as testing the materials that had been brought up with the slurry from just before the rig blowout. I can tell you just from looking at the video that the rock we're seeing down there in that chamber is completely different from the type we were cutting through."

Lee turned to her, "How different?" She hadn't told him any of this.

She tilted her head in a half-shrug, "If I could get an actual sample, I could tell you more, but just from the look, I'd say that the rock these things are crawling over has never been subjected to the kinds of heating and pressure they should have endured at that depth. We were cutting through mainly sedimentary and sub-continental granitic rock here, with a greater proportion than usual of the latter because we're in the African Rift Valley, and it was all showing the usual signs of heating and pressure."

She flicked a hand at the screen, "I can't see much detail and the colors are off due to the atmosphere down there, but that stuff there looks more like mainly sedimentary rock, like you get in the continental platform or sub-continental slope regions. It's rock that should all be at the surface or a max depth of just a few kilometers, and we're definitely beneath that."

"So what does it mean?" Duke asked.

Angeline spread her hands, "I don't know. It doesn't make any sense to me either, but you get me a sample and I might be able to tell you."

Lee reached out and put a finger on the tablet screen, "The bigger question right now for me is, what the hell is that black thing?"

Bill blinked at him as the table fell silent.

Lee continued, "I mean, beyond what it looks like, because..." he trailed off, unwilling to finish.

Dan spoke up, "A demon."

All eyes turned toward him. He'd said it with confidence, not as if he were simply offering up a guess.

"A demon," Lee repeated after several beats.

He looked around the table and noted that Bill, Frank, Dan – and even Angeline - all wore the same expression; they weren't shocked or disbelieving. Only Duke and himself looked skeptical.

He gave Angeline a brief assessing look and locked eyes with Bill, "Demons, seriously? You really think..." he paused as Bill shrugged and their lack of reaction dawned on him, "Wait a sec. You guys are not surprised by all this."

Now Bill began to look uncomfortable, "Lee..."

Duke started to bluster, "This is bullshit. Pure, spring-fed, steaming bullshit. There's no such thing as fucking demons, aside from my ex-wife," he flicked a glance at Angeline, "Pardon me."

Lee raised a hand and Duke fell silent with a disgusted snort.

Lee spoke to Bill, "You know something. You've seen or heard about this before." His voice rose, "What the fuck is going on here? I know what these things *look* like, but are you seriously telling me," he pointed at the screen, "that you think we punched a hole through..."

Bill nodded slowly, "To Hell, yes."

Seven

"YOU'RE ALL OUT OF YOUR goddamn minds," Duke spat the words, "You're telling us you think that there's actually a Hell and that it's sitting only eight kilometers below East Africa? Bull. Shit." He glowered at everyone.

Bill leaned in and put up a placating hand, "Duke, Lee, just hang on a sec. We're not saying that we believe this is the literal Hell, but we're not saying that we don't, either."

"But it sure looks like it," Dan said.

Lee shot a glance at the security man. He certainly looked as confident as he sounded.

He turned to Angeline instead, disbelief in his voice, "You don't buy this, do you? You're more of a scientist than I am."

She didn't answer him directly. She merely nodded at Bill's tablet, "Maybe if you showed them, Bill."

Lee narrowed his eyes at her, wondering how far out of the loop he'd been on this whole thing.

Or rather, how far in she was.

He switched his attention to Bill again, "Show us what?"

Bill reached around the tablet and tapped an icon on the side of the screen. A new window opened up.

His finger hovered over the screen, "This is old, and the quality is shit.

The sound cuts in and out, so just bear with it."

He hit the screen and an image ballooned onto it, showing a wide white room and some people wearing light gray, loose-fitting body suits with helmets and face shields. They were standing around a table in the center of the room, frozen in the middle of doing something to a man lying on the table. It looked like some sort of makeshift operating theater.

Before Lee could ask anything, Bill tapped the screen, and the image came to life. Immediately, loud shrieks erupted from the tablet speaker, guttural screams that sounded like they were scraping the flesh from the screamer's throat.

It was the man on the table who was screaming.

Screaming and twisting, his body convulsing, rising up and banging back down onto the table, over and over.

The people around him jerked and dipped almost in time, trying to control the flailing man's movements. Half a dozen voices speaking another language rode over each other. The clanking of metal could be heard, and a tray of instruments clattered to the floor somewhere in the room.

The sound cut in and out, making everything seem to be happening in staccato bursts, though the grainy image wasn't interrupted. The quality of video looked to be at least twenty years old.

The camera moved around, shaking and bobbing, obviously held in someone's hand. It moved closer to the table and an arm came out from under the camera, motioning to people to step aside.

It moved in and focused down on the man on the table. The arms of several people were holding the man's limbs down and it seemed that he'd broken through frayed straps that dangled off the sides of the table. His head was a blur as it jerked wildly from side to side. All that could be seen of his face was a white smear with streaks of black across it.

The camera came to within a couple feet of the man and he suddenly stopped convulsing and stared directly at the camera for a second. Then there was a loud bang, and the image went completely dark. Another voice started screaming in the darkness before the sound stopped, cutting off this new shriek, and the video ended.

There was silence around the meeting table.

Lee stared at the dark image on the tablet for several seconds, feeling sweat prickling on his scalp, "What the hell was that?"

Bill took a deep breath, "For lack of a better word, that…was a case of possession."

"*Possession?*" Duke scoffed, but some of the certainty had drained from his voice. He'd been as shaken by the video as Lee.

Bill hit the slider bar at the bottom of the video playback window. He drew his finger across and pulled the video back five seconds, to the instant where the captive man's face could be seen, "We think so, yes."

Lee stared at it, feeling his skin crawl and his insides contract.

The man's face was drained of all color, appearing almost as white as the walls around him. The only contrast was his eyes and mouth. The mouth was open impossibly wide and showed only a black maw with stained teeth that looked too large in the shrunken features. And the eyes…

The eyes were both completely black – wide open in either terror or rage – and solid, glossy black.

Lee blinked and looked away. He reached for his coffee and noted his hand shaking. He clenched his fist.

Bill laid the tablet screen-down on the table, "That language you were hearing was Russian and that video was shot in 1992."

Lee hazarded a guess, "Kola?"

Bill nodded, "Yes. The official reasons given for closing down their deep bore were that the Soviet Union had collapsed and funding had dried up, and that the temperatures they had encountered were too much for their equipment, but the real reason," he tapped the back of the tablet, "was something else entirely."

Lee stared at him, "You know this for a fact."

"Yes. We know this. We have their data and this, as well as several other videos showing shit that's even worse."

"Like what?"

Bill's eyes took on a thoughtful cast, "Like recordings from a Japanese project where they stuck a microphone down their deep bore and recorded…"

"What?"

"What sounded like the unending screams of people being tortured."

Despite himself Lee felt a chill go through him.

Duke whispered hoarsely, "A crock of shit. I heard rumors about that stuff. It was just heat stress on the pipe echoing up top. I've heard weird shit too-"

Lee turned to Angeline, "You've known about this for…how long?"

She wouldn't meet his eyes, "Lee, it's…this is so much bigger than you think."

He leaned in, his eyes boring into the side of her head, "You've known about this…whatever this is, since the very beginning, haven't you?" His gaze roamed around the table, "You all have."

Duke's brow furrowed, "What's going on here?"

Lee barked a bitter laugh and swept his hand around at everyone, "Duke, you're not getting it. This whole project wasn't about setting any records or anything like that. It was about this," he pointed at the tablet, "and only this."

He spoke to Bill, "Let me guess. Somehow, Copeland got wind of the Kola situation and figured there was an angle here for him. He's not really the religious type, though, so-"

Frank leaned forward suddenly, "If I may?"

Lee spread his hands, "I'm all ears."

The physicist put his hands on the table, his fingers intertwined, "I'm also not the religious type of person and I do not think we have literally found the doorway to Hell…"

Dan snorted softly.

Lee sniffed, "Then what, pardon the expression, the hell is at the bottom of our hole? And what is that video all about?"

Bill said quietly, "Let him speak, please, Lee."

Lee looked at Angeline. This time she looked back, "Hear him out, Lee."

"Okay, fine. Go ahead."

Frank started again, "Let me rephrase. I said I don't think we found a doorway to anything like a biblical hell, but I think it is a doorway."

"A doorway?" Duke asked.

"Yes, and I'll have to ask you to bear with me as I make certain assertions here. The theories and math do back me up, but it would take weeks to explain it all in detail."

He looked around, but no one seemed inclined to comment, so he went on, "There are several theories in particle physics currently connected to the idea that we live in a multi-verse; that our universe is but one of many, perhaps millions, perhaps even an infinite number, that are nested next to each other, or overlapping each other, lying over each other like layers of onion paper."

"I'm already lost," Duke muttered.

"Brane Theory," Frank continued, "asserts that the three-dimensional reality we inhabit is limited to a 'brane', or membrane, that is one of many inside higher-dimensional space that we call 'hyperspace', or 'The Bulk'."

Lee put up a finger, "I know a little about the idea of other dimensions, but aren't they supposed to be tiny, like sub-atomically small?"

Frank nodded enthusiastically, "Yes, that's one idea, but there is another that says the additional dimensions could be as large and potentially infinite as the three that we know. I happen to favor this idea, because it explains why gravity is such a relatively weak force compared to the other natural forces and also why the cosmological constant is also very small."

Duke spoke hesitantly, "The...the what?"

Frank waved a hand, "It isn't important to know that, sorry. However, what is important for us is that these dimensional branes can, in some models, be seen to interact with each other – to flow through each other and influence each other – and the points where these branes intersect-"

Lee finished the thought, "Gives us those doorways. I've seen Star Trek."

"Exactly," Frank bobbed his head, "It is my theory that the shimmer we saw at the bottom of this hole marks the boundary, one point where our brane of existence meets another. In fact, I think that the existence of this boundary is not limited to this spot either."

"So the Kola team found the same thing," Lee said.

"Yes. They must have encountered it and punched through it as well."

"But that's practically a third of the world away from here," Duke said. He was catching up to the topic.

Frank turned to him, his hands describing an arc in the air, "If branes are infinitely large, their areas of intersect could be at least planet sized, if not immensely larger. They could appear at any angle, any configuration, due to the natural laws that govern each brane."

He held up a fist, the fingers loosely separated, "Imagine this is the earth, rolling along quite happily in our brane." He made his other hand into a similar loose fist, "And this is another place – another planet perhaps – rolling along in its own brane, very different from ours, with different natural laws, even."

He brought the hands together, the fingers of each intersecting until he had a double fist in front of him, "You could have the potential of a planet-wide series of intersect points, in fact, a surface of intersection like a sheet that, in this case, exists under our crust at varying depths across half the planet or more."

Lee glanced around the table at the others. It was apparent they'd all heard this explanation before, even Angeline appeared to have, and he vowed to quiz her about it later.

Duke said, "I think I'm with you so far, maybe, but where do hell and demons come into all of this?"

Bill spoke this time, "Maybe there is no Hell, as we've been taught to think of it. Maybe our ideas of a classical Hell stem from old knowledge of this intersection with a different reality."

"Or maybe it is actually Hell," Dan interjected.

A flicker of distaste flitted across Frank's face, "I prefer to think of it as something less supernatural and more something that's *other*-natural. Those creatures that appear to us as demons, could simply be people inhabiting another realm, one with different rules, though I think not too different from ours."

"How so?" Lee asked.

"Well, they may look very different in a purely superficial way – larger, pitch-black in color, sporting tails and so on, but their body symmetry is basically the same as ours. They have a head and four limbs in roughly the same ratios as ours. This implies that their evolution has been driven by at least some of the same forces as ours."

Lee shifted in his seat, "So you're saying that 'Hell' for us, as it has been depicted in art, the Bible, Dante and so on, may be just the result of people's encounters with these…demons or whatever throughout ancient history?"

Frank shrugged, "It's possible that people in the past may have encountered intersection points closer to the surface and possibly even crossed over. Our intersection point is at a depth of eight kilometers, but Kola's was at twelve. Some may be only meters below the surface, or perhaps even above ground. Miners or people exploring deep caves may have encountered it."

Duke shook his head, "Now that is definitely bullshit. Something like that would make the news no matter when it happened."

"Maybe it did," Angeline spoke up, "You just heard the list of sources. Have you read Dante's descriptions in his Divine Comedy?"

Duke looked at her blankly.

She went on, "His account of what he called his tour of Hell and his descriptions of the demons he encountered seem to mirror the creature down our hole."

Lee was tapping his fingers on the table in front of him, "A coincidence?"

Frank nodded, his brow furrowed in thought, "Possibly, but it would be an enormous one. It's hard to tell much with these images, though. We're looking at things from above and have little to go on for scale. Also, there's-"

"They look like they move funny too," Duke said, "kind of jerky."

Frank nodded again, "I have a theory about that. In addition to the possibility of different physical laws being at play here, there may be a time element as well."

"What?" Duke asked.

"Time may function differently there as well, and our equipment is catching only fleeting glimpses of things, like…a series of snapshots that are being compressed into a movie. This gives me greater confidence in the theory that this place," he indicated the screen, "exists in a different dimensional plane, rather than a different physical place in our own universe."

Lee shook his head, "Wait a sec. You said the branes could be infinite in size, right?"

Frank nodded.

Lee went on, "Then surely even venturing out into space would be risky for us. If there are brane intersects here on Earth, there would be-"

Frank interrupted him, eyebrows raised, "No. It's a good assumption, but the theory doesn't support that. Given facts about gravitation that I cannot outline for you here in less than a few hours, suffice to say that brane intersection points seem to require some sort of specific gravity well – not too large and not too small – in order for the boundaries between membranes to allow material or energy to transit."

Lee furrowed his brow, "You're saying that Earth's mass is…"

"Just about right to allow the branes to intersect and the barriers to form. Venus also. Mars would be too small and the outer planets too massive."

"Lucky us," Duke muttered.

Lee shook his head in wonderment, "It's…too big. It's too much to believe, surely."

Bill flipped his tablet over and went back to the screen showing the Endeavor video feed. He pointed at the image coming from the bottom of their own hole, "Yet there it is."

Duke snorted, "Yeah, so there it is. So what? Granted, it's the discovery of the century, but what's next, aside from your article in *Scientific American* or whatever," he flipped a hand at Frank.

The physicist squirmed in his seat, "Well, we have to get better images and more helpful data to start, before we can even guess at what this really is. From a sheer scientific perspective, this will knock the lid off everything from cosmology to quantum physics, religion, you name it."

Bill nodded agreement, "Yep. Can you imagine the effect something like this will have on everyone who doesn't work in a lab or with a telescope? Religion, Philosophy, History, everything."

"Our understanding of everything will certainly change," Frank agreed.

Duke flung a hand at the tablet, "It sure as hell changed things for that Kola guy in the video, didn't it? Anyone thinking of that? He certainly looked like his worldview had shifted."

Lee was reminded of their own mystery, "That's right. Whatever we're dealing with here, it obviously is dangerous. We still don't know what happened to our own people, but we've already got a dead guy in the cooler, the circumstances of which we can't come close to explaining."

Frank said, "That's why we need more information."

Lee read into it, "Those crates you guys arrived with," he looked at Bill, "Better equipment, cameras and sensors, that sort of thing?"

Bill hesitated only a moment, "That…and a bit more."

Lee flicked a glance around the table. He knew what was coming; the size of those crates told him there was clearly more than a few more cameras and tiny sensors brought along. Also, the fact that the hole they bored here was much wider by far than any deep bore needed to be. It all led to one conclusion.

He shook his head even as he said the words, "You're not serious, Bill. You're not going to-"

Bill looked resigned, but resolute, "Yes we are." He looked around at everyone, "We're going to go down there."

Eight

LEE SCUFFED HIS FOOT ON the deck, watching the last section of prefab wall slide into place around the well. It was suspended from the refurbished deck crane's arm and being guided into place by two rig hands.

The crew had managed to monkey the damaged deck crane's arm and its hydraulics and cables into something that was serviceable again by cutting their way into the workings and hooking in power from the main rig generator. That had taken a day and a half to accomplish, but the work they'd been able to do since then had made the time spent worthwhile.

Lee turned to Frank, who was supervising the placement of all the equipment they'd brought in the helicopter, "We on track so far?"

Frank replied but kept his eyes on the men fitting the last wall section in place, "Yes. I think we'll be ready to head down tomorrow morning as planned," he ducked his head to check his tablet.

Lee ran his eyes over the odd structure taking shape before them, "What's in those walls again?"

Frank looked up from his tablet, "It's nothing more, really, than an updated Faraday Cage; a room that can be insulated from outside electrical interference, as well as protect the outside environment from anything that discharges from the well."

Lee eyed the tanks attached to one of the walls already in place, "And it'll be airtight as well?"

"Not completely, no, but close enough. Aside from the initial discharge of whatever it was that blew out when the doorway was first breached, sensors have detected nothing in the past couple of days coming out of the hole and we want to keep it that way. Therefore, for protection both ways," he flicked his touch-pen forward and back to indicate he meant both in the hole and on the surface, "this room will act as something like an airlock."

Lee looked intently at the physicist, "You really think that we can do this, and that's it's worth doing?"

"Worth it? Definitely. Think of what we can potentially learn here; biology, chemistry and physics of all types will benefit."

It was obvious to Lee that thoughts of the possible social and religious ramifications never even occurred to Frank. It was all just about the science.

"And as to the 'can we do it'?" he asked.

Frank waved a hand, "Without a doubt. The environmental considerations, such as temperatures and pressures, are not too much of a challenge. They are, in fact, much less severe than we imagined and prepped for."

It was again a reminder to Lee that Endeavor had known about the possible existence of a dimensional doorway long ago and had undertaken this entire project just to confirm it and capitalize on it somehow. He'd been meaning to nail down both Bill and, especially Angeline, about that for the past couple of days, but had been busy getting the rig and its crane secured and ready again.

He said, "I think some famous guy once said that 'Just because we can do a thing, it doesn't necessarily follow that we *must* do it', or something like that."

Frank gave him a genuinely bewildered look, "If we adhered to that line of thinking, we'd still be shitting in the woods and waiting for lightning strikes to cook our food."

The comment seemed so out of character for the physicist that it caught Lee by surprise. He grinned, "I suppose you're right."

"I am."

He said it matter-of-factly, but there was nothing of ego in it. Frank didn't seem to Lee like a guy who was in on a big conspiracy. He was just a scientist, as tunnel-visioned and committed to this project as he would be to any other. Lee didn't know whether to admire or pity him for it, as it either made him simply naïve or maybe just self-involved. Either way, Lee had a hard time resenting the guy.

Frank had returned to examining his tablet and Lee cleared his throat to get his attention again, "Ahh…"

Frank looked up, "Yes?"

"About this time thing you were talking about?"

"Yes?"

Lee frowned, "I'm trying to get my head around it. If time operates at a different speed over there," he nodded down at the wellhead, "then how come we see things at the same speed on our video and data feeds?"

"We don't, at least not exactly," Frank pursed his lips, "It's a bit of a mystery to me too, but you recall that the video feed looks like it's chopped up, kind of jerky?"

Lee nodded slowly, "Yeah."

"I think it's an aberration connected to electromagnetism; the speed of light and so on…something seems to be acting as a compensator. The speed of light – and therefore electrical impulses in an unimpeded medium – must remain constant," he pointed down at the wellhead, "perhaps even across dimensional barriers."

"I don't follow you."

Frank turned to him and held up his hands to demonstrate, "It's like the old experiment where you shine a beam of light through an impeding medium, like a tank full of water. When the light goes through the tank, it slows down by a few millionths of a percent. Yet when the light emerges out the far side, it somehow regains its original speed again, without any apparent extra input of energy."

Lee winced trying to imagine it, "That's giving me a headache."

"Really? I find it fascinating."

Lee shrugged, "Well, I'll take your word for it about that stuff, but what about the physical discrepancies? Our cables and equipment penetrate the barrier as well and, if time is flowing at a different rate, how does the cable continue to spool out at a constant rate without backing up or suddenly reeling out at an incredible rate?"

Frank pointed at Lee's chest, "That is the million-dollar question, and I don't have an answer for it yet. However, I would surmise that the barrier somehow compensates for it as well. It obviously has to in some way," he raised an eyebrow at Lee, "Perhaps within the barrier, all physical laws from either side can act without constraint."

Lee gave him a twisted grin, "You mean all things may be possible in there? Now you're sounding like Dan."

Frank just snorted and shook his head, "God and the Devil are too simplistic for my taste, I'm afraid," he went back to looking at his tablet.

Lee was going to ask more, but his phone burred in his pocket, and he fished it out. He saw it was from Bill, *Just the guy I also need answers from...*

He put a finger up to Frank, "Excuse me," and turned away.

Frank had his face buried in his tablet and didn't even seem to notice.

Lee walked a few feet away, "Yeah, Bill, what's-"

"Get back to camp right away," Bill rasped, "We have a situation." He sounded stressed.

"A situation?"

"Maybe another of our missing guys. Get back here. We need your jeep." He hung up.

Lee stared at the phone for a moment, *One of our missing guys?* Images of the first man stumbling across the ground toward him and Duke came to mind, *Shit. Not another one.*

He waved to Frank, who didn't notice him anyway, and spotted Duke on the other side of the wellhead, keeping an eye on the crane arm. He waved, pointed to his chest and then in the direction of camp.

Duke got the message and waved him on, indicating he would stay at the rig.

Lee headed down off the rig two steps at a time and jumped into his jeep. He hit the starter and aimed the vehicle down the dirt road toward camp, his mind filled with mounting dread.

He still had his phone in hand and hit the quick dial for Angeline. The number went straight to voicemail, and he swore. He hadn't seen much of her for the past two days and then only in meetings with others around. She hadn't come by his room the past two nights and the one time he dropped by hers, she didn't seem to be there – at least, she hadn't answered the door.

Their relationship was complicated at the best of times, and they often found themselves on opposite sides of the table when it came to company policy issues, but their respect for each other, as well as their mutual attraction, kept things on an even keel. Recently, though, he was beginning to feel that they might be further apart than he realized. They certainly weren't communicating as well as they should, either professionally or personally.

Some hard discussions were probably coming up for them. Of course, people who need to talk should actually be in the same room together at some point...

A few minutes later, he pulled up to camp, spotting Bill and Bobby the medic together, talking to what looked like a local. Whatever they were talking about, it didn't look congenial; the local was very agitated.

Bill grabbed the door handle before Lee even stopped the jeep. He jumped in and Bobby and the local guy leapt into the back.

Bill pointed out the windshield, "Follow the road west to the highway that runs toward Manyovu. We're heading to a small village at the junction."

Lee hit the gas, "Yeah, I think I know it. I've seen it on the local maps. What's up?"

The local man patted the back of Lee's driver's seat impatiently and spoke with heavily accented English, "A...man came to our village. He was sick...very sick."

"What kind of man?" Lee asked.

"He wore the blue shirt of your company. We thought he was mzungu," the man said.

Lee looked at Bill, "White man?"

Bill shook his head, "In a modern sense, yes, it means white person, but really it means 'someone who wanders'."

Lee looked at the man in his mirror, "When did this man come to you?"

"Five days ago," the man avoided Lee's eyes.

Bill blurted, "Five days ago? You didn't say that before. Why did you take so long to tell us?"

The man looked like he might bolt from the moving jeep, so Lee tried to calm him, "It's okay. We just want to know what happened."

The man gulped, his eyes darting back and forth, "We took him in…he was very, very sick. Then he died for a while."

Bobby jerked his head at the man, "He what? What do you mean he 'died for a while'?"

"And no one came to tell us," Bill said accusingly.

The man patted Lee's seatback again, almost frantic, "You must hurry." He spoke to Bill, "He died soon, and we were afraid that we might be blamed for his death. We…we are farmers. We did not know how to help him. Our *mganga*…our *daktari*…tried to help with some white medicines, but the man went away from the world after only an hour." He made a floating motion with his hand.

"So he did die, then," Bobby said.

"Yes. We buried him at the edge of the village and hoped that no one would come looking for him."

"Then what's our rush now?" Bobby asked.

The man looked at Lee in the mirror, his eyes dark, "He came back again."

There was stunned silence in the jeep.

Bobby met Lee's eyes in the mirror. They were both thinking the same thing, about their guy in the cooler at camp.

Lee asked carefully, "When the man came back, what happened?"

"It was today, in the morning. He walked into the village. There were some women at the water pump. He…" the man broke off.

"He what?" Bill prompted, "What did he do?"

"He attacked them. He grabbed one woman and shouted at her. He…bit her on the face, like he wanted…wanted to eat her."

"Jesus Christ," Bobby whispered.

The man continued, "The woman's son grabbed the bucket from the water pump and hit him on the head. The man fell down but he did not sleep. We had come from hearing the screaming and six of us held the man down. We carried him to the cement building that holds the water pipe and put him

71

inside. All the time he was screaming at us, speaking words we couldn't hear and trying to bite us."

"He's still in there now?" Bill asked.

"Yes. Our daktari will not see him. He says the man is *shetani*...we all know it."

Lee steered the jeep around a shallow washout in the dirt road and asked Bill, "Shetani? I don't know that one."

Bill's face was grim, "Devil. It means devil."

"Please hurry," the man said again, "We must hurry."

Despite the rough road, Lee pressed the gas a little harder.

*

It took another ten minutes of jerking and bouncing to get to the intersection with the highway.

The man's village was basically a collection of wood and concrete buildings around the intersection, surrounded by dry fields and spindly trees. Lee marveled at how people could make a life in such inhospitable conditions, but they'd been doing it in this part of the world for millions of years already.

The man pointed past Lee's head out the windshield, "There. There is the pump and the pipe house."

Just to one side of the intersection that cut through the village was an open space with one small concrete structure about four meters on a side. Next to that was a concrete slab with a metal pipe sticking up out of it, looking like a glorified fire hydrant, the source of the village's drinking water.

Several people were standing around the open space, milling about and talking. Lee noted that no one was near the concrete building. They approached and clustered around the jeep as it pulled up.

The local jumped out and started talking to them. It was obvious that the villagers been tasked with watching the building while one of their number had run to the Endeavor site.

He translated quickly while Lee and the others got out, "They say that the sheta- ah, the man screamed for much time after I left, saying nothing

72

that they understood. Some people here can speak English as well as French, so it wasn't one of those. Then they say he became quiet and has not spoken since."

"And nobody bothered to check on him?" Bobby spoke with anger in his voice, "Where's your doctor – your daktari?"

The local man answered, "He will not see this shetani again. He says it is a matter for God now."

Bobby muttered to Lee and Bill, "People find some sick and injured man who then falls unconscious, and they fucking bury the guy without calling a proper doctor. Then he wakes up, digs himself out somehow and they just slam him in a goddamn oven."

He pointed at the concrete shack, "It must be hot enough to fry eggs in there. That's why he went silent. Jesus Christ."

He started for the shack and Bill and Lee hastened to keep up.

The local came after them, "You must be careful! He is a man no longer."

Bobby spoke over his shoulder, "Well he isn't any devil, I can tell you that. If he's anything he's probably a true corpse now."

The man stopped, but called after them, "If he is not shetani, he is also not a man. He is only mzungu now, a wanderer between worlds."

The words stuck in Lee's mind, reminding him of the guy they'd found out in the scrub, literally wandering the countryside and hollowed out of mind and spirit.

Despite the heat, he felt cold inside.

The three men made it to the building. There was a shovel handle pushed through the thick hasp on the door and fresh scars in the wood, like it had been subjected to some force while in the lock.

Bobby made to grab it, but Bill put a hand on his arm, "Hold it. What if they're right and he's crazy or something?"

Bobby scowled at him, "If he wasn't when they stuffed him in here, he will be by now from the heat. Come on, we have to get him out."

Lee was looking back at the fearful villagers behind them, "Wait a sec."

Bobby put a hand on the shovel handle, "The guy could be dying as we speak, Lee!"

Lee put a hand on the door, "Just a sec. Let's say the guy was just sick," he waved a hand at the villagers, "They say he was raving and trying to bite people. Does that sound like anything you know?"

Bobby paused. He took a moment to think about it and drew a deep breath, "Yeah. Rabies."

"So what if the guy has rabies? It's still prevalent in Africa, right?"

Bobby furrowed his brow as he thought, "If he was already displaying symptoms like uncontrolled movements and mania, he's as good as dead anyway, I guess, but we don't know yet. We have to-"

Bill interrupted, "But doesn't rabies take, like, weeks or months to develop?"

"Generally, yes, but it can take as short as a few days to as long as a year, depending on a number of factors."

They all looked at each other for a few beats.

"So what do we do?" Bill asked.

"We go in anyway," though Bobby sounded less sure now.

Lee asked, "You got anything to knock him out if he's dangerous?"

"I have some Midazolam. It's fast-acting and works well as an anticonvulsant and muscle relaxant." He dropped his bag and rummaged around for a moment, bringing out a syringe and a small bottle.

He held them up, "Can we go in now?"

Lee grabbed the shovel handle, "You keep that stuff ready. Bill and I will handle the door and the guy if necessary."

"Right."

Lee put his ear up to the door and listened. He could feel the heat radiating off the metal from inches away. Bobby was right, if the guy had been in there for any time at all, he was probably already beyond help.

"I don't hear anything," he carefully started sliding the handle out of the hasp, keeping one hand against the door in case the guy inside lunged at it or something.

The handle slid free quietly and he kept it in his hand. With the other, he grabbed the door handle and slowly pulled it open.

In contrast to the bright day outside, the inside of the building looked pitch black. The sun was almost overhead and didn't penetrate the open doorway at all.

"Damn, no flashlight," Bill muttered.

"Our eyes will adjust," Bobby said and stepped through.

Lee followed, with Bill behind him.

The concrete walls were almost a foot thick, and Lee expected it to be somewhat cooler inside, but it was sweltering. A few pinpricks of light stabbed down from above, showing them that the roof was thin, corrugated metal. That explained the heat, but it also allowed some dim light to penetrate the gloom.

A few seconds inside was enough for their eyes to start to adjust and Lee could see the convoluted bulk of the water pump and its pipes sitting in the center of the shack, which was one room. The floor was a sand-covered concrete slab and their feet made crackling sounds as they moved.

Bobby was in the lead, squinting into the corners, "I don't see anyone, do you?"

Bill angled to the right and peered around the corner of the pump, "Nope. Not over here. Maybe-"

A piercing shriek split the thick air of the shack and a form hurtled at them from the left. Bobby turned just in time to meet the attacker and get his hands up before the impact drove him back past Lee.

The two bodies crashed to the floor and slid on the sand right up to the wall. Lee and Bill jumped forward and tried to grab a flailing leg or arm, but the attacker was thrashing around too much.

Bobby had hit his head on the floor when he fell and was momentarily stunned, just barely managing to keep a grip on his attacker's arms. He'd dropped the syringe and bottle of Midazolam, which had smashed on the floor under him.

The figure was on top of Bobby, screaming and twisting wildly. Lee and Bill could see the man's head lunging in and out, trying to bite Bobby in the face, but it was all in shadow and hard to track.

Bobby's voice cut through the screaming, "Get...him off...of me!"

Lee and Bill made an attempt to grab the man's shoulders, but the attacker reared back violently. Lee staggered to one side but managed to keep his feet. Bill fell backward and struck his head on the side of the pump, collapsing to the floor.

In the moment, Bobby released his hold on the man's arms and rolled to the side, trying to get out from under him, "Lee! Get him off! Aah!" he yelled in pain as the attacker grabbed a handful of his hair and yanked his head back, almost snapping his neck.

Lee didn't have time to think. He still had the shovel in one hand. He raised it and brought it down high on the attacker's back. The heel of the spade struck between the shoulder blades and the tip hit him in the back of the head.

The man fell off of Bobby, rolling away. Bobby pushed himself away in the opposite direction, sliding up against the wall.

The man wasn't down, though. He leapt to his feet and ran straight at Lee, arms outstretched and yelling something unintelligible.

Lee reacted instinctively. He brought the shovel up in an effort to ward off the attack and the man ran straight into the pointed blade of the spade. The force pushed Lee back against the wall and the end of the shovel's handle slid through his fingers and impacted with the wall behind him.

The attacker kept coming, the sheer force of his rage driving him forward. The blade cut through his already ripped shirt and sunk deep into his stomach. The handle splintered with a loud crack and the man fell to the floor in front of the doorway. He lay on his side and a gout of dark blood vomited from his gaping mouth. It hit the floor in wet lumps, like jelly.

Mortified, Lee knelt at the man's head, thinking he was dead, but he saw the man's mouth moving, bloody saliva dripping from it. His body shuddered and the man rolled over onto his back, the broken handle of the shovel sticking straight up out of his upper abdomen.

Lee stared into the pale face as Bobby crawled up beside him. Even in the light from the open door, the man's eyes were completely black. His bloody mouth opened and closed, the purple lips pulling back over bloodstained teeth as he tried to speak. He noted the man's greasy blond hair and realized with a shock that this was the young man they'd seen in the rig video, the one by the rail when the blowout occurred.

He didn't look young now.

Bobby leaned in closer, and the man's head twisted his way suddenly, the teeth snapping at him.

Bobby jerked back and Lee angled his head, "Better check Bill."

Bill's own voice responded from behind them, "No, I'm all right. Just smacked my head."

He crawled up beside Lee and Bobby and the three men looked down at the man on the floor, whose mouth was still moving.

"What's he saying?" Bill asked.

Lee fought down his revulsion and stared at the man's bleeding, bubbling mouth, "I don't know, but he looks to be in the same shape as that guy the other day," he glanced across the body at Bobby.

Bobby gingerly put a hand on the man's arm, "He's burning up. I felt it when he was on top of me. He's like a furnace."

Lee placed a hand on the man's chest. It felt like he was on fire inside.

He looked down at the ruined face. The lips were pulled back into what looked like a grim smile, but still moving.

He leaned closer.

"Watch it, Lee," Bill warned.

"We have to know what's going on here." Lee carefully put his hand on the man's forehead to prevent him from making a sudden lunge and put his face close to the man's ear.

He whispered, "Who are you? What happened to you?"

He drew back. The man's mouth was still moving around that odd smile.

He leaned in again and put his ear over the man's mouth.

The lips kept moving, the whisper hoarse and bubbly, "G-giza iasubiri. Giza iasubiri."

Lee pulled back, *What the…?*

"He says, 'Darkness awaits'." The voice came from the doorway behind him.

Lee turned.

The local man stood there, his eyes wide, "It is Swahili. He says that darkness waits for you."

"Kula…" the blond man spoke again.

Lee leaned down and heard, "Kula wanaume…ni mlan…mlangoni."

A bubble of blood burst on the man's lips as he started to laugh. The laugh started low and rose in pitch, quickly becoming a high shriek; a screaming cackle of madness that echoed in the concrete room and buzzed their eardrums before suddenly stopping.

Lee looked down again.

The man was dead, the mouth stretched wide in a rictus of a smile, the black eyes turned to gray.

In the sudden silence, Lee thought he could hear his own heartbeat echoing off the concrete walls.

He looked up at the villager, the unspoken question in his eyes.

The man swallowed, "He...he said, 'The eater of men is waiting at the door.'"

"What does that mean?" Bill asked, his voice rough and shaky.

Lee looked outside, past the cluster of villagers, in the direction of the drilling rig somewhere over the dusty hills, "I don't have a clue, Bill, but tomorrow morning we're heading through a door of sorts, aren't we?"

Nine

"JUST LIKE THE OTHER GUY," Bobby snapped off a glove and stepped back from the table, "See for yourself."

Lee had spent the past fifteen minutes against the wall of the medical room, avoiding looking at the table. Now he walked over and hesitantly leaned in, looking into the dead man's insides with an expression of distaste.

He didn't have any idea what he was looking at, but everything was unexpectedly grayish brown in there, rather than red. He tried to keep from breathing in.

He pointed, "It's like looking into a stew pot or something."

"Yep, this guy was fried on the inside, just like the other one. Even his blood is clotted and brown."

"It wasn't when he puked at that water shack."

"No, but it was already clotting even then. What he threw up looked like strawberry jam instead of blood."

Lee moved away from the table, feeling a little dizzy, "So what does it all mean?"

Bobby snorted, "You're asking me? I don't have a clue." He pointed at the body, "There's no way this guy should have been able to attack us, no way he should have even been moving around, for Christ's sake."

"Like you said, just like the other guy."

"Yeah, I'm more inclined to believe you and Duke about that now, and I'm starting to think that those villagers were right in assuming this guy was dead when they buried him five days ago. He shows even more deterioration than the first guy."

Lee pulled the plastic sheet over the body, "It just doesn't make any sense."

"You got that right." Bobby pulled off his other glove and tossed it into the trashcan with its partner, "What do we do about this, Lee?"

Lee started for the door, "Bill is probably finding out about that right now. He's been talking to Corporate since we got back."

He pointed at the body, "Put him in the cooler with the other guy for now, Bobby. Both of them have to go back to the 'States as soon as possible."

He left without waiting for an acknowledgement from Bobby, grateful to be away from that odor of cooked insides and rotting meat. There was no one in the rec area or the kitchen, despite it being early evening. Everyone was working at the rig to make sure they were ready to go in the morning, and the camp felt abandoned.

He made his way to the central trailer housing the offices and saw that the communications room was that only one with a light showing under the door. He heard Bill's voice inside and rapped twice.

"Come."

He pushed it open and found Bill sitting with Dan Crowley. It was immediately apparent that the atmosphere was tense; both men looked simultaneously awkward and relieved to be interrupted.

Lee stopped in the doorway, "Sorry, am I intruding?"

Bill waved him in, "No, it's okay."

Dan immediately stood, "I was just leaving anyway."

"Not on my account?" Lee said.

Dan flicked him a plastic smile, "Never," he looked back at Bill, "I have a lot to prep for tomorrow anyway."

He slid past Lee and went out.

Bill pointed to the empty chair and Lee sat, shooting a thumb over his shoulder, "What's up with him?"

Bill waved his hand, "Nothing. Just a bit of tug-o'-war about tomorrow."

"Uh-huh."

Bill sighed, "Corporate wants to go ahead with the exploration, but Dan thinks we should get our shit sorted out up here first, like finding the rest of the missing men and doing a better job of securing the site, especially in light of the fact that at least one of our lost workers has disrupted a local community."

"I don't really like the guy much, but I can't say I disagree with him."

"Aw, he's all right. A bit stiff, but name me a serious security coordinator who isn't."

Lee gave Bill a level look, "So tell where you sit on this; Corporate's side, or the sane side?"

"Not you too. That kind of talk isn't constructive, Lee. I need – Corporate needs - to know that everyone involved is on board."

Lee could see the plea in Bill's eyes, that he be 'on board' as much to help make Bill's life easier as to protect his own future with the company.

It had been a tough couple of days for all of them and he respected Bill as much as any man he'd ever worked with, "Speaking honestly?"

"Of course."

He pointed over his shoulder, "As much as I hate to say it, in my gut I'm with Crowley," he put up a hand as he saw Bill open his mouth, "but you and I go back a long way and I owe you my loyalty as my friend and mentor, no matter my misgivings. If you need my support, you know you'll have it."

Bill settled back in his chair, "Thanks, Lee. It means a lot." He reached down a pulled an amber bottle from a drawer, "Jesus Christ, I really need a slug right now, you?"

"I thought you'd never ask."

Bill handed him the bottle and he took a healthy swig. The scotch trickled down his throat like hot honey and went a long way toward cleaning out the memories and smells of the medical room, "Oh shit, that's good."

He handed it back to Bill, "Can't be easy."

"What?"

"Treading the thin line between the corporate world and reality."

Bill grinned wryly, "You have no idea," his smile faded, "What about our guy today? Same as the other one?"

"You wouldn't believe it if you saw it yourself. I did and I'm not sure I do."

Bill took another swig, "That makes about as much sense as I figured it would."

A silence stretched between them as Bill handed the bottle over again.

Lee took a sip and asked, "What are we going to find down there, Bill?"

Bill waited a few seconds before replying, "Maybe the answers to a lot of big questions."

Lee almost responded with, *From your lips to God's ears*, but that sort of stuff usually felt awkward coming out.

He decided to go with, "Let's hope that's all."

*

A light knock came on his door.

Lee was just on the edge of sleep and jerked awake, "Yeah?"

The door opened and Angeline poked her head around, "Can I come in?"

His room was dark and the hallway light behind her made her hair look like a halo around her head.

He pushed himself up in bed, "Yeah, sure." The movement made his head swim a bit, *Maybe a couple swigs too many of the scotch.*

She slipped in and came to the side of the bed, sitting down next to him, "Whew, smells like a distillery in here."

"I, uh, had a couple shots with Bill."

"I suppose you both needed it. I heard from Bobby about the guy you found today."

"I told him not to say anything to anybody."

He could hear the smile in her voice, "I'm afraid I demanded it."

"It's fine. I would have told you myself if I'd seen you. You've been as rare a sighting as a white rhino the last couple days."

If she heard the admonishment in his voice, she pretended not to, "Just been busy, that's all. So what happened?" She shifted and lay on her side across his legs.

He felt the heat of her body and tried to keep his mind on telling her about their encounter in the village, as well as the results of Bobby's crude autopsy. She listened while idly drawing small circles on the covers over his thighs, which made it harder for him to concentrate on relating the horrors of the day.

"Sounds awful," she said as he finished, "I can't imagine," she moved her hand up his leg and began to rub him over the covers, "Almost nightmarish."

He knew what she was doing. It was something she did very well. This time, he tried hard not to be in the mood, though.

He put his hand over hers, stopping her, "Can I ask you something?"

"What?" she asked in that arched, guarded tone he knew so well.

"This whole project...you've really known about it since the beginning?"

A pause, "Yes."

"Tell me about it."

She sighed, "Brent came to me almost three years ago with his plan to drill here. I spent a couple weeks doing online research on the site, plus a couple other places along the rift valley, but I quickly realized it would be a waste of resources. There were no indications of oil or gas anywhere around here and I told him so."

"And?"

"And he showed me the material – the videos and drilling reports – from the Kola Project, as well as a couple others, and told me what he really wanted to do."

"And you went along with it, just like that."

She tried to pull away and sit up, but he kept a grip on her hand.

She slumped back onto his legs, "No, not just like that. I couldn't see the point in it and told him pretty much the same things you've been saying, but you know Brent. His mind was made up from the start and he didn't care what I or anybody else said."

Lee was forced to agree, "Yeah, I know Brent. Still…"

"Why didn't I fill you in?"

"Yeah."

Another pause during which Lee tried not to think she was fabricating an excuse before she answered, "A couple of reasons. You're already known around Endeavor as the 'difficult child', the one who needs watching. This would have just been another thing for you to get into Brent's face about."

"I was doing that anyway."

"Yes, but it was easier to just let you assume the project was simply for notoriety, fame, the record books, and all that. Can you imagine the row that you'd have created if you'd known the real story?"

Lee could easily imagine that. "Why not just fire me and have one less problem to deal with?"

"Because you're damn good at your job, you idiot, and Brent knows that. The guys on the rigs, from the deck hands to the supervisors, all respect and like you. With Bill on the Board and you in the field, Endeavor has been running more efficiently, and more happily, than anyone could have wanted, and this economic environment isn't one in which we should be rocking the boat, you know?"

Lee knew she was stroking him a bit, and not just literally, but it was nice to hear anyway, "And?"

"And…to be honest, I didn't believe it all myself and I'm not sure I do now, whether it's all about doorways to other dimensions or even Hell itself, but I admit the scientist in me is intrigued either way."

He supposed he could understand that, "Okay, fair enough. So, what are we really trying to accomplish here, Ang?"

She moved up the bed toward him, her hand starting to work on him again, "Lee, I don't know what we're trying to accomplish as far as the bore goes, but I do know what I'm trying to accomplish here and now."

She moved up to him in the dark and kissed his bare chest, making her way up his neck to his mouth as her hand kept busy down below.

He had a great many questions still rolling around in his head, but they all just seemed to drift away, like they always did in situations like this.

Sometimes, he figured, it was just better to keep your mouth shut – or open, as the case may be…

Ten

LEE AWOKE TO THE SOUND of a helicopter thumping overhead. He glanced at his watch and saw that it was five-thirty. They had a briefing at six before starting the descent.

He reached over to nudge Angeline, but she was already gone. Not unusual, as they both strived to keep their relationship discreet, no matter where they were. It wouldn't do for anyone to see them skulking around each other's bedroom, though Lee didn't really care. It seemed to be a bigger deal for Angeline, but he suspected it was always a bigger issue for women, especially those high on the corporate ladder.

He jumped out of bed and headed for the shower. Despite having missed some sleep, Lee found himself feeling energized and eager for things to get going, the way he usually did at the start of a project.

He finished and made his way to the rec room, noting as he went that there didn't seem to be anyone else around, not even in the kitchen, *I guess I'm last again.*

He entered and glanced around, nodding at each person in turn. They were clustered at the two games tables. Bill, Dan, and Frank were at one, Duke and Bobby were at the other and the three rig hands involved with the descent were sipping coffee and leaning on one of the billiard tables.

But no Angeline, *Hmm, I'm not the tardiest today after all.*

Duke waved him over and Lee sat down, grabbing the coffee Duke handed him, "Guess I slept in a bit. You hear the chopper this morning?"

Duke gave him a knowing look, "We're in the big leagues this morning, baby."

Lee sipped, "Huh?"

Bill suddenly stood up and raised a hand in greeting, "Brent! Welcome to our hole in the ground."

Lee spun in his chair to see Brent Copeland coming through the door from the office area. Angeline was right behind him.

Everyone stood and shook hands with the Endeavor CEO as he made his way past the tables, smiling and clapping shoulders.

He grabbed Lee's hand and gave it a couple hard pumps, "Lee, how are you? I hear you've had a couple rough spots so far."

Rough spots? Two dead and seven missing, not to mention a trashed rig, are a couple rough spots?

Lee put a smile on his face, "Good to see you, Brent. Surprised, though. Thought you were in Germany?"

"And miss the discovery of the century, maybe of all time?" Brent waved a hand around, "Not on your life," he dropped Lee's hand and stepped over to Bill's table.

Lee looked at Duke, who simply gave him raised eyebrows. The two of them sat back down and Lee watched Brent glad-hand everyone else.

Brent Copeland was only a few years older than Lee and about the same height. A spattering of white at his temples was the only sign of middle age on him. He was fit; thick in the shoulders and still flat in the stomach, though it was mostly his hectic lifestyle that kept him trim.

Endeavor had been his father's company, started out of Oklahoma in the late seventies with one mortgaged drilling rig and a leased service rig that could extract any oil the drilling rig found. The senior Copeland had worked his ass off for twenty-five years, building it into a solid entity with a regional reputation, but had died of a heart attack on one of his rigs ten years ago, leaving thirty-three-year-old Brent as CEO of Endeavor at that point.

No silver-spoon slouch, Brent had worked his way up through the company honestly, spending high school and then college summer breaks on the rigs doing every lousy, dirty job there was to do, finally moving into the senior offices when he graduated. He'd been seen as a steady, supportive scion all through his youth, helping the company to grow well under his father.

When the old man had passed, however, Brent finally flexed his muscles with the Board and had pushed and pulled the company into becoming an internationally renowned entity through aggressive acquisitions and a reputation for having the hardest-working rigs in the business. In ten years under his control, Endeavor had grown from a regional drilling company worth millions to a global corporation with fingers in many pies worth billions.

Lee had enormous respect for him, coupled with a certain level of wariness; Brent always had a surety, a manic energy and almost messianic aura about him that was unsettling with too much exposure. He was an engaging person, but was reputed to have a ruthless side, which made him rather normal as far as billion-dollar CEOs went, Lee assumed.

Brent and Angeline finally sat at the table with Bill and the others. Lee tried to catch Angeline's eye, but she wouldn't look at him, seeming to be engrossed in her tablet.

Funny how the subject of Brent's arrival didn't come up last night.

"Now that we're all here," Bill said, with a nod at Brent, "why don't you start us off, Dan?"

Crowley reached over and hit the switch on a portable wireless projector that was in the middle of their table. The wall behind him blossomed into a field of blue with the Endeavor logo in the center.

He tapped his smartphone and the image changed to a live feed from the hole, showing the ocher rocks and slightly misty atmosphere, though in greater detail than before. What it didn't show was any of the black creatures.

He said, "As you know, we removed the drill string and the first camera platform a couple days ago. These images are from the new high-rez camera we put down yesterday."

He slid his finger over his screen and the image zoomed in, "You can see here," he pointed, "there's a ledge of some sort almost directly below the opening we're going through. It looks to be about seventeen or eighteen meters – maybe sixty feet – above the floor of the cavern, or whatever that place is down there. It appears to be almost flat and has an outcrop along its front that should shield us from view while we get set up. I think it would be a good base of operations for us."

He looked at Brent, who nodded in agreement.

Dan continued, "The platform has already delivered some of the supplies we'll need," he pointed at some square objects, obviously crates, on the ledge, "and, with the stuff we'll be taking down with us, we should be outfitted for a number of hours."

"How long, exactly?" Lee asked.

Frank Arden stood up, "The environment suits have carbon-composite tanks, which are lighter than aluminum, but higher-pressured, and can carry up to two and a half hours of air. Each person will have two refill tanks as well, so just using the tanks alone, you're good for seven or eight hours."

"What's the air like down there if the tank fails?" Duke asked.

Frank waved a hand at the video image, "The new sensors have provided us with a lot more information. The air down there is surprisingly like ours, but you wouldn't want to have to breathe it for too long. It's hotter, of course, which would severely dehydrate you, but wouldn't cook you inside."

Lee flicked a glance at Bobby at those words, reminded of the two men they'd autopsied. Bobby raised his eyebrows back at him.

Frank went on, "The problem with long-term exposure are the levels of methane, CO_2, and oxygen. The levels of nitrogen and trace gases are almost exactly that at the surface, at about seventy-nine percent total, but the distribution of trace gases is different. There's not a trace of argon, for one thing, which our atmosphere has. The big difference for us, though, is that both the CO_2 and methane are slightly higher, while the oxygen is lower."

Lee was mystified, "But CO_2 and methane are both organic compounds, right?"

Frank nodded, "Yes. It has been known for some time that the immediate subsurface of the earth acts as a carbon and methane sink for the atmosphere, but we are far below any organic levels here – well, except for the creatures we've seen – so it's surprising, to say the least."

Duke rumbled, "Those black things are crawling around all over the place and they sure as hell look organic to me."

"Yes, but for the levels we're seeing, there must either be an enormous number of them or other organisms down there, or they have been in place for a very long time."

Brent said, "Well, they're there anyway, so life of some sort is in place and obviously thriving." He sounded excited.

"What's the oxygen level?" Lee asked.

"Just over eighteen percent, almost three percent lower than we're used to."

"That doesn't sound too bad," Duke said.

Frank looked at him, "It's bad enough. Nineteen and a half is considered dangerous to humans over prolonged periods, and combined with the higher methane and CO_2, you would find you'd rapidly develop a headache and feelings of panic, followed by disorientation, unconsciousness and, finally death within an hour or two, depending on the level of exertion."

He noted the grim looks that passed between people, "However, in short doses, such as when exchanging tanks, or even with tank failure, which is unlikely, you'd be fine for up to even ten or fifteen minutes at a time with no long-term effects. In fact, I estimate that you could extend your total time down there to almost ten hours by relying on local air every once in a while."

He bobbed his head at Brent and sat down.

Dan nodded at Frank, "Good to know, Doc," he went back to his part of the briefing, "Each of us will have, as Frank says, three tanks of air, as well as a supply of water, a firearm and any portable scientific equipment you need to carry, so our loads won't exactly be light."

"Video equipment?" Duke asked.

Dan tapped his temple, "Built into the helmets, along with sensors. We'll record everything. Any more questions?"

Duke shifted in his chair, "How tough are these suits, anyway? I mean, how much can they take?"

Frank shrugged, "Well they're not body armor, if that's what you mean, but they are tough. The outer shells are lightweight and can't stop a bullet, but the Kevlar underlay can keep out smaller caliber rounds. Is that what you're asking?"

Duke nodded, "Good enough, I guess. Just want to know how much we can rely on our equipment if we get into scrapes."

Brent spoke up, "No one down there's going to be shooting at us, Duke."

He said it with such certainty that Lee glanced at him, *How does he know?*

"Any other questions?" Dan asked.

No one spoke.

"One more thing," Dan said, "There are a lot of big wigs on this project," he flashed a tight smile around the room, settling finally on Brent, "and while Mr. Copeland here is the boss, he has agreed to make me the de facto leader of this expedition and I'm responsible for everyone's safety. Once we step off that platform down below, I'm the final say on things, okay?"

Somewhat surprised, Lee kept his eye on Brent. The CEO looked satisfied with the arrangement, but he knew his CEO. Brent Copeland had a hard time taking orders from anyone, *Let's see just how long that situation stays static once we're down there.*

Bill spoke to Frank, "What can you tell us about actually going down?"

Brent spoke, "Yes, I can understand the issues with breathing down there and everything, but I admit I'm a little more concerned about the transit itself and with penetrating the...the 'barrier' I think you called it in your report?"

Lee was impressed; Brent seemed to know pretty much everything about the project and its issues so far. Then again, this had apparently been his pet project for several years now.

Frank awkwardly got to his feet again, "We'll proceed from here to the rig. The suits and supplies are all there and ready to go. We've been piping fresh air down the hole for the past few hours, so we expect we won't need to use our suit air until we get to the hot zone, which is at about three kilometers. We'll need to use suit air while we pass through that, but it begins to cool off again rapidly at four point five kilometers, so we won't make much of a dent in our overall air supply."

He pointed at Bobby, "We'll get suited up in the airlock and, while we do that, Bobby will shoot us all up with a sedative-"

"A sedative?" Duke blurted, "Why?"

Bobby shrugged apologetically, "It's a long, hot trip down there in a dark, narrow pipe. Even the most stable of us will begin to experience signs of claustrophobia fairly quickly, I think. The sedative is Midazolam, the same thing I had for that guy in the water shack. It's fast-acting and has a short duration. I can adjust the dose so that it lasts pretty much for the trip down."

Lee asked, "What about the actual barrier penetration? Do we have any idea what will happen to us?"

Bobby shrugged, "I don't have a clue," he looked over at Frank.

The physicist blinked several times, "It's likely that…it's surmised that we will experience some sort of disorientation. No one really knows what the effects may be, as no one has done anything like this before."

Duke tapped on the table to draw attention, "The camera rigs and sensors sure go screwy for a few seconds."

"But they continue to function afterward, albeit spottily," Frank said, "so we know that electrical and mechanical properties must at least be similar."

Angeline finally spoke up, "So the electronics work, but what about us? We are attempting to penetrate a barrier between two different dimensions, right? There's apparently life there, but how do we know that the biomechanical or chemical processes – the laws of nature that govern life, in other words – will operate the same? We could all simply die the instant we cross over."

That got everyone's attention.

Frank said, "We are assuming it's a different dimension, but it may not be. It could simply be a doorway to another point in our own dimensional space where the rules are the same, perhaps even somewhere else on – or in – Earth. The atmospheric conditions are similar enough and the small discrepancies could be just that it's a subterranean pocket of primordial atmosphere."

"But we don't know that," Lee said. "You said that even time might be different there."

"No, we don't anything for sure," Frank admitted.

Brent sighed and stood up. Everyone grew silent.

He moved to the front of the room, "The risks are significant, to be sure, and nothing will be said if anyone wants to back out. You have my word on that."

His eyes roamed the room, locking onto each person as he spoke, "However, we are poised on the edge here; the edge of discovery such as humankind has not seen for decades – possibly ever – and discovery has always entailed risk."

He waved a hand around the room, "The whole history of this company, in fact our whole history as humans, has been about discovery and risk…and people have never backed down from it. Every time we've been faced with doubts, or obstacles, we've overcome them. Everything we have achieved in our existence, from fire and the wheel," he pulled out his smartphone and dropped it on the table, "to the technological marvels we treat as commonplace today, has come to us through the acceptance of risk and the surmounting of our challenges."

He put both hands on the table and leaned forward, "It's simply what we do as a species," he looked around at everyone again, "I know I'm in, but I won't order anyone else to go."

Bill jerked in his seat, "Wait, you can't go, Brent."

Brent smirked at him, "Why the hell not? This whole project has been my baby for almost three years."

"You're the CEO, for Christ's sake. If anything happens to you-"

Brent snorted, "Things will trundle along without me just fine. In fact, I don't doubt some of the Board members would want me to go and get lost in another dimension."

Lee watched the exchange with interest. It was no surprise that Brent was also considered to be a difficult child by many of the directors. Most of them had been in place since his father's time and they often felt that Brent's aspirations for the company, as well as his brash approach to running it, were contrary to established company culture. However, they'd all grown much richer during his tenure, and it was hard to stay angry with an expanding wallet in your pocket.

Bill tried a compromise, "We have to go down in two groups. How about if you go down with the second group. That way-"

Brent shook his head, "No way, Bill. I intend to be the first one to set foot on those rocks down there. You can't stop me and if you try, I'll have to fire you," he gave Bill an exaggerated grin.

Bill gave him one back, "You can't fire me. I'm on the Board now."

"Oh yeah, right. I guess it's a stalemate then."

Bill threw up his hands, "Fine. I tried."

Brent put a hand on Bill's shoulder and gave it a squeeze, "I appreciate the concern, though." He looked up at everyone, "So it's settled. Any other dissenters?"

No one spoke.

"Okay, then," he clapped his hands, "I say we get started."

They all rose as a unit and started filing out. Brent went first, with Angeline and Frank next to him. Brent was discussing the descent with Frank as they passed Lee.

Lee caught Angeline's arm as she went by, "Got a sec?"

Duke took the hint and followed everyone else out.

Lee waited until the others were all gone, "You knew Brent was coming?"

"Yes," she looked him in the eye for a few seconds, then her gaze flicked away, "If you didn't think he'd be here for this, you're not paying attention. This is his baby, as he says."

"Truth is, I didn't think of it at all. Been a little busy," he took her arm as they headed out of the room, "Ang, I'm a bit…concerned."

"Concerned, as in worried? Calm, cool Lee Mitchell is worried?"

He nodded, "That we're rushing this. We have no idea what we're going to be facing down there – assuming we survive the transition, that is."

"I thought you were the optimist between us."

"I'm not joking, Ang. We have two dead guys with no clue as to what killed them, seven men still missing and something that blew the top off this whole rig when we first breached that barrier."

"Are you saying you want out?"

"Hell no. I'm in, of course. My concern is that…you look like you're in as well."

"I am."

"But-" he started.

She reached up and put a finger on his lips, "Don't give me any of that sexist gallantry shit. I'm the chief geologist and there's no way I'm missing getting a first look at the geology of what could be a whole other reality, or at least another planet, for God's sake."

"And the fact that we don't even know which of those two it may be doesn't even bother you?"

"You're going. Does it bother you?"

"No, but I always thought we considered me to be the stupid one."

She laughed, a rare sound, "Don't worry, your reputation is secure," she raised her eyebrows, "Now, shall we go discover a new world?"

He relented, as always, "After you, I guess."

Eleven

EVERYONE HAD TO STRIP TO their underwear and put on a tight-fitting bodysuit. Angeline used the drill shack to change, but the men all just stripped and zipped on the rig deck.

Next came the environmental suits. These were carbon fiber segmented pieces covering the limbs, chest, back and abdomen, over a thin Kevlar under skin that allowed the suits to bend easily at the joints. Less bulky than an astronaut's outfit, but thicker than a diver's dry suit, they resembled Star Wars storm-trooper armor more than anything else, except they were light gray in color and had a clear helmet more like that of an astronaut.

Internal heating and cooling systems were housed around the front and sides of the torso sections, leaving the back unencumbered to hold the air tanks. The helmets had internal heads-up displays, communication gear and built-in cameras that allowed a view of the user's face, as well as a one hundred-eighty degree view out the front. The person up top monitoring the video feeds would be able to see and hear everything the suit user did.

The suits were troublesome to get into, but once on, they were surprisingly light and easy to move around in. The team spent a few minutes under Frank Arden's tutelage getting used to all the systems and walking around the deck checking their suits' capabilities.

Duke rapped his chest plate hard, "It's like a super-dense plastic." He stretched his arms and shoulders, testing the flexibility, "Jesus Christ, I feel like a real spaceman in this thing."

"You'll be going where no spaceman ever dreamed of in a few minutes," Brent said.

That sobered everyone up quickly.

Dan Crowley keyed his helmet mic with his chin, "Everyone hear me?"

They all acknowledged they did, and he said, "Okay then, first group to the platform."

The team would use two platforms, one above the other, with five meters, or about seventeen feet, between them. The borehole was five feet in diameter, giving each platform room for four people at a time, along with some equipment. Dan, Brent, Lee, and Frank would go down on the first platform, with Bill, Angeline, Duke, and Bobby on the one above.

Dan held the door to the airlock open for them. Brent and Frank walked through without looking back, but Lee turned and waved at the others, "Beam me up, Scotty."

"That's *down*," Duke corrected him and waved back.

Lee went through with Bobby, and Dan closed the door behind them. There was a soft whooshing sound, signifying they were now isolated from the outside world.

He glanced around the inside. The walls were as plain on the inside as out. He eyed the platform as his group prepared to mount. It looked like an old-fashioned elevator cage, only round, with a flat floor made of some composite material and a mesh cage around it made from the same insulating material as the airlock walls.

The cables supporting it went up through the roof and disappeared into a series of rubber and carbon fiber seals that effectively prevented anything inside from escaping, but it wasn't perfectly airtight, of course. The cable had to be able to raise and lower freely through it.

The second platform was off to the side in two pieces, waiting to be connected to the drop cables after theirs had descended. The three technicians who would be running the drop were waiting by a console to one side of the airlock. They each nodded to him.

"Okay, guys," Bobby stepped forward with a hypo, "Ready?"

"Not really, but I don't want to go mad halfway down," Lee muttered.

"Me first," Brent thrust his arm out.

Lee watched as Bobby loosened the glove on Brent's sleeve and bent to inject the sedative into a vein close to the wrist. Brent dipped his head in and spoke to Bobby for a second then pulled away, shaking his hand, while Bobby moved on and did the same to Frank and Dan.

Bobby warned them, "Better get settled before this takes effect."

They made their way onto the platform and started getting into their slings as Lee moved forward to take his shot.

Bobby gave him a queer look for a moment, as if he were about to say something, but then just tapped the hypodermic and slid it into Lee's wrist.

"How fast will this work?" Lee asked.

"You should be feeling it in less than thirty seconds, so get mounted."

Lee hastened over to the platform and stepped into his sling, which was suspended from the mesh cage and would allow him to remain upright, but supported for the entire descent, saving his leg muscles and his energy. There were several boxes on the platform between them, so it would be a tight, crowded, dark trip down and he was grateful for the sedative.

Or was he?

He realized with mild surprise that he wasn't as concerned about it all now as he was a moment ago. A feeling of malaise was overtaking him.

He shot a thumbs-up to Bobby, "Wow, this is good shit, Bobby."

Even Dan seemed looser. He waved at the technicians, "See you guys on the bottom."

The techs turned away to focus on their console. Lee had only a moment to look up at the seemingly slim cable that was holding them all up over a five-mile drop into darkness before everything jerked and they started down, *What, no ceremony? Oh well.*

They descended very slowly, and the thought flickered through his mind that this trip was going to take forever, but then they jolted to a stop, and he remembered that they had to pause while the team above got connected to the cable.

After what seemed like no time at all, though, they started down again. He glanced at the chronometer on his arm, surprised to see that six minutes had already elapsed.

Brent's voice came over the suit radio, "Everyone settled and feeling good?"

A chorus of laconic yeses came through.

Lee looked up and saw nothing, but it took him a moment to recall that the other platform above them would block out any light from the top. He tapped his light with his chin, and it flared on, showing him the sides of the borehole rushing by. The cage bottom was ringed with a thick nylon and rubber bumper all around that brushed the sides of the bore as they went, causing the cage to vibrate.

Lee found the sensation vaguely relaxing but supposed that was the sedative.

"Douse that, uh, light Lee," Dan said calmly, "Batteries. We'll use the…the cage light…here somewhere…where the hell is it, ah got it."

A light came on overhead and Lee flicked his own off.

Dan's voice came again on broadcast, "Hey…you guys up there?"

"Yeah?" Bill's voice drawled.

"Hit your cage light before…before you all pass out up there."

There was a series of muttered questioning sounds and curses before Lee's group saw a thin arc of light come on from around the floor of the platform above.

"All right, good job, uh…guys," Dan's voice faded, and Lee saw him slump in his sling. Frank looked like he was already relaxing into it, his helmeted head drooping, while Brent seemed to be gazing around at the sides of the borehole.

Lee felt heavy and a bit fuzzy now, *Gravity must be getting stronger, I guess, or something? A nap sounds like a good idea. Nothing to miss anyway for a while…*

*

The heat woke him up.

He didn't think he'd been sleeping, but it now seemed that he wasn't on a beach in Mexico after all, as he'd been sure he was a moment ago.

It just felt like it.

He realized he'd been dreaming and looked at his chrono. It showed that they'd already been in descent for sixty-one minutes. The cage light still showed the walls of the bore moving by quickly. The sound he'd thought was the slow rushing of Mexican surf was the noise generated by the platform's bumper against the sides of the bore as they went down.

Shit, I've slept through almost half the trip already.

He looked at the others on his platform. Brent was awake and gave him a lazy wave, which he returned, but Dan and Frank were still slumped in their slings.

They all had their suit helmets open still but would have to close them soon from the heat. His body felt cool, but the air was stiff with heat and his face felt hot. He hit the switch for the broadcast mic and heard a humming that seemed to be coming from Brent, as well as a couple people snoring lightly.

"Hey guys," he spoke softly.

"Huh? Whazzat?" came Bill's voice.

He heard Angeline clear her throat and saw both Frank and Dan jerk erect in their slings.

"Lee?" Duke asked, "You guys okay?"

Everybody responded with affirmatives and Lee added, "I just wanted to make sure everyone has their cooling units on. It's getting a lot hotter now."

"Been getting hotter for a while, "Brent said. "I've been awake for a while, listening to you lot snore at me."

"The cooling units are, uh, automatic," came Frank's voice, "It's now showing us at…fifty-two degrees Celsius, so your units should all be functioning already. You can increase or decrease cooling…function with your heads-up."

It was quiet for a moment while everyone checked their suits. It took a long time, as everyone was groggy from the sedative.

Angeline asked, "Where are we?"

Brent answered, "Just shy of halfway, three point eight klicks down."

Frank said, "We're getting close to having to…seal our suits for good.

Our coolers have kept us fine so far, but it'll soon be too hot to breathe comfortably-"

"Already is," Duke muttered.

"Yes," Frank agreed, "but the sooner you seal your suit, the more of your internal air you'll use. I'd say hold out as long as you can…but we don't want to risk heat, uh, exhaustion for the sake of…uh…"

"We get you, Frank," Bill said, "I think we should all seal up now anyway. In our current condition…"

"I agree," Dan announced, "Everyone seal up." His voice sounded slushy.

The sound of faceplates snicking down filled their ears. It seemed immediately cooler as soon as Lee lowered his again.

Bobby's voice came over, "Ah, that's better."

Lee's cage suddenly rattled as the platform hit a small ridge on the side of the metal bore pipe and everyone made fumbling grabs for their sling straps. As lightly sedated as they were, the reality of the long drop still below them wasn't far from their minds.

The platform above hit the same bump and they all heard Angeline let out a squeak and a laugh, "I'm glad I'm high now, or I'd be terrified."

Frank came on, "Try not to think about it too much. We'll be down sooner than you think."

Both platforms subsided into silence as people went back to playing with their suit displays, snoozing or otherwise trying not to think about what they were doing.

Lee watched the sides of the bore slide by. It was mesmerizing. *We're on a long, quiet, slow fall…to the bottom of the earth…wait, that's not right, that would be…*

He nodded off again as they dropped inexorably toward the barrier.

*

Seventy-five minutes later, Lee woke to a beeping sound. It was coming from Dan Crowley's chrono.

Dan tapped his arm to shut off the alarm and alerted everyone, "Morning people. We're five minutes from barrier penetration. Everybody okay?"

100

Slushy voices groused at him, but everyone came awake and seemed relatively refreshed.

Duke rumbled, "That Mida-Mina-whatsit stuff worked pretty well, Bobby. Feel like I've had a good eight hours."

"Just don't try any fast movements for a bit yet, Duke," Bobby warned, "You'll likely have some vertigo for a few minutes until it's all out of your system," he added, "Let me know, everyone, if you have a headache or dizziness."

Affirmatives came over the broadcast from everyone but Angeline.

Lee jerked his head up involuntarily to look at the platform above, "Angeline? You with us?"

"Huh? Yes…I'm fine. Just a bit woozy still."

Bobby broke in, "I estimated the dosages for everyone based on body size. You may have gotten a bit more than you needed. Just relax and it'll pass before long."

"All right, Bobby. Thanks…and I'll try not to remember that you overestimated my body size."

That got a laugh from both platforms.

Brent raised a hand at Arden, "Frank, I've been checking the readings on my display for a few minutes now. It all seems a little wonky. What you got?"

Frank fumbled his chin around his helmet, bringing everything up on his own display finally, "Got it all now," he spoke a bit louder, though he didn't have to, "Everyone, you can call up the direct feeds from the sensors by tapping the orange lights on your chin panel."

Murmurs and clicks followed for a few seconds.

"Temp and pressure are right where we expected," Duke said, "The same we've gotten this whole time…temp has climbed a bit, but still only seventy-two degrees here. Unbelievable."

"Still too hot for us, but it should fall to below sixty again once we penetrate the barrier," Frank added.

"Look at the field-meter reading," Brent said.

Frank checked his, "It's…wow, just passing fourteen kilovolts and heading for twenty."

"What's up?" Bill asked.

"Static electricity is building fast down here," Brent said, "I've been watching it for a while."

"We noted that on the readings up top all week," Duke said.

"Yes, but the levels were not fluctuating," Frank said, "and they were steady in the ten to fourteen kilovolt range. These are…there it goes, past twenty."

"Do we worry?" Bill asked.

Brent answered before Frank could, "No, I don't think so. It looks to be leveling off at about twenty…two or three for now."

Lee saw the physicist reach out tentatively and touch the side of the cage. His voice came over, "The platforms are insulated, as are our suits, so it shouldn't be a concern. However, we should be monitoring it as carefully as we do the atmosphere and temp readings."

"What causes static electricity down here?" Bobby asked.

Frank said, "Tectonic force can generate substantial electricity and we are in the Rift Valley, so there is slow, but definite movement in the deep earth of this region."

"It may be something else, though," Brent said.

Frank's helmet bobbed, "Yes. The barrier itself may by partly electrical in nature."

Duke came on, "That would explain the weird effect on the sensors and cameras."

"If it's the barrier, we'll find out shortly," Brent said, "We're…three minutes from it. Duke?"

Duke was going to coordinate the last stage of their descent and alerted the men up top, "Tommy? We looking good?"

The reply came fast, as the top techs had been monitoring them constantly, "You're all looking good on monitors, Duke. Everyone feeling okay?"

"We're all good. Looking at barrier penetration in…about two point five minutes now."

"Roger, one-forty-three seconds…mark."

"Take us down to one-third speed," Duke said.

"You sure? That'll add another…five minutes to the trip."

Airtime was an issue on this expedition and any time saved on the trip down was more time they could spend on-site, "Fine, keep us at one meter per second until we're thirty seconds out, then go to one-third."

"Roger that, Duke," they signed off.

"Good thinking to wait on slowing us down a bit, Duke," Bill said.

"I don't think it'll make much difference anyway, fast or slow," Brent muttered. He was clearly impatient, "Penetration is going to be rather startling, I would think."

"It usually is," Angeline's voice came through loud and clear.

That got a hearty bark of laughter from everyone, and they settled into prepping themselves and their respective equipment for the next phase.

Staying busy helped keep their minds off the fact they were about to possibly pierce the edge of reality and move into an unknown realm.

Twelve

"OKAY…WE'RE ALMOST THIRTY SECONDS out from the barrier," Duke rumbled, "Deceleration to one-third right…now."

Right on cue, everyone felt their stomach drop slightly as their descent slowed markedly.

"Everyone okay down there?" the voice from the operator on the surface buzzed in their helmets.

Duke answered, "We're all good I think, Tommy. Keep it steady but be ready for a stop if I call it."

"Roger that, Duke. You're now going to be…ninety seconds from penetration at one-third speed. Time enough for a coffee and sandwich."

Duke took the small joke and ran with it, "Last chance to back out everyone."

They all chuckled in appreciation of the levity.

Lee looked around. Dan and Frank were checking their equipment, but Brent seemed to be just waiting. He was still letting his sling take most of his weight, but Lee noticed the man's leg shaking like he was impatient, which Lee imagined he was. *For a guy on sedatives, he looks more like he's been on a caffeine drip.*

Frank was looking at his tablet, "Bottom camera working fine. I can see the shimmer now. It looks almost like we're coming up on a pool of water, but shinier, like mercury. There's a…purplish light in the center, likely where the cable cuts through it."

He tapped the screen, "Looks like it's reacting to the cable. I'm seeing colors and textures, but it's definitely not solid."

"Too late to mention I can't swim?" Bobby asked.

Brent broke in, "Everybody looking good, Bobby?"

As the team medic, Bobby's displays could show him everyone's bio readouts. They could hear him clicking buttons, "Everyone's heart rate and breathing are up about where they'd be if we were watching porn, but no obvious probs, boss."

Lee was hearing his own pulse in his ears, *Here we go*. He arched his neck and looked up at the bottom of the platform above, "You guys okay up there?"

Bill answered, "Fine. Just feeling ripped off that you guys get to go through first."

Brent spoke, "You ready on the brake if we have any problems, Duke?"

Duke was on the upper platform so that he and the team above could stop the drop if the lower platform had any obvious difficulties going through the barrier. Duke would have an extra seventeen seconds to act and there'd hopefully be no problems with communication if there were trouble.

Duke had a hold of the manual control for the cable and answered, "Taking control of descent now, boss," he spoke to the men above, "I have control, Tommy. Remember, if there's some kind of time gap thingy, we may drop out of communication."

"Roger that, you have cable control, Duke."

Frank spoke, "Twenty seconds now. Get a grip on something. We don't know if it'll be rough."

Lee saw Frank grab his support sling, so he did the same. Dan and Brent hung onto the side of the cage.

Duke's voice came over, "Ten seconds to lower platform penetration… Five…four…three…two…here we go."

It felt like the world turned upside down, but only on the inside.

Lee felt a sudden wave of nausea pass through him. He was dizzy and lurched to the right. If he hadn't been in the sling and hanging on, he'd have hit the deck of the platform.

He reflexively closed his eyes, but that increased the vertigo, so he opened them and tried to focus on the figure of Brent directly across from him. It didn't help that Brent also seemed to be in distress, his legs buckling under him, rocking back and forth in his sling.

A noise so loud it was more a vibration rattled Lee's ears. He pulled his arms up in an instinctive effort to block out the sound, but before he could get his hands up it was gone.

The vertigo passed at the same time, and everything was quiet again, except for muted gasping and coughing coming from the others. It felt like his ears were plugged. He swallowed and the pressure equalized with a loud click in his head.

Bobby's voice came over, sounding tinny through static, "Everyone okay? Whatever you do, don't throw up. You'll be stuck with it in your suit."

"And gum up the works, too," Frank added.

Brent waved a hand unnecessarily, "We're all okay, I think. Suit lights are all blinking at me, though."

"Do I stop drop?" Duke asked.

Frank shook his tablet, "Electrical seems to be shaky. My computer's down but looks like it's coming back. Check your suit systems."

Lee tapped his chin board, relieved when everything lit up and his heads-up display brightened with data.

"Stop drop, Brent? We're getting close," Duke warned. His voice sounded like it was pitched higher.

The second platform was only a few seconds from dropping through the barrier.

"Naw, we're okay," said Brent.

"I concur," Frank added, "No stop. Just hang on."

Lee looked up in time to see what looked like a sheen of rippling silver hanging above them, as if someone had stretched a sheet of plastic wrap across the borehole. It reflected his helmet light like the sun on water before suddenly flaring into an explosion of violet light as the upper platform made contact with it.

The light was intense, but brief, followed by a wave of pressure that pushed against his suit, pressing him back into his sling and vibrating the platform. The cables rattled and Lee felt a chill at the sudden thought that they might snap like the ones on the original drill platform.

Everything held, though, and he breathed a silent sigh of relief, even as he heard the sounds of the team above dealing with their nausea.

"Fuck me, what the hell was that?" Duke boomed, "I almost lost my breakfast."

"That was awful," Angeline said.

Bill commented weakly, "Feels like someone wrung out my insides."

Bobby came on, sounding hoarse, "Deep breaths and a couple swallows of water should fix us up, guys."

They all took a few sips and it seemed to help.

Dan said, "Everyone good?"

Bill answered, "That's a relative term right now, but we're still alive."

Tommy's voice intruded from the surface, sounding like he'd taken a few hits of helium, as if his voice were compressed somehow, "You guys were offline for a moment...getting readings on everyone now. Looking good."

Duke muttered, "You try dropping through that shit, Tommy, and then tell me if you're good. I feel like I've been fucked hard and put away wet."

A rasp of static, followed by, "Oh, so you're feeling normal then, boss."

That got Duke chuckling.

Frank said, "I think you should retain control of the platforms, Duke. With the voice distortions, it seems there is a time element involved here. They seem slightly sped up to us while we no doubt sound slower to them. If the effect increases, or there's some other issue we're not aware of, we should be the ones controlling our descent."

Lee cut in, "But we're talking to Tommy, and we've gone through the barrier already and were even on opposite sides of it for a few seconds. Time seems almost normal."

"Right now. That shimmer may only be part of the barrier," Frank said, "The effect may be gradual, but increasing as we continue."

Dan interrupted, "Check your equipment, people." He pointed at Frank's tablet, "How we looking?"

Everyone started running through their own checklist as Frank reported, "Camera is showing…something weird."

"What's that?" Brent demanded.

"The walls of the bore…they're gone. We're not in the pipe anymore."

Everyone looked around. It was completely black beyond the platform lights, but they could easily see that the walls of the borehole were not sliding past them anymore. Instead, they saw only a field of darkness all around.

"Lights," Lee said, and those who didn't already have their lights on hit their switches.

It made no difference. The darkness was total and seemed to swallow their beams only a few meters away.

Frank said, "We are likely still inside the barrier here, but despite this void or whatever this is, I'm still reading something that looks like the opening to the chamber coming up. Should be in about twenty seconds. Temperature is now…sixty-two Celsius, pressure is one point one-two of sea level, atmosphere showing same gas ratios as before; not immediately poisonous, but not healthy either."

He tapped the tablet, calling up the camera view again, "Here comes the chamber, everyone."

Lee had already noticed a subtle change in the light on the platform. The harsh bluish-white glare from their lights was being replaced by a softer yellowish-orange glow seeping up around them. It seemed to push back the darkness, but only slightly.

Lee turned his own light off and saw Frank and Brent do the same.

Dan spoke loudly, "Duke, halt the drop once you guys are free of the bore. We'll take a look around first to see if it's safe to continue to ground level."

"Righto," Duke acknowledged, "You guys get that up there, Tommy?"

There was silence for a few moments before Tommy answered, his voice pitched almost to a high squeal, "Rogerboss. Yousou…funny… waitingfory…"

Communication was getting spotty. Lee was going to comment on it when what seemed like the whole of existence was suddenly lit up like a stage. Their platform slid out of darkness, and they were abruptly dropping through open air.

The light was overwhelming. After two and a half hours in stark blackness with only their narrow lights, it was like opening their eyes to a sunlit morning.

"Holy shit," Lee muttered to himself.

He heard Brent's softly spoken, "It's wonderful."

"Marvelous," Frank breathed.

Lee saw Dan stiffen and grab his sling as if suddenly surprised or shocked. He murmured something that Lee couldn't make out.

"What was that, Dan?" he asked.

The security man didn't move, but answered stiffly, "Nothing. It's just…a bit higher than I realized."

Lee looked out and down from the platform, startled to see that they were dangling what appeared to be twenty stories over the rocks below. His eyes went instinctively to the cables holding them up, even as he realized the moment of panic was foolish. The fact was they were now only sixty or seventy meters from the ground, whereas for most of the trip, they'd been kilometers above it on the same cables. It was easy to fool yourself that that wasn't the case when you were surrounded by the walls of the borehole. Now, swinging free and clear in the air, it was a different thing.

Lee never had a fear of heights, but suddenly felt very vulnerable and exposed, "I'm with you on that, Dan."

A chorus of oohs and aahs erupted from the group above as they emerged from the borehole, followed by several gasps of alarm as both platforms swung slightly in one direction.

The borehole wasn't completely vertical and deviated from it by quite a lot in several directions over the length of its decent. It wasn't noticeable while traversing it due to the gradual nature of the deviations, but it meant that, as soon as the platforms were free of the hole somewhere in that black void just above, the supporting cables pulled to one side and the platforms followed them. It hadn't been obvious while in the dark, but it certainly was now.

Duke called topside, "I'm stopping, Tommy. Repeat, all stop."

No reply came.

"Just as I thought," Frank said, "If there's a time difference, they may get our messages still, but greatly slowed down or greatly delayed.

Duke hit the brake switch and the platforms vibrated to a slow stop and hung in space, slowly swaying from side to side.

He muttered, "At least the electricals still function."

Frank murmured, "Electrical signals through the wiring don't travel at light speed, but fast enough that even a major time shift may not disrupt them too much, and the power source is up top besides."

"What about the voice signals, though," Brent asked, "They're electrical too."

Frank patted a box attached to the cage next to him, "It might be because of the wi-fi, but I'm not sure."

Everyone clung to the sides of the cages or to their sling straps. Their nervousness gradually abated, though, as one by one, they took in more of the scene around them.

"My God," Bill whispered.

"It's…it's beautiful," Angeline said.

Frank murmured in awe, "It's…not a chamber at all. It's a…a world of its own."

Even Duke spoke softly, "What the hell…what is this place guys?"

They were hanging above a landscape that looked like it was plucked from a rocky desert bathed in a sunset glow. On one side of the platforms was a cliff face about ten meters away that marched off into the distance in two directions, disappearing into a bronze haze at what could have been a dozen kilometers away. Near the bottom of this cliff was where their intended base camp was going to be.

On the other side of the platforms, encompassing the full one hundred eighty degrees of the view, was a rough plain that spread out to the limits of eyesight. It was crosshatched with ravines and craters and strewn with boulders and rocks that looked to be from the size of baseballs to trucks.

In the middle distance were two massive vertical outcroppings that looked like towers. They stretched from the ground to a sky above that looked washed-out and metallic, off-white at the zenith and darkening to orangey brown at the horizons. There was no visible light source, but the sky looked slightly brighter in the direction behind the towers.

Behind them, the cliff face extended upward and disappeared into that diffuse sky like the towers several hundred yards above the second platform, yet that couldn't be the case at all. The platforms had just penetrated through that haze to this place.

Lee called up, "Duke, what do you guys see happening with the cable?"

Duke and the others all looked up, tracing the cable with their eyes to where it abruptly disappeared into nothingness. It looked as if it were cut off only several yards above them. There was no sign of the borehole, or the black void through which they'd traveled only moments before.

"Lee, it's…you wouldn't believe it. The cliff goes up at least another hundred meters and is cut off by some sort of dense fog or cloud, but the cable only goes up about three meters. It just stops in the sky, like it's going through something solid, but the cliff…the cliff goes well beyond that. Giving me a headache looking at it."

Frank flicked his tablet view to the overhead camera that pointed directly up. He showed the screen to Lee, "That's what it looks like. Cable ends just out of reach, but the cliff goes up a lot higher."

Lee examined the image then shifted his view to the plain. There was something not quite right about it. The plain before them faded into the distant haze, but just before that, it appeared that the horizon wasn't flat; it had a very slight, but definite curve.

Perspective was off and, with no frame of reference such as trees or recognizable structures, it was difficult to decide the scale of things. The horizon could have been anywhere from two to twenty kilometers away and the stone towers in front of them between tree and skyscraper size.

He asked Frank, "You got a laser clinometer with you?"

"Yes, I do, of course."

"Good. We'll need it to find out the scale of this place once we're down. It's obviously a lot larger than we thought and we're not going to be able to explore much with the time we have."

"Speaking of getting down," Brent said, "we are descending, yes? Time's a-wasting."

"Just a second," Dan put up a hand, keeping the other firmly on the side of the cage, "This place is a lot bigger than we figured and there could be all sorts of unknown dangers down there."

"Dan," Brent said with a warning tone.

"I hear you, Mr. Copeland, but I'm in charge of safety, as we agreed. Let's at least check out the immediate area."

He pulled a set of binoculars from the kit by his feet and began scanning the ground directly below them, "I don't see any of those creatures around anywhere, but they have been in the vicinity a few times over the past few days." He altered his aim to look at the outcrop that was to be their base, "The equipment we lowered ahead of us seems unmolested."

Lee held out his hand, "Let's have a look."

Dan looked at his hand for several seconds before deciding to hand over the binoculars, as if he regarded them as his sole property, "Here."

Lee took them and panned around below the platforms. It looked utterly deserted down there, "I agree. Nothing visible below but rocks."

He angled the binoculars to look out across the plain at the distant towers. The view was slightly blurred due to the turgid atmosphere, but he could see dark specks moving among the boulders and crevasses.

He handed the binoculars back, "Look at that base of that second tower, the one on the right."

Dan took a look, "Yes…I see them."

"What is it?" Brent demanded.

Dan pointed, "Some of those creatures it looks like. Scores of them."

Frank was squinting in that direction, "I can't see anything, but if they're there, it gives us a start on calculating the size of this place."

Dan nodded, "Right. If those things are man sized or slightly larger, then they have to be at least two or three miles away and given their comparative size…that would make those towers about…"

"A hundred meters tall or more," Lee said, "just over three hundred feet, at least to where they disappear up into that white haze, and that horizon is looking to be maybe…eight to ten kilometers away, given our current elevation?"

Dan pursed his lips, "I agree."

Frank said, "I'll get a more accurate reading on things when we're down."

"So let's get down, for Christ's sake," Brent groused.

Lee spoke to the group up top, "Duke? You guys got binocs up there?"

Duke answered, "I'm looking now, Lee. I see those things by the tower, too. And there's something else you should see."

"What?"

"Take a look off to the left, halfway between the cliffside and that first tower. The place with that big jumble of rocks and mounds."

Dan swiveled in that direction. He panned around slightly for a few seconds and suddenly froze, "Dear God."

"What is it?" Lee asked.

Dan handed him the binoculars, shaking his head slightly, eyes wide.

Lee took them and peered in that direction.

At first, he didn't see anything but a brown blur with black dots, until the auto-focus kicked in and everything became clear.

The chaotic geometry of the landscape gave way to straight edges and curves, and what looked like angled shadows became apertures.

It looked like a city made of stone.

And hundreds of the creatures moved about within it.

Thirteen

"FUCK ME," DUKE MUTTERED.

He was controlling the drop manually and hit the brake when the lower platform was still forty feet above their destination.

Lee saw it too, "You got that right."

"What is it?" Brent asked, moving to the side where Lee was peering over.

Lee pointed, "We're too far out from the ledge."

"That's not possible," Brent said, "We lowered the advance supplies right down onto it."

"Well, it isn't directly below us now, plus we're swinging back and forth a bit."

Brent watched the ledge draw closer then farther away as the platforms slowly swung. Even at the closest approach, they were still too far away from the ledge to land on it. For some reason, since they'd planted the first supplies things had changed, and the borehole was no longer directly over the ledge.

This was compounded by their back-and-forth motion. As the length of cable from the borehole overhead increased, so did the amount of sway that the platforms experienced. There was only a slight wind, but it was enough to have the platforms slowly swinging through an arc that amounted to almost ten feet back and forth.

Brent drummed gloved fingers on the side of the cage, "Well, what can we do about it?"

"Only one option that I see," Duke said, "Drop us all the way down to the base of the cliff. We can climb up and get the supplies on the ledge later."

Bill joined Duke at the rail of their platform, "That'll leave us visible and exposed to any of those creatures down here."

"It's all we can do, though," Duke said, "and if this wind picks up or changes direction, it may send us into the cliff behind us here. We've got to get down somewhere fast."

Lee had been watching the ledge slowly approach and recede, "There may be another option."

Brent looked at him, "What?"

Lee stuck his head through the mesh and looked up at Duke, "How much climbing cable do we have?"

"Plenty, but…hold on now," Duke leaned over the side of his cage and shook a finger down at Lee, "You aren't thinking of…no way, man."

"What?" Angeline asked.

Lee explained, "I think I can get us to that ledge. With the swing we have going on now, at its closest approach it'd be only about six feet from us. Get me close enough and I can jump onto the ledge with a line and then haul you over to it."

He looked up and could see Duke shaking his head inside his helmet, "You're out of your damn mind. You miss and-"

"And I'll just dangle under the platform until you haul me back in."

Nobody responded for a few seconds and Lee knew they were chewing on the idea.

He pressed the case, "If it turns out not to be doable, we just lower everything to the base of the cliff and take our chances on not being detected anyway."

Several more seconds passed before Brent asked him, "You really think you can do it?"

"Long jump champ in high school."

Duke added, "Two decades ago!"

Brent stared hard at Lee, "All kidding aside, you can do it?"

"Yeah, I think so."

"You *think* so?"

"I can do it."

Never one to waste time on decisions, Brent nodded, "Good enough. It's worth a try anyway. Let's do it."

Both Duke and Bill grumbled, but they pulled out a length of climbing cable from one of their boxes and passed it down.

The climbing cable had small loops at each end and Lee fastened a loop to one of the utility clips on the waist of his suit. Dan ran the other end through the side of the cage and anchored it by winding it around the base of the short pillar that held the main drop cable for the platform.

He opened the door on the side of the cage, "I'll run it around my own waist and act as your belay point, alright?"

Lee eyed him, "You've done this sort of thing before?"

"Like this? Never. Have you?"

"Uh, no."

Dan didn't even crack a smile, "Then we'll learn together."

He pulled the slack of the cable in, looping it over his free hand until he had about five or six meters coiled up, "That should do you for the jump without giving you too far to fall in case you miss."

Lee nodded, "Yep, just enough to hang myself with."

He moved to the edge of the cage and put his hands on both sides of the open door, "Anytime, Duke."

Duke sounded resigned, "Roger, Lee."

The platforms jerked as Duke started lowering them at one-eighth speed. They descended slowly and the first few times the platform swung close to being in line with the ledge, Lee was tempted to jump, but he was still too high.

"Lee, be careful," Angeline's voice came into his helmet.

Like I won't?

He was going to respond to her, but Duke's voice came over, "Hey, if you miss, can I have that sweet '69 Mustang of yours?"

That broke some of his tension and he laughed, "Tell you what; you time this right and if I *do* make it, you can have the car."

"I'll hold you to that."

Lee gripped the sides of the cage and got ready to pull himself out, waiting for the optimum moment when the platform was at its closest and not too high, nor too low, to give him enough room for the jump.

He waited until the platform was about five feet higher than the ledge, which would ensure he could get more distance from his jump.

He barked into his helmet, "Okay, Duke. Hold it there."

The platform jolted to a halt.

Lee watched while they went through another swing out and back, "Uh-oh, we're off the line now."

The wind had picked up a bit more, increasing the slow swing, which should have brought them even closer to the ledge at the end of each arc. However, either the downward motion of the platforms or a shift in the wind direction had altered their trajectory. The platforms were now no longer swinging in an arc that brought them directly toward the ledge. Instead, they were off by a few degrees now and the closest approach saw the platforms gliding by the side of the ledge, coming no closer than ten or twelve feet.

A much farther jump.

"Too far out," Duke said, "Can't do it."

Lee kept his focus on the front edge of the outcrop, the closest part of the ledge now, "I can still do it. Our height will add distance to my jump."

"Don't do it," Angeline warned, "We can wait-"

"If we wait, we'll likely end up smashed on the cliff," Lee said.

The new direction and increasing wind was bringing them closer to the rock wall behind them each time.

Duke hit the button on the controller, "Screw it, I'm putting us on the floor."

"No, wait!" Lee yelled as the platforms jerked and started downward again.

It was now or never. They were at the top of their arc nearest the ledge and would never be closer. He ran two steps and launched himself away from the gate.

Dan saw what he was going to do and raised a hand as if to stop him but didn't say or do anything other than that. He just stood and watched Lee sail past him.

Lee put everything he had into his leap, feeling his thigh muscles cramp with the effort. He threw himself up and out, stretching his arms and continuing his run in the air, as if that might help him. He hadn't counted on the extra weight and slight restriction of movement the suit caused, not to mention the now downward motion of the platform, but he thought he could still make it.

Duke immediately hit the brake, stopping their descent, but the platforms were hanging freely in their cables and Lee's action in pushing off caused them to react by moving slightly in the opposite direction.

He was halfway across to the ledge when he realized he wasn't going to make it after all. His helmet filled with the startled cries and gasps of everyone else as they also saw it.

Instead of landing on his feet and rolling forward, he smacked chest-first onto the edge of the outcrop, completely halting his momentum. His breath whooshed out and his arms bounced off the hard rock of the ledge. There was nothing to grab onto and he immediately started to slide off.

"Lee!" Angeline's voice shrieked in his helmet.

Lee scrabbled frantically at the lip of the ledge, his gloved hands clawing for any hold and his legs scraping at the side of the cliff for purchase. He had only a second before he lost his grip totally.

His body slid down, and the chin of his helmet cracked on the lip of rock. Just then, he felt his right leg catch on something at the knee, halting his slide. He didn't waste the moment and pushed off with that leg. His scrabbling fingers found a small protrusion just before the lip of the ledge and he glommed on with every ounce of strength in that hand.

For two seconds he hung there, feeling his own weight pulling him down, along with the added drag of the cable connected to his waist.

"Lee, just let go!" Bill bellowed, "Dan's got you. He can haul you back up!"

Lee flashed on the image of Dan just standing there watching him run by, not even trying to stop him, *To hell with that. He might just conveniently drop me.*

Slowly, agonizingly, he put more pressure on his right leg and pushed himself up the side of the cliff edge. Feeling around with his left foot, he found a toehold and did everything he could to practically weld that foot to the wall. Once he felt secure, he hooked his right arm over the lip at the elbow and started to lever himself up, keeping his legs rigid and stretching his body upward as far as possible.

In a second, he found another small protrusion with his right hand and pulled himself a bit farther, feeling his back and shoulders begin to spasm. Despite the cooling of the suit, sweat ran freely down his face, stinging his eyes, but he just closed them, hung on and grimly pulled himself up.

Before he knew it, his upper body was horizontal on the ledge, and it felt as if an iron weight was taken off his back. He brought his right knee up to the ledge and rolled over onto the flat surface on his back, gasping. His suit read his increased body heat and kicked up his cooling.

As he caught his breath, his ears became unstuffed, and he heard the others' voices riding over each other.

"Oh, thank God…"

"…damn stupid…"

"…one lucky sonova…"

"…ope his suit's alright…"

He put up a hand, "Guys. Guys! I'm all right. Give me a sec."

Duke's voice cut in, "Hate to rush you, but can you pull us over? Our swing has picked up some."

Lee rolled over and looked up. The platforms' arc of swing had doubled, either from the wind or maybe his action in pushing off. They were only an arm's length from the cliff face at that end of their arc.

He pushed to his feet and grabbed the cable at his waist, "Hang on, Duke, keep lowering. I'll tell you when to stop. I can't stop your swing, but maybe I can slow it a bit and get you back in line with the ledge."

"Righto, you crazy motherfucker."

It took several more swings, but Lee was able to gradually guide the platforms back into an arc that brought them over the ledge, while Duke slowly got them down to within a few feet above it.

On the last swing in, he dropped the platforms and the lower one hit the ground with a crunch. It slid back toward the edge a bit, following the momentum of the upper platform, but ground to a stop well short of the lip.

Brent, Dan, and Frank jumped off to help Lee hold everything in place and everyone above gave a short cheer.

Duke and Bill dropped down another couple lines and the four men below managed to pull the upper platform in line with the lower as Duke tapped his controller to bring it down on top with a light thump, despite the remaining bit of side-to-side motion.

"Right on the money," Lee said. He dropped his cable, arms almost numb with exhaustion, "We're down."

"Thanks to you," Bill said.

Duke commented dryly, "All I'm thinking of is driving that sweet ride of yours, Lee. I guess it's mine now."

Lee laughed lightly, "The way I'm feeling now, if I had the keys, I'd hand them over."

"What are we waiting for," Angeline said breathlessly, "Let's go."

"Hold on while we secure you," Lee reached up and started flipping latches that would secure the cages to each other. There were four, spaced all around the platforms, and he sidled around to do them all. Dan joined him and they had them quickly secured.

Once that was done, Bill opened the side of their cage and hit the switch on an extendable ladder, which slid down in segments, stopping just above the ground.

He gestured to Angeline, "Ladies first."

She appeared at the top of the ladder, "Thank you. I can't wait to be off this thing."

A minute later, everyone was finally on the ledge, shuffling around with tablets or smartphones held high, taking photos, looking at the view or scuffing the rock, depending on their area of expertise.

They had arrived, barely making it, but they were down.

Fourteen

EVERYONE CONTINUED MILLING AROUND FOR a few moments, taking in the sights, and getting used to feeling their feet on the ground again. No one spoke, except to utter small expressions of awe.

Duke came up to Lee and squinted at the scratches on the front of his suit, "You're lucky these things really are tough. We heard you hit the rock even from up there."

Lee shrugged and was going to say something flippant, but Duke put a hand on his shoulder and leaned in, "Next time, I go. Got it, boss?"

Lee saw the earnest look in Duke's eyes, "Yeah, alright. Once was enough for me anyway."

Duke grinned and turned away, muttering, "Bloody crazy son of a bitch."

Lee saw Angeline examining the rock of the ledge. He went over to her and poked the button on his suit arm that was labeled for her radio channel only, "Hey."

She rose and saw him pointing at the frequency panel. She hit the button for him and punched him lightly on the arm as he drew up, "You idiot. You could have killed yourself or something," she looked at the scratches on the front of his suit, "Is your rig okay?"

He spread his arms, "Seems to be."

"Better have Frank check it out."

"Okay, mom," he flashed her a grin, but she'd already bent to run her gloved fingers over the rock again.

He squatted next to her, "What do you make of it?"

She spoke almost to herself, "The texture looks baked and slightly crumbly, but very much like sedimentary rock. There's a thin layer of powder over the surface, more granular than dust. It looks like the surface of the rock has been pulverized at some point."

She stood and showed him her dusty fingers, rubbing them back and forth, "You can feel the grit, even through the gloves. Very friable."

He gave her a rueful grin, "I know, I felt it pretty closely on the edge over there. Hard to hold onto. So any ideas?"

"I'll let you know when I know."

"Alright," he turned to go, but she reached up and grabbed his hand.

He turned back, "Yeah?"

"No more silly stunts, okay?"

"Hey, I got us down. Someone had to or we'd have all ended up smeared on the cliff face or risking exposure down below."

"Yeah, well, I'm serious Lee. I think we're going to have our hands full as it is down here without the possibility of injuries or worse."

He could see she was really concerned, "Yeah. Okay, you're right. Sorry. I'll leave you to it."

He left her and walked back toward the others. Dan was bent and working at opening one of the larger cases they'd sent down before, while Frank was walking around, almost in a circle, staring at his tablet, as usual. Bobby and Duke were fussing with several of the supply boxes, which contained their water, some energy bars, and the medical kits.

Lee approached them, "Need a hand?"

Duke waved, "Join the party."

With everyone else occupied, Brent left the group and walked over toward the edge of the outcrop. There was a waist-high lip of stone running along the edge that would serve to keep them hidden from below, but it also impeded their view of the area below them.

Dan saw him, "Hold on there, Mr. Copeland. That edge might crumble.

Nothing's been checked out yet."

Brent waved back at him, "Right. Sorry," he walked back as the others finished unloading.

He watched everyone fuss over their equipment for a few beats and cleared his throat.

They all straightened and looked at him.

His words echoed in everyone's helmet, "If you don't mind, I think we should say a few words."

Duke raised a hand, palm-up, "Go ahead, boss."

Brent waited for a bit, as if weighing his words, "Lee took a bit of the wind out of my sails by being the first to land here," he paused and everyone chuckled, "but, um, wherever we have ended up, I make no claims on this place. I only marvel at the achievements of humanity; our drive, our resilience, and our ingenuity, in allowing us to accomplish this thing."

He looked up at the white sky, "We stand on a new shore of discovery, as many have who sought knowledge before us. Whether that discovery is one of a scientific or metaphysical nature – or perhaps a combination of both – it is at this point that we tremble," he glanced at the edge of the outcrop, "literally on the precipice of knowledge."

He brought his eyes back to the team, focusing his gaze on each of them in turn, "All of you have brought us here and our names will surely resonate through history."

He paused, looking as if he was going to continue, but then waved a languid hand, "I guess that's it."

It seemed simultaneously anticlimactic and profound.

"That's good enough, Brent," Bill said.

The others voiced agreement and went back to their tasks.

Lee noticed Frank still circling and frowning at his tablet, "What's up, Frank?"

Frank came over and tilted the tablet toward him, "Take a look at this. The readings now are completely different than when we were up higher."

"How so?"

Frank lowered the tablet, "The atmospheric levels are all different. It's as if we've gone down to a layer where the gas ratios change."

"So what's it say now?"

"Well, it says that the amounts of CO_2 and methane are down by just a tiny bit, but the oxygen is up by almost two percent...O_2 is now at nearly twenty percent and CO_2 is almost what it is at the earth's surface – just over four hundred seventy ppm."

"That's good, right?"

"It might make all the difference for us," Frank reached up and grabbed his faceplate, "Hang on."

Before Lee could do anything, Frank slipped his faceplate up and took a tentative breath of the native air.

Lee lunged for him, "Wait!"

Frank pulled back, "No, no. It's okay, I think." He took a deeper breath and let it out, "Whew, it's really hot, but I think the air's good."

Everyone else had heard the exchange and came running over.

Dan seemed the most put out, "Frank, what the hell are you doing?"

Frank showed him the tablet, "Sensor feed on the cages is telling me the atmospheric mix is different here than up by the borehole. O_2 is richer and might even be higher down at the level of the plain."

"How the hell is that possible?" Bill asked, "There's not that much difference in pressure or elevation, and no greenery that I can see anywhere."

Frank gave an exaggerated shrug, "I don't know. Oxygen is a bit lighter than CO_2 – at least where we come from. Its molar weight is thirty-two as opposed to forty-four for CO_2, so it makes no sense that the O_2 should be more concentrated closer to ground level. The only explanation I can imagine is that there's a strong oxygen-producing source down here right at ground level or...perhaps the oxygen isotopes have different densities here, though that makes no sense to me. Whatever the reason, though, the air here is breathable for us. It's within safety margins and that's what matters."

He held his arms up and spun in a circle, "It's cooler too, for some reason I can't figure out. It's only" he checked his readings again, "fifty-one degrees C now. That's still really hot and will dehydrate us over time if we're not careful, but it means we can go much longer without using our suit air. In fact, if we just crack our faceplates open a bit so we don't lose much in terms of cooling, I don't see why we couldn't go indefinitely on native air, at least at ground level."

"Let's see," Brent pulled his own faceplate open and sniffed, "Hmm, smells a bit funny, but doesn't seem too different than up top. Sure is hot, though."

Frank nodded enthusiastically, "Yes, but now it's only a hot day in Death Valley, not like sticking your head in a furnace."

The rest of them slowly opened up their own helmets and sampled the air, keeping an eye on each other for signs of ill effects.

After several moments, Bobby asked, "Everyone feel okay?"

The general consensus was that everyone seemed fine, though Duke complained, "Tastes like shit and makes my throat hurt a bit."

Frank answered, "That's the slightly higher methane and especially the heat. It's super dry here, as well as hot, so try to breathe through your nose as much as possible. That will save your throat. If it gets bad, close up your helmet for a while every so often and make sure to stay hydrated."

Angeline spoke, "I'm almost afraid to ask, but…what does this mean for us?"

Brent could barely disguise the glee on his face and in his voice, "It means we can stay down here almost indefinitely. The guys up top can just ferry us food and water."

"You're not serious, Brent," Bill stared at him.

Brent spread his arms, "Why the hell not?"

Lee heard Dan's voice in an almost whisper, "*Hell* is right."

Brent continued, "This is a whole new world down here," he glanced at Frank, "or over here, or wherever. Considering what we had to go through to get here, I'd say it's almost mandatory that we stay as long as we can. Find out as much as we can."

Bill said, "Key word there, boss, 'mandatory'. You making it so?"

Brent looked at him, appearing to be genuinely bewildered, "No, of course not, but how could any of us call ourselves explorers or scientists and not want to stay?"

Everyone lapsed into silence, alternately staring at the ground and flicking glances at each other.

Brent added, "Naturally, depending on whatever we find here that might change our minds about that, what do you say?"

Dan raised a hand, "Just one thing," he pointed at Lee and Frank, "We've taken enough risks already. As I'm responsible for safety, I want no more of that kind of thing, okay?"

Everyone shrugged or nodded their agreement, but Lee couldn't get one thought out of his mind, *I don't know how he feels about Frank, but he seemed fine with me taking a risk.*

He went along with the sentiment, "For me, I'm quite happy to not do that kind of shit again."

Silence reigned for a few more seconds before Duke broke it, "What the fuck, I guess we send up for some tents, then."

Bill said, "Speaking of 'up', we haven't heard anything from them in a while."

Duke arched his neck and aimed his face upward unnecessarily, "Tommy? Al? You guys there?"

No answer came.

He tapped his communication panel with his chin and tried again. Still no answer.

He lowered his head, "You guys try."

Brent spoke, "This is Copeland. Anybody up top read us?"

They waited for several seconds, but no voice answered.

Frank pointed at each of them, "Everyone check your units."

They all hit their switches and took turns trying to communicate with the techs up top, but the only reply was airy static.

"What the hell's going on?" Bill said.

Frank spoke slowly, "Communication was spotty, even up by the hole, but now seems to be totally gone."

"But we're hearing each other fine down here," Angeline said.

Lee turned to Frank, "Some kind of damping field or an effect of the changes in atmospheric gases?"

Frank frowned, "I don't know. I'll have to check it out."

Brent pointed at him, "That's your Job One, Frank."

Frank nodded and pulled up his tablet, already sweeping at the screen.

Duke said, "So we're totally cut off?"

Lee let his eyes follow the cables from the platforms up to where they disappeared into the white haze far above, "Looks that way."

Fifteen

"WE HEAD BACK UP," DAN sounded almost angry.

Lee looked at the security man. Dan was sweating and licking his lips, even in his air-conditioned suit, though his helmet was currently open, which could have accounted for the sweat.

Frank was already shaking his head, but Brent beat him to it, "No way. We're here and we're not in any trouble. We stay."

Dan's voice rose slightly, "We have no communication with topside. What if we have a problem?"

Brent started to bristle, "We didn't spend three years, forty million dollars and come all the way down here just to-"

Dan put up hand in a calming gesture, "Mr. Copeland, I'm not saying we abandon the project. I'm just saying that maybe-"

"Maybe you're being hasty, Mr. Crowley," Frank intervened, "We know we had communication up higher, and we know that atmospheric conditions have changed. Logically, if we really need to communicate and continue to have difficulty down here, we only have to ascend back up to the hole in order to-"

Dan rounded on him, less patient with the scientist than with his boss, "That's an unfounded assumption. For all we know, the situation is just as bad up there now. We don't know anything about this place, its effect on our equipment, or even on us."

It was close to getting out of hand and Lee cleared his throat.

They all stopped and looked at him.

He turned to Duke, "You can still control the platforms manually yourself, right?"

Duke nodded, "Yup. I can get us back up anytime, even without communication with topside. Once we start back up, they'd know we were coming."

Lee said, "Okay. To be honest, everyone, I'm with Dan on this. We're really in terra incognita here and we've already had a couple of problems."

"A couple?" Brent blurted, "I see only one, and it may be temporary."

Lee pointed at the scratches on his suit, "A couple days ago the borehole was directly over this ledge, right Duke?"

Duke nodded, "Yep. We lowered the crates straight down onto it."

"And yet today," Lee continued, "We were dangling a couple yards from it and the camera feeds from the first looks down here a few days ago showed the ledge with the view closer to the other side, so it's moved what, maybe fifty feet or more?"

He swept a hand at the opposite side of the ledge and looked at Frank, "What does that tell you?"

The physicist swallowed and craned his neck to follow the cable up to where it disappeared into the sky, "We have...a wandering borehole."

"A what?" Brent asked.

"I've been thinking about it myself," Frank said, "I believe it gives us further proof that the barrier we breached was one between dimensional space, rather than simply between up top and down here in the physical sense, if you follow me."

Bill pointed upward, "So we're not simply five miles below the drilling rig?"

Frank shook his head, "I don't think so."

Lee suddenly put up a finger, "Hang on a sec," he started away from the group, heading for the far side of the ledge.

"Where are you going?" Duke called after him.

"Just seeing something," he replied, "I've been wondering where the original drilling platform and all the slurry went to," he jogged over to the far side and peered over the edge, "And there it all is."

The others joined him at the edge and looked down.

The entire side of the cliff face was streaked with multicolored stains and at the bottom lay a huge pile of metal, the remains of the drilling platform. The thousands of gallons of thick slurry had either dried up in the heat or been absorbed into the rocks, leaving only lurid stains. There wasn't even a chemical smell in the air.

Lee said, "I was wondering where all the equipment went. It wasn't up here or under the spot we came through."

Frank was nodding, "Further proof we have a wandering borehole. When the drill first punched through, it was completely over on this side of the ledge."

They all plodded back toward the platforms, and he continued, bringing his gloved hands together as if applauding, "I believe that the two brane *surfaces*, for lack of a better term, may act like tectonic plates, slowly moving over each other," he slowly slid one palm over the other, "perhaps reflecting differences in time or spatial motion between the two branes."

Duke squinted upward at the spot the cable emerged from, "So what does that mean? If they move far enough, will we lose the borehole?"

"I don't think so. As I said up top, the two branes are more like sheets coming into contact with each other. The area of overlap may be thousands of square miles or more."

"*May* be," Dan muttered.

Frank shrugged, "It's a supposition, but I don't see any reason so far not to give it credence. This shift has been occurring for about a week now, apparently, yet we still made it through to here and were off by only a couple meters. In fact," he turned and indicated the far side of the ledge, "The pace of change seems to be on the order of less than seven or eight centimeters, or just over three inches, per hour."

"What about the cable and the platforms," Lee asked, "Would it affect our ability to get off the ledge when we depart?"

Duke answered, "It shouldn't. We have a few more kilometers of cable up top, so unless we stay down here for weeks, we won't run out or end up having the platforms dragged off the ledge. I can control the cable payout from down here, so I can keep giving us more slack as needed."

Brent said, "So then we're fine, right?"

Duke shrugged, "For now, but we will have a problem after more than a few days, I think."

Brent frowned, "How so?"

"Whenever we leave, the instant we lift off from here the platforms will be dragged into line with the borehole. Right now, it was a challenge to land with only a ten-foot gap or so between the two. In a few more days, that gap might be fifty feet or more."

"We'd be sent flying like a couple frisbees through the air," Brent said, "I get you." He spoke to everyone, "So we have a definite deadline here anyway, it seems."

"How much time to ensure a safe liftoff, do you figure?" Bill asked Frank.

The physicist narrowed his eyes in thought, "At the apparent rate of motion, I'd say no more than five days. That would translate to a displacement of about another ten meters, or roughly thirty-three feet or so."

"Assuming a steady rate of change," Bill said.

Frank nodded, "Yes. Assuming that. Beyond that distance, the stresses on the cable when we lifted off from here might be too great and it could snap, or smash us into the cliff, depending on the direction of pull."

Lee turned to Brent but spoke to everyone by looking around at the group, "So five days is the max, then. As I was saying, I'm with Dan on concerns about our security, but, until or if we encounter any serious problems, I guess we should take as much advantage as we can and learn what we can while we're here."

Brent put a hand up, "And that means that we start making preparations for heading to that city or whatever that is over there," he pointed at the distant jumble of rock structures.

"I agree," Frank blurted, "If these creatures are sophisticated enough to build shelters on a large scale, we have to-"

Dan interrupted, "I don't like it. We can't go running around down here without making sure we're secure and can get back out. We still have a communication problem."

Again, Lee was disposed to agree with Dan, though he seemed to be the only one. He said, "How about this; we do both. Angeline, Bobby, Frank and Brent, you guys sort out our gear for a trek to that…settlement over there. Duke, Dan, Bill, and I will work on the communication problem, okay?"

If Brent objected to Lee making decisions for the group, he didn't show it, except for a quick narrowing of the eyes that only Lee caught. It passed quickly, though.

He gave Lee a plastic grin and turned away, clapping his hands, "Right, you guys tackle that. The sooner we can get communications sorted, the sooner we can get on with things." He touched Angeline on the arm and the two of them headed over to the crates.

Bobby hesitated, shooting a look at Lee before following them.

Duke spread his hands, "Okay, so what can we do?"

Frank hadn't followed the others to the crates and pointed up the cable, "Is there some way we can get back up there to check the conditions out?"

Duke put his hands on his hips, "I suppose I can disconnect the platforms and then one of us can be hooked up and raised back up to where the borehole was – is, I mean. If we can communicate from there, we can tell Tommy what our situation is so they don't panic."

Lee said, "Then I think we should do that fast. They have to be wondering why they haven't heard from us."

Bill spoke up, "They must know we're okay, though. They haven't tried to haul the platforms back up yet. And we know that the wired communication still works, because the cable control unit functions, right Duke?"

He nodded, "Yeah, but it's hard-wired data communication only."

Lee seized on that, "No way to tap into that, is there?"

Duke shook his head, "No easy way. I could probably do it, but it would mean cutting into the cable and messing with the wiring, not something we might want to do with our only lifeline unless we have no choice."

"Can we disconnect the platforms from the cable?" Lee asked.

"Easily enough," Duke said, "and it would normally be a job of just a couple minutes, but the remote cable control unit is hard-wired to both the upper platform and the cable, which means that the control unit has to remain physically connected to both the cable and the platform to work at all."

Lee studied the platforms, "No way around it?"

"I don't think so, but I can run an extra two hundred meters of cable down, which would be enough to raise a person back up to the borehole when it's retracted. The platforms would still remain attached to the bottom of the cable and the rest of us can just hang on to the cable and haul the passenger back to the ledge afterward."

"Let's give it a shot," Bill said.

Duke hit the button and ran the extra cable down from the borehole. It came smoothly, which meant that Tommy and the guys up top must not have been too worried about them, though they must have been wondering what all the cabling was for. Lee, Bill, and Dan kept pulling the cable in to the ledge and coiling it up at their feet.

To hold the passenger, Duke disconnected one of the slings from the upper platform and secured it to the cable. Now they had a way for someone to be transported up to the borehole.

By the time they were finished, Brent and the others had rejoined them, and everyone was standing around the coils of cable. All they had to do was decide who that would be.

"I'll go," Duke volunteered.

"You can't," Lee said.

"Why not?"

Lee pointed at the cable control unit, "You have to run this."

"Anyone can do it."

Lee shook his head, "Not down here, not in these conditions. You're best qualified when it comes to one of us hanging off that thing."

"I agree," Brent said. Dan was also nodding.

"Who then?" Duke asked.

"I'll go," Lee said.

Bill stepped forward, "No way. You've already risked your neck for us once today. I'll do it."

He looked around the group, "All of you have specific tasks to perform on this adventure. I'm just along because the Board wanted oversight. Well, I'm overseeing this."

He walked over to Duke, who was holding the sling next to the pile of coiled cable, "Hook me up."

Duke looked at Brent, who shrugged, "Okay, if you're sure, Bill."

"I am."

Duke gave Bill a serious look, "It's going to be a bit wild up there. There might be no way to control your swing if you get caught in a wind."

"You guys will be holding onto the cable, and you'll haul me in."

Duke pointed at the control unit, "This thing only works so fast, you know."

Bill patted his arm, "It'll be okay. Let's get to it."

Duke looked doubtful but hooked him up and rechecked that the sling was firmly attached to the cable.

Lee put a hand on Bill's shoulder, "Bill, I really wish you'd let one of us-"

Bill hit the mute on his helmet mike and smiled at him, speaking low so the others wouldn't hear, "What, one of you younger guys? Aside from you and Duke, I didn't see anyone rushing to do this," he leaned in closer, "Keep an eye on Brent and Dan for me while I'm gone, huh?"

"What do you mean?"

Bill angled his head at Dan, "Our security man is really worked up about this whole thing. I suspect he's a true believer in the religion side of this under all that muscle. And Brent-"

Lee saw Dan edging forward, as if wanting to hear what they were saying. He clapped Bill on the shoulder and stepped back, "You just be careful, Bill."

He saw Bill mouth the words as he moved away, *Ask Bobby.*

Dan came up beside them, "All set?"

Bill gave Duke a thumbs-up, "Ready to fly," he moved close to the lip of the ledge.

Everyone crowded around Duke, their eyes on Bill and the coils of cable at their feet.

"Righto, here we go," Duke pressed the retract button, "One-quarter speed."

The cable above Bill jerked slightly and began to draw upward, taking up the several yards of slack that sagged in the air just off the side of the ledge. Lee and Dan bent and grabbed up a couple loops of the excess cable each, ready to brace and dig in if there was a problem. Lee took up station closest to Bill, with Dan behind him.

The cable grew taut, and Duke said, "Hang on Bill, you're going to swing a bit."

Bill grabbed the cable in front of his face just in time. He was abruptly lifted up and out over the edge, moving at about a foot a second.

His feet kicked involuntarily, and everyone heard his startled "Whoah!" before he remembered that the sling was carrying his weight.

He immediately started to spin, but Lee and Dan had a firm grip on the cable below him, feeding it between their hands slowly and keeping the line taut. His spin was stopped, and any swing was kept to a minimum, so he simply hung just below the cable as it stretched and pulled up and away from the ledge toward the invisible point in the sky where the borehole was.

Duke hit his mike, "You okay, Bill?"

Bill released his grip on the cable with one hand and waved. His voice came over their helmets, "I'm okay. Just a bit…uh, unnerving to be suddenly hanging here. Too, uh, late to change my mind, I suppose?"

"You'll be okay," Duke said, "Just hang on and don't look down."

They saw Bill re-grip the cable with both hands as his reply came over, "Don't worry, my eyes aren't leaving this cable."

He lapsed into silence for a few seconds and the team watched him ascend slowly upward. He was already about ten meters higher and had moved about four meters out from the line with the edge of their outcrop.

Frank called out, his voice loud in their helmets, "Secure your faceplate, Bill. You'll likely be going back through layers with lower oxygen."

"Roger that."

They heard the click as he closed his faceplate.

"I'm monitoring your suit data," Frank said, "Switch your inputs to ambient."

"Okey doke," came the reply.

Frank walked forward and held up his tablet as Bill's readings came in, "Look at that, temp is climbing and O2 is falling." He looked up at Bill's dwindling form, "It doesn't make sense."

Angeline pointed up, "He's swinging a bit."

Bill's voice came over their helmets, "Uh, it's…indier up here…rting to swi…"

Lee and Dan gripped the cable tighter, but all they could really do was keep it steady down below. As Bill got farther away, his side-to-side motion increased.

"Want to abort, Bill?" Duke asked.

"No…kay so far."

Frank said, "He's only about halfway up and communication is getting choppy."

Lee said loudly, "Bill, see if you can talk to Tommy yet. Maybe you don't have to go all the way up."

*

Bill was gripping the slim cable tightly. He knew it could easily hold him, since it had carried both platforms down, but dangling alone from a sling made the six-foot swing he was experiencing feel much worse than it had on the platform.

Lee's message was chopped up, but he got the gist of it, "Roger Lee."

He kept the radio on broadcast and said, "Tommy, Tommy, you guys hear me? Come in, please."

Everyone heard it and held their breath.

Nothing.

Bill tried again, "Tommy? Come in Endeavor topside. This is Bill. We're down safely but having communication troubles. Repeat, communication trouble. Do you read?"

Only static came through.

Frank's voice came in, "Swi…your direct…annel, Bill."

"What's that?"

Frank repeated it and Bill got it, "Roger…switching."

Bill chinned the button for a direct line topside, "Tommy? This is Bill. Do you read?"

He strained to hear anything and thought he detected a faint click, but that was all. Maybe he needed to get right up to the invisible barrier, wherever that was.

He sighed and his eyes followed the cable to where it abruptly cut off in mid-air. That was too disconcerting, so he lowered his gaze and looked around, tracking the horizon and being careful not to look directly down.

The place that looked like a stone city was still there and he could just see small black figures moving around. He turned his head the other way and looked down just far enough to see the others on the ledge. They looked impossibly far away. He was suddenly aware of the drop beneath him, *Oops, don't do that.*

He felt tremendously exposed and vulnerable, hanging up here. His pulse thrummed in his ears and his stomach started to flutter.

He tried the direct channel again, "Tommy, Tommy. It's Bill. Come in."

Still nothing. Not even a click.

He tried the broadcast channel again, just to be sure, but only got an eerie echo of his own voice back.

This is a bust. We should...

He was focusing on listening and his gaze had traveled to the rock towers in the middle distance. He noted, almost absently, that there were several black specks in the sky, lazily circling over one of them.

What the hell are those, birds?

At the same moment, he realized they couldn't be birds at this distance, unless they were birds with fifteen-foot wingspans.

As he watched, the three specks turned as one, just like birds in formation, and started coming in his direction, rapidly getting larger. Very quickly they were close enough for him to see some detail; vaguely human shaped torsos, with thick limbs and long, ropey tails that switched and snatched at the air.

They looked like the creatures they'd seen on the ground, only these were flying.

And coming straight at him.

He watched for several more seconds, waiting for them to veer away, a tremor growing in his chest.

They didn't turn away. They got larger. They were obviously coming straight for him.

Feeling the beginnings of panic, he pointed frantically across the plain and yelled into his mic, "Lee! Brent! There are…things coming my way! Do you see them? Pull me in!"

He started kicking his legs and tried to grab at the cable stretching below him in a futile effort to pull himself back down, but he was still slowly ascending.

*

Lee and the others watched Bill get pulled closer to the point where the cable disappeared into the white haze. They all heard Bill's voice getting fainter and choppier the higher he went. Finally it faded out in a short, electronic buzz that cut off after half a second.

Brent had pulled out the binoculars and was watching, "He looks okay so far, just kind of looking arou…hold it."

Duke shot a look at him, "What?"

Brent's brows furrowed over the eyepieces of the binoculars, "He's… twisting around or something, pulling at the cable. What the hell is he doing?"

Lee said quickly, "Is he in trouble?"

Brent handed him the binoculars, "I don't know. Have a look."

Lee kept one hand on the cable and took the lenses. He peered up at Bill's small, twitching figure, "He's…it looks like he's trying to pull himself back down or something."

The lenses allowed him to catch a glimpse of Bill's pale face and the panic on it was plain. He saw Bill point frantically out into the air and altered his aim, sweeping a line from Bill to the towers in the middle of the plain.

He saw them at the same time that Angeline said, "What are those?"

Everybody looked out across the plain. There were three black figures swooping through the air in their direction.

"A-Are those birds?" Duke asked.

Lee adjusted the focus, bringing the figures into stark clarity, "Jesus Christ."

Brent grabbed the lenses from him, "What?"

"They aren't birds," Lee's voice was full of dread, "They're...they look like men of some kind, like those other creatures."

Angeline's voice rose high, "They're heading straight for Bill!"

Lee still had one hand on the cable. He started pulling hard, "Duke! Reverse! Bring him back down!"

Brent put out a hand, "No! He's closer to the borehole than to us! Keep him going up!"

Duke paused, unsure what to do. He looked at Lee helplessly.

Lee's mind raced, but he realized that Brent might be right. If Bill made it back to the hole, he would possibly disappear into it.

He waved at Duke, "Kick it up!"

Duke hit the button to retract the cable upward at the maximum speed of one meter per second. The cable jerked and pulled out of Lee's and Dan's hands, rapidly building up to top speed.

Brent pointed up, "I think it might be too late, guys."

Angeline shouted uselessly into the air, "Look out!"

Lee looked up just as the first of the large figures flew right into Bill.

*

Bill was twisting around in his sling, trying to keep his eyes on the approaching figures and signaling to his friends below. They looked like they finally caught on to the danger, as they suddenly started gesticulating wildly.

The cable jerked and his speed greatly increased. He gripped it tightly and glanced upward.

He was close to the top. The cable ended in mid-air about fifteen feet above him. If he could hold out for just a few seconds...

A piercing shriek cut the thin air, loud enough that he could hear it through his closed helmet. He looked up just in time to see one of the creatures almost upon him, rocketing at him incredibly fast.

It was a monster, almost twice his size, pitch black and gnarled with muscle. He threw one arm up as his vision filled with huge orange eyes blazing at him over outstretched talons.

It smacked into him, driving the breath from his body.

He didn't even have time to scream.

One of the creature's clawed hands clamped onto his raised left arm, crushing the bones within and dislocating it at the shoulder. The other hand drove deep into his stomach, punching through the Kevlar and composite armor like they were cardboard. He could briefly feel its long taloned fingers worming through all the way to his spine. The tail wrapped itself around his body with a pressure that crushed his ribs instantly.

Electric shocks traveled all through his numbing body as he looked into eyes the color of magma. Thick black lips drew back over long fangs and he saw something that looked like glee in there, before everything mercifully dwindled to a few errant sparks in the darkness as his consciousness faded.

*

Lee and the others watched in shocked horror as the first creature slammed into and swarmed over Bill's body. Even from a hundred feet below, they could see it tearing into him, shredding the armor and the sling like tissue paper.

Angeline was screaming and Lee could only yell, "Nooo!"

The other two creatures flew higher, circling around the cable. One of them swooped in and swung an arm at it, severing the steel and composite fibers in one swipe.

The cable dropped and pieces of the sling fluttered down as the first creature tore Bill's body away from the falling cable. It flapped enormous batwings twice and flew even higher, before dropping the body and veering away.

The team watched Bill pinwheel down through the air to finally crash at the foot of the cliff like a broken doll.

Angeline's anguished scream followed him all the way down.

For a moment, everyone was transfixed with horror and disbelief, looking down at Bill's crumpled form far below. It had all happened so incredibly fast.

Dan suddenly said, "Oh shit," and pointed upward.

The others tore their eyes from Bill's body and followed Dan's arm.

The three creatures had paused, hovering in the air far above, their massive wings beating rhythmically, and were looking down at them.

Then, as a unit, they dove and arrowed straight for the team.

Sixteen

"MY GOD!" BOBBY SAID, "WHAT do we do?"

Duke grabbed his arm, "Run!"

He pushed Bobby ahead of him and yelled at Frank and Brent, "To the platforms! The cage! Get going!"

Lee reached over and grabbed Angeline by the shoulders. She looked like she was in shock, still gazing down at Bill's body far below.

She looked up at him, tears streaming, "What's going on? Bill! He's-"

He shouted into her face, "Bill's gone! Get to the cage!"

He spun her to face the platform and gave her a push in that direction.

Brent reached back for her, "I've got her!"

They all ran to the lower platform, which was topped by the upper one and surrounded by the carbon-fiber insulating cage. It might provide them with some protection.

Lee looked up. The creatures had halved the distance, looking like huge birds of prey swooping in for a kill.

He saw everyone except Dan make it to the cage and start ducking in.

He looked back, expecting to see Dan right behind him, but the security man had headed in the other direction, away from the cage and toward the boxes of supplies.

He called after him, "Dan! What are you doing?"

Dan didn't stop. He only yelled, "The crates! Weapons!"

Lee wasted no time. He waved back at the others, "Close the door!"

Duke was making sure the others got inside and roared, "Lee! Get back here!"

Lee ignored him and charged after Dan.

Duke watched them for a second as Brent and Angeline crowded past him into the cage.

He made sure they were in and pulled the mesh door closed, staying outside, "Get down!"

Then he turned and ran after Lee.

Angeline saw it and yelled, "Duke! Lee! Get in here!"

Duke heard her but didn't answer. He put everything he had into running back across the outcrop. He saw Dan throw open the top of one of the containers, and Lee running toward the security chief.

The whooshing sound of heavy wings was right behind him.

He opened his mouth to yell when he was struck from behind by a massive weight. Lines of icy heat ripped across his lower back, and he was launched forward, flying through the air.

He crashed to the ground and somersaulted into a shoulder roll, coming up on his feet.

Ignoring the fire in his back, he spun, arms up, and came face-to-face with a monster.

There were no other words for it.

It was a couple feet taller than his own six-foot-five. The only colors on it were blazing orange eyes and the white slash of a gaping mouth that revealed fangs two inches long. Primitive, heavy brows swept up from the flaming eyes into pointed knobs on top of its forehead that looked like horns, alongside narrow, pointed ears that stuck out from the sides of its broad, flat face.

The body was twice as wide as his, roped with muscle. Thick, leathery batwings filled the air around it, abruptly folding in on themselves to disappear behind its broad, humping shoulders. Blood he knew was from his own back dripped from black talons on six-fingered hands. Those hands hung at the ends of long arms that almost reached its knees, knees that impossibly bent backwards like the hind legs of a horse.

The legs flexed and the creature stalked toward him with a leer on its misshapen face that screamed hunger.

Duke stumbled backward in shock. This thing was an impossibility he could barely get his head around.

But this thing, or one of its buddies, had murdered Bill.

He straightened his shoulders against the pain in his back and lowered his chin, "Alright motherfucker, come on."

The thing reared its head, roared, and charged, its ragged mouth open and talons reaching for him.

Duke lunged forward, ducked under the first swipe of the creature's outstretched arm, and drove his shoulder into its middle.

It was like hitting a concrete wall.

He bounced off it, the shock jolting his whole body. He was flung backwards by its momentum and slid across the rough ground on his already damaged back.

The thing was on him in a second.

*

The other two creatures converged on the platforms at the same moment, one crashing heavily onto the upper deck and the other coming down right in front of the cage door.

As if knowing they had no opposition, they ignored the people inside the cage and focused on the struggle between their partner and Duke.

The one on the ground took a step toward the fight and Angeline whispered hoarsely to Brent, "It's after Duke too."

Brent breathed back, "So? What can we do about it?"

She blinked at him, a strange look coming over her face. Then she shouted out at the creature, "Hey! Over here, asshole!"

The creature paused and looked back over its bulging shoulder. It simply stood there watching them for a second.

"Why isn't it attacking us?" Frank asked.

He was rewarded with a black, clawed hand suddenly slamming down from above onto the door of the cage, rattling the whole structure.

They all dropped flat, limbs intertwined.

"That's why!" Bobby shouted.

A groaning sound came as the creature above grabbed the decking of the upper platform and started to pull it up. The front clamp holding it to the lower platform snapped off with a pang!

It started to peel the deck back like the lid of a tin can and all they could do was huddle inside and watch.

*

Duke locked his elbows straight, keeping his hands on the upper arms of the creature on top of him, just managing to keep its slashing claws from coming too close.

It was like wrestling a raging dolphin. The creature's flesh was rock hard with muscle and perfectly smooth, hard to keep a grip on. He dug his fingernails in and hung on, but he was being dragged back and forth across the ground as the creature's gnashing fangs came ever closer to his face.

Suddenly there was a boom and the thing reared back, breaking his grip. He tensed for another lunge, but the creature seemed no longer interested in him. It was straddling him, had him at its mercy, but it was looking at something beyond him.

A gout of yellow fluid spurted from its upper chest at the same time he heard another boom. It snarled and stood up straight, seeming to have forgotten about Duke altogether.

It took a step forward, its clawed foot passing right over his face, and he didn't waste the chance. He rolled to the side and got to his feet as quickly as he could, following the creature's gaze toward the crates at the other end of the outcrop.

Dan and Lee had found two large automatic rifles and were firing at the thing. Two more booms sounded and two more spurts of yellow exploded from its chest. The creature uttered a grunt and staggered back half a pace.

Lee yelled, "Duke! Get away!"

They couldn't open fire wildly with him near the creature. He glanced

145

back at the platforms and saw the other creatures, one standing in front and the other hammering at the top of the cage.

He moved away to put his back up against the cliff and yelled, "Gimme one!"

Lee quickly tossed the one he was using slightly to one side, and it landed about halfway between them as Dan opened up on Duke's creature. Round after round pocked the thing's chest and shoulders, but it kept moving slowly forward.

Duke dove forward and grabbed up the rifle Lee had tossed. He rolled and came up on one knee. Figuring that Dan and Lee had this one under control, he took aim back at the one on top of the platform.

It was moving back and forth, alternately pounding on the deck and grabbing the edge.

He flicked the rifle to single-shot and aimed at the creature's head, which was the farthest point away from the people below.

The one standing in front of the cage quickly saw what he was doing and launched itself forward, scampering across the ground like a cat, using all four limbs.

Coming straight at him.

He ignored it, took a breath, and fired.

The armor-piercing round hit the creature on the platform high on its forehead and one of its horns exploded in a spray of yellow.

Its head rocked backward, and it released its grip on the decking, grabbing at its head with both hands. A sound like a howl of pain came from it and it dropped back onto the deck.

The one running at Duke skidded to a halt in a cloud of dust, reversed and ran back toward the cage. It leapt up onto the second platform and Duke saw it duck down, as if it were examining the fallen one.

He swiveled and took aim at the one that had attacked him. Its back was to him now and it was still advancing on Lee and Dan.

"Hit the horns!" he yelled and popped off a shot that hit the creature in the back of the head.

It stopped then and turned back to face him. Yellow ichor was dripping from a dozen wounds on its body, but it seemed to feel little effect from them, even from the shot in the back of its head.

He aimed at one of the protuberances on its forehead, but before he could shoot, it abruptly unfurled its wings and leapt into the air, its eyes glaring at him with naked hate and a snarl rattling its throat.

He pulled the trigger, but the thing was fast away and rising, and the bullet struck it low in one leg.

It screeched and looped up and around, diving back toward him.

He threw himself down as its clawed feet passed only inches overhead. He heard both Dan and Lee continue to fire as he rolled over onto his back, gun up and ready to fire.

It was gone, already a small figure high in the sky.

Lee ran over, breathless, "Duke! Are you alright?"

Duke spat and sat up, pointing, "The other two, on the platform!"

Dan pounded by them, and Lee pulled Duke to his feet.

They all ran toward the platforms and could see the team inside crowded against the door of the cage.

Brent pointed behind them, "They jumped off the platform and went over the edge!"

The three men skidded to a stop at the edge of the outcrop, just past the platforms.

Lee saw them and pointed with his rifle, "There!"

Two black figures were gliding low across the ground. One was slower, its flight path a bit erratic.

Duke pointed upward, "That other one is heading away too."

They looked up and saw it was now a speck winging its way back toward the towers, the same direction as the other two.

Brent opened the door to the cage and the team emerged. Angeline ran straight to Lee, while Bobby ran over to Duke and grabbed his arm.

He pointed at the ground, "Sit, Duke."

Duke dutifully collapsed and Bobby bent to look at his back.

Brent and Frank walked over to the lip of the outcrop by Dan and Lee.

Lee turned to meet them, "You guys okay?"

Brent nodded, "Yes, thanks to you three."

Lee shook his head, "Not me. Dan here is the one. If he hadn't made straight for the guns, we'd all be hamburger now I think."

Brent tilted his head at the security man, "Good job, Dan."

Dan didn't seem to hear him. He was still staring at the far-off figures nearing the towers, breathing hard through his nose, his jaw muscles working.

"Dan, I said thanks," Brent said.

The security man still didn't seem to hear him.

Brent reached out and touched Crowley's arm, "Da-"

Dan spun and brought his weapon up, "What?"

Lee could see Dan's eyes were wide, his face pale and sweaty. It was the face of real fear, bordering on terror and panic.

Lee imagined he looked pretty much the same himself right now, but it was startling to see it on Dan's face. On the face of a man who'd probably seen lots of action in his time.

Scratch that; he did say he was basically a button-pusher. Maybe he wasn't just being humble. But then again, he was pretty on top of things and damn handy with that rifle.

Dan was an enigma, to be sure, but right now they had a lot of shit to deal with.

He reached out and put his hand on the still warm muzzle of Dan's rifle, "What the hell are you doing, man? They're gone. Calm down."

Dan glared at him for a second then turned and stalked away without speaking.

Lee was about to go after him, but Brent put a hand on his arm, "Let him go. His blood is still up. He's kind of an intense guy."

Lee gave him a sour look, "Really? Hadn't noticed."

He made to pull his arm away, but Brent clamped on more tightly, "I mean it, Lee. You guys just saved our asses. Thanks," he waved at Dan's retreating back, "He'll cool off in a bit."

Lee angled his head to indicate the distant towers, "It's not him I'm worried about."

He pulled away from Brent and went over to Duke and Bobby. The medic was slowly peeling away the shreds of Duke's Kevlar and the bodysuit underneath to reveal the damage.

Lee squatted by them and winced when he saw the deep scores on

Duke's lower back. The creature's claws had sliced clean through the Kevlar, leaving three cuts across his waist and one long gouge across the bottom of the armor that protected his upper back.

He winced in sympathy, "I bet those smart."

Duke's snorted, "You ain't kidding. Feels like someone poured boiling water on me."

Bobby pulled a bit of fabric out of one groove and Duke hissed, "Jesus, Bobby, you're fucking killing me."

Bobby grabbed up a bottle of spray anesthetic, "That thing almost did. You have three gouges here and if it had cut you any deeper it would've hooked your spine out. Thank goodness you have a generous layer of fat in the way."

Duke spoke through clenched teeth, "That's muscle, asshole. Only three cuts? Those fuckers have six fingers."

"Then you're really lucky, boss."

Lee watched Bobby begin to clean sand out of the wounds and felt his own back begin to twitch.

He stood up, unable to watch more, "Is he going to be okay, Bobby?"

"If he stops whining and lets me work," Bobby nodded, "A couple butterfly bandages and a staple or two and he'll be okay."

Lee put a hand on Duke's shoulder, "You are one tough piece of jerky, taking on a monster like that, man."

Duke swiveled his head around, "Wasn't my plan, but…" He flinched as Bobby hit a soft spot. "Ow! Fuck, Bobby!"

Bobby kept working, "Hush, you big baby."

Lee left them and headed back to the others, all the time keeping his eye on the sky around that central tower.

Frank, Angeline, and Brent were in front of the platforms, heads bent together in deep discussion. They all looked up as Lee came near, their faces a banquet of dark emotions.

Angeline asked, "Is Duke alright?"

Lee shrugged, "Bobby says he'll be fine, but that thing took a couple chunks out of him."

"I'll see if I can help," she turned away quickly with a strange look on her face. Lee had the sudden feeling that she didn't want to talk to him right now.

He shrugged it off, *We're all shaken up at the moment.* He tilted his head at the other two, "So, we're pretty fucked right now, huh?"

Neither of the men responded. Brent was tapping his thumbnail on his front teeth, seeming to be deep in thought, while Frank looked totally defeated.

He addressed Frank, "Any ideas?"

Frank spoke with despair, "The cable is cut. We have no way to get back up, no way to even communicate with topside and even if we could, it would take them days to mount anything like a rescue-"

Brent snapped at him, "No 'rescue' is necessary, Frank, but it will come anyway. I told you that. The guys up top will by now have noted that all the data feeds are gone. They'll try to figure out if it's a software or signal problem for a bit, then they'll do the reasonable thing and retract the cable. Once they see that the platforms are gone, they'll come back down to check us out, either with cameras or another cage."

"How?" Frank blurted, "There are no more platforms up there! Are we going to all just hang onto the camera cable with our bare hands and be pulled up?"

He was close to losing it, Lee realized. "Hold on, Frank. Brent's right. We're not stuck down here; at least not for too long. The guys up there will figure something out. It may just take a bit of time, that's all."

Frank snorted derisively, "Yeah, and in that bit of time, what happens to us? Do we all end up like…like Bill?"

Lee felt his jaw clench in reaction to Bill's death and he narrowed his eyes, ready to explode back at him.

The scientist saw it, though, and hastened to apologize, "Oh, Mr. Mitchell, I-I'm sorry. I know you two…that Bill was…"

"Like a father to me in this company, yes," he put a hand on Frank's shoulder, "and maybe we can stick with just Lee from now on?"

Frank gave him a grateful smile.

Brent sighed, "We're all strung out. Let's not get at each other's throats here." He cast his eyes at the cliff edge just past the platforms, "We…should see what we can do for Bill in the meantime, don't you think?"

Lee thought they might have more pressing concerns to deal with, but it was an unexpectedly considerate thing for Brent to say, "Yeah. I guess so."

He felt a lump looming in his throat and coughed to cover it as a sudden thought occurred to him, "Hey Frank, these suits…I barely felt my impact with the cliff edge before. Is it possible that…" he looked past the platforms.

"What, that Bill could have survived the drop?"

Lee didn't even want to say it, for fear of both hope and disappointment. He nodded.

Frank shook his head, "Highly unlikely. You jumped about four meters. He fell about sixty. Even if the suit could protect his body, the internal damage from the impact would-"

Lee put up a hand, "I get it. Thanks."

As much as he didn't want to see Bill's twisted remains again, he left the other two and stepped over to the edge of the drop. He took a breath and looked down, afraid to look at the tiny, broken figure, but knowing he had to.

His brow furrowed in puzzlement.

Bill's body was gone.

Seventeen

"TOMMY!" AL'S VOICE CUT THROUGH the hot air of the late afternoon.

Tommy ran out of the drill shack and dashed back over to the console by the airlock room, "What is it? Get something?"

The video and audio feeds from the team below had stopped almost from the moment they'd penetrated the barrier, but the data stream had continued with its temperature, pressure, and electrical readings.

Four hours had then passed with no signals and no movement of the cable up or down, so Tommy had figured things were going well despite the silence. Then two hours ago, the cable started retracting at the slowest speed and Tommy thought the team might be on its way back up, but it abruptly stopped after only a few minutes and the data stream ceased at the same moment.

They hadn't heard a peep from the team since.

Tommy glanced at his watch for the hundredth time. Just coming up on two hours since they'd lost the data stream. With Duke and everyone else down below, he was in charge up here now…and he didn't have a clue what to do, so he'd run up to the console when he heard Al shout, hoping that things were coming back online.

Al just shook his head as Tommy skidded to a halt beside him on the deck, "Nothing. I thought for a moment we had something, but now everything is flat again."

"What was it? What did you get?"

Al gestured at the console, "Just a blip. A squelch of static on the audio feed."

Tommy felt his pulse slowing as hope was once again dashed, "Not a voice?"

"Just noise. Could have been static build-up letting loose, with all the higher electrical activity down there. Sorry to get your hopes up, but I thought it might be them coming back online."

Tommy put a hand on Al's shoulder, "No, it's okay. I want to know every time there's so much as a squeak from down there."

The two of them looked at the flat lines running across the console screens for several moments before Al said, "Tommy, when do we pull the plug? We're getting awfully close to their estimated O2 limit. They should have signaled they're coming back by now."

Tommy was torn. He desperately wanted to just haul the platforms back up, but with no signals coming up at all, he didn't know if the platforms were even still there. For all he knew, they'd lowered the team into a pool of magma or something, though that short retraction of the cable two hours ago had told him Duke was still down there doing something.

That was the only reason he hadn't hauled the whole thing back up already. If the platforms were still attached and he hauled them up prematurely, he might be stranding some or all of his bosses at the bottom of a deep hole if they weren't on the platforms and the audio and video communications were still out.

And if that happened, they'd likely run out of oxygen before the top team realized it and were able to send the platforms back down.

Al tapped the console in thought, "I still think we should at least retract enough to get back above the barrier. That's where the interference started. Then we'd know."

Tommy nodded, "Yeah, I know. I'm dying to do that too, but without knowing what they're doing down there, we could really screw them up. If they're in the middle of something, we could damage the platforms or some equipment."

"We can't keep just sitting here. I think it's worth the risk, Tommy."

Tommy closed his eyes. They'd tried everything technically possible to re-establish contact over the past six hours and nothing had worked. It gnawed at his insides over every second of those hours that, at any moment, the team could be in trouble but unable to communicate.

He sighed and checked his watch again, "Just a bit longer. That Frank guy said that there may be some kind of time thing at play down there, like time might go slower for them or something. If that's the case, they may be nowhere near their O2 limit."

Al frowned, "But you don't know that. We have no idea what's-"

Tommy put a hand up, "I know. How about when we hit that lower O2 limit up here, we retract cable at least up to the barrier and see what we can. I'll take the responsibility if there are any problems."

Al looked like he was going to object again but just took a deep breath and nodded.

Tommy turned away, leaving Al to stare at the flat lines scrolling across the screens. His guts churned as he walked away, trying to figure out what, or even if, he should do something.

Just a few minutes more, he thought, *then we'll start hauling it up.*

He had no clue that it wouldn't make any difference anyway, since the platforms were no longer connected to the cable, nor did he have any inkling that the six hours for them had been only a few minutes for the team below.

*

"What the hell could have happened to him?" Duke asked.

All the team, except for Dan, who was still over by the crates, were clustered at the edge of the drop, staring down at the spot where Bill's body had landed.

Bobby pointed out at the towers, "Those things. They must have taken him. The two that jumped off from here were flying low. One of them could've-"

"But why?" Angeline asked, "Of what use... oh my God," she put a hand to her mouth, "You don't suppose that...that they..." she couldn't

154

finish it.

Lee didn't even want the thought of what she was implying to be in his head. His mind was swirling with grief and blind rage about Bill.

He spoke with anger, "We don't know why *anything*, damn it. We don't even know what 'they' are!"

"We sure as hell do," Dan spoke from behind them. He'd finally decided to rejoin the team.

They turned to face him. Lee noted that he was cradling his rifle and was now sporting a thick belt around the waist of his suit that had a large, silver handgun attached, as well as several palm-sized boxes.

Duke said, "Oh yeah? What are they then?"

The security man nodded slowly, "You all know. You just don't want to say it."

Frank said, "Enlighten us, then."

Dan almost growled it, "Demons."

Frank guffawed reflexively and said, "Bullshit."

Lee looked at the scientist in amazement. It was the harshest word he'd heard him use so far down here.

Duke echoed Frank's skepticism, "Fucking fairy tales."

Dan pointed at Duke, "You were closer to them than anyone! Nine feet tall, horns, tails, fangs, fucking *flying* for Christ's sake!" He hefted his rifle, "And a dozen fifty caliber bullets in the chest and head didn't put one down! Does that sound like a fairy tale?"

Lee put up a hand, "Simmer down, Dan. You have to admit, it's pretty far-fetched."

Dan rounded on him, "Fuck you if you can't see it, Lee," he ran his eyes around the group, "We're in it, down here. We're in Hell - actual, real Hell - whether you want to admit it or not."

"That's-" Duke started to say.

Dan turned his way, the barrel of the rifle sliding down from the crook of his arm to his hand, "How fucking obvious does it have to be to you all? We're five miles underground, in a place full of murdering, giant black demons that look like they came straight out of a medieval painting!"

"That's enough, Dan!" Brent barked.

Dan looked like he was going to explode for a second, but instead spun on his heel and stalked away to the front of the outcrop. He cradled his rifle in his arm again and raised his binoculars, looking for all the world like a sentry on duty, scanning the sky and the ground between them and the towers.

Lee stared at Dan's back, remembering Bill's advice to keep an eye on both Dan and Brent.

He glanced over at Brent. The CEO looked highly stressed, but they were all stressed right now. Bill had told Lee to talk to Bobby about the two men and he resolved to do that as soon as he could get him alone.

Frank broke the tense silence, "We don't know that we're really even underground here and I doubt very much that we are. The environmental readings tell us that we must not be."

Lee kept his eye on Dan, but addressed Frank, "So what do you think this is, then?"

Frank craned his neck to look up at the white haze above, "That has all the indications of being a sky of some sort. The atmospheric gradations would indicate that. If it were an enclosed chamber – even an enormous one – you would likely see less stratification of gases," he shrugged, "but it would appear to be a very compacted layering of atmosphere, like if you took Earth's, which is about sixty miles thick, and sandwiched it down to less than a mile, yet kept the pressure relatively low."

"So this is likely not Earth?" Angeline asked.

Frank shrugged again, "If this is an atmosphere around a planetary body of some type, it obviously means this would have to be a different planet than ours, but I'm not completely discounting the idea that we are in some sort of vast underground world. I just don't have enough data yet, and, as this could very well be a different dimension, natural laws could vary greatly from ours."

Duke said, "Like in allowing creatures that weigh hundreds of pounds – and trust me, those black things are heavy - to fly around like fucking butterflies."

"Then what does all this mean, Frank?" Brent sounded exasperated.

"It means that I don't know where we are yet, but that we should assume that things will be very different from what we know."

Duke grunted, "Tell me about it."

"However," Frank shot a glance in Dan's direction, "I'm loathe to attribute any of this," he waved a hand around, "to the supernatural yet."

Given what he'd seen so far, Lee wasn't so sure of that, but the fact was, they were in real trouble, "Regardless of where we are, we're in a pretty tight spot right now and we need everyone together, using all of our wits, okay?"

Everyone nodded.

Lee called over to Crowley, "Dan! Can you join us for a sec?"

The security man turned and looked over his shoulder, his expression unreadable.

For a moment, it looked like he would ignore them, but he turned and trudged back to the group, "Have you decided to accept the fact of where we are yet?"

Lee tried to head off another confrontation, "Let's just say that we're open minded on the subject right now, fair enough?"

Dan regarded him flatly for a moment, "I guess," he sighed, and his shoulders slumped, "I'm...I apologize for my behavior. It was not professional."

Angeline reached out and put a hand on his arm, "It's okay, Dan."

Duke blustered, "Yeah. No hard feelings. We all owe you."

"That's right," Lee said, "If it weren't for your fast action in getting the weapons out, not to mention even thinking to bring them to begin with, we'd be in a lot deeper shit."

One corner of Dan's mouth twitched up, "Thanks," he raised the rifle, looking at it wistfully, "though it doesn't look like these are going to be as effective as I thought."

Duke still had his rifle and brought it up, "I don't know. We just have to be choosy with our shots, aim for the head and especially those horn things."

Dan raised eyebrows at him, "We had trouble with just three. What if an army attacks?"

Lee saw an opportunity to weld the security man back into the group, "Then we need your tactical knowledge. In this situation, what would you suggest we do?"

Dan nodded slowly as he thought, "Assume those first three will report

157

that we are here. That means that this ledge is blown as a place of cover for us."

Frank interrupted, "But all our supplies, all our equipment, even our water, is here."

Lee shook his head, "Dan's right. We can't stay here unless we can find some way to defend it."

Dan went on, "If attacks came solely from the ground below, we could probably manage it, but since these de-...these things can fly, we have no protection whatsoever. We're as exposed as we would be on the open plain."

Brent spread his hands, "So what's our option?" Lee noted that the CEO's fingers were shaking slightly.

Dan brought up his binoculars, "I have found a possible alternative."

"What?" Angeline and Bobby both asked.

"Something that looks like a cave near the bottom of the cliff face, approximately a quarter mile away," he pointed with the binoculars out past the platforms.

"And you were going to tell us when?" Brent asked.

Dan shrugged, "I just saw it and I can't tell from here how deep it is, or even if it is a cave. It might be just a shallow cleft."

They all pondered that for a moment, weighing the risks of moving against those of staying.

Lee waited for Brent to say something for or against the idea, but the CEO seemed at a loss. He simply stood, looking at the ground and tapping his thumbnail on his teeth.

Someone has to decide, Lee thought. He turned to Frank, "Regardless of what we think those black things are, do you think they're organized in any way?"

Frank nodded, "Undoubtedly," he pointed at the distant windowed structures, "They have constructed dwellings, choosing to live together, which implies some sort of social organization," he angled his head at the platforms, "and when one of their number was severely injured, the others halted their attack, which they would have probably won, and helped it. That implies social cohesion that comes with more highly evolved organisms," he shrugged, "But I'm not a biologist or psychologist."

He inclined his head at Bobby, and everyone turned to the medic.

Bobby's eyes widened, "And I am?" He shook his head, "I peddle bandages, guys, that's all. Break an arm and I can help you. The socioeconomics and relationships of aliens or demons is a bit over my paygrade."

Lee looked at Brent, "What do you think, boss?"

Brent's mouth twisted in an expression of dislike, as if he didn't want to make the decision, "I think we should..." his mouth worked, "...stay here."

"I agree," Frank said.

"Well I don't," Duke blurted.

"Me neither," said Bobby, "if we can find a safe place-"

"There is no safe place in Hell," Dan muttered.

Lee ignored his comment and turned to Angeline, who'd remained silent, "What do you think, Ang?"

She swallowed, her eyes flicking up to meet his briefly, before lowering again, "I...I'm not sure at all, but," she looked at Brent, "I agree with Brent. I'm sorry, Lee."

Lee just stared at her, but she continued to avoid looking at him.

Frank spoke, "As I said, all of our supplies are here, and we know that we beat them off once with only three of us armed. If all of us had weapons-"

"You'd shoot your own damn foot off," Duke boomed. He flung a hand at the city, "If Dan's right and they come back with a lot more, we'll be sitting ducks up here."

Lee watched as Angeline slowly sidled closer to Brent in what looked like an unconscious move, *So that's how it is.*

He stepped in between everyone, hands up in a placating gesture, "Hold on. We seem split down the middle here. I suggest a compromise."

He turned around slowly, but everyone seemed content to listen.

He nodded at Frank, "I'm as reluctant as you to leave all our gear behind, especially as we don't know shit about this place yet." He saw Dan shift like he was going to interrupt and continued, "But I agree that we should at least check out the possibility of another place to hole up, since this one is now known to those things."

He waited for someone to disagree, but everyone just nodded at him or looked at the ground, "So I propose that some of us scout out that cave, while the rest of us consolidate our supplies into those we absolutely cannot do without, in case we do have to abandon this ledge." He looked around again, "Does this sound reasonable?"

No one argued.

"Okay then," he continued, "Dan and I will scout the cave-"

Duke stepped forward, "I'll go too."

Lee glanced at Bobby, who just shook his head.

Lee put a hand up to the big man, "I don't think so," He pointed at Duke's bandaged back, "You're in no shape to go clambering up and down this cliff."

Duke scoffed, "Bullshit, Lee, I-"

"Besides," Lee cut him off, "I would really like you to be up here to help protect everyone else if those things come back."

That seemed to mollify the engineer, "Oh, yeah, okay."

Lee turned to Copeland, "You want to come, Brent?"

The CEO took a step back, "Huh? No way, Lee. I'm…I'm not sure I'd be anything but a burden to you out there." He looked like he was trying to focus on Lee, but his eyes kept darting around.

"Want me to come?" Bobby asked.

Lee shook his head, "No, Bobby. I need you here to help prioritize supplies, especially the medical stuff, and keep Duke healthy."

Duke uttered a scoffing chuckle but didn't say anything.

Lee turned to Dan, "So I guess it's just you and me." He purposely didn't ask Angeline, but he noted she didn't volunteer either.

"Fine, let's go," Dan said and abruptly headed toward the platforms.

Oh, okay. Looks like we're going right now.

Lee called after him, "Give me a minute."

Dan spoke without turning, "Only a minute."

Lee spun and headed over to Bobby as the others headed toward the supply crates.

It was time to start getting some answers.

Eighteen

TOMMY CALLED OVER TO THE closed door of the airlock, "Al!"

A few seconds later, Al stuck his head in, "Yeah?"

Tommy chewed the inside of his cheek, feeling the ragged flesh inside there. He'd been gnawing on it for the past hour, "It's time, I think."

Al came in, nodding, "Yeah. We haven't had a click or a beep at all for the past hour."

Tommy tapped his watch, "And they must be reaching the limit of their air by now."

"At least for us, it's been..." Al glanced at his own watch, "...over seven hours now."

Tommy dropped his head in resignation, "Yeah."

"But there is that time thing the science guy talked about. It might not be seven hours for them. Could be only a couple-"

"Or it could be the other way around and they've been down there for a full day already. We could draw up a bunch of suffocated corpses."

Al cast a glance into the black hole their bosses had disappeared into. The cable assembly wasn't so much as quivering, "So what do we do?"

Tommy figured at this point it didn't matter much one way or another. Two out of three scenarios meant death was likely for the team. If time below ran the same as above, the team would be running out of air soon, and if it ran faster, they were likely dead already. Only if it ran slower would the team have more time, but the question was, how much time? Minutes? Hours? Days, for that matter?

It wasn't worth the risk. The best-case scenario had him pulling up the platforms and stranding the team below, but if they had more time, that might not be the end of it. Maybe there would be enough of a time gap to allow the platforms to be lowered again...

"Fuck it," he decided, "We yank it up."

"If you say so," Al sounded doubtful.

Tommy pointed at the console, "Here's what we do; we send a message down – maybe they hear it or maybe they don't – giving them ten minutes to get back on the platforms. Then we haul up. Sound okay?"

Al shrugged, "What do you want me to say?"

Tommy shook his head, "Just say I'm doing the right thing, is all."

Al just looked at him.

*

"Got a sec?"

Bobby turned to Lee, his brow furrowed, "Yeah, sure. What is it?"

Lee led them farther away from the others and kept his voice low, "Before he went up, Bill told me to ask you something."

"He did?" Bobby looked totally confused, "What?"

"About Brent."

Bobby's eyes narrowed. He swallowed and looked suddenly guilty, "Oh?"

Lee gave him a wry look, "Come on, Bobby. We're in deep shit here. Bill's dead, our security guy's freaked and our CEO doesn't look to me like he's in total control of himself. All the way down the hole he appeared antsy while the rest of us were swooning, and his hands are shaking now. What's up?"

Bobby's head dropped, "Uh...I'm not supposed to say anything."

"Bobby, our lives are all at stake here."

He took a deep breath, "Alright. He...has MS."

Lee felt a shock go through him, "Multiple *Sclerosis*?"

Bobby made a shushing motion with his hand, "Yeah, but nobody knows, I guess. He just told me this morning. He brought his meds with him and told me he's been self-administering them for the last year or so, aside from the odd injection."

"How bad?"

His face was glum, "Apparently, he has what's called 'Fulminant' MS, the rarest and most aggressive type."

"What are the meds for?"

"Depression, muscle spasms," he paused, "motor control and cognitive degeneration. He has them all."

"So that explains the shaking I've been seeing and his darting eyes? He can't seem to focus on one thing for long."

"The symptoms can worsen with high temperatures," Bobby looked decidedly guilty now.

"What? Jesus Christ, Bobby. How could he even come to Africa, let alone come down here?"

Bobby hissed back, "There was nothing I could do about that. I found out *after* he arrived this morning. And he only told me because he needed an injection, and he swore me to secrecy."

"Well, he absolutely shouldn't be down here."

Bobby sniffed, "Huh. You go tell him that. I just gave him a shot he asked for. The other drugs he takes himself. He wouldn't even let me give him the sedative, as it might have conflicted with his medications."

Lee's jaw dropped, "You mean he was fully conscious all the way down that hole?"

"Yeah. He told me to pretend to shoot him up."

"Fuck, Bobby." Lee shook his head.

"I'm sorry, Lee, but-"

Lee raised a hand, "No, it's alright. At least I know now. Just do me a favor."

"Anything."

Lee angled his head at Brent, who was deep in conversation with Angeline, "You keep a close eye on him and let me know if anything comes up, okay?"

"Yeah, I will."

Lee clapped him on the shoulder, "Thanks, Bobby. You guys take care of each other up here."

"We will. You just watch it going down there."

"You bet."

Bobby went to join the others at the crates, passing Brent and Angeline on the way. Angeline flashed a look at Lee, and he flipped her a wave.

She patted Brent on the arm and turned toward Lee, obviously intending to head in his direction. He wasn't sure he wanted to talk with her right now and set out after Dan, who was waiting by the platforms.

Angeline caught up with him, "Lee."

He didn't stop, but said, "Yeah?"

She matched his pace and spoke quietly without looking at him, "Lee, I know you must be wondering…"

"How long?" He tried to keep his tone level.

She knew what he was asking, "It's not like that. It's…we have this arrangement. He has his life and I have mine and…"

"So for a while now. All through our thing?" he flapped a hand back and forth between them.

She grabbed his arm, stopping them both, "Don't you dare judge me, Lee. We're all adults here and I know you've hardly been lonely on your jaunts around the globe over the years."

The ridiculousness of them having a petty squabble about their sexual relationship suddenly struck him and he laughed, "Hah, you're right, Ang," he put a hand on hers, "Look, it's fine. It really is. Brent's an okay guy, for the most part. I'd say be careful, but you're a big girl. For now, let's just get our asses out of this predicament and then we can all have a grown-up conversation about it, deal?"

She looked like she was going to say more, but flashed him a quick smile, "Yeah, okay. Deal."

"Great. Just do me a favor."

"What?"

"Keep an eye on Brent. He's not…something's not right with him."

"We're all upset about Bill."

He shook his head and glanced over at Brent, who quickly averted his eyes and turned away, like he'd been watching them, "No, it's not that. It's…" he paused; this was not the time to get into it, "I'll tell you when I get back."

"Just get back."

"I will. Don't worry."

He turned away and left her standing there.

She watched him for only a moment before heading back to Brent.

Lee approached Dan, who was waiting impatiently beside a mound of the remaining cable, "Okay, Let's go."

Dan bent and went back to pulling in the cable that remained from Bill's failed attempt to reach the borehole. It had been left dangling down the side of the cliff off their outcrop since Bill had fallen.

Lee gave him a hand hauling in the last of it, "What do you figure?"

Dan kept pulling on the cable, piling it up at his feet, "I figure we check this out, make sure it's okay, anchor it to the platforms and use it to rappel down this side." He didn't look at Lee, just kept pulling up the cable.

"Sounds good," Lee saw the remains of Bill's sling bump over the lip of the ledge, followed soon after by the severed cable end, "Hang on. That's it."

Dan dropped it and they went over to examine the last couple meters of stiff cable.

Dan bent and held up the part where Bill's sling had been attached with clamps. The sling straps were still connected to the cable, but all had been cut through neatly. They were dark with bloodstains, and he dropped that section, wiping his hands on the Kevlar around his abdomen.

Lee didn't want to look at the sling remains and went straight to the end of the cable. It, too, was cut cleanly across.

He pointed at it, "Those things must be incredibly strong and have razor-sharp talons. You can't cut this cable with heavy shears."

"Uh-huh."

Lee dropped the end, his voice bitter, "Bill never had a chance."

"None of us do."

Lee glared at him, trying to keep his impatience with the man in check, "Dan, if you're so certain that we're all doomed, why even try? Why bother shooting at those things? Just lay down and let them have at you."

Dan grabbed up the cable end and peered at it, "I'm still alive, aren't I? We may all face certain death here, but I'm not about to give up my life easily," he glowered at Lee, "nor even yours. That's my job and I'll goddamn well do it as long as I can."

Despite himself, Lee was impressed, "You want them to work for it, huh?"

"You bet I do."

Lee sighed and leaned back, his eye traveling up to the point in the sky where the last meter or so of cable dangled, the length remaining after the creature had severed it.

It was gone.

"Shit," he said.

Dan was still bent over the coil of cable and looked up at him, "What?"

Lee ignored him and called over to the others, "Hey, guys!"

Everyone jogged over. Bobby asked for them all, "What is it? A problem?"

"Maybe a big one," Lee pointed up into the air.

They all saw it immediately.

Frank said, "The cable's gone."

Duke muttered, "Jesus Christ, Tommy must have pulled it up after our data signals all ceased."

"Well, that's a good thing, right?" Angela said, "They'll know we're in trouble then."

Bobby snorted, "And what exactly are they going to do?" He turned to Duke, "There are no more platforms to use."

Duke's eyes were narrowed in thought, "Tommy will figure something out."

Angela put her hands on her hips, "And how long will that take?"

Duke shook his head, "I don't know, a couple days to rig up even something rudimentary, I'd think."

"A couple of days their time," Bobby said, turning to Frank, "while how much time passes down here?"

Frank shrugged, his suit shoulders coming up to his ears, "I... don't know the exact time difference. We have no way of comparing without communication, or until we get back ourselves."

"If the time thing's even real," Dan said, "Regardless, we probably have to bank on at least a couple days down here, right?"

Lee glanced over at Brent. The CEO hadn't said a word through the entire discussion and, judging by the calm look on his face, didn't seem at all put out by the situation.

He spoke up, "Boss? Brent?"

Brent jerked like he'd been deep in thought, "Huh?"

Lee tried to keep exasperation out of his voice, "What do you think?"

Brent blinked at him several times, appearing to not understand the question.

Lee was going to ask it again, when Brent said, "I think we continue with the plan. We prepare for a move and you guys scout out the cave. It's all we can do at the moment anyway. If rescue is coming, it's a couple days away, so we better make ourselves secure."

Everyone was quiet for a few beats then Dan clapped his hands, "I agree." He looked at Lee, "Ready to descend?"

Lee looked around at the others. Frank was looking at the ground nodding and Angela was just staring at Brent with a strange look on her face. Bobby and Duke's expressions probably mirrored the one on Lee's face – resignation.

He nodded at Dan, "I guess so."

"Then let's get at it," Dan grabbed at the cable and started to haul it toward the cliff.

Lee spread his hands at the others, and they all turned away to get back to their tasks. Duke shot Lee a tense look before turning and mouthed the words, *Be careful.*

Lee nodded and bent to grab a loop of the cable Dan was pulling.

They struggled to drag it to the edge and dropped the end over. Between them, they fed the cable over until it looked like a few meters of it had pooled on the ground at the bottom.

"That should do it," Dan said, dusting his hands, "Can you secure the other end?"

Lee followed the remaining cable to the still sizeable pile near the platform and pulled several loops of it through the wall supports of the cage, tying them together. The platform weighed many times more than a man and would provide a good anchor.

He walked back to Dan, "That should do it. All ready to go, I guess."

Dan watched him approach and leaned into Lee as he drew near, "You wanted to know why we're here?"

It was an unexpected question and Lee stopped. He'd completely forgotten about their earlier conversation.

He shrugged and waved over at Brent, "I... don't have a clue. Because our boss wants to leave his mark on posterity?"

He meant it as a rueful joke, but Dan didn't smile, "Nope. Why does anyone go to Hell?"

Lee just stared at him, unable to respond in any way that made sense to him.

Dan answered himself, "Because they deserve to." He winked at Lee, "I'll go first."

Nineteen

THE TRIP DOWN ONLY TOOK three minutes.

The rest of the team came back to the edge and nervously watched them descend, their heads swiveling back and forth from cautious glances at the haze overhead to their comrades below.

The carbon-fiber cable was slicker and stiffer than climbing rope and a bit harder to handle with their suit gloves, but Lee had done some climbing in his twenties and Dan had a military background, which was news to Lee, and he said he could do it with his eyes closed, according to him. This proved to be the case when he rappelled to the bottom so fast Lee was only halfway down when Dan's feet touched the rock of the plain.

Duke's voice came over as soon as Lee hit the ground, "You guys watch each other's back down there."

Lee craned his neck and waved up at the row of heads poking out over the ledge, "You bet. You guys do the same."

He turned away to see Dan already striking out along the base of the cliff in the direction he'd seen the possible cave entrance, "Hold up."

Dan ignored him and just kept going, so Lee hastened to catch up. *Okay, it's going to be like that, I guess.*

Several yards along, they passed the spot where Bill had landed on the jumbled rocks. Lee told himself not to look, but he did anyway.

A few scratches from Bill's suit and a long, thick runnel of dried blood over one small boulder were the only signs of the tragedy. Lee felt a fresh welling of sorrow and anger looking at the maroon stain.

Dan just walked on by. If he noticed, he gave no indication.

Lee resolved not to think the worst of the security man, but it was tough not to. He was simultaneously an arrogant prick and weirdly vulnerable, especially in his apparent fear of this place.

The going was very rough and the two of them were hard-pressed to even keep their feet. The plain wasn't as flat as it appeared from above. Razor-edged boulders of every size dotted a cracked and creased land full of trenches and crevasses. Some of these were many feet deep, dropping away into shadows, and many of the boulders were more than head-height. If it weren't for the presence of the cliff on their left to keep them moving in a straight path along its base, they'd have been lost in minutes.

Additionally, the heat was still incredible, even with their suit coolers on full and their faceplates open just a crack. Just walking on the flat was an exertion, let alone hopping over trenches and pulling themselves around boulders and over jutting slabs of rock.

Even with the heat, though, Lee felt like he had more energy. He supposed Arden was right and the gradations of gases continued all the way down to the level of the plain. He quickly realized that his breathing was easier here than it had been even on the outcrop above.

He switched on the ambient environment readout on his heads-up display and saw that the O2 level was now half a percent higher than it had been on the ledge. It was amazing that such a small change in elevation could make such a big difference.

He hit his mic, "Hey, Frank."

Arden's voice came back immediately, "Yes? Go ahead."

"You were right. The oxygen is even higher down here."

Frank was silent for a moment and Lee imagined him checking his tablet for Lee's environmental readings, "You're right. It is. That's good to know. I'll keep monitoring you."

"Roger that," Lee clicked off the broadcast switch and stepped up close behind Dan. It might as well get to know his traveling companion a bit better.

He raised his voice, "Dan."

Dan angled his head over his shoulder, "Yeah?"

"So you, ah, you're a true believer, huh?"

"A believer?"

"God and the Devil, Heaven and Hell, the whole works."

Dan stopped and turned around, "That obvious, huh?"

"Yeah, it kind of is."

Dan turned away and resumed walking, "My dad was a preacher in Nebraska. I was pretty much raised in the pulpit."

That was easy, "Yeah, I guess I get it then."

Dan took a few more steps before replying, "No, you don't."

Lee thought about it and realized he was right, "No, I don't suppose I do." He lapsed into silence and looked at Dan's back.

Dan kept walking, but he wasn't really seeing the ground in front of him. He was seeing the ground of their backyard in Nebraska. Lee's question had called him back to his youth and images flooded into his head unbidden.

As he stumbled along in an alien desert that might or might not be Hell, he was seeing the rutted grass of their family home; the big tree next to the house and the wide stump beside that, the one used as a chopping block and…he tried to push the memories away, but they rushed in again. The memories of countless times his father had bent him over that stump, yanked his pants down and told him how evil was bred into him by his mother, who'd abandoned them both, The countless times his father had stripped the skin from his backside with his belt, punctuating each harsh word with a swipe of the leather while Dan watched his tears of pain and shame drip onto the stump and disappear into the wood.

The tears had evaporated but the shame had remained.

Elbowing out all the other images was the memory of the last time it had happened; when at the age of fifteen and finally as tall as his tormentor, he'd refused to take it anymore and had turned, grabbed the belt from his father, wrapped it around the old man's neck and twisted and twisted and twisted until…

He squeezed his eyes shut as he stumbled along, banishing the image of his father's purple, bloated face to the bottom of his brain once more.

Swallowing bile, he opened his eyes again to focus on this new hell they were in and saw the obstacle right in front of them just in time.

He stopped short and pointed at the ground in front of him, "Didn't see that from up top."

Lee came up beside him and looked down. They were at the edge of a wide trench that ran perpendicular to their path. It was about six feet deep, eight feet across, and appeared to extend well out into the plain on their right and ended under a pile of boulders at the foot of the cliff on their left.

They'd have to jump it. Not an impossible feat, given that it was only about two and a half meters wide, but encumbered by the suits and any gear the team would be carrying, it might be tricky for some of the members if they all came this way.

Lee looked to their left. A few meters closer to the cliff the trench narrowed, and the gap was closer to only half as wide.

He pointed, "That'll be easier for everyone to get across if we find your cave. Come one."

They moved over to the narrow spot and Lee jumped over the gap with no problem. Dan came soon after, but he appeared to misjudge the distance and didn't clear the far edge by much. The crumbly rock gave way under his heels, and he started to fall backward.

Lee reached back and hooked a hand under the chest plate of Dan's armor, pulling him forward, "Got you…lean forward."

Dan jack-knifed his body forward, but the effort cause one foot to slip backward and it went over the edge. He crashed down on one knee but stayed above the trench.

He slowly got back to his feet, "Thanks. That was close."

Lee examined the leg of Dan's suit, checking for damage, "Not a far fall if you went in, but this whole landscape is a damn obstacle course as dangerous as those demon things. We'll have to be careful. Even a twisted ankle could be a big problem here."

"So you admit they're demons," Dan resumed his point position, and they started forward again.

"I admit that's what they look like, that's all."

They walked a minute or so farther and Dan suddenly asked, "In the face of all this, why aren't you ready to believe?"

Lee gave it the consideration such a question was due, "Well, if I buy into the idea of Hell and demons, I'd have to accept the whole shebang, right down to the talking snakes and flaming swords and shit, and I just can't get myself that far."

"You can accept Frank's theories about alternate universes or dimensions or whatever but can't believe in the physical manifestations of Good and Evil."

"Let me just say that I think the cosmos is more complicated than can be boiled down to a simple moral dichotomy."

Dan was silent for a few paces and Lee tried to probe him a bit more, "But you believe in the existence of Evil as a physical presence in the universe, or as the built-in nature of some human souls."

Dan jumped over a narrow crevasse, "I do. The Devil is a real influence on the mortal realm. You can see his hand at work consistently through all of human history. As to the nature of some people's souls…" he trailed off.

"Yes?"

The image of his father flashed across Dan's mind again, "I think evil is in the bones of some people."

Lee thought about it, "I can't go that far either. I think evil is merely in the skin. It is simply learned, like racism, intolerance, or any other aberrant thinking."

Dan flicked a glance back at Lee, "How about things like malevolent dictators or sociopaths?"

Lee saw where he was going, "The cause is learned in the former case. Kids aren't born racist, for example, they learn it from their parents, teachers, media or whatever."

"And sociopaths?"

Lee shrugged, though Dan couldn't see him, "Those guys earn it through chemical imbalances or physical development issues – bad wiring just comes with the package in some people I think."

Dan glanced back again with a knowing look, "What if it's Satan doing the wiring? What if Satan is the cause; an electrician who deals in the currents of evil?"

173

That gave Lee pause for a moment, "For what purpose?"

"To disrupt God's plan. To harvest souls in the war against Heaven."

"Now there it all starts to sound like Bible-thumping hysterics to me again. No offense."

Dan walked in silence for a bit and Lee feared he'd gone too far. He was about to attempt an apology when Dan said, "Fine, putting all that stuff aside, though, what did you make of that video of the Kola engineer?"

"The possession?"

"You said it, I didn't."

Lee shrugged again, "I have a hard time getting my head around that. We don't know what went on there, maybe the guy just snapped, too much time on the rig, personal problems, who knows?"

Dan stopped again and turned, "You're rationalizing so as not to face a potentially uncomfortable truth. Fine, but what about our own men? The two guys from the first crew you found? I heard all about it. Dead men cooked inside and walking around, even talking? What part of that shit can't you get your head around? How much evidence needs to stack up?" He raised his eyebrows at Lee before turning away and resuming the trek.

Lee followed him in silence. In truth, he had no ready explanations for anything he'd experienced over the past few days. Despite all logic, he knew deep down that both those men were dead – long dead – while still walking. He told himself he didn't believe in demons, yet he'd shot at three of them less than twenty minutes ago and one of those had killed his friend.

The rational part of his mind knew there had to be an explanation, but a deeper part, a kernel of him closer to his core, worried and fretted that maybe there wasn't one. Maybe, at some point, you just had to take things on faith?

He was lost in the thought and almost ran into Dan when the security man suddenly stopped with a hand up, "I think it's here somewhere," he pointed at a craggy boulder near a small rise in the land, "It was just beyond that boulder, if that's the one I saw from above."

Lee glanced back in the direction of their ledge. It was high enough that he could see it over the jumbled rocks that obscured the ground-level view. The platforms were just visible, but he couldn't see anybody moving around.

It was only a couple hundred yards away but felt much farther.

He heard Dan start forward again and turned to follow.

The ground rose slightly toward the big boulder Dan had spotted, which allowed them to gradually see more of their surroundings. It didn't reveal much, however, just a seemingly endless crenelated landscape interrupted only by those far-off, tall stone towers.

He squinted and thought he saw a few dark spots circling around them but couldn't be sure. In the back of his mind he also knew that moving in this direction brought them closer to that place that looked like a settlement of some type, though he couldn't see it from here.

It was frustrating and unnerving, knowing they were so close to places of potential danger. In fact, any number of creatures could be hiding in and around the boulders and trenches surrounding them and they'd never know.

Until it was too late.

Dan rounded the boulder and called out, "There it is."

Lee walked up beside him and gazed at the side of the cliff.

It certainly looked like a cave; a big one, in fact.

Twenty

"PUT THOSE OVER HERE, I guess," Duke flipped a hand at the small pile of supplies they were gathering by the platforms.

Bobby dropped the two boxes he was carrying, "We really should have thought about bringing duffels or knapsacks or something. We can't carry half the shit we need like this."

Duke pursed his lips, "I know. I don't think we're going to be able to bring even this bit of stuff with us."

The team had combed through the crates and had managed to limit their essentials to just about two hundred pounds of water, energy bars, medical supplies and, given what had happened so far, every weapon and box of ammunition they found, which turned out to be quite a lot.

Dan had planned that side of it well, though how he knew they'd need .50 caliber rifles, hundreds of rounds of ammunition and even some small explosives was beyond their understanding.

Duke picked up one of the boxes of ammo, "That Dan is a jerk, but I'm sure as hell glad he came prepared."

Brent brought over another box of medical supplies, "That's what I pay him for."

Duke idly scratched the stiff bandages across his back, "Yeah, I guess."

Angeline joined them, "You think we can bring anything else? Frank

176

is upset we can't pack any of his equipment," she waved a hand back at the physicist, who was looking down at several boxes with his hands on his hips.

"The essentials are what we need to survive," Brent said, "He can program most of his stuff to just collect data here as easily as anywhere else. It'll do the same job no matter where it is."

Frank overheard them and came over, "It's not that. It's that I don't know if I'll be able to recover the data if we leave the stuff here."

Brent said, "Doesn't it upload to your tablet automatically?"

Frank tapped the screen he seemed to never be without, "Yes, but not all of it." He hit the screen with a bit of frustration, "And the hotspot wireless communication isn't working since we lost the cable connection," he frowned over at the platform.

"Well, you'll have to make do," Duke said, "This shit here is about all we can carry, at least on a first trip."

"Speaking of which," Brent said and hit his mike, "Dan, Lee; you guys hear me?"

Lee's voice came back, "We hear you. How you guys doing up there?"

Duke said, "We got it pretty well handled. More importantly, how's it going with you guys?"

Lee's answer wrestled with static, but was audible, "It looks good. The cave is pretty big and goes back a ways. Should keep us hidden."

"Should we start moving it over then?" Angeline asked.

Dan's voice broke in, "The cave is fine. It's the getting here that's a bit tough. It's a rough hike."

"Is it doable, though?" Brent asked.

"It's doable," Dan said.

Lee broke in, "Duke, maybe we can bring more stuff over if you start using the cable to lower some of it down first. Once it's at the bottom, we can make a couple trips and it'll go a lot faster."

"Will do. We'll start right away."

"Hold on," Brent broke in, "I'm still not convinced that we should be abandoning this outcrop."

Lee said, "We're not abandoning it. Think of this as just a temporary relocation until we get a better handle on things down here."

Silence stretched for several moments while Brent thought about it. He finally said, "Okay, if everyone else agrees."

He looked around. Bobby, Angeline, and Duke were nodding. Frank just shrugged.

He relayed to Lee and Dan, "I guess we're heading to the cave."

"Just one thing," Dan said.

Brent answered, "Go ahead."

"We can't see more than a few yards down here. Maybe someone up there should keep a lookout for us all while we're doing the move, so we don't get surprised."

"Good idea," Brent said, "We're on it."

They signed off and Brent turned to Duke, "See? That's what I pay him for, asshole or not."

*

Lee stood at the mouth of the cave and squinted, surveying the surrounding area. After the relative darkness of the cave, the hazy white sky seemed overly bright.

He had to admit the cave was a better refuge than the ledge. It was spacious, set a few feet higher than the level of the land, which afforded a pretty good view, and its entrance was at an angle into the cliff. From half the surrounding area, it didn't look like anything other than a slice of shadow from a rock. Unfortunately, from the direction of the towers, it was much more obvious, which presented a problem.

Beggars can't be choosers, Lee thought, *it should serve well enough for a while and at least provides protection from attacks from above.*

After informing Brent and the others of the cave, Dan went back in to check it out further. The man was a perfectionist, Lee thought, as he heard him moving around behind him in the dim, inner reaches of the cave. The main cavern was shallow, penetrating only about ten meters into the cliff, but there were several smaller spaces branching off to the sides and Dan wanted to make sure there were no hidden dangers.

The security man seemed more relaxed now, as if the discovery and confirmation of the cave as a place of refuge made him feel more self-assured; like he'd accomplished an important task, which Lee supposed he had. He couldn't shake the feeling, though, that as competent and stolid as Dan seemed on the outside, he was still somehow shaking on the inside. He presented outwardly as calm and prepared but had revealed himself to be thin-skinned and an almost tortured person in some ways.

For some reason that Lee himself couldn't define, Dan's religious beliefs made him seem to be less a person to depend upon and more one to be worried about. Lee had to admit, though, that they were all displaying unsuspected sides to themselves on this journey. Added to the fact that some of them were holding secrets, it didn't give him much confidence in their ability to stick together as a group.

He heard Dan approaching from behind and left the view to walk back into the cave, "Good job finding this place. You may have saved us again."

Dan's voice echoed hollowly, "I may have extended our survivability by a bit, but that's a far cry from being saved."

Oh yeah, I forgot; we're all doomed, "Well, I'll take it anyway."

There was a moment's pause before Dan said, "Thanks, though."

Even in a lighter mood, Dan wasn't disposed to idle chatter.

Lee was getting impatient to get back to the outcrop. They'd been away too long, "Seen enough?"

Dan suddenly emerged into the dim light from the side, "Yes. I think this will do nicely," he threw a thumb over his shoulder, "Unfortunately, there's no back exit, so we could easily get boxed-in here, but that also means nothing can come at us from our six."

Lee noted he said nothing, rather than nobody.

Dan walked up to him, dusting his gloves, "We should be able to fit everything we have in here and, as long as we can keep the location secret, we should be safe."

"Fine. Let's get back. The sooner we're off that ledge, the better."

Dan took the lead as they headed back out of the cave. Right outside the mouth was a small drop to the ground and they both reached up to pull their faceplates back down to cut the sudden glare from the hazy sky. It wouldn't do to break an ankle here.

Lee was right behind Dan and saw his arm go up halfway to his faceplate, but then stop. The security man's body went rigid, and he just stood there at the lip of the cave.

Lee was going to ask him what was up, when Dan sucked in a ragged breath and suddenly staggered backward toward Lee, gasping, "Dear Jesus protect us."

Lee rushed forward, grabbing Dan's outstretched arm and steadying him, "What is it?"

Dan turned to him with eyes wide, "We're in trouble."

Lee pulled himself around Dan and looked down over the lip in front of the cave, expecting to see one of the monsters.

It was worse.

Bill was standing there, looking up at him.

Twenty-One

LEE'S FIRST FEELING WAS SHOCK, followed by immense relief. Bill was alive!

He moved instinctively toward Bill, but Dan was still in front of him, and his arm shot out, blocking Lee, "Don't!"

Lee tried to push past him, "But that's Bill! He survived the fall."

Dan seemed to have shaken off his own momentary shock. He grabbed the side of Lee's chest plate to hold him and pointed down, "Did he? Look at him."

Lee looked…and a cold worm of dread slowly crept through his guts.

Bill's helmet faceplate was wide open, and his pale face was slack, mouth gaping, jaw working slowly. Part of his face, the left temple behind the eye, was a mass of red jelly.

And the eyes…

They were totally black, glittering like insect eyes.

Those eyes looked up at him. They could have been looking anywhere, but Lee knew they were focused right on him.

The gaping mouth widened slightly into something like a smile, *"Lee…"*

The voice was Bill's, but it sounded like Bill had swallowed a cup of gravel.

Lee's shocked gaze tracked down Bill's suit.

Dried blood crusted the Kevlar at nearly every joint, the suit was cracked and splintered in places like fiberglass. There was a gaping hole in the Kevlar over his stomach. Bill's left arm hung at an odd angle and was bent slightly backward at the elbow.

Every inch of him looked like it would have him screaming in pain, yet he was just standing there, his smile a black slash in his white face.

He felt Dan release his grip and heard him unclip the pistol he had at his side.

Lee couldn't believe this wasn't Bill. He held his hand out toward the figure, "Bill? Are you okay?"

Dan cocked the gun and whispered, "That isn't Bill Owen. Not anymore."

Lee angled his head back, but kept his eyes on Bill, "What?"

"If that's even Bill's body, he's not in there anymore. He's just a puppet now, maybe like those other two men you met above."

Lee stared at Bill for a few seconds, seeing him standing there like a statue, not swaying, not rocking slightly like people did when they stood still.

Not even breathing.

No, not like a statue; worse than that.

Hollowed out somehow, like a mannequin.

He knew that Dan would say his spirit or soul was gone. Lee simply saw it as a complete lack of life.

He felt cold sweat break out all under his suit as the realization struck him. He knew that inside Bill was cooked just like those other two men.

Cooked and walking around.

Bill's head jerked slightly, more a spasm than a conscious action. He aimed those eyes up at Crowley, *"Dannn..."*

Dan whispered hoarsely, "Yes, demon?"

Bill's smile broadened and Lee could see the shattered teeth inside, "You...know us."

Dan said, "Yes, I do, but I will not hear you, demon."

Lee saw the muzzle of the pistol come into view beside him and a fresh surge of adrenaline coursed through his body, *That's Bill!*

But he knew that it wasn't.

Dan whispered, "Resist the devil and he will flee from you."

The gun boomed and a black hole opened up in Bill's forehead.

The head didn't even twitch and no blood came out. Bill just kept smiling.

Dan grabbed Lee's arm, "Didn't think that would work. Come on. We need to go, right now," he started pulling Lee backwards.

Confused, Lee made to follow him, but Bill spoke louder, calling Lee's attention back to him, *"Lee…you…I…and the othersss…all belong herrre."*

"Come on," Dan pulled on Lee's arm, "Shut your eyes and ears to it." He shouted down at the Bill thing, "You belong only to your father, the Devil! And you want only to carry out your father's wishes!"

The Bill thing's smile dropped a bit. It moved then, reaching up to grab the lip in front of the cave.

It began to pull itself up using only one arm, as if its body weighed nothing.

It stood erect in front of the cave now, effectively blocking the way out, and its face creased into a deeper smile, *"Weee…are coming."*

"Let's go!" Dan yanked Lee further back into the cave. He fired again and Lee heard the hollow *ponk* sound of the bullet hitting the Kevlar under the echoing report of the gun.

They stumbled away from the thing, deeper into the cave, knowing there was no back door of escape.

The Bill thing shambled after them, its gravelly voice calling, *"Leeee…"*

Lee kept his eyes locked on the approaching figure and chinned the broadcast switch in his helmet, "Duke! Bobby!"

Duke's scratchy voice came back immediately, "…eah?"

"I think you're about to have guests! Get the weapons!"

That was all he could manage. His back bumped up against the rear of the cave. There was nowhere to go.

Dan fired again at the Bill thing, apparently to no effect. It kept walking slowly forward, a black shape silhouetted in the light from the entrance, saying over and over, *"Leee…Leee…"*

Dan yelled at him, "Shoot it, for God's sake!"

Lee still had his rifle slung across his back. He'd forgotten all about it.

He pulled it around and took aim at the Bill thing. At least in the dark, it was easier to tell himself it wasn't his friend.

He started firing.

*

Duke heard the distant *pok-pok* of shooting and dropped the box he was carrying, "Bobby, with me! Angeline, Frank, Brent! Get in the cage!"

Frank made a move toward the cage, but Angeline snatched up one of the rifles and ran in the other direction, toward the front of the outcrop.

Bobby watched her go, shrugged at Duke, and grabbed one too, "Maybe we all ought to have one?"

Duke ground his teeth and gripped his own rifle, pointing at Bobby to go with Angeline. He kept waving Brent and Frank in the direction of the platforms, "Get under cover!"

Brent ignored him and grabbed up the binoculars from their pile of supplies, aiming them back at the towers.

There were at least a dozen of the flying things in the air heading their way.

He lowered his aim and scanned the floor of the plain between the towers and their ledge.

A great many black forms were loping and scrabbling their way through the trenches and over the rocks toward them.

He dropped the glasses and yelled, "Guns alone aren't going to do it!"

"It's all we got," Duke said and tossed his rifle at Brent, "Can you shoot?"

Brent shook his head, "Not yet, but I will."

Duke bent and took another rifle from their supply pile, as well as a few small metal boxes labeled as explosive, "Stick with Frank at the cage and shoot anything that comes near."

Brent nodded and trotted back to the platforms. Frank was already by the door of the cage, his arms loaded with his tablet and other electronics.

Duke charged up to the outcrop, "Angeline! Get back to the cage!"

She had stationed herself near a gap in the rocks where she could see out, "No! The more guns the better!"

He knew there was no arguing. Besides, she was right, "Okay, fine, but let me take point here. You go to the platform side and watch for Lee and Dan. They may need covering fire if they're heading back."

He turned to Bobby without waiting to see if Angeline went, "Bobby, you head to the other side. This way we can guard both flanks and the middle," he raised his voice, "Just one thing; if they make it onto this ledge, let's not shoot each other in a fucking crossfire."

Bobby waved and headed over to the far side of the ledge.

Duke peered through the gap in the outcrop. What he saw made his blood go cold.

Dozens of the huge black creatures were already nearing the foot of the cliff below them in a roiling mob, climbing all over each other in their haste. He glanced up and saw several of the flying ones circling, just like hawks do before diving for a kill.

He palmed one of the explosive boxes, "Get ready everyone!"

*

Lee and Dan were right at the rear of the cave. Dan had given up on his pistol and was using his own rifle as well now. Lee had his back against rock and was pulling his trigger repeatedly, not wanting to waste ammo on a full auto setting.

The Bill thing had followed them back and had moved out of alignment with the cave mouth, so now it was in darkness as well and virtually invisible. Lee could only track it by the sound of its gravelly voice intoning his name over and over.

He knew most of his shots were missing and he stopped firing, "Fuck it! Can't see a thing! Lights on!"

Lee chinned his helmet light at the same time as Dan and the blue-white flare of illumination lit the entire back half of the cave…

And the Bill thing's face only an arm's length away, right in front of him.

"Jesus Christ!" he yelled and threw himself to the side, just as the

185

creature reached out with both hands, gloved fingers clawing through air where Lee's head had been a second before.

He rolled away, his light strobing the cavern, and the creature turned to follow him. He scrabbled backwards, trying to keep his face aimed at it so his light would add to Dan's and present clear shots.

Dan saw his opportunity, then. The Bill thing had turned away to follow Lee, taking its gaze off the security man. It seemed more focused on Lee for some reason and its side was to him now.

He dashed forward and jammed the muzzle of his rifle into the side of the Bill thing's open faceplate, right into its temple, "God calls you back!"

He pulled the trigger.

The fifty-caliber round crashed through the side of the creature's head and blasted all the way through, just behind the face. The pressure exploded both black eyeballs, which burst in yellow geysers.

The creature's head canted over to the opposite side, and it reeled away, spinning, to fall against the back wall of the cave.

Lee got to his feet as Dan rushed up to him, shouting, "Now's our chance!"

He kept running right past Lee, making straight for the mouth of the cave.

Lee looked back, *Surely, it's down for good now.*

His light showed him the creature slowly getting back to its feet, its face a gray and yellow ruin from the nose up. It was blind now, arms up and grasping at the empty air around it.

But it was still smiling.

Time to get the hell outta Dodge.

He spun and ran after Dan toward the front of the cave.

*

Brent hovered by the door of the cage and looked at Frank, "What the hell are you doing?"

The physicist was wrestling with one of the larger crates they'd moved over to that side of the ledge, "Help me get this open! No, wait!" he rose and pointed at the cable Lee and Dan had used that was still dangling over the side of the ledge, "Pull that up! I have an idea!"

Brent knew better than to question. He dropped his rifle and started hauling the cable up hand over hand.

Duke cursed as his rifle clip went empty yet again. He'd been firing down into the approaching mass of creatures one shot at a time, taking careful aim at a head each time.

The results were mixed at best.

For every hit that seemed to score with a creature collapsing, twice as many other hits didn't seem to do anything and those creatures would keep relentlessly loping toward the base of their ledge.

He told himself that those were clean misses, but he knew they weren't. It seemed that the only shots that got results were ones that struck the creatures' horns or eyes. Any other headshot was as useless as a body shot – and those were as useless as misses.

He heard the deep bangs of both Angeline and Bobby to either side and hoped they were getting a better average than he was. It seemed they might be, as none of the creatures had managed to make it up to the ledge so far.

So far.

He looked up and saw the winged ones circling overhead and wondered if they were feeding information to their grounded cohort. For some reason they hadn't attacked yet – hadn't even swooped lower than about a hundred feet - but Duke doubted it was because they'd been stung the last time they came down.

No, they just looked like they were waiting; maybe waiting for the swarm below to break over the top of the ledge, or…

He peered out through the gap in the rocks, using the rifle's scope like a monocular lens, and swept it back and forth across the ranks of black creatures below.

He spotted it right away.

A creature completely unlike the others moved through the swarm, making its way forward. It was twice the size of the others, with an elongated body supported by four backward-bending legs, a thicker tail than the others, a set of sinewy arms protruding from its mid-torso and what looked like immense, crab-like pincers sprouting from its shoulders. It was more arachnoid than humanoid, and its head seemed to be all mouth, impossibly wide with teeth like spikes.

Then he saw another coming behind it…and another.

Interspersed here and there through the swarm were also some things that looked like humans. They were smaller, wore ragged clothes and had pale faces, and all those faces were upturned to look straight at the ledge as they marched steadily forward alongside the black creatures.

"Fuck me," he whispered to himself.

He settled himself and took aim at the head of one of the larger creatures. In his telescopic sight, the thing looked like it was right in front of him, and he had to steady his breath, watching it bob up and down, getting closer with each bob.

The creature had the same horn-like protuberances as the smaller versions and he timed the shot well, just as the head was sliding downward across the scope's field of view.

He squeezed the trigger and saw the horn explode in a yellow spray.

The monstrosity stopped short, its head jerked to the side as one of the pincers came up to scrape across its face. Its mouth stretched wide and a roar like a jet plane came from it.

Immediately, it started to swing its arms wildly about, striking out as if blind. It didn't go down, but instead seemed confused. Its pincers swept back and forth, slicing the air – and slicing through anything near it.

Creatures near it fell like lopped saplings as the massive claws took their heads off or sliced into their bodies. Those fast enough darted away, creating a ring of space around the thrashing behemoth.

Duke yelled at the others, "Definitely the horns! There are two giant things coming up fast! Get them while they're down there and they'll do more damage than we can!"

The remaining two bigger creatures split off, one to each side. He drew a bead on the one heading toward Angeline and started firing, "Bobby! Big one headed your way!"

He heard Bobby and Angeline pick up the pace of their shots and saw small explosions all over the head of the large creature on Angeline's side.

One of its eyes burst in a yellow fountain, but the creature just shook its head and continued forward. It was quickly out of his sight around the corner of the outcrop. In seconds it would be right below Angeline's position.

He hoped she would be able to take care of it.

While he was focused on the larger creatures, some of the smaller ones had reached the base of their ledge and were clambering up. Duke swung his rifle back to begin firing into the swarm again, but a leering black face suddenly rose right in front of him as a creature reached the top.

He jerked the trigger in shock and the round went straight into the thing's mouth, exploding out the back of the head. He may not have killed it, but it toppled backward off the ledge to disappear.

It was immediately followed by two more, though, clawing their way over the front of the outcrop, talons skittering and leaving gouges in the rock.

Duke reeled back, firing blindly at them on full auto, hoping that a barrage would knock them back.

It barely seemed to slow them and several more pulled themselves over the lip right behind them.

He yelled, "We've been breached!" and grabbed up one of the explosive canisters he had at his waist, pulled the ring on top and tossed it at the group advancing on him. It landed in the middle of them, and Duke threw himself down, hands over his head, hoping the canister wasn't just a smoke bomb or something.

He was only about thirty feet away and the blast lifted his body several inches off the ground. The noise was so intense he felt the sound travel through his body as a wave of heat passed over him. The side of his suit was scorched, and hot gravel pelted him, but most of the blast went overhead and dissipated quickly.

Duke rolled away from it and came up on his feet, feeling dizzy and disoriented. The ground by the edge was littered with smoking black creature parts, but already he saw the taloned hands of several more clawing at the rock to pull themselves up.

His ears felt stuffed with cotton, and it took several seconds for him to hear Brent's voice calling him, "Duke! Duke! Get back to the cage!"

He turned and saw Brent waving to him from in front of the platforms.

Frank was behind him, bent over one of the crates they'd hauled over and Bobby was still at the side of the ledge near them, firing down into the swarm on that side.

Duke saw Angeline backing up slowly from her side of the ledge, still firing down at the massive creature scaling the cliff there. As he watched, one of the large pincers cleared the top and smacked down into the rock of the ledge. The heads of half a dozen smaller creatures popped up right beside it.

He shouted, "Angeline! Get back here!"

She turned toward him and ran, but behind her, more of the creatures crested the lip and started after her. The big one pulled itself up, roared and strode forward.

They were all faster than she was and would be on her in seconds.

Duke grabbed out another of the explosive canisters and pulled the ring, yelling at her, "Duck!"

He tossed the canister as Angeline threw herself flat out into the dirt in a cloud of dust, her suit scraping across the rock.

It sailed over her head and hit the larger creature in the chest, bouncing off to one side. It was still in mid-air when it went off.

The blast tore off the pincer on that side and shredded three of the smaller creatures as well. The big one staggered sideways, roaring in either agony or rage, and collapsed to its backward knees. Yellow fluid coursed out of the stump of its upper arm, but it used its other pincer to push itself back upright.

Duke ran forward and grabbed Angeline's outstretched hand to pull her up. As he did, he looked at the big creature and saw its head lower to focus on him.

Yellow ichor was still flowing from its severed arm, but it took a step toward them as its smaller brethren flowed around it like it was rock in a dark river.

Duke tugged at Angeline's arm, "Well, that pissed it off, I'd say."

Angeline was shaking her head, "What was that? Can't hear anything."

He pulled her and they both ran as fast as they could.

Brent was standing in front of the platforms, waving them forward, "Hurry up!"

He pointed at the ground in front of them, "Don't step on the cable!"

Duke saw that the cable was laid across the ground in an arc about five meters away from the platforms.

They leapt over it and ran to the cage with scores of creatures closing in. Brent continued firing past them at the advancing swarm.

Frank waved them on, "Hurry! Get inside! Seal your helmets!"

They crowded into the cage without asking and flipped their faceplates down. Brent came after them with his mouth moving, but the sound of the approaching swarm drowned out his words.

Brent slammed the door of the cage and Frank put his finger over a switch on top of a white box that was sitting in a crate between his feet. Duke saw that one end of the cable was spliced and connected to the box.

Frank's voice crackled over the helmet radio, "Everybody down!" and hit the switch.

Duke pointed at it as he dropped, "The portable gen-"

Several of the creatures crossed over the cable at the same instant and one of them trod on a thick wire attached to the end.

The world outside was lit first by a blue-white flare of light that scored the team's retinas even through their faceplates and everyone clenched their eyes shut. It was quickly followed by a brilliant yellow flash that seemed to happen everywhere at once. A wave of pressure and heat washed over them, much stronger and longer than the explosive canisters had been.

It felt like the whole world was on fire for a moment. Their suits absorbed most of the effects and the helmets spared their eardrums, but they were physically pummeled by a shockwave.

*

Lee and Dan ran awkwardly through the ruined landscape, dodging boulders and leaping narrow crevasses. Their suits made fast progress impossible, but the noise of the battle and interrupted bursts of yelling over their helmet speakers spurred them on.

They didn't bother detouring to the narrow spot when they crossed the wider crevasse, they both just leapt over it, rolled in the dirt, and came up running again.

Lee kept himself in good shape, but he found he had to strain to keep up with Dan, *He's no desk-jockey, that's for sure.*

He glanced back over his shoulder, fearing he might see Bill coming after them, but he couldn't see past the last boulder they'd rounded anyway. Part of him wondered if Bill would just appear in front of them somewhere at any moment.

He thrust that thought out of his head and focused on the cliff they were approaching. Clouds of dust billowed into the air above it and they heard a muffled explosion and the rapid *pop-pop* of rifle fire from the ledge. He wanted to radio the team up top to find out what was happening, but he couldn't spare the wind to talk and besides, he figured they didn't need the distraction at the moment.

They came around one of the last big boulders and were nearing the spot again where Bill had landed. Now they could see the part of the swarm on this side attacking the outcrop. Scores of black bodies clambered up the cliffside in front of them.

Lee and Dan both skidded to a stop and brought their rifles up. They knelt and began firing into the bodies on the cliff wall, focusing their aim on those nearest the top.

Lee pointed at a large insectoid one closing in on the ledge, "What the hell is that?"

He caught a glimpse of one of the team firing down at the creature and directed his own bullets into its back. Dan kept up his own barrage at the mass of climbing creatures, swinging his rifle back and forth on full auto. Black forms tumbled off the rock and fell, only to be replaced by others.

Suddenly, the sky overhead was rent by a brilliant double flash of light – one white and another yellow. The air above seemed to beat down upon them and they both dropped to the ground.

A ball of fire expanded in the air right above them, scorching the backs of their suits and pushing them flat onto the ground.

Lee could see flames licking the ground around him and realized the roar he was hearing was coming from him.

If this wasn't actual Hell, it sure felt and sounded like it.

Twenty-Two

AFTER FIVE SECONDS, THE WORST of it was over and the team up top opened their eyes to see curling wisps of flame rolling through the air in the distance, expanding in every direction. They flared and sparked here and there before winking out at the edge of vision.

Everyone got to their feet and saw some of the creatures fleeing over the sides of the outcrop. The ground in front of them was littered with charred and twisted figures – the creatures that had been closest to the platforms.

Duke looked up and spotted a couple of the flying ones very high up and apparently making their way back toward the towers, "What the hell was that?"

Frank stood up, "Uh, I guess that was me. I spliced the cable into the generator and Mr. Copeland attached a piece of metal to the cut end, wrapped with some ten-gauge copper wire and run out over the ground."

"What, hoping to electrocute them or something?"

Frank shrugged, "It was all I could think to do. I knew that electricity would work here, but because of the high static readings we had I was just worried that the atmosphere would somehow dampen any field generated and that the portable generator wouldn't be powerful enough."

"Looks like it was," Bobby said dryly.

Frank looked up, "Yes. That was unexpected. I think perhaps that the arc may have ignited pockets of methane in the air – there is a higher concentration of it here - and that may have offset the slightly lesser concentration of oxygen. I didn't expect that to happen at all."

"Lucky for us it did," Angeline said.

Duke added, "Lucky for us those grenades I tossed didn't do it beforehand, or we might have ended up like those things," he indicated the smoking corpses outside.

"Shrapnel grenades versus an extended, high-intensity electrical arc," Frank said, "No contest. The heat of the arc was easily-"

"Thanks Frank," Brent interrupted the physicist, "You saved our asses, no matter if it was an accident."

Duke was looking around at the black figures on the ground, "Not many here. I think we mostly just scared them off for a bit. They'll likely be back."

Brent hit the switch on the generator and opened the cage door, "Yes, the sooner we're off this rock the better."

They clambered out, carefully avoiding the corpses, and stood in front of the platform.

Their helmets squelched with static, and Lee's voice came over, "You guys okay up there?"

"Lee!" Angeline said, "Where are you?"

"Right down here. Where's the cable?"

They all ran to the ledge on that side and peered down. Lee and Dan were standing at the base of the cliff, weapons dangling from their hands, looking up at them.

Duke flipped open his helmet and shouted down, "We're okay for now! Frank used the cable to fry those bastards! They're gone for the moment, but-"

Brent finished over the broadcast frequency, "But they'll be back in short order, you can depend on that. Dan?"

Dan keyed his mic, "Yes?"

"That cave work out?"

Dan glanced over at Lee before answering, "It's...good, but there's a problem."

"What's that?"

Lee answered, "Bill showed up there."

Silence for one second, then a jumble of voices asking questions.

Dan waited for them to quiet and said, "It wasn't Bill."

"What?" Duke asked, "Was it, or wasn't it?"

Dan's voice was firm, "It only looked like Bill. It was a demon wearing Bill Owen like a suit. Bill is gone."

Brent asked, "Lee?"

Lee spread his hands, "I don't know. It...wasn't the Bill I knew. As to whether it was a demon...at this point I'm not inclined to disagree with Dan."

Angeline interrupted, "Where is he now?"

Dan pointed behind them with his rifle, "We left it at the cave. Not dead, but full of holes and blinded."

"Jesus Christ," Bobby murmured.

"He never showed up," Lee said dryly, "though we really could have used his help."

That got a snort from Duke and even Dan angled his head at Lee and flashed him a tight grin.

"Anyway," Lee said, "the ledge up there is useless to us now. We better get our stuff and you guys down here before those things come back."

"Wait a sec," Brent said.

Everyone looked at him, but he spoke to Lee and Dan, "Things have changed. If Bill was a demon and found you there, then the cave is compromised as a refuge as well."

Dan answered, "Yes, but it's more defensible than the ledge. It has only one point of access and offers complete protection from above. That ledge is completely exposed."

"Anything's better than this place," Duke muttered, "I say we get to the cave." He turned to grab up the cable, "This thing safe now?"

Frank nodded, "Yes, it should be. The power is off."

Duke paused, *"Should be?"*

Frank crouched and grabbed a section of the cable, "See?"

Brent raised a hand, "Hold on. Not so fast."

Duke turned back to him, "What?"

"I don't think we should be in such a rush to leave here now."

Duke glowered at him, "Why the hell not?"

Lee started to speak, "Brent-"

Brent cut him off, pointing up at the white haze overhead, "The cave is known to these creatures and this ledge is closest to our point of entry. When the guys up top figure out what to do, this is where any rescue is going to come to. We successfully fought off an attack twice-"

"Barely!" Duke thundered. He thrust a finger at the towers, "Whatever those things are, they aren't animals. They might have been scared off once, but I don't think it'll work again."

"And we have no defense now," Frank added.

Brent looked at him, "What? Frank, you just-"

Frank shook his head inside his helmet, "I said the power was off, Mr. Copeland. I meant it's off for good. The generator is blown. The feedback fried it."

Stunned silence from everyone.

"Can you-" Brent began.

"No, I can't fix it."

Lee broke in, "That settles it then."

Brent looked up at the sky again, "But what about the borehole? We shouldn't get too far from it."

Frank waved a hand in the direction of the cave, "It's a wandering borehole, remember? It's slowly moving in the direction of the cave anyway. In a couple of days or so it may be closer to the cave than to here."

Bobby blurted, "In a couple of *days*? How are we going to hold out here for that long?"

Duke patted his arm solicitously, "Calm down, auntie. Tommy will figure something out long before that."

Dan broke in, "Mr. Copeland, what everyone is saying is correct. The cave is a better option for us at the moment and it's not too far from here if rescue comes soon."

Lee added, "But we'd better get moving fast."

Everyone waited, holding their breath. Brent Copeland was their boss, after all.

Brent took a deep breath, "Okay, fine. Fuck it, let's go."

Lee said, "Start sending stuff down. Only the bare essentials."

Duke looked at Bobby, "The medical stuff, ammo and water?"

Bobby pointed at the pile of boxes by the platforms, "Some were crushed, but most are intact."

"Fine. We'll send these down first," Duke waved a hand at the front of the outcrop, "Can you and Angeline keep an eye out?"

"We will," she said and breezed by them, "Come on, Bobby."

They headed toward the gap in the outcrop.

Duke spoke to Arden, "Sorry, Frank. Your equipment still has to stay here. At least for now."

Frank shrugged, "That's okay. I'm at a point now where I'd rather just survive than do experiments, trust me."

"You and me both."

Duke bent and grabbed up a coil of the cable, "I guess we can tie a box on every couple feet or so and lower as much weight as we can in one go."

A sudden, loud scraping noise came from behind them, accompanied by a low, rattling grunt.

Everyone spun around in surprise.

One of the giant creatures was hauling itself over the opposite lip of the outcrop. It was the injured one with the missing pincer.

It pulled itself onto the ledge and smashed its remaining claw onto the ground, shaking the rock beneath their feet.

Duke dropped the cable, "Fucker was hiding over the ledge all this time!"

He pulled his rifle around from his back and started firing, even as the creature charged.

Its severed pincer was still leaking, but it was just a fast as before. It covered half the distance across the ledge in seconds.

Angeline and Bobby started firing from the creature's flank, but it swept its good claw out and Bobby was tossed aside, crumpling in a heap. Angeline had moved in behind it as it passed but stopped firing and rushed to Bobby.

Brent brought his weapon up and fired once at the creature's head, but he was panicked, and the bullet struck its shoulder. Duke took more careful aim, but the creature was so fast it was difficult to line up a good shot. In seconds it would be on him.

Lee and Dan heard the shots and startled gasps up top. They looked up and Lee yelled, "Duke! Angeline! What's happening up there?"

Dan pointed off to one side, "Look! Another one coming!"

One of the winged creatures swept down from the sky, seeming to come from nowhere. It glided across the face of the cliff and dove straight toward the team up top.

Both Lee and Dan began firing, but it had already disappeared behind the ledge. Their bullets merely chipped rock off the cliff face.

The flyer landed on the upper deck, rattling both platforms. Frank was standing immediately in front and ducked low, startled by this new attack.

Duke swung his gun around, "Brent! The big one! Frank! Get down!"

Brent continued firing at the big creature closing in. His rifle was on full auto, and he simply sprayed bullets at its face. Most missed, but one round struck it in the eye and the creature reared back, skidding to a stop and clutching its face.

Duke fired off a short burst at the creature on the platform, but it launched itself back up in a blur and he missed completely.

Before he could fire again, it darted forward and swooped down, going straight for Frank.

Before the scientist could move, its outstretched talons clamped onto his helmet and yanked him straight up into the air.

Frank's legs kicked wildly, and he started screaming as the talons pierced the neck of his suit, his voice distorting in their helmet speakers.

Duke raised his rifle but checked himself. He didn't want to hit Frank.

Brent turned away from his creature and shouted at him, "Shoot!"

"I can't!" Duke yelled in frustration through gritted teeth.

Frank's voice was a high shriek buzzing their eardrums now. Duke winced against it and brought his rifle up to take careful aim at the creature's bobbing head. It was already fifteen meters above them and still climbing.

His finger tightened on the trigger just as Frank's scream abruptly cut off and he saw the physicist's helmet separate from his body.

Not just his helmet, Duke realized. A long streamer of dark red followed the falling body down to the ground. It crashed at his feet, and he could hear the bones inside snapping like someone wadding up paper.

A patter of liquid sounded on the back of Duke's helmet as Frank's blood spattered down upon him. He was momentarily frozen in shock and horror looking down at the headless body, blood still pumping weakly from the torn collar of the suit.

Pure rage flared up in Duke's mind, blotting out everything else, "Fuckers!" he screamed and flicked his rifle to full auto.

He sprayed the sky after the creature, which was a rapidly dwindling spot now in the sky, making its way back to the towers with its prize, Frank's head, in its claws.

*

Down below, Lee and Dan saw the flying creature ascend with something in its hands.

Lee shouted fruitlessly up at the ledge, forgetting to use the radio in his panic and frustration, "What's going on up there? Goddamn it!"

He turned to Dan, "We have to get up there!"

The security man could only shake his head, "No way to do it."

Lee ground his teeth, "GodDAMN it!"

Above them, the firing and unnatural roaring went on.

*

Lying on the ground and clutching his side, Bobby saw the big creature take another step toward Duke and the others.

He shouted weakly, "Look out!" and fired at it again. He'd been still firing at the giant creature and every kick from the rifle was agony.

Angeline rose from beside him and resumed firing as well. She slowly made her way back out into the middle of the ledge, firing as she went.

The creature was now stuck in the middle, with Angeline behind it, Bobby to one side and Duke and Brent peppering it with bullets from the front.

It could still move fast, though, and Angeline was standing between it and the opposite edge of the outcrop.

Duke saw it start to turn and knew what it was going to do.

He shouted, "Angeline! Get back!"

She was too slow to react, or maybe didn't even hear him with all the firing and roaring.

The creature veered away from the men and lunged for her. It reached forward and wrapped both its sinewy mid-torso arms around her, pulling her close to its chest. Her rifle clattered to the ground, and she started to scream.

The men had no choice but to stop firing, for fear of hitting her.

Duke rushed forward, shouting, "Angeline!"

Brent grabbed his arm, "It's too late!"

Duke shook his hand off and charged after the creature, but it was already nearing the far side.

Its four legs launched it off the edge of the outcrop and it dropped out of sight with her flailing in its arms like a rag doll.

Her radio was still on broadcast, and they heard her scream like she was inside their helmets all the way down to the bottom, when the sound cut off.

They all rushed up to the edge and saw the creature loping across the ground, still holding Angeline, heading toward the distant structures they called the town. Her mic was still active, and they could clearly hear rhythmic rustling, scraping and the occasional muted grunt as the creature ran.

But no sound from Angeline.

Twenty-Three

"WE HAVE TO GO AFTER her!" Lee shouted.

The remaining team members were clustered at the base of the cliff below the ledge now. Duke, Bobby, and Brent had lowered the cable with as much of their water, medical supplies, and remaining ammo as possible and then climbed down to ground level to meet Dan and Lee.

One trip was all they thought they could risk.

Lee knew that Angeline had been taken but had no idea where. He and Dan hadn't seen anything from their position on the ground and Brent and the others said they lost track of the creature carrying her when it was about halfway to the jumbled structures of the settlement. It seemed to just melt into the landscape, along with all the others.

Angeline's radio was still functioning, and they could occasionally hear rasping and grunting coming over the broadcast frequency, but never anything resembling a voice, and never a response to their calls.

Once they were all on the ground, only an appeal to the safety of everyone allowed Brent to keep Lee and Duke from immediately setting out after the creature that had taken Angeline. Bobby had several suspected broken ribs and wasn't in any shape to go anywhere but wanted to join them.

Only Dan and Brent were against going.

And Lee was furious and terrified for Angeline, "Brent, all our shit is down now! We have to go after her! We have to do something!"

Duke was fed up with waiting too. He clutched two rifles in his hands, "Enough of this. Let's just go, Lee."

"I'm in," Bobby said again.

"Go where?" Dan asked calmly.

Lee blustered and pointed out across the plain, "Out there! You said it was headed toward that town-"

"Hold on!" Brent stood with his hands on his hips, "I said no way, at least not yet."

"Not yet?" Lee exploded, "What on earth would you be waiting for?"

Duke said, "Lee, goddamn it, let's just go. We know where that thing took her."

Dan stuck his jaw out, "You do? Really? Where?"

Duke tossed his head over his shoulder, "To that city place. It was making a beeline for it."

"When it started out," Dan scoffed, "It disappeared before it was halfway there, you said, just like all the rest. It could have gone anywhere."

Duke looked like he was going to go ballistic, his dark face creasing around his flashing eyes, "It's a place to start and I'm not afraid of these things, unlike some of us."

Dan bristled, "Any man who isn't afraid of losing his soul is a fool."

"Bullshit," Duke said, "You've been scared and spewing supernatural crap about these things since we saw them on camera up top."

Dan nosed up to him, "And why wouldn't I be? Take a look around you, Duke. Anything about this place or those things strike you as being natural?" He angled his head at Lee, "Ask him what he thinks now after meeting Bill Owen again."

Everyone looked at Lee and he was momentarily nonplussed. He had no idea what he believed right now. All he felt was impotent anger gnawing at his insides.

His eyes wandered over everyone, "I don't know if that was Bill in the cave, or something that just looked like him, but I know that we shot it point-blank at least a dozen times, including through the head, and it didn't go down. I'm not sure if that makes it a demon, some kind of other-dimensional thing, or just a hallucination, but it was an atrocity in my book, regardless, and we can't allow that to happen to anyone else."

He stared at Brent and gripped his rifle so hard his fingers went white, "We've had two friends murdered by those things and now Angeline is gone. I don't care where we are or what the deeper meaning of all this is. I just want to get Angeline back and get the fuck out of this place, putting as many of those things down as we can."

"Fucking A," Duke muttered.

Bobby pointed at Duke, "What he said."

Brent stepped forward making a patting motion with his hand, "Simmer down, everyone," he looked Lee in the eyes, "You know that going after her will likely mean that more of us die?"

Lee felt his blood rising again, "If we don't, she's definitely going to!"

Brent turned away, "She's probably dead already. She hasn't made a sound since that thing took her off the cliff."

Lee felt his insides clench up. He'd been ignoring that fact himself, telling himself that her unit was damaged, but it was still broadcasting sounds, which meant that she was either unconscious, or...

He didn't care what the reason was. No matter what happened, there was no way he could leave this place and live with himself without knowing if she were alive. And if there was even a slim chance she was, he couldn't leave without her.

He spoke to Brent's back, bringing all the bitterness and betrayal he felt to his voice, "I can't believe I'm hearing this shit from you, Brent. You and Angeline..." he couldn't finish the sentence he wanted, so he settled for, "You're a coward," he looked at Dan, "Both of you."

Dan immediately stepped forward, but Duke moved quickly to get between him and Lee. His attention was on Dan, though, so he missed Brent.

Before Lee could react, Brent spun around and punched him in the face.

Lee was wearing the helmet, so Brent's knuckles connected mostly with the chin guard, but the blow rocked him, and he stumbled backward a few steps.

He came to his senses to see Brent dancing around and shaking his hand, "Ow! Fucking Christ!"

Brent stuffed his throbbing hand under his suit's armpit as best he could and shook a finger from his other hand at Lee, "Who's the coward here, Lee? Who didn't want anything to do with this from the start? Not Angeline, that's for sure! She knew goddamn well what was at stake and was prepared to accept any and all risks-"

"To keep her damn job!" Lee countered, "To stay in your favor! You're the damn boss, for Christ's sake! You dragged her into it!"

Brent straightened from massaging his gloved hand and fixed Lee with a shocked expression that quickly melted down through understanding and finally to pity, "Is that what she told you? Oh, Lee...she played you all through this as well as she played me."

"What the hell do you mean?"

Brent shook his head, "Lee, this whole project was Angeline's idea. She sold me on it."

"Horseshit!" but even as he said it, Lee knew that what Brent was saying was true; he could see it on the man's face.

"Lee, she came to me three years ago. She showed me the Kola data and the video, along with all the other stuff from the German and Japanese attempts. She worked on me for days. She got me to do it."

She lied to me the other night, she outright lied to me. Lee found to his surprise that he wasn't shocked. He didn't have to ask Brent how she got him to do it. If she really wanted something, Angeline could always get it. The question was, why did she want this?

For Brent? For herself?

Duke wasn't as familiar with Angeline's powers of persuasion, "Brent, why the fuck would you want to do...all of this?" he waved his hand around.

Brent looked at him for a long time before answering, "At first, for the science, the glory of discovering something completely new, something world changing." He looked at Dan, "Later, maybe even to find something like an essential truth to our existence, a reason for everything to be, before...." he trailed off.

Lee knew the real reason behind it all. Brent had finished without adding, *before I die.*

Brent cleared his throat and gave Lee a rueful look, "That's how

204

Angeline explained it to me anyway."

Lee didn't know whom to feel sorrier for; himself, Brent, or Bill, Frank and all the other men lost so far in this nightmare.

So far.

His shoulders slumped, his anger suddenly gone. All of this was because of one woman's appeal to a man's ego and his fear of mortality.

In the face of that, all Lee had left was his own appeal, "Brent."

"Yeah? You want to take a shot at me now?"

"No. I want to go after Angeline. I want all of us to."

Brent saw right through him, "You don't want to, Lee; you *need* to." He stepped toward Lee, "You need to save everyone. It's a thing with you. It radiates off you like a pheromone or something. It draws people in, and they don't even know how or why. It's what's made you the company golden boy, this complete loyalty people have toward you."

"Maybe because I give as good as I get," Lee said, "and I gave it to you as well. I wedded my life to you and your vision for this company a long time ago."

"And I gave it back to you."

"Yes, you did, but you seem to have forgotten how it's supposed to work somewhere along the way. The people, Brent; the *people* make this company great, not the product or the bottom line, and you're throwing them away here."

Brent held his hands out, "That's not what I'm trying to do here, don't you see? If we can unlock Mankind's greatest mystery, vanquish our greatest fear, then we will have given-"

"But at what cost, Brent?" Lee waved a hand around, "The lives of everyone around you?" he pointed at Brent, "Your own life, maybe even your soul?"

He stopped and the two of them stared at each other. Brent looked like he was about to launch into another justification, but then gave him a resigned look, "Maybe you're right, Lee, but I have…considerations that you don't."

Lee nodded slowly, "I may be aware of them."

Brent searched Lee's face for a moment then sighed, "You're going to go anyway, aren't you."

Duke nodded, "You bet we are."

Dan stepped forward, blustering, "Mr. Copeland has organized and underwritten this entire operation. His word-"

Brent put a hand up, "Dan, stop." He looked at Lee, "I want to get Angeline back as much as you do, you know."

Lee had trouble believing that, but kept his mouth shut. He inclined his head at Brent, inviting him to continue.

Brent stared hard at Lee, "I love her, you know. I always have," he paused and grinned sheepishly, looking at the ground, "Or, I should say I love her as much as she'll allow any man to love her."

The words were hard for Lee to hear, but he was surprised that, deep down inside, they didn't really hurt much at all, "And you knew about…"

Brent took a step toward him, "Oh, I knew all about you guys from the start. Angeline was always very honest with me."

At least with you she was, Lee thought, but then regretted it. He and Angeline had never spoken of commitment, and he knew he was certainly not one to judge.

Brent went on, "It used to drive me insane that I never saw her much when you were in town. Didn't you ever wonder why I allowed my chief engineer to go gallivanting all over the world all the time? Or that I was rarely around when you were both at Corporate?"

He hadn't and Lee was disappointed in himself for how blind and naïve he'd been, "Brent, I-"

"No, that's enough for now. Maybe after this is over, we can have a duel or something and settle things. First things first," he turned to Dan, "I guess we go see if we can find our teammate."

"Finally," Duke muttered, "if all the lovelorn handwringing is over."

Dan looked like he was going to object again, but something in Brent's eyes maybe told him it would be useless.

He took a deep breath, suddenly all business again, "Fine. We'll leave all the medical and other supplies here for now and bring every weapon we have."

I'm coming too, guys," Bobby said.

Duke frowned at him, "You're in no shape to go anywhere."

"Like hell I'm not! A couple cracked ribs, is all," he pointed at one of the boxes, "You help me get this tin can off and tape me up a bit, I'll be as good as new."

Lee spoke before anyone else could object. They'd wasted enough time already, "I guess we're all going then."

*

They each had a hard-shell knapsack that they filled with smaller weapons and explosives, and each man had either a rifle or shotgun and a pistol to carry. It was going to make the trek awkward with the uneven footing, but everyone wanted to be well armed.

They set out with Lee on point, followed by Duke, Bobby, and Brent. Dan brought up the rear and was carrying the most in firepower and ammunition. Lee didn't feel completely comfortable having Brent and Dan behind him and couldn't even tell himself why he felt that way, but he told himself not to let his resentments cloud his thinking.

Duke spoke over his shoulder to Dan, "I have to say, you sure know how to pack for a hike in Hell. You always travel with this much stuff?"

Dan's answered quietly, "I had a bit of a heads-up."

"Oh yeah, I forgot. How you doing, Bobby?"

Bobby sucked in the hot air, "Doing fine." They'd only been walking a few minutes, and every breath was a lance of pain through his chest, but there was no way he was going to let Duke know that.

"Well, you let me know if you need a piggy-back."

"And you let me know if you need to stop for a pee break."

Duke grunted, "Huh, little do you know I've pissed myself in this suit three times already."

Lee was only half listening to the banter. His eyes swept the view ahead from side to side, checking the shadows behind every rock, the depths of every crevasse or hole in their path, and scanning the sky for signs of those flying creatures. He heard the others stumbling behind him but kept all his attention on the sides and in front, trusting Dan to keep their six covered.

Even if he didn't completely trust Dan to look after the team, he trusted him to look out for himself.

It was hard going. There was no trail to follow; no path through the jumble of boulders and cracks, no scratches on the rocks, not even any prints in the sand and dust, which didn't make sense. Hundreds of those creatures had traipsed through here just minutes before, but you would swear nothing had been over this ground in years, if ever. It was as if those things walked above the ground, their clawed feet leaving no trace of their passing.

He thought back to Bill's appearance at the cave. Had he been actually standing on the ground? Or just slightly above it, hovering like a…a specter of some kind? Bill had lifted himself up to the lip of the cave with one hand as if he weighed nothing.

Maybe he didn't.

Maybe these things were hallucinations, more phantoms than reality, but not in the spirit sense.

No, that couldn't be right. Their bullets certainly damaged the creatures, and several had been torn apart by the explosives. Duke said the one he'd wrestled was heavier than a man.

So they had mass. They could affect – and be affected by – their environment.

So what did it all mean? These things could move through their environment without leaving a trace, could lift themselves one-handed effortlessly, yet weighed more than a man.

There were too many questions with the answers teetering on the edge between science and the supernatural. He'd started out closer to Frank Arden's side of things, but the longer he was here, the more he was finding himself leaning toward Dan's way of thinking.

Demons, monsters…the Devil, even?

Or…what, aliens? Other-dimensional beings? Were they in Hell or in some other kind of reality?

He didn't know which possibility was worse, but he knew that either way, things could end in death.

Death, at least, was multi-universal.

*

It was quiet.

Angeline came awake and opened her eyes to a dim, close-up view of a stone floor. She was lying on her side. The air was hot, but the stone felt cool.

She lay there for several moments, afraid to move, and listening keenly for any sound. Her whole body ached, and her head pounded in time with her pulse.

There was an acrid smell in the air that she knew was the scent of the demons. She vaguely remembered it emanating from the body of the giant creature that had taken her. She'd felt like she was going to smother in the smell of its hot body as it carried her away from her friends.

The odor was all around her. She angled her head to sniff her arm and realized the smell was coming from her. She was covered in the thing's oily sweat or maybe some other kind of secretion.

It made her gag, and she pulled her head away, feeling the stone beneath her scrape her arm. She slowly pushed herself stiffly up to a sitting position. The small sound of her movement echoed hollowly.

There was light from somewhere, but it was feeble, just enough to show her she was in some kind of enormous space. She could barely make out what looked like walls at the edge of vision.

She squinted. On either side, it looked like the walls were lined with statues of large, misshapen creatures. Other than that, there seemed to be nothing else in the enormous space.

She looked down and saw that she was wearing only her bodysuit. Her armor was gone, including her helmet. She had no way to contact the others.

A look up showed her the white haze that served as a sky in this place far above, so perhaps the room was open at the top, more like an amphitheater of some kind.

She was exhausted and dizzy. Without her suit, she'd been breathing the lower-oxygen air for who knew how long while unconscious and her mouth and throat ached from sucking in the stifling dryness.

The beginnings of despair threatened to well up inside her. No suit meant no communication, as well as no oxygen supplementation or water, and she could be anywhere. The others might never find her.

If they were even looking.

Or even alive.

Angeline was not one for regrets, but she wished now that she had listened to Brent three years ago when he'd balked at the idea of doing this. She'd couched it in terms that would appeal to his ego and his fear of encroaching death to get him on board then.

She'd known something was up with Brent and had learned about his illness from its earliest stages. It allowed her to half-convince herself then that she was pushing the drilling project to help him find a reprieve from the MS, if not even a possible cure. She'd also dangled the ideas of eternal fame in front of herself as much as him, but her own reasons for wanting to undertake this whole enterprise were baser – money, power, and professional achievement.

If Endeavor were successful in punching through to another dimension – and it now seemed they were – then she would be at the helm to take the world in a new direction. If their discoveries could somehow end up helping Brent, so much the better, but even if they couldn't, at least he'd live forever in memory as the man who had done it.

And she could carry on well enough without him.

She had no regrets about that; both she and Brent knew enough about each other to dispense with something as useless as regret. But she had to admit that the cost now was growing too great for even her to absorb - Bill, Frank, the men on the rig and now perhaps Lee and the others.

Lee.

He'd told her it was all okay, had spoken even lightly about it, but she'd seen the hurt in his eyes.

And now he and the others might all be dead too. It was almost too much to bear.

Almost.

Scratch that. During the planning and set up for this project, it had all seemed so distant, almost just an academic exercise. Now Bill and Frank were gone, maybe the others too, and she was finding that her reasons – all those important justifications she'd fed herself over the past couple of years – had abandoned her.

Despite her desire to do this, she really had no idea what they had done or where they were, in an alternate reality? A literal hell?

Regardless, she suddenly found, after all this time, that she didn't care. She just wanted out.

As she sat in silence contemplating her predicament, she gradually became aware of a growing sound at the edge of hearing, a susurration of air, like a far-off bellows. She'd assumed it was the normal low hiss of blood in your ears that you heard when you were alone, but this was slower; it was rhythmic, like the wind rising and falling.

Or like breathing.

Coming from all around her.

She peered around and a trickle of ice ran down her spine when she realized that the shapes lining the walls weren't statues.

They were alive.

Even as she looked, they pulled themselves away from the walls and started to advance toward the middle.

Toward her.

Angeline stood and backed up a pace, stopping abruptly when her heel hit the edge of something. She tottered but managed not to stumble backward.

A liquid rustling noise came seemingly right next to her ear, and she turned.

And saw a horror.

She opened her mouth to scream, but a wall of hot blackness hit her in the face, pushing its way into her mouth and down her insides, pressing her body to the floor.

Filling her up even as it emptied her out.

Twenty-Four

"DIS."

Dan whispered the word so low that Lee almost missed it.

He looked at the security man, "What?"

Dan pointed at the crude structures spread out before them, "Dis, the city that surrounds and guards the lower precincts of Hell. The Roman poet Virgil referred to it in his Aeneid. Dante also mentioned it in The Divine Comedy. Even the Egyptians and Greeks wrote about the Underworld and depicted parts of it as a city."

Duke gave a low whistle, "Wow, you really know all about this shit, don't you?"

Dan murmured, "I had somewhat of a...classical education, you might say."

The team were crouched behind several large boulders next to a deep trench that cut across their path. On the other side of the trench, the plain sloped away in a slight decline. About two hundred meters down the slope was a low, stone wall that stretched away into the haze in either direction. On the other side of the wall were the rough stone buildings they'd designated as "the city".

The perspectives in this place were confusing. From the ledge where they'd first arrived, the city looked to be just a mile or so distant at most and not much more than a village that might house a couple hundred people. But they'd traveled at least a mile across the plain before finding the trench and still the city appeared to be a good hike away.

And closer up, it was immense. Not high; the highest of its crude structures were perhaps only three or four stories, but it was much more than a village. It extended to the limits of visibility, spreading out behind the wall and continuing down the slope of the plain to disappear into infinity it seemed.

The area between them and the wall was riven with shallow trenches and dotted with boulders here and there. There was also an assortment of the black creatures, as well as a few of the things that looked like humans in ragged clothing wandering around, apparently aimlessly.

Thankfully, none were close to the team at the moment.

"It's big, but it doesn't look like much," Duke commented.

Lee said, "I read Dante in school and from what I remember, Dis was described as a great city of white, with towers, moats, and bridges, surrounded by an iron wall. This," he pointed, "looks more like something out of The Flintstones."

Dan shrugged, "I imagine that Dante took some poetic license in his descriptions, but if you're looking for towers, they're right over there." He indicated the two massive stone columns about half a mile away on the right. They appeared to be about a hundred meters on a side and dwarfed everything else in view, disappearing up into the white sky, cut off flat at the top, as if by a knife, just like the cliff by the borehole.

Lee said, "Dis was also said to be bounded by the River Styx, which ran all around it."

"What do you want from me," Dan frowned, "This whole place is full of trenches that could be described as moats." He inclined his head, "Those there are certainly towers and this sure as shit looks like a city in Hell to me. Maybe Dante gussied it up a bit or maybe when he came here, he came from another direction and saw a river and prettier buildings. Who knows?"

"Quiet everyone," Brent said, "We have to figure out where Angeline is and how we get to her, right?"

"Wait a sec," Lee said, "Maybe Dan is onto something."

213

Duke looked at him, "What?"

"I've been thinking about this a lot on the way here."

He looked around at the others and everyone just gave him expectant looks in return.

"Go ahead," Bobby said.

"Okay, so, regardless of whatever we think this place is, why don't we assume that both Frank and Dan are correct."

"How can they both be right?" Duke asked.

Lee's eyebrows rose, "Because it's the only thing that makes sense, both from a scientific and religious perspective. Let's assume that this is a real place in another dimension basically rubbing up against our own, like Frank said. It's a place where these beings live," he tilted his head at the city, "have a functioning society, where the physical laws are different enough to allow things to exist that to us might seem like fantasy, but they're just as real as the physical laws and things that we take for granted at home."

Brent nodded and added, "And maybe our supposition is right; that throughout human history, the odd person has come into contact with this place, people like Virgil and Dante, maybe some of the people who wrote the Bible, and they described it in the only ways they could, by using the frames of intellectual or religious reference they had available to them in their times, is that what you're saying?"

Lee said, "Yes, that's it."

Duke scoffed, "Only a few guys? Out of thousands of years?"

"Maybe not just a few," Lee said, "There could have been many, but the average uneducated Joe might not have been able to articulate what he'd experienced and been designated a loony or…" he paused for a moment as a thought occurred to him, "…maybe thought to be *possessed* or something, just like that guy on the Kola video."

"Hey, that's right," Bobby said, "If someone couldn't handle the experience, it might drive them around the bend."

"Or perhaps he was possessed by something from here, just as our own two men were," Dan spoke in a low voice, "Just like Bill."

Lee decided to let that one slide for a minute and continued, "And maybe most people who come into contact with this place *can't* escape and write stories about it, they don't survive to report on it. People go missing every day around the world and are never heard from again - hundreds, thousands of people."

They all looked toward the city and saw the stumbling figures that looked like ragged people dotting the landscape, "Maybe a lot of them actually end up here."

"Mzungu," Duke said, "that Swahili word for wanderers. If anyone ever fit that description, it's those poor saps there."

"But," Dan said, "the Biblical descriptions tell us that Hell is a place of eternal punishment, for those who turn away from the grace of God-"

He stopped suddenly, staring ahead, and pointed, "Look."

The others followed his finger and saw a small group of the human-looking figures near a large boulder about halfway between the team and the stone wall around the city. On the other side of the boulder, one of the bigger black creatures was approaching. Easily twice the size of the humans, it rounded the rock and casually reached out to grab one of the humans by the neck. In an instant, it twisted the head off the human and dipped its own face down onto the pulsing stump of the neck briefly before dropping the body to the ground.

It walked on, still carrying the head.

It happened so fast everyone was stunned. What was even more shocking was what the other humans nearby did. Most apparently ignored the scene and just continued stumbling around as the black creature sauntered off, but several crowded around the collapsed body and bent, as if examining it closely.

"Holy shit," Bobby breathed, "Did you see that?"

"What the fuck?" Duke whispered, his voice shaking, "Those...most of those other guys didn't even do anything. They're just walking around out there!"

Lee was reminded of something, "It's just like what you see up top with wild animals. Lions or cheetahs take down a member of a zebra herd and once they do, the other zebras just stand around like they know they're safe now, even with a lion chowing down on their buddy a few yards away."

Brent was nodding his head slowly, "They know the rules and accept

215

them. Predator and prey mutually agreeing to fulfill their roles."

"That fits too," Lee said, "Nothing we've seen here detracts from anything you've said, Dan, or what Frank said. This place has different physical laws and maybe it has a different morality as well."

He pointed at the black creatures, "I'm guessing those things don't even see us as sentient beings. Maybe they see humans as prey, or sport. They obviously don't hesitate to kill us. I'm not saying that they're semi-divine or fallen angels or whatever. They're simply beings of their own continuum, functioning as the top dogs in their realm. In our own world, we've managed to opt out of the food-chain, but here…"

Brent finished for him, "But here, we're most definitely in it and we don't occupy the top spot."

Dan spoke slowly, almost to himself, "So Hell is a real place after all…"

"But maybe not a supernatural one that metes out eternal punishment to damned souls," Lee said, "It's one that can kill anyone who comes here. We're still alive, as far as I can tell. We're not disembodied souls, and Bill and Frank were killed right in front of us."

Bobby was staring at the bloody heap out on the plain, "And disembodied souls don't spout blood like that, as far as I know."

Dan's lips were set in a thin line, "Or, it really is the Hell we learned about. Nothing I've seen so far tells me I'm not looking at the supernatural," he swiveled his head at Lee, "certainly nothing that explains Bill Owen at the cave."

Lee blinked at him. That one was the big question for him too. No matter what physical laws might exist in another dimension, it was hard to explain away a dead man – three dead men, in fact – walking around and talking.

He spoke carefully, aware of the thin line they were all treading here, "I think it was Arthur C. Clarke who once said that any sufficiently advanced technology is indistinguishable from magic. Maybe what we have here is a reality that is not necessarily technologically advanced, but different enough from ours to appear to be almost magical."

Dan looked like he was going to launch into a debate, but Duke broke in, "I don't see how the fuck it matters one way or the other. Okay, so we agree it's a real place that we've interpreted differently in literature through the ages. It satisfies both scientific and religious worldviews and doesn't contradict either. How does this help us?"

Lee turned back to Dan, "What do you know about Dis?"

Dan furrowed his brow in thought and licked his lips. He was still coming to terms with everything he'd just seen, "Virgil called it a…a desolate realm and a city of vacant halls, whereas Dante spoke of it as a place where the obdurate were punished, rather than those who committed venial sins."

"Yeah, obdurate," Duke said. He whispered to Bobby, "He means guys like you."

Bobby punched his shoulder, wincing at the pain in his own body.

Dan continued, "Virgil gives the impression of Dis as a place for the lost, but Dante placed people of malice within its walls…and the impression he left with was that it was crowded."

"What about the modern religious interpretation?" Lee asked.

"Pretty much what we all grew up with as a vision of Hell; piles of corpses, capering demons, instruments of torture everywhere and, hanging over all of it, the shadow of Satan."

Bobby put up a hand, "I vote we go with the Virgil version."

"You and me both, bud," Duke said.

Lee noticed Brent's leg shaking, like he was impatient. He suspected that wasn't the case, but it called attention to their immediate concern, finding Angeline.

He pointed at the city, "Regardless of which version it may actually be, if Angeline is in there, we'll never find her. It's huge."

"So what do we do?" asked Bobby.

Lee was studying the broad sloping plain in front of them, watching the wandering beings that looked like lost people.

"Maybe," he said, "we ask a local?"

Twenty-Five

THEY CLIMBED DOWN INTO THE trench running in front of them. It looked like it angled a bit closer to the wall a few hundred meters along and would provide some cover. Moving single-file and keeping their heads just below ground level, they started to follow it to where it branched off and led further down the incline toward the city. They were hoping to get as close as possible to the stumbling human figures without being seen by them, or by any of the black creatures.

They'd only moved a few meters along when Lee stopped and put up a hand. They all halted in half-crouched positions, trying to keep their heads below the lip of the trench.

Duke hissed, "What is it?"

Lee's brow was deeply furrowed, "You guys hear that?"

"Hear what," Dan said.

Lee cocked his head, "That...grinding sound or whatever it is."

They all held their breath, listening.

Bobby said, "I hear it. It sounds...close." He moved to the side of the trench, his head tilted and hands up, fingers splayed as if tracking the sound, "It's...it sounds like it's coming from all arou-Jesus!" He jumped away from the wall and stumbled back against the other side with wide eyes, "Holy shit! It's alive!"

They'd all been so intent on keeping an eye on the top of the trench walls that they'd missed it.

Brent leaned close to the wall and sucked in a breath, "Oh my God, there are people in here."

Duke whispered in disgust and awe, "Sweet jumping Jesus...what the hell?" He backed away from the wall of the trench and stood against the opposite side, "What in God's name?"

The trench wall on the side closest to the city was lined with the faces of people, all apparently alive, their mouths slowly moving, their eyes clenched tightly closed. They were almost invisible, covered in layers of grime the same color as the soil, like they were made from the same material. They barely protruded from the wall, looking like they were made from the soil itself.

Yet they moved, and the earth around the dusty faces undulated and shifted as their bodies squirmed beneath them deeper in.

"God is nowhere near this forsaken place," Dan intoned, as he regarded the faces with distaste.

The group all backed away against the opposite wall of the trench. Now they could hear them as well. The noise wasn't so much a grinding sound as a low moaning, just above the level of hearing.

It was the sound of pained breathing from hundreds, maybe thousands who couldn't draw a deep breath, reduced to shallow gasping under the weight of the dirt imprisoning them.

Bobby stared at the twisting faces, "It's...horrible, a torture. We have to help them." He took a step and reached toward one of the softly moaning faces.

Dan grabbed his arm and pulled him back, "Don't! You'll end up there as well. They'll pull you in."

Bobby goggled at him disbelievingly, "What are you talking about?" He tried to shake off Dan's grip, "We have to help these people."

Lee saw it. In the instant that Bobby's hand came closer to the wall, the eyes of one of the faces cracked open slightly, two slivers of white in all the brown, and the soil around the face flexed and split, bits of it crumbling off and falling to the floor of the trench. Something dark and glistening showed through the cracks, looking like rivulets of old, coagulated blood under thin, varicosed veins. The cracks subsided when Dan pulled Bobby away and the glistening wetness underneath disappeared.

But it looked as if something had been close to pushing its way through to the outside for a moment there. He didn't want to think what would have happened if Bobby had gotten closer, and carefully put a hand on Bobby's shoulder, "I think Dan's right. We shouldn't get too near."

Bobby spun to face him, "What are you talking about, Lee? Look at these people. We-"

Dan still had ahold of Bobby's arm and gave it a jerk, "Listen to me, Bobby." He flung his free hand at the squirming wall, "The damned suffer many different tortures in Hell, but one thing they all share is a desire to drag others into the same torment they endure."

"Bullshit," Bobby spat back at him, "Psycho bible-thumping bullshit, is what that is."

Duke stepped forward, "I agree, Bobby, this is all bullshit as far as I'm concerned, but what the hell are we going to do?" He inclined his head at the wall behind him, "There are hundreds here. Are we going to dig them all out?"

"And have them turn on us and pull us in there with them," Dan said.

"You don't know that," Bobby said, but his voice became weaker, "You can't."

Dan spoke gently, "But I do. If it's one thing I know, it's all about the tortures of Hell...and the fates of the damned, as well as their desire to not suffer alone." He gave the wall of faces a dark look and spoke through gritted teeth, "Trust me on this."

Everyone was silent for a moment as they contemplated the sad horror they were witnessing. Lee kept his hand on Bobby's shoulder in case the medic tried to jerk out of their grasp, but he saw that Dan wasn't about to let that happen. The security man's knuckles were white around the grip he had on Bobby's sleeve.

They were all appalled and frightened by what they were looking at, but he wondered again why Dan in particular seemed so close to the edge of terror here.

Duke said, "Come on, Bobby. There's nothing we can do for these poor bastards here, but if we can grab one of the ones up top, we might be able to find out what happened to Angie."

Bobby looked as if he was going to argue further but then his shoulders slumped, "Okay, okay. Fine, but...let's just get the hell out of this place."

Lee and Dan slowly released their grips, ready to grab Bobby again if needed, but the medic just put both hands up to his ears and started walking away along the side opposite the faces. He kept his eyes on the floor of the trench.

Duke shot a glance at Lee and mouthed, "I'll handle him."

Lee nodded back as Brent and Dan pushed past him. He watched the team's backs as they all moved away, hugging the wall of the trench and keeping their eyes averted from the gasping faces. The sound of the strained breathing all around them seemed so much louder now and he wanted to plug his own ears against it but settled for just following along with his own eyes on the ground.

His insides quivered with disgust and fury as he went.

*

The number of faces in the wall dwindled as they went and after a few hundred meters there were no more. But the pall they cast over the group was palpable.

Duke walked ahead with an arm around Bobby's shoulders, perhaps as much to console him as to keep him under control. Dan and Brent walked close together in the middle, obviously talking between themselves while keeping eyes on the wall and the top of the trench. Lee brought up the rear, consumed with his own concerns about everyone else, his fears about this place and misgivings about their plan, which seemed less certain to succeed with every step he took forward.

He looked ahead and saw that the trench would soon begin to curve to the right, away from the city, which wasn't the direction they wanted to go. As much to distract the others as himself, he quickened his pace and passed Dan and Brent to reach Duke and Bobby, "Hold up everyone."

They all stopped, remaining semi-crouched to stay below the lip of the trench.

Duke said, "Yeah? Far enough, you figure?"

"It's got to be. We'll be heading the wrong way in a few minutes," he nodded at the curve ahead.

"Well then let's take a look," Duke moved to the wall of the trench and slowly stuck his head up. Several seconds later he ducked back down and whispered, "Bingo, I think." He waved the others forward.

They all crept to the wall and stuck their heads up. One of the wanderers – a man - was just a few yards away, walking parallel to the trench.

"How about him?" Duke asked.

The man looked to be middle-aged with a white-streaked, scraggly beard. He was wearing the tattered remains of a suit jacket that hung off his frame, his pants were shredded below the knees, and he was barefoot. He shuffled along with a vacant expression on his grimy, sunken face.

"As good as anyone, I suppose," Lee said. He looked at Brent, who merely shrugged.

Duke put his hands on the lip of the trench, "Just tell me when."

Lee, Dan, and Brent each chose a direction to survey their surroundings. It took a few minutes, as the wanderers nearby seemed to just be stumbling around in every direction. Just as one would turn away from them, another would alter his or her direction and be able to see them if they stuck their heads up too far. Plus, the occasional black creature would lope past at a distance, and they would all duck and freeze, expecting to somehow be detected.

"Come on, come on," Brent hissed impatiently. It was only a matter of time before one of the locals came close enough to see them huddled in the trench, or their target moved too far away. Already, the scraggly man was double the distance from them and getting farther every stumbling pace.

Finally, the moment came when nothing was nearby, nor seemed to be looking their way.

"Go!" Lee said.

Duke pulled himself out of the trench, ducked low and dashed to the man as fast as he could. The man never saw him coming.

Duke ran up and swung an arm around the man from behind. He spun him and hoisted him off the ground, throwing him over his shoulders in a fireman's carry. In a few seconds, he was retracing his steps to the trench.

The man never uttered a sound, but a nearby female wanderer turned around and spotted Duke just before he leapt back into the trench with his prize.

She made an inarticulate squawk like an animal and raised her arm to point in their direction. All she did, though, was draw attention to herself.

Bobby was peeking over the lip of the trench and, as he watched, one of the black demons appeared out of nowhere and raced toward her, moving much faster than a human sprinter. It swept by the woman without even stopping and lashed an arm out. Its talons sliced through her middle and she toppled to the ground in a bloody spray.

The creature never broke stride and thumped away toward the walls of the city, clutching something red in its claws.

Duke still had the man on his back and wheezed, "Got him. Was I seen?"

Bobby swallowed his bile, sickened, "Yep, but…I don't think we have to worry."

Brent looked at the human wreckage hanging off Duke's shoulders and wrinkled his nose, "Jesus, the guy stinks."

"Tell me about it," Duke said, "I think half his weight is the shit in his pants."

Lee slapped Duke's arm, "Let's get back to where we were, fast."

Hunched over, they jogged back about fifty meters to put as much space as possible between them and the site of the abduction, in case anyone else had seen them, yet not far enough to encounter the faces in the wall again. The area around them was clear, so they climbed back out on the side opposite the city, passing the ragged man between them like he was no more than a duffel bag of clothes.

They laid him up against a boulder where they couldn't be seen from the direction of the city and stood around looking down at the man, if 'man' was the word for it.

"Jesus Christ, he barely looks human," Bobby murmured, "Let me see him."

He bent carefully, mindful of his own injuries, and did a cursory examination of the man, who just laid there with his eyes rolling, gasping for breath. He looked terrified.

"He's nothing but skin and bone," Bobby said as he prodded the man gingerly, "Rheumy eyes, thready pulse…half his teeth are gone. All the signs of severe malnutrition." He looked over his shoulder at the others, "This guy is weeks into a cycle of starvation. It's a wonder he's not dead."

Dan said quietly, "Maybe he is."

Bobby noticed the man's eyes had stopped roaming and had focused on him.

He leaned in, wincing at the odor coming off the man, "Can you hear me, sir? Do you understand me?"

The man's eyes widened, and his mouth stretched open, as if to scream. His tongue was swollen and blackened.

All that came out was a hoarse whisper, "U-Uomini? Si-siete uomini?"

Bobby pulled back and looked up, "What? What is that, Spanish?"

Dan shook his head, "It's Italian. He said, 'Are you men?'"

They all looked back down at the ragged man. His eyes were closed, but his chest still rose and fell in a jerky, hitching motion.

He'd passed out.

Twenty-Six

"SO WHAT THE HELL DO we do now?" Duke asked.

Dan said, "We're too exposed here. We should take him to the cave."

Brent immediately objected, "It'll take us half an hour just to get back there and we'd risk being seen the whole way."

Lee wasn't in a hurry to get back to the cave either. He wondered if they'd encounter Bill again there and was in no rush to do that.

He said, "We've already wasted enough time as it is. We've got to go on to find Angeline."

He turned to Bobby, "Can you do anything for this guy?"

Bobby was still examining the man and shrugged, "I don't know. I have some mild stimulants, but almost anything I give him might kill him in the shape he's in."

Duke pulled out one of his suit's flexible packs of water, "Maybe just start with this. Guy looks like a dried-out husk."

Bobby pulled the drinking tube off the top and held the spout to the man's lips. The water just ran off his lips and down his chin at first, but after a couple seconds, the man's eyes cracked open and he slowly brought a hand up, trying to grab the pack.

Bobby let him have it and sat back, "Let him take what he can for now."

The man sucked at the spout greedily. They could hear the water gurgling its way down to his stomach.

"He might lose it all if he takes too much," Duke murmured.

"Do you think it matters at this point?" Bobby asked.

Suddenly the man lurched forward, clutching his middle, and coughed weakly. He dropped the pack, but Bobby snatched it up.

He put a hand on the man's shoulder, keeping him steady while rasping coughs rattled his skeletal frame. He didn't throw up any of the water, though.

After several seconds, the man raised his eyes and looked up at them, "Am...ambrosia dal cielo," his voice was weak, but his eyes were clearer, "Gra-grazie."

Dan said, "It is Italian."

He leaned closer to the man, "Signore, chi e lei?" he spoke over his shoulder, "I asked who he is."

The man's eyes widened again, and his mouth quivered, "S-Sono... sono..." he trailed off, a look of confusion coming over his cracked and sallow face, "...sono...Sta-Stefano. Mi chiamo Stefano..."

His head dropped and he heaved a sigh, mumbling to himself, "Stefano...Stefano..." His shaking hands reached out for the water and Bobby gave it back to him.

He drank again and said, more firmly this time, "Grazie." He looked up at Dan, "Sei di casa?"

Dan was momentarily confused, "From...home? No, wait, he thinks we're from Italy."

He crouched and spoke to the man, "No signore. Siamo Americani e Britannici."

The man's eyes looked around the team, "Americani...I speak...s-some English."

Lee bent down, "Sir...Stefano, how did you come here? What is this place?"

Stefano looked confused, "It is difficult...to remember...I was at a... festa, a party. I walked home. It was dark...I walked on a different road. I saw a light...I fell...and I was here."

"When was this?" Brent asked.

Stefano frowned, "It was...just today? Leri – yesterday?" He put a hand to his head, "I do not know. There is no night here…no time…no time…"

Lee stood up and tapped Dan on the shoulder. They all stepped back, leaving the man to mutter to himself about time.

Duke said, "Unless it was some kind of wild, Italian come-as-your-favorite-homeless party, this guy's been here a lot longer than a day or two."

Lee pursed his lips in thought, "A retro party as well. Look at his jacket. My dad used to have one of those. Something's off here."

"No kidding," Brent said, "This poor asshole may not be of much help to us."

Duke shot a thumb in the direction of the city, "By the look of it, no one here may be. They all look like this guy, or worse."

Lee was frustrated, but he had a nagging hunch something was off. He bent down again and fingered the wide lapel of Stefano's tattered jacket, "Sir – Signore, can I ask you, what year is it?"

"Che cosa?"

Lee hooked a finger at Dan, "Can you ask him?"

Dan gave Lee a strange look, but squatted down, "Signore, che anno e?"

The man paused, brow furrowed, "E, sono…" his eyes darted about as he searched for the answer, "…diciannove…ottantacinque."

Dan frowned at Lee, "He says it's nineteen eighty-five."

"What?" Brent exclaimed.

Lee inclined his head at the man, "Ask him…who the Prime Minister is."

Dan did so, "Chi e il Primo Ministro?"

Stefano answered, "Be…Bettino Craxi. *Il Cinghialone*…The Big Boar."

"That settles it," Duke muttered, "He's bonkers."

Dan agreed, "Yes, he's very confused. He says he's only been here a day or two, and while he's clearly been here longer than that, it certainly hasn't been nearly forty *years*."

"Unless it has," Lee said.

"What?" Duke said.

"Like Frank said before, as well as other things, time may function

227

differently here."

Duke nodded, "Yeah, maybe, but I still don't see-"

Brent interrupted, pointing down at the man, "So then maybe he's right. From his perspective, he's been here a short time – not days, just by looking at him, but maybe weeks or even months – while time on our side has progressed more quickly, decades instead of weeks."

Duke shook his head, "So what? What the hell difference does that make to us?"

Brent tilted his head, "I don't know. Maybe none…maybe everything," he turned away, tapping his teeth.

Lee squatted in front of the man again, "Stefano, we need your help. We are looking for our friend, a woman. She was taken by one of the larger, uh, creatures here. We don't know where she is-"

The ragged man reached out, his fingers clawing at Lee's chest plate, "No! E pericoloso, danger…dangerous. If your friend was taken, she cannot be helped. You must leave."

"We can't leave without our friend."

He pulled Lee closer, his voice shaking, "You must. If you can leave, you must…before…before you become…one of us."

"What the hell does that mean?" Brent turned back, bending down. He grabbed Stefano's chin, "Look at me, what do you mean, 'one of us'? What is this place?"

Stefano's eyes darted back and forth between Lee and Brent, "Questo posto e la morte…la morte. This place is death…forever death."

Lee felt a chill go through him.

Brent released the man and stood up, "Bull," he looked at the others, "This guy's batshit."

The man focused on Lee, "No. No, veramente…I speak the truth."

"Tell me," Lee said softly.

Stefano put a hand on his own thin chest, "We…people come here. The demoni…they prey on us. They eat us…and drink our blood. Those who run, who cry or scream, they are taken quickly."

His head dropped again, and he snuffled, "We learn…not to be noticed. We learn how to survive, but to do that…" he looked up again with desperation on his face, "You must understand, there is no food, no clean water. To survive, we must…we must…" he trailed off again.

Lee pulled away instinctively. He didn't need the man to fill in the blanks; he'd seen what some of the wanderers had done when the demon had beheaded one of them and could easily guess how people would survive here by living off the scraps the creatures – the demons - left behind. He tried not to let it affect how he saw this poor man; tried to feel pity for him, but it was difficult.

Duke whispered in disbelief, "Are you fucking kidding me? They eat each other here?"

Stefano overheard and nodded, "I…belong here now. I was not a believer before, but now…now I know that I am in Hell…and that I belong here."

Lee swallowed his own feelings of revulsion and bent to the man again, "We have to find our friend. Can you help us? Tell us where she might be?"

Stefano didn't look up at him now, "She is gone from you already and you do not want to find her again."

"Why not?" but he had an inkling that he already knew what the answer would be.

Stefano raised tear-filled eyes to him, "It is a horror to live in this place, but we are the lucky ones. If the demoni kill us…when they kill us… then it is worse."

"Worse how?"

"Then we come back. The ones they kill…always come back."

Brent reached down and pulled lightly at Lee's shoulder.

Lee stood, "Anything else we can do for him, Bobby?"

Bobby brought out a couple energy bars, "Just these, maybe?"

Lee nodded, "Yeah," and turned away to where Brent and Dan had their heads together, talking privately.

He joined them, "Brent?"

Brent turned to him, "I don't know. That time stuff notwithstanding, he barely knows who or when he is. We're not likely to get much more from him."

"Maybe, but-"

Brent flipped a hand at the ragged man, "The guy's a psycho, a babbling, self-admitted *cannibal*, for Christ's sake, and Bobby's giving him food now. The best thing we could probably do for him is put a bullet in his head."

Lee flicked his gaze to Dan, "What do you think?"

Dan wore a grim smile, "What I've said all along. We are in Satan's dark domain here and the longer we stay, the more likely we are to end up like him," he pointed at Stefano, who was nibbling at one of Bobby's energy bars with tears streaming down his face.

Duke stepped closer, "Well, I'm still not sold on the idea that we're in Hell just yet, but if there is one, that guy has surely been through it, and I know one damn thing."

"What's that?" Brent asked.

"If Angeline's still alive, there's no way we're leaving her here to turn into that," he pointed over his shoulder, "or worse."

Brent narrowed his eyes, "And if I order us to leave?"

Duke sniffed, "Last time I looked, we were either in another dimension, or in Hell, and none of us is the CEO of shit here."

Brent gave him a wry smile, "Just checking. I'm not in a hurry to leave yet anyway."

Lee stuck out a hand, "Hold on everyone," he looked at Brent, "So I take it you're still in with staying until we find her?"

Brent's smile widened, "Oh yeah. I think there's a lot here to discover yet."

Dan blurted, "Mr. Copeland, do you understand-"

Brent spoke over him, "What I understand, Dan, is that, regardless of what Duke here says, I still pay your salary and I say we stay."

"Until we find Angeline," Lee said.

"Right," Brent amended, "Until then."

He put a hand on Dan's shoulder and led him away a few yards. Lee watched them go with an uneasy feeling in the pit of his stomach.

"Lee," Duke said beside him.

"Huh?"

"What should we do?"

Lee just shook his head at Duke and strode over to Stefano again,

"Sir…Stefano."

The man was taking small bites of the energy bar, sobbing openly, "Grazie…grazie. It is like…tasting Heaven. I had forgotten anything can taste so…delizioso."

"Sir, when the…demoni take someone away, where do they take them? Do you know?"

The man nodded slowly and raised a hand. He pointed at the towers, "There."

Lee looked over his shoulder at the looming masses of stone, "There? Not to the city?"

"No. There, but you must not go. Please, my friends, do not go." He kept chewing on the energy bar and nodding slowly, "Not go, not go…"

Lee stood up and the man's eyes didn't follow him. He remained against the stone, savoring the energy bar, nodding and crying and repeating the words like a mantra.

"Okay," Bobby said, "Now we have a place to investigate."

"And at least it's not the city," Duke said, "It would have taken us years to search that place."

Lee squinted up at the nearest tower, which disappeared into the white haze about a hundred meters above them, "I'm not sure this is going to be any easier."

Twenty-Seven

THEY LEFT STEFANO WITH HIS energy bars and a water pack at the boulders and dropped back down into the trench. Stefano watched them go with an expression of infinite sadness in his eyes, though whether it was because he feared for them or because he knew the food and water went with them was anybody's guess.

There were misgivings about leaving the man behind, but they knew that bringing him along would not only slow them down, but also possibly increase their risk of being discovered. The last they saw of Stefano, he was still nibbling the energy bar and staring up at the white sky, mumbling to himself and crying.

The main part of the trench seemed to run generally in the direction of the nearest of the towers, so they decided to take advantage of it. It would provide them with cover for much of their journey and they had yet to see any of the black demons or the humans using the trenches to get around.

They made it past the branch they'd used to kidnap Stefano before Duke mentioned it, "Why do you think none of the people here use these trenches? It's got to be better than just wandering around in plain sight."

Lee was in front and picked his way around a small boulder that almost blocked the path, "Beats me. Maybe some do at first, but I kind of doubt they continue after a while. Most of them out there look like they don't give a damn."

"Yeah," Duke squinted up at the lip of the trench, "it's like they're in a daze or half-asleep or something."

Bobby was behind Duke and said, "It's the malnutrition, the heat, and the exhaustion, I'd guess. After just a short time here, your reasoning ability would begin to deteriorate quickly. Plus, if you didn't have a clue how you got here, you'd probably never be able to find your way out again and just... give up after a while."

Brent overheard and chimed in, "I think it's that predator-prey thing you mentioned, Lee. They know the score and submit to their fate like dumb animals."

"It's more than that," Dan said from the rear, "They are damned souls, and they know it. They have lost all hope for redemption and accept the judgment of God."

Duke rolled his eyes, "Oh, that shit again. Dan, you can't tell me that Stefano there was a damned soul. He was just a guy who was in the wrong place at the wrong time and stumbled across that barrier or whatever."

"Or perhaps he was supposed to end up here," Dan persisted, "There is a deeper truth to this you're not seeing, any of you."

Bobby countered, "He was no incorporeal spirit or phantom, Dan. He was as real as we are. You touched him yourself."

"Maybe we aren't as real as we seem either," Dan said, "Maybe spirit to spirit contact feels as real as the physical. For all we know, we died the instant we crossed that barrier, and all of this is merely the start of our eternal damnation."

That shut everyone up immediately.

Lee decided a little less talk was in order, "Tell you what, guys, let's see what happens when we try to re-cross that barrier to get home. Then we'll find out for sure. In the meantime, let's just keep it down, shall we?"

They proceeded in silence as the trench wound its way back and forth across the plain, never holding a straight line for long, but generally trending toward the tower. Each of them kept one eye on the path and the other on the rim of the trench above them, while their minds were consumed by the questions about this place and its denizens.

Twice, they had to suddenly halt and press up against one side or the other when one of the wanderers appeared close to the trench. Both times the person staggered away just a few feet from falling in and never saw them. The wanderers apparently kept enough of their wits about them to keep from stumbling into natural calamity.

Finally, it looked like the trench was the nearest it was going to get to the tower before veering away and Lee halted, "I think this is it, guys."

They all collapsed against the wall of the trench. They could feel the heat from the rocks even through their suits.

The going had been mostly level, and their suits were still helping to keep them cool, but the emotional and physical tolls were beginning to tell on them. Despite his driving need to find Angeline, Lee was feeling on the edge of exhaustion and was particularly concerned about Brent and Bobby.

Bobby was not letting on about his physical distress, but it was clear to everyone that his injuries were giving him a hard time. He wasn't so much breathing as he was wheezing, and he was beginning to stumble.

Lee nudged Duke and nodded at Bobby, who was bent over looking at the floor of the trench.

Duke reached over and put a hand on Bobby's shoulder, "Hey."

Bobby straightened, but couldn't keep a wince from creasing his features, "Yeah?"

"Do me a favor. Give yourself a shot of painkiller, close your helmet and turn up your oxygen for a bit. It'll make the going a lot easier for me."

"For you?"

"Yeah, 'cause if you don't do it, I'll end up having to carry you in a few minutes, either because you'll pass out, or because I'll knock you out."

Bobby waved a hand weakly, "Yes mom. And will you read me a story when you tuck me in tonight?" But he immediately closed his helmet and fumbled in his pack for some meds.

Duke watched him to make sure he followed through, and Lee shifted his attention to Brent.

The CEO was in close conference with Dan, as usual. The two had dropped back a bit and were standing with their helmets close together, but there was a casual air about them. Lee was less interested in what they might be talking about, though, than in Brent's physical condition.

He noticed that Brent kept the fingers of his right hand hooked around the side of his chest plate most of the time. It looked like a natural position, but every time he shifted and removed them, the fingers were shaking. He also noticed that his CEO had adopted a jerky kind of head motion at some point, like his muscles were locked and he had to slightly force movement. His every motion appeared less smooth, more deliberate.

Duke had climbed partly up one side of the trench to keep watch, so Lee sidled up to Bobby and tapped his private channel, "How you doing?"

Bobby sounded better, "The O2 is helping a lot. I'm doing okay."

"How about our boss?" Lee inclined his head at Brent.

"Humph, you noticed his stiffness?"

"Yeah. Hard not to, now that I'm looking at him."

"It's most likely the heat and exertion, like I said. It worsens his symptoms."

"Okay. Should we be worried?"

Bobby tilted his head slightly, "I don't really know. I don't know shit about MS and Brent wasn't exactly forthcoming about the details of his condition."

"Alright, just checking. You up to this next part?"

Bobby straightened, "You bet, just…"

"What?"

"Don't tell Duke he was right about the meds and oxygen. He'll hang it over my head forever."

Lee flashed him a tired grin, "Our secret."

He left Bobby, even less at ease now about Brent than before. If his physical symptoms were worsening here, what about his cognitive functions?

Brent seemed to feel something was up. He strode over to Lee, "What's next? A plan of attack?"

"Something like that. How you doing, Brent?"

"Me? I'm fine, why?" he eyed Bobby, "He and Angeline been telling tales about me?"

Angeline? Does everyone know about this but me? "No, I-"

"I've seen you watching me off and on since we got here, Lee. I'm choosing to see it as your concern for your boss's well-being."

Lee didn't know what to say. Guys like Brent generally didn't want anyone to see them as weak and certainly didn't want people gossiping about their private lives.

He decided to make light of it, "Well, you're the oldest dog in the pack now, Brent, so naturally-"

Brent laughed, "Don't worry about me, bud," he eyed the tower, "Let's just focus on getting in that thing and then I'll race you to the top."

Brent moved back to talk with Dan and Lee watched him go, *He seems like the same old Brent, but...*

A hand on his shoulder startled him and he turned around.

Duke asked, "Just what is our plan of attack, Lee?"

Lee craned his neck and slid his eyes up the side of the immense tower. They were still about a hundred and fifty meters from it and down in the trench, but it filled the field of view on that side.

Up close, it looked less like a natural feature and more like something constructed, or maybe something carved out of a natural feature. It was stone, but there were gaping windows and alcoves, and wide ledges that looked hand-hewn all the way up to where it disappeared into the white. He could see several of the dark winged things flying around it like seagulls circling a tall ship and the odd one would dart into one of the alcoves.

The tower was as wide as a football field at its base, making it twice the size of a New York skyscraper, and there was no way to tell how tall it actually was. It could stop at the limit of the white haze or be miles high.

How long would it take to construct something like this, hundreds of years? Thousands? He had yet to see any signs of technological or even mechanical culture here.

Or was there some other mechanism used in a different dimension with different rules? Clarke's maxim about magic came to mind again - maybe here you could wish something into being, for all he knew.

Regardless how it was made, it was huge, and he tried not to feel discouraged, but the thought intruded, *Maybe the city would have afforded a better chance to find someone. This thing is big enough to be a vertical city itself.*

And it was one of two. Its partner was out of sight on the other side, but from a distance, had looked to be equal in size to this one.

Lee tried not to let their task daunt him. They had to find Angeline – they were going to find her – before he would entertain any thoughts about leaving this place.

Duke was waiting patiently for him to think his way through it. Lee turned to him, pointing up, "Those black things; some of them fly into it and don't come out, and others emerge from other places. I think this thing is hollow, just like a big building."

"Yeah…so there have to be entrances…?"

"At ground level as well for the walking demons."

"Maybe there aren't," Duke said, "The walkers might use the city and the flyers might use this place."

It was a possibility that Lee didn't want to consider, as it would mean they might never gain access unless they could clamber up the outside to one of the windows, and the lowest of those looked like it was at least five stories up, "Think positive, Duke, we…"

Lee stopped as he slowly became aware of a tremor moving through the ground underfoot, a tremor that was rapidly growing in force. He could feel his feet vibrating.

He said, "You feel that? An earthquake?"

Duke shrugged, "I don't know."

A shower of sand slid down the wall of the trench next to them and Duke said, "Maybe we should-"

Bobby's voice suddenly intruded over their radios, "Oh my God."

Lee looked up and saw Bobby staring at them, his wide eyes visible through his faceplate, "Yeah?"

Even as he said it, he realized that Bobby wasn't looking at them, he was looking past them, at something behind them.

Bobby pointed, "I think I know why the locals don't use these trenches to get around."

Brent and Dan were facing Lee and Duke's direction and saw it too.

Dan shouted, "Out of the trench! Now!" he pushed Brent toward the side wall and started boosting him up.

Lee and Duke turned around to follow Bobby's shaking finger to see something massive rounding a bend in the trench and heading straight for them. All they could see through a large cloud of dust were three enormous black heads that looked vaguely canine, with three sets of jaws filled with fangs inches long gnashing and snapping at each other as the creature or creatures pushed forward down the trench.

Duke and Lee stood frozen for a split second, before Bobby shouted in their helmet radios, "Move your asses!"

The thing emerged from the dust momentarily and Lee could see that it was one creature, one giant thing with three heads, and his mind tried in vain to make sense of what he saw. It was as high as an elephant and seemed to have scores of clawed feet beneath it and along its sides, pulling it forward at incredible speed. It undulated like a snake, sliding over boulders and the uneven sides of the trench easily. A row of tall spines ran down its back and swayed back and forth behind the heads with each twist of its long body.

That was all they could see before adrenaline kicked in and both Lee and Duke scrambled to the side of the trench behind Bobby, who was painfully pulling himself over the lip. Brent and Dan had already made it up and each had a grip on Bobby's arms, trying to help him up.

Duke and Lee both leapt up and grabbed the lip of the trench, but Duke's weight caused the edge to collapse, and he lost his grip, sliding back down to the bottom in a shower of dirt.

Lee was lighter and hauled himself over the edge quickly. He'd seen Duke fall, though, and immediately rolled back and extended his arm, shouting, "Grab me!"

Duke stepped back and cast a glance down the trench at the approaching monster. It was only fifteen meters away and six blazing orange eyes were locked on him. One of the heads opened its mouth and a roar like a great machine came out of it.

Panic galvanized him and he reflexively jumped up without thinking, arms outstretched.

His left hand caught Lee's arm at the elbow, and he hauled himself up while Lee rolled away from the edge, dragging Duke with him. Their combined action brought Duke over the lip to fall onto Lee and they both continued to roll away from the edge.

One of the creature's heads rose above the lip and snapped at them, foam and liquid spraying from its jaws, but it quickly sank back into the trench as the thing careened on without stopping, the roar of its passage shaking the ground and buzzing their eardrums.

Seconds after it passed, the team were swamped by a cloud of dust that billowed out of the trench. The dust slowly settled as the vibration diminished.

Duke and Lee got to their feet and the team watched the cloud of dust boil out of the trench like smoke from an old locomotive as the creature made its way toward the distant cliff.

Brent coughed and spat, "What the hell was that?"

Duke said, "It looked like a bunch of giant dogs fucked a dragon or something."

Dan said quietly, "I…think that was Cerberus."

Duke looked at him, "No kidding. What the fucking hell is a Cerberus?"

Lee said, "The Hound of Hell that guards the gates, that Cerberus?" he looked at Dan.

Dan nodded, "Yes. Cerberus patrols the outer regions and prevents souls from escaping the Underworld."

"But wait," Lee put up a hand, "Cerberus is a Greek or Roman myth, isn't it? Not Christian."

Brent said, "That so-called 'myth' almost bit Duke here in half. I'd say that goes a long way to proving that people from those times must also have come here and gotten back with tales of this place and its creatures."

Lee was trying to find some rationale for what they were experiencing, "The Bible doesn't mention Cerberus or any of the Greek or Roman Underworld figures, does it?"

Dan shook his head, "No, but from the earliest accounts in history, most cultures held very similar ideas about the afterlife and the Underworld, with succeeding civilizations perhaps borrowing from older stories and refining them. Some of them mention demons that resemble combinations of earthly creatures – chimeras – but not all of them."

"So maybe different people encountered different things here and they just added their own experiences of this place to the lore, so we got a distorted, patchwork picture of it?" Lee suggested.

"Yes, I admit it seems that maybe a lot of our mythology stems from here."

"So you admit the idea of Hell as a place where souls are punished is a myth?"

Dan frowned, "I admit nothing, but it seems-"

Bobby's voice whispered into their helmets, "Guys, while you're arguing theology, we should maybe consider this new problem we have now."

"Which is?" Brent asked.

Bobby inclined his head, and the others followed his gaze across to the plain on the other side of the trench.

Dozens of the wanderers were standing there, staring at them with their mouths hanging open. Several of them slowly raised their arms to point at the team.

Far behind the wanderers, closer to the wall surrounding Dis, were the dark forms of several of the demons who were also frozen in place. Their apparent attitudes, however, didn't suggest shock or surprise. They suggested predators that had just sensed prey nearby.

For a moment, it seemed that all movement on the plain came to a halt.

Then the moment ceased, and the demons immediately broke into a run and started charging across the plain toward the team.

Twenty-Eight

"RUN!" DUKE YELLED.

They turned as one and made for the only place they could: the looming side of the stone tower.

Brent and Dan ran pell-mell toward the tower, heads down and not looking back. Duke helped Bobby, who was much slower, and Lee was behind them, staying close to help Duke if necessary.

Lee cast a glance back over his shoulder and saw that there were at least half a dozen of the black creatures and that they could all run twice as fast as a human. Already, two of them were nearing the far side of the trench and he had no doubt they'd be able to leap its gap like a kid jumping over a crack in a sidewalk.

He looked ahead and saw that Dan and Brent were almost at the base of the tower. The ground was now sloping down toward the structure, as if its weight had depressed the land around it.

Another glance back showed him that he, Duke, and Bobby would never make it in time. They had only covered half the ground to the tower and the demons were all on this side of the trench now and running on all fours, their longer limbs eating up the ground between them and the team.

They'd be on them in seconds.

He sped up, coming alongside Duke, "Got any...of those...bombs still?"

Duke kept both hands on Bobby, almost dragging the medic along, "Side pack there."

Lee dug into Duke's pack without breaking stride and pulled out two of the small boxes, "Got 'em!"

"Push...red button...five second timer...I think."

"Got it!" Lee slapped Duke's shoulder, "Don't look back!"

Duke surged ahead and Bobby called out, "Lee! Stay with us!"

Lee ignored him. He looked ahead again and saw that Dan and Brent had reached a large opening in the base of the tower. Dan pushed Brent inside and turned back, dropping into a crouch.

That was all Lee had time to see. He could already hear the heavy thumps of the demons coming up behind him. Every instinct he had was telling him to pour on the speed, but he was the only thing between Duke and Bobby and those things.

There was no time to figure things out. He thought he could hear hoarse, grunting breathing right behind him.

He pushed the button on one of the boxes, held it in his hand for a count of two and just dropped it, hoping the timing worked and that one of the demons wasn't already close enough to get him before it went off.

Right on his count of five, a concussion lifted him and threw him forward into the air. A wave of heat blew by, and the ground rushed at him.

He landed on his feet, but momentum threw him forward out of control, so he just clutched his rifle close and rolled with it, hitting the ground hard and tumbling twice before coming up again on all fours.

He was dizzy and his ears felt clogged, but he could hear the *pop-pop* of a rifle somewhere close. He looked up to see Dan at the opening, firing past him.

Duke and Bobby had made it to the tower. Duke practically dropped Bobby and spun around with his own weapon already in his hand. His mouth was open, shouting something Lee couldn't hear and he started firing too.

Lee didn't bother looking back. He either had a chance or no chance and he didn't care which at the moment. As soon as he got his feet under him again, he put every ounce of power he had into making his arms and legs move as fast as possible, expecting at any moment to feel razor-sharp talons dig into his back.

Seven seconds later, he reached the opening, surprised to still be alive. Duke frantically waved at him to get down and he threw himself to the ground, sliding on the rough rock and coming up against a side wall of the opening.

He could hear the rapid fire of Dan's and Duke's guns still going. He took one deep breath before pushing himself up and bringing his own rifle around, just as they both stopped shooting.

"That's all of them, I think," Duke said. He turned to Lee, "You okay?"

"Fine, I-"

"New problem!" Dan shouted, looking up.

They followed his gaze and saw two of the flying demons diving directly on them.

Duke pushed Lee away from the opening, "Get to Bobby and Brent!" He didn't look to see if Lee complied. He raised his gun and joined Dan in firing almost straight up at the diving monsters.

Lee spun and looked deeper into the opening. It was a tunnel of some kind that quickly faded to inky darkness just a few yards in. Brent and Bobby were nowhere in sight.

Suddenly Brent appeared out of the gloom, wind-milling his arm, "In here! Back here!"

Lee shouted at the others, "Duke! Dan! Get back here!"

As that moment, a huge black form crashed to the ground right outside the opening. Its wings snapped, and its own bones burst through its skin, splashing yellow blood everywhere.

Duke and Dan stopped firing and Dan said, "The other one backed off. It flew into an opening above us."

Lee started to follow Brent, "Come on!"

The three of them ran into the dark after Brent. They had no idea where they were going, but Brent's light snapped on and they saw they were in a long, curving corridor that angled slightly upward. A few steps more and they saw Brent's light jerk to the left and suddenly disappear.

His voice came out of the dark, "This way!"

They all went left and found they were in a much narrower tunnel.

Brent's jittering light was aimed ahead, and they could see Bobby leaning up against the side, his hands on his thighs.

Brent stopped and turned back to face the others, "Hold up, guys."

He turned off his light and they were plunged into darkness.

They all tried to catch their breath as quietly as possible while listening for sounds of pursuit. Thirty seconds of silence told them they might be okay.

Dan's voice came out of the dark, "We shouldn't stay in one place."

Brent whispered, "I figured we should hole up a second and get our bearings before we knock ourselves out running into walls or whatever."

"Think we got away with it?" Duke asked.

Lee was straining to hear anything from behind them, but heard nothing, "I think so. Everyone okay?"

"Duke threw me around like a sack of potatoes, but I'm okay," Bobby groused.

Duke hissed back, "If you didn't run like a sack of potatoes, I wouldn't have to toss you around."

Lee asked, "Brent? Dan?"

"We're okay," Brent answered, "just winded." His voice was shaky, and Lee frowned to himself in the dark.

Dan said, "Seriously, we should not stay in one place. They know these tunnels and we don't. We need to find a bolt hole so we can-"

"What we need," Lee interrupted him, "is to find Angeline, so you're right, we shouldn't just stay here."

Dan lapsed into silence and Lee could imagine him fuming.

"That's right," Brent said, "Everyone okay to move on?"

Duke muttered, "I guess so. Those things are going to be around no matter if we stay put or wander the joint."

"Which begs the question," said Lee, "how come we're still alive?"

"Because you blew the shit out of them," Brent said, "That bomb you threw took out two that were breathing down your neck and slowed the other ones down long enough for Duke and Dan to blast at them."

"We didn't kill them, though," Duke said, "but the bomb may have given them second thoughts. They headed back across the trench."

"Maybe to get reinforcements, is my guess," Dan said.

"Could be," Duke whispered, "If they weren't pissed off at us already, they sure as hell will be now."

"But why aren't they after us in here?" Lee asked, "This is their place, and they outnumber us thousands to one."

Brent said, "Maybe because it is their place. They know where we are, they know they can have us at any time, and they know-"

"They know we'll come looking for Angeline," Lee finished.

Dan sighed, "Maybe it's just because they don't give a shit either way. They're demons at worst, or possibly extra-dimensional beings at best. Why ascribe human rationale to their actions? They serve a higher will, a sinister will, and if they see us as anything at all, it's as prey or playthings...like cats with mice, that's all. Our souls are fodder for them."

"Back to that again, huh?" Duke said.

Dan's voice was a harsh whisper, "When are you going to realize it yourself? They know it doesn't matter what we do, how long and to where we run. We're trapped here and the end is inevitable."

Bobby hissed, "Well, I'm not ready to just throw in the towel, whether this is Hell or not. We're here to get Angeline and I say that's what we do."

"Me too," Duke said, "so...where do we go?"

"Good question," Lee mused, "Stefano said they bring people here, but for what purpose and where would that be?"

Duke said, "Wherever it is, we shouldn't take long deciding. Those things are likely to be back soon."

"Shh," Brent said, "Maybe they're already here."

Everyone froze and listened in the dark.

They heard a light, regular scraping sound, like something being dragged across stone. It was regular, like a metronome.

Footsteps.

Something was in the corridor outside their narrow tunnel, stalking them, listening, peering into the dark, possibly even smelling them, for all they knew.

The sounds got slowly louder, and the team held their collective breath as the noises echoed all around them.

Suddenly the scraping stopped, and they could hear a liquid rattling sound, like water in a pipe.

Breathing.

It was in the narrow tunnel with them.

Brent nudged Dan and whispered, "Get ready."

He hit his light and the tunnel flared blue white.

One of the winged creatures was only a few feet away, its massive black bulk filling the tunnel. Its orange eyes narrowed in the sudden glare, but its mouth opened in a rasping snarl as its arms came up, talons reaching toward them.

The team reeled back in surprise, but Dan was prepared and fired a burst straight at the thing's head. Bullets chopped into its features, but it didn't fall.

Duke brought his own weapon up and took aim at the top of the thing's head. It was jerking from side to side as Dan's bullets struck, but it was confined in the narrow tunnel and couldn't move much.

It lurched forward another step and Duke pulled the trigger.

The first two rounds bounced off the demon's furrowed forehead, but the third hit one of the stubby horns, which exploded into yellow jelly.

The creature's angry roars turned to pain, and it clutched its face, dropping to its backward knees in the tunnel.

Dan lowered his aim and put another burst into the thing's midsection. The bullets punched into the black flesh like they were breaking through thin armor, but still the creature didn't go down. It dropped one hand to its stomach and used the other to pull itself forward, still coming at them.

The team slowly backed up, away from it, and kept firing until it finally collapsed face-first onto the floor, its long wings folded over its back and covering it to its feet.

"Jesus Christ," Duke said, "I put half a magazine into it."

Suddenly, the creature heaved a deep breath and rolled itself over onto one side. It was leaking yellow from a dozen wounds and one eye was gone, but the other glared at them, as orange as a bright ember.

Its mouth opened, spilling yellow blood, and a voice grated out, sounding like sticks in gravel.

"What is that?" Bobby asked, "Is…is it talking?"

The creature made the sound again and spat a wad of yellow onto the floor. It's one eye narrowed and it croaked, *"Heh mora zha ympa."*

Duke looked at Dan, "What the hell kind of language is that?"

Dan shook his head, "I...I don't know."

The creature tried again, *"Non podo morrer."*

Lee whispered, "What the...that sounds different, almost like Latin."

The creature's eye widened, *"I...cannot die. You cannot...kill us."*

"Now that sounds more like it," Dan said. He shoved the barrel of his rifle up under the thing's jaw and intoned, "We come against the Devil, his demons and all those he is using for his evil purposes."

Duke stepped forward and put the muzzle of his rifle against the remaining horn, "I'm just coming to get my friend, but two birds with one stone, you know?"

The creature stiffened, its muscular arms clenched, and one clawed hand dug into the wall of the tunnel, scoring the stone, while the other slowly rose as if to strike.

"Uh-uh," Duke said and prodded the remaining horn with his rifle, "I'll take the other one off. You say you can't die, but we've blown a couple of you apart already. We'll find out if you can die."

The creature didn't reply, but its raised hand slowly dropped to the floor. The eye narrowed again, and a smile creased its pocked and bleeding face.

Brent hissed, "What are you doing? Blow it away."

Duke shifted, his shoulders bunching as if he wanted to pull the trigger, but he shook his head, "Wait. This fucker can *talk.*"

Lee pushed forward and looked down at the enormous demon, "You have our friend, you understand? A woman, a female."

A few seconds ticked by, and the demon said, *"I...understand."* Its gravelly voice echoed metallically in the tunnel.

"Where is she?" Lee said.

No reply.

Duke pressed his muzzle against the horn and rasped, "You talk, and you bleed. I think you can die. Now where...is she?"

Bobby pointed at the creature's body and breathed, "Look at that."

Dan and Duke never shifted their gaze from the demon's eye, but Lee and Brent looked down.

The creature's wounds were healing themselves as they watched. The leaking blood had stopped, and the holes were sealing themselves up, the chitinous flesh drawing together. Already, some of the holes were no more than puckers in the skin and even the damaged eye was opening, revealing a milky orb underneath.

Lee stared at the creature's damaged horn. It wasn't showing any signs of healing…yet.

He aimed his own rifle at the other horn, "So you can heal. Talk, or we'll extend your recovery as long as necessary."

The demon laughed, a deep, grating rumble, *"You…may try, but I will… tear into your weak flesh and suck…the life from you…while you watch."*

Dan was staring as the demon healed itself and whispered, "Our Father, who art in Heaven, hallowed be thy name…"

The orange eye focused on him, *"I know those words…many of your kind…speak them here…as we devour their blood and hearts. Words or no words…they taste just as sweet."*

Dan continued whispering the prayer, though his voice wavered now.

Duke shifted his aim to the demon's good eye, "Last time; where is she?"

The demon slowly pushed its face forward until its eyeball rested against the muzzle of Duke's rifle, *"So…you don't miss."*

Brent said, "What are you? What is this place?"

The eyeball shifted to him, *"We are…Sirrush. And this place…is your death."*

"Maybe," Duke said, "but not before yours." He jammed his muzzle sharply into the eye and the demon jerked its head away with a grunt.

"Our friend," Lee repeated, "Where is she?"

"Your friend…is already nothing more…than a Revenant, but you will find her…in the Ekerla…*below,"* the demon's eye rolled down to indicate the floor, *"Be wary of her…and her new master…the Eater of Minds."*

It started laughing again, a deep, dry chuckle that vibrated in their chests.

Duke raised an eyebrow at Lee, "Heard enough?"

"Yes, I have."

They pulled their triggers simultaneously. Lee's blast tore off the other horn and Duke's punched through the demon's good eyeball, spattering yellow ichor across the wall.

The creature's head dropped to the floor while its laughter still echoed through the tunnel.

"Not the most engaging conversationalist," Bobby said dryly.

Lee turned his gaze away from the demon's shattered face, "No, but we learned something."

Duke stood, "Yeah, that these guys are bigger assholes than we already thought."

Lee nodded, "And that Angeline is here, somewhere below us." He looked at Brent and Dan, "You coming?"

Brent gave him a crooked smile, "Wouldn't miss it," he patted Dan on the shoulder and headed back out of the tunnel, keeping his hand over his light.

The security man had his eyes locked on the demon, but he slowly rose and followed Brent as he headed back toward the bigger tunnel.

"Great," Bobby sighed, "We're heading even further underground. Five miles isn't enough."

Twenty-Nine

THEY RE-ENTERED THE WIDE TUNNEL that led to the outside, but instead of heading out they went left, deeper into the tower.

The floor rose slightly but steadily, and a few paces farther in they realized it wasn't completely dark. They could see alcoves along the right wall every five meters or so and some of them were letting in diffuse light.

Brent turned off his light, "That must come from outside."

Lee cast a glance into one of the door-sized niches as they went by. It curved away sharply, and he couldn't see very far, but the light definitely got stronger farther in, "Like windows. Let's keep it in mind in case we have to make a hasty exit."

Duke muttered, "Yeah, but those flying uglies use those too. Wouldn't want to bump into one on your way out."

"Let's hope they're only flyers, not climbers," Bobby whispered, "and only use the ones higher up."

It was nerve-wracking progress. The ceiling above them started low, but as they moved inward, it rapidly rose to disappear into the echoing heights, even as the tunnel widened, and the number of alcoves and side-passages increased. The team were constantly swiveling their heads to keep track of all the nooks and crannies where enemies could be hiding, while casting constant glances above their heads for any sign of the flying demons.

"This place is like an enormous termite mound," Bobby commented.

"And what do termites do to invaders?" Duke said, "Tear them limb from limb."

Bobby gave him a sour look, "Thank you for that. Just when I was starting to warm up to the place."

They were still climbing, moving inexorably farther away from the ground, and the number of apertures to the outside was increasing as they went. It was getting brighter, and they had already given up on being able to stick to shadows. If something came their way, they were totally exposed, and their only hope would be to fight it out.

"We're spiraling inward as we go," Lee said, "but it's getting brighter somehow."

Dan was in the lead and abruptly stopped with a hand up, "Hang on."

He shifted around, looking back in the direction they'd come, a questioning look on his face.

Duke brought his weapon up, "What is it?"

Dan turned and looked ahead up tunnel. It was even brighter up there, "Do you hear that?"

They all listened.

Somewhere ahead was a noise, so low it was almost undetectable. It was a dry rasp, like the wind skittering dry leaves down a distant street.

Or like claws on stone.

A lot of claws.

Bobby sniffed, "Smell that?"

There was a scent in the air as well. Not exactly unpleasant, it was an earthy smell, but not like soil or stone. It had a metallic tang to it that stirred something in the back of the mind.

Bobby had smelled it before, "I know what that is. It's the same smell as the insides of those guys we found."

Lee recognized it now too and the memory brought a grimace to his face, "Yes, the smell of cooked blood."

Dan gestured with his rifle, "Well, whatever they are, the sound and the smell are coming from up there."

A sudden series of scraping noises came from behind them, Startled, they all spun and crouched.

Something was coming up the tunnel from behind. It was still out of sight around the curve but would be in sight in seconds from the sound of it.

Lee spotted a wider alcove a few yards ahead and pointed silently. The team dashed over to the opening as quickly and quietly as they could, cramming themselves into the space.

Bobby went in first and only made it a few paces in before coming up against a dead-end wall, "Oof. This is as far as it goes, guys."

The others pushed in as best they could, backs toward the rear of the small space and weapons clutched and held high, ready to fire.

The alcove wasn't very deep, but it curved back into the wall as it went, providing extra cover, and it was very dark. As long as nothing looked too closely, they might be invisible.

The scraping got louder and now the floor was vibrating as something heavy approached.

Lee and Duke were nearest the front, with Dan and Brent sandwiched between them and Bobby. Lee held up a hand with fingers extended in the signal to wait, knowing that the others would be able to see his silhouette.

Everyone held their breath.

A few seconds later, something huge lumbered past the alcove. Its feet scraped the floor as it shuffled, long claws scratching the stone as each foot was brought forward to thump down heavily with each step.

Twice the height of a man, its black body bulged with muscle atop legs that were as thick as Duke's torso. Its shoulders were six feet across, and Lee's jaw dropped when he saw that they supported two horned heads that swung from side to side, with four orange eyes that scanned the entire tunnel as it went along.

And the heads...

The heads were each bisected by enormous vertical gashes running from between the horns to what would be their chins and lined with curving fangs as long as a human hand. They were more mouth than anything else.

The heads swiveled constantly and, for an instant, one of them swung over and locked onto their alcove, the eyes seeming to bore through the dark right into Lee's. The fangs opened and gnashed together with a sound like knives clashing, dripping white foam down its front.

Lee's grip tightened on his rifle, and he was on the edge of leaping forward and firing, when the creature's head swung away, and it continued past without missing a step.

They waited another thirty seconds as the scraping and thumping moved away. Despite his suit's coolers, Lee felt sweat running down his back and his face, but he didn't dare move, certain that the thing would reappear at the slightest noise.

Silence finally returned to the tunnel, and they stumbled out of the alcove.

"Jesus Christ," Duke breathed, "Did you see that fucking thing?"

Lee swallowed, his throat dry, "Yep, I sure did." As big as the six-limbed demons were, that monstrosity made them look like juveniles in comparison.

Brent said shakily, "We couldn't see it clearly. What did it look like?"

Duke answered, "Like it could rip an elephant in half." He turned to Lee, "Did that fucker have *two heads*?"

"It did indeed." Lee looked around at everyone, "Something's weird, though."

Bobby huffed, "Seriously, you're just noticing weird here?"

Lee shook his head, "No, I swear that thing looked right at me. One of its heads was facing this way and…for a second, I saw its eyes shift, like they locked onto me as it went by."

"Well it obviously didn't see you," Brent said, "or we'd all be dead now."

Lee had no answer and just murmured, "I guess so," but in his mind he was certain; the demon's eyes had no apparent pupils, but he had a feeling – he just knew – that the thing had focused on him for a split second.

Dan interrupted his thoughts, "We got lucky. Come on, let's get moving."

He took point and Lee followed close behind, but he couldn't shake the image of that massive head and those orange eyes boring into his.

They proceeded more slowly, moving half-crouched, nerves humming with the anticipation of sudden attack. It was apparent to everyone now that the creatures they'd been seeing, as terrible and mind-bending as they were,

were not the only things here. Each new encounter brought worse horrors they had to consider.

Twenty meters farther along, the corridor stopped at a T-intersection, with side-tunnels disappearing in either direction. There didn't seem to be anywhere else to go, so the team moved up to the left corner and Dan and Lee stuck their heads around.

It was a gallery of sorts, continuing at least thirty meters, or a hundred feet, in that direction, with a low ceiling and wide, waist-high apertures cut out of the rock all along the right side. The floor still had a definite upward slant and disappeared around a distant curve to the right. A look behind showed that it went a similar distance in that direction as well, with apertures along the same side and with a downward trend to the floor.

The rasping noise was much louder now, seeming to come from all directions.

Duke edged forward and took a look through one opening in the rock. The others saw his head tilt up as he said, "Holy shit."

They crept up beside him and looked.

The entire interior of the tower was a massive open space. They were peering from one aperture in a row of at least a fifty on the same level and same side. Fifty meters directly across from them was a similar row, and above that and on either side stretched row upon row of openings ascending in a slow spiral all the way up to where the walls disappeared into the same white haze that was outside.

The light permeating the space was coming from the haze above, as well as from some of the apertures in the ranks of galleries that apparently led to the outside. Compared to the dark tunnels, it seemed as bright as a sunny day at the higher levels.

Duke nudged Lee and angled his head at the other side. Lee looked and saw that some of the apertures held dark shapes that shifted restlessly, no doubt occupied by some of the flying creatures. He nervously glanced in each direction down the hallway they were in and didn't see any, but there were surely some of the creatures on their side, possibly on the next level above or below.

Dan craned his neck, taking in all the levels, "It's like a cathedral in here."

Bobby hissed at him, "Yeah, only the gargoyles are on the inside."

Duke whispered back, "Shit. You could fit a couple cathedrals in here. This place is a giant fucking rookery for these flying things or something. Where the hell would Angeline be in all of this?"

"I'm not sure," Brent said, "but I think down there would be a good place to start."

They all gazed down.

Two stories below them was the floor of the tower. It was fifty meters on a side and cloaked in relative darkness. The intense rasping noise was coming from there, as was the pervasive metallic smell.

That level of the tower was below the outside ground level and no light penetrated from any alcoves to illuminate it. Only the glow from the haze far above and that filtering in from the lowest of the apertures gave any hint of what was there.

Enough did, though, for them to see that there were many of the walking demons down there. Their black bodies were almost indistinguishable from each other as they moved about in the shadows, but it seemed that there were many more different kinds than the ones they'd met so far.

The humanoid ones were the most common and there were a few of the larger six-limbed types among them, but there were also some that appeared to crawl on the floor with thin, extended bodies and others that hitched along on multiple legs like giant spiders. A couple of the behemoths with two heads could also be seen.

The only thing they all seemed to have in common was their black color. They were constantly in motion, bodies sliding over each other as they milled about. It was hard to see where one creature ended and another began.

"It's like a fucking demon orgy or something," Duke whispered.

Lee pointed, "Yes, but look. There in the middle. There's a clear space."

They all stared at the floor. The demons seemed to range over most of it, except for a portion near the center, where there was indeed a large empty space they all appeared to avoid, congregating around it, but not intruding into it.

That part, a rough circle about ten meters across, was also jet-black, but shiny, like a pool of oil.

And it was moving. Its surface curled and roiled like a glutinous, bubbling tar-pit.

Like something was moving around under it.

"I don't like the look of that," Bobby said.

"Maybe it's like their toilet?" Duke ventured.

"That is the Remorga," a deep, grating voice intoned from behind them.

They reacted as a unit, heads jerking around and weapons whipping up.

A winged demon filled the corridor, its one orange eye blazing down on them. The other eye was crusted over with dried yellow blood. Its arms were up, and its taloned six-fingered hands were hanging over their heads.

The demon.

Their demon.

The one they'd already killed. The first eye they'd shot out was now healed.

"You!" Duke blurted.

He raised his rifle, but the demon brought a hand down and grabbed the barrel, pushing it downward and twisting it out of Duke's hands. He couldn't release it fast enough and everyone heard something snap in his hand or arm.

Duke sucked air through the pain and stepped forward to swing with his other fist, but the demon batted the blow aside and grabbed him. It pulled Duke to its chest and held him there with one hand around his neck and the other holding the rifle.

Everyone else stood with their weapons aimed at the thing, but they didn't dare pull their triggers. Duke would be shredded, and the creature would likely not be killed – again.

Its voice grated in their ears, *"I...invite you...to shoot."*

Duke held his injured arm and gasped, "Y-You're dead."

"As I said...you cannot kill us," it tightened its grip on Duke's neck and he squirmed in pain, *"but your kind...is not as strong."*

It dropped the rifle with a clatter and jabbed the talons of that hand into Duke's side, *"You can be...ended in so many...interesting ways."*

Duke hissed as the talons penetrated the Kevlar and dug into his side.

The creature's eye widened, *"Your weapons...can damage, but not kill.*

However," it pushed the talons in a bit more and Duke tried to stifle a yelp.

"Alright!" Lee said and held his free hand and rifle up in the air, "We won't shoot. Let him go."

Duke spoke through gritted teeth, "Fuck that, Lee. Fill this asshole."

Lee looked at the others, "Weapons down."

They all hesitated.

"Down!" he commanded.

They all lowered their rifles. Lee noted that Dan was the last one to do so. The security man's eyes were wide and rolling about. Lee feared he would let loose with a volley and end up killing Duke, so he stepped in front of the demon.

The demon's eye narrowed and it spoke directly to Lee, *"Here is...the Ekerla. You cannot escape. If you resist...you will die...badly."*

"And if we don't resist?" Lee asked.

The demon ignored the question, turning away, *"Follow."*

It still had Duke in its clutches, hugging him to its chest like a child with a doll.

They had no choice, as far as Lee was concerned. They still had their weapons, but that thing had Duke and they still had no idea where Angeline was.

He started after the demon, "Come on."

Bobby and Brent made to go as well, but Dan grabbed Brent's arm, his voice trembling, "Boss, don't..."

Brent shook him off, "We're in it now Dan. I'm curious to find out where this ends," he flashed Dan a crooked smile and a wink.

Every instinct Dan had was telling him to run, but his job was to protect his boss and besides, where could he escape to in Hell? They were here and they were all damned, as far as he was concerned; had been since they'd made the decision to come here.

But a man who knew he was damned had nothing to lose...and maybe some small measure of forgiveness to gain.

He took a deep breath and jogged after the others, still keeping his rifle at the ready.

Thirty

THE CREATURE LED THEM IN the opposite direction, past the corridor they'd arrived in and down the slanting tunnel. They were headed to the bottom level of the tower, the one filled with demons.

Lee was right behind the creature and ran his eyes up and down the thing's body. Aside from its still missing eye and truncated horns, there seemed to be no sign of the damage they'd inflicted with their automatic rifles.

A miracle?

A different kind of physical reality?

His mind wrestled with the question of which was more likely – or less unbelievable – science or the supernatural.

These things were physically real. He heard the creature's wings brushing against the stone of the tunnel walls; he'd felt its heaving body and smelled its yellow blood in the narrow tunnel near the entrance when they'd gunned it down.

Yet it had taken more damage than any physical being should be able to and survived. Not only survived but had almost completely healed in less than ten minutes. He had no doubt that given a little more time its other eye and even its horns would regenerate.

The tunnel they were in curved gradually to the left as it descended, and the apertures allowed them to see that they made their way around one quarter of the tower before emerging onto the expanse of the bottom floor.

The gathered demons seemed to have been expecting them. By the time they arrived onto the main level, the creatures had cleared a corridor between them that led straight to the black circle in the middle.

Still clutching Duke to its chest, the one-eyed demon strode through the ranks with the team in tow.

Lee felt his blood pounding in his ears. They were in the middle of it now, surrounded by hundreds of the huge creatures, with no way to escape. They could pounce at any second and it would all be over.

But they weren't pouncing. None of them were moving at all, in fact. The only motion was their heads, slowly turning to track the group as they walked through the crowd.

Eyes darting from side to side, the team all had their weapons up ready to fire, but no one was fooling themselves; they might be lucky to get off one or two shots each. When an attack came, it would be over before they could all draw a breath.

Bobby edged up to Lee as they walked, "It ain't looking good, Lee."

Lee was perplexed, "We aren't dead yet, though, and I don't know why."

Bobby muttered, "If there's an empty buffet table at the end of this walk, I'm all for being the rude guest and going out with a bang."

Lee said, "If there's an empty buffet table here, I've got news for you; we aren't the guests."

He glanced back at Brent and Dan. Brent was walking as if in a daze, staring up at the ranks of demons with an almost admiring look on his face. Dan was simply staring straight ahead, as if seeing nothing.

Like a man walking to the gallows, Lee thought.

He heard a low rumbling sound and realized their guide was speaking – murmuring - to itself as they neared the black circle. He strained to hear, but the sounds made no sense, though he thought he caught the word the demon had uttered up above once or twice – 'remorga'.

As they neared the center of the floor, he heard the same sounds coming from the other demons all around them, starting low, but gaining in volume as they neared the black circle, which Lee could now see was more of a wide, shallow pit containing some black liquid.

Their one-eyed guide reached the edge of the circle and stopped, unceremoniously dropping Duke to the floor.

Duke collapsed and Bobby pushed forward to him, "Duke, you alright?"

"Just dandy, thanks," he muttered. He was still clutching his injured arm to his chest, "I think that fucker broke my wrist."

Lee knelt beside them, "Could as easily have been your neck."

Duke rubbed his bruised throat through the Kevlar, "Tell me about it."

"At least it's not your jerking-off hand," Bobby said as he rummaged in his bag and brought out a roller bandage, "Sorry, all I have."

Duke let out a shaky sigh, "I'll take it anyway," he held his arm out and Bobby started wrapping his wrist.

Lee stood and looked around. The demons all seemed to be ignoring them. Their bodies were all turned to face the pit and their black faces were all angled upward. They seemed to be speaking in unison, as if performing a chant.

The words they were saying kept growing in volume, becoming more distinct, but no more comprehensible. The only one Lee recognized was that one, remorga, that seemed to come after every string of sounds.

He stepped a pace back to talk to Brent, but the CEO was still gazing around with wonder on his face. He didn't seem worried at all.

The demons' voices were loud enough now that Lee had no fear of talking in a normal volume, "Brent. *Brent*." He grabbed Brent's arm and shook it.

Brent shifted his gaze to Lee, speaking as if to himself, "Isn't it fantastic? Look at it."

What? Lee shook Brent's arm again, "What the hell are you talking about? Brent, they're lining us up for dinner here."

Brent's eyes focused on him, "I don't think so, Lee. Why bring us here? Why not kill us a half dozen times before this? There must be a reason."

Duke said, "I think I'm looking at the reason guys."

Lee turned back to see the liquid in the pit now bubbling higher, humping up as if something was emerging from beneath.

The demons' chanting had become louder, and they were all rocking their heads from side to side now, as if caught up in something. The noise rose rapidly to a crescendo, hundreds of deep, grating voices speaking as one, echoes overlaying echoes as the noise reverberated around the immense interior of the tower, the tone and volume at a point where the team were wincing in their helmets.

Suddenly, after one sustained sound, they all stopped, and the echoes slowly died. The roiling liquid in the pit was spinning now as it rose higher, but it didn't spill over the edges of the pit onto the floor. Instead, it was coalescing, solidifying; something wasn't coming up from beneath it, the liquid *was* the something.

One-eye bellowed into the echoing silence, *"Q'amanis a Remorga!"*

The hundreds of demons all around them repeated, *"A Remorga! A Remorga!"*

The shape in the pit gelled into solidity and spoke with a voice that made the tower tremble, *"Remorga cho renhira."*

The team stared up at the thing.

It was vaguely humanoid and resembled the flying creatures more than anything else, but it was twice the height of even the tallest of the demons. It had four thick arms that ended in clawed hands as wide as a man's chest. It had no legs; instead its trunk simply extended down into the gelatinous pit it was part of.

It raised its two upper arms and massive wings unfolded from its back, spreading across half the floor as it spoke again, *"Remorga cho renhira."*

Its black, blocky head tilted down, and blazing orange eyes focused on the team from under beetled brows that swept up into horns two feet long, *"Remorga has come."*

The surrounding creatures murmured in unison, *"Remorga,"* and One-eye stepped away to disappear into the throng around the pit.

Silence fell in the tower.

Lee's insides felt like ice. *Is this their God?*

Duke and Bobby slowly stood up next to him, eyes wide and mouths gaping at the enormous creature.

Brent moved to step forward. Dan grabbed his arm, but he pulled away and looked up at the demon, "We are-"

It ignored Brent and brought one arm down to point straight at Lee with a finger as thick as a man's wrist, *"I know...who you are and...from where you come."* Its voice vibrated in their chests.

Brent tried again, "I am the leader-"

The creature's finger flicked to one side, hitting Brent in the chest. He flew backward, crashing into Dan, and the two fell to the floor.

"I lead here," it boomed.

Lee looked over his shoulder as Brent and Dan got back to their feet, "You okay?"

Brent's armor had taken the hit, but he was bent over, wheezing, his breath knocked out. Dan was supporting him.

Brent waved weakly, "Yeah...okay."

Lee turned around to face the creature again and jerked back with a start. It had leaned down, and its enormous head was now within arm's length.

His mouth was dry, but he swallowed and forced a calm voice, "We only want-"

The creature reared back, standing straight and towering over them, *"I know what you want. To claim your friends."*

Lee realized his whole body was clenched in anticipation of a blow, which didn't come, "We do not wish to intrude. We intend to return-"

A long arm shot up, pointing to the haze a hundred meters above them, *"To your own level of existence; to breach the barrier...to your own... dimensional brane."*

Lee was jolted. The creature was using...

It brought its arm down again, *"Yes, I am...what your kind here call... the Eater of Minds. I take the atma...the consciousness, and make it my own. I grow...and learn...and I know,"* it spread its hands, *"everything."*

It pointed behind the team, *"See my works."*

Lee and the others turned around to look back down the path between the ranked demons. There was a figure there coming toward them; one of the walking creatures, except...

It was Frank.

Frank's head atop a demon's body.

It strode calmly straight toward them, a black, muscular, genderless body…surmounted by Frank's white face and completely black eyes, his mouth split in a wry smile.

"Holy shit," Bobby breathed.

Duke said, "Twisted mother*fuckers*."

Brent backed to one side, away from the creature, but stared at it with open curiosity, while Dan sank to his knees, mumbling to himself. Lee tapped his com button for Dan's channel and heard him reciting the Lord's Prayer again.

He switched it off, feeling like an eavesdropper, but also uncomfortable with the consideration that Dan might be right after all. He couldn't imagine anything in science being able to achieve what he was looking at, let alone anyone wanting to.

As the Frank-thing drew near, Lee focused on the neck, where the pale skin of the physicist melded with the smooth black of the demon body. There was no line; one flesh simply melted into the other. Somehow, he knew that if he looked closer, he wouldn't see anything as crude as stitching; it would look like some kind of fractal blending, an interweaving of flesh right down to the cellular level.

Fighting revulsion and rage, he swung around to face the giant demon. Even beyond what had been done to Bill, this was an abomination, an assault on his moral senses. That a quiet, reasonable man with a mind able to contemplate the cosmos should be turned into this thing…

He opened his mouth to shout his condemnation, but Dan beat him to it. He rose before the Frank thing reached them and shot a hand out. Lee saw that his glove was clutching a small gold cross on a chain.

Dan shouted up at the Frank-thing, "I command the evil and unloving spirits to be bound! To be confused and powerless! I command-"

The Frank-thing reached out with one long arm and grabbed Dan by the neck, picking him up effortlessly. Dan's feet kicked uselessly in the air and his voice became a harsh gurgle, but he still had the cross in his hand. Even as he struggled to breathe, he brought it up in a roundhouse move, ramming it into one of Frank's eyes.

The eye popped, gushing black and yellow liquid over Dan's glove, but the smile on Frank's face never faltered. It drew Dan's flailing body up high above its head and slammed him down to the stone floor at its feet. There was a splintering sound that Lee hoped was the armor and not Dan himself.

Dan lay motionless on the ground. The Frank thing didn't even look down. It just yanked the cross out of its ruined eye and dropped it to the stone floor next to Dan with a clink. Its remaining eye kept staring straight ahead, but Lee thought he saw one corner of its mouth turn up slightly, as if it enjoyed what it had done.

Duke tried to lunge at the thing, but Lee and Bobby grabbed him and held him back.

Lee whispered hoarsely, "Duke, it isn't Frank in there. It could kill you."

"You are correct," the huge demon said, *"Your...colleague is with me now. Everything he knew, everything he was, is me now."*

Duke flung a hand at the Frank-thing and yelled, "Then what the fuck is the point of that anyway?"

"In his own words," the demon's face cracked in a smile, *"an experiment."*

Dan stirred and moaned.

Lee and Bobby bent to him as he sat up and Lee said, "Dan. Dan, you okay?"

Dan shook his head and rubbed his neck, "Feels like my head was almost twisted off." He stopped when he saw the Frank thing and scowled at it, "A vile abomination. An offense to God."

"No arguments from me there," Lee said.

He left Bobby to see to Dan and turned around to face the demon, "What do you want from us? Why are we here?"

Its flaming orange eyes widened, *"You came here."*

"I mean, why haven't you killed us? Why bring us down here?"

The eyes narrowed, *"To learn. You are not like most of the others of your kind."*

"What can you learn from us?"

"More of your...origins. Most who have come before knew little of where they were from and only possessed...superstitious fears of this place.

I wish to learn more."

It raised a hand to indicate the Frank thing, *"This one knew much, but the constructs of its knowledge...its understandings of reality...are unfamiliar to me."*

Lee said, "To learn from us, is that all? Why kill? Why do you torture and steal the minds of people?"

"Lee!" Dan rasped hoarsely from behind him.

Lee looked back, "What?"

Dan was being supported by Bobby and Brent. He still had a hand to his neck, but his eyes flashed with anger, "You're chatting with a minion of Satan! The Devil doesn't learn. He lies!"

He'd picked up the soiled cross and held it up, "I abjure and renounce you, vile serpent! Our adversary the Devil prowls like a roaring lion, seeking someone to devour! Only that!"

The demon laughed, a raw, rattling noise that seemed to come up from the pit beneath it, *"Otherworlder, I have heard these names of Satan and Devil before from your kind. A petty construction of small minds that seek to grasp what is beyond them. They are...a fiction."*

"You lie!" Dan screamed, "You are a fallen entity, disgraced in the eyes of God!"

The demon roared laughter and spread its arms and wings wide, *"God! You speak of gods here!"* Its voice reverberated around the tower.

It lowered its head and leaned forward, *"Look around you and perceive. There are no gods here, save one, as I understand your meaning of the word God."*

Dan seethed with outrage, "Again a lie. You say you want to learn. God needs nothing of learning; He is all-knowing!"

The remorga placed a wide hand on its own chest, *"I make no claim of Godhood, nor of possessing all knowledge, but I serve one that could."* Its orange eyes narrowed as it stared down at them, *"Indeed, this one,"* it waved a languid hand at the Frank thing, *"possessed a deeper conception of reality than my own, but of yours I might learn more as well. Your understanding is limited, but you are correct in one manner."*

"How's that? Duke asked.

The demon smiled widely, revealing long, glassy fangs and a black tongue, *"To learn...I devour."*

Thirty-One

THE REMORGA'S WORDS WERE LIKE icicles down Lee's spine. They were in the midst of hundreds of the creatures, facing a monster the size of a two-story building. He knew they had no way out and figured the others knew it as well.

Duke exclaimed, "You're going to fucking *eat* us? You can choke on my bones."

The remorga smiled again, *"I have no use for your crude flesh. I will consume your minds. Your thoughts, your knowledge will become mine. What remains of you after, if I cannot make use of you,"* it pointed at the Frank thing again, *"I shall give to my children to dispose of."*

A thought occurred to Lee, "Our friends, this one and the other named Bill; you control them?"

"I do, as I do all in my domain. I see all, know all that they do."

"And our other friend, the woman?"

"She is mine as well."

Lee's heart sank at the same time as his rage flared. He knew it was a vain hope that Angeline might still be...human, but he'd had to ask.

He aimed his rifle at the remorga and spoke through gritted teeth, "Where is she?"

"She is near."

"Show her to me!"

Brent moved up beside him, "Lee, she's gone. Why-"

Lee rounded on him, "Because I give a shit, Brent!" He lowered his voice to a whisper, "If we're too late to save her, maybe the least we can do is put a bullet in her brain and hope it gets her out from under this thing's control."

Bobby came up to them and whispered, "I vote we all put bullets in our own heads right now. I don't want this asshole getting my memories of Janine Adams at the junior prom."

"Just wait," Lee said.

Duke murmured, "You have an idea?"

The remorga rumbled, *"Behold...your destiny,"* it raised a hand to indicate the path through the demons back to the tunnel.

They all turned and looked.

One of the flying demons was coming through the ranks, pushing a human figure before it; a thin, bent caricature of a human.

Stefano.

The emaciated man stumbled along, shoved and half-carried by the demon. As he came nearer, the team could see that he still had a half-eaten energy bar clutched in one hand and tear streaks on his dirty face.

Lee looked up at the remorga, "What? How did you-"

"I know all here," it said, *"I see and hear everything. This one,"* it held a hand out at Stefano, *"shall serve as...a demonstration."*

"You bastard!" Bobby yelled, "He's done nothing!"

Remorga's eyes widened, *"I offer..."* it swiveled its head to Dan, *"salvation. A life eternal now...in me."*

Before Dan could answer, he was shoved aside as the flying demon pushed Stefano between them.

Stefano fell to the floor at the edge of the pit and his demon stood behind him, as much to prevent his escape as to keep the others from getting too close.

Stefano rose to his knees, almost gibbering in terror, speaking a torrent of Italian and English in desperation, "Aiutami, help me. Imploro, I cannot harm...non uccidere..."

His rolling eyes caught sight of Lee and the others, and he held his hands out to them, beseeching, "Aiutami! Aiutami! Not kill! Not come back-"

One of the remorga's enormous hands rose from behind Stefano and clamped down on his head. He collapsed to the floor and his voice suddenly cut off.

Lee tried to lunge forward, but the iron arm of Stefano's guard demon swung down, blocking him. Duke started forward from the other side, but the demon's wing snapped out, clipping him under the chin and sending him backward into Bobby.

The remorga raised its arm, pulling Stefano upright. Its hand completely covered Stefano's head.

Stefano started screaming, weak, muffled cries that sounded half-animal. His body shuddered, though his arms and legs went limp. He was like a rag doll being held upright by the head.

Suddenly the creatures all around them began chanting again as one, *"Remorga atma toma...Remorga atma toma...",* their combined voices echoing around the tower interior in a thrumming rhythm.

The team could still hear Stefano's muffled voice pleading for help inside the oily flesh covering his head, but his pleas were weakening.

It was over in seconds. Stefano's cries ended and his body stopped twitching. The remorga's hand released him and he dropped to the floor.

"Mentara," it commanded, *"Arise."*

Stefano slowly rose from the floor, his black eyes turned up, staring at the remorga blankly.

The remorga pointed back down the aisle between the demons, *"Saro. Go and feed."*

The Stefano thing turned slowly and started walking toward the exit to the tunnel, its unblinking eyes black pools in its pale face. It never even noticed Lee and the others clustered to one side as it shuffled by.

Lee ground his teeth in frustration. Another person – another soul – gone, consumed by this thing.

He whispered to Duke, "We have to stop this," he lowered his eyes and showed Duke the one bomb he still had attached to his equipment bag.

Duke's voice was heavy with hate, "I'm with you on that," he nodded and held up four fingers, indicating he still had four himself.

"Count of three and toss on my mark," Lee murmured.

"We're a bit close, boss."

Lee's mouth twisted, "No choice. You'd rather the alternative?"

Duke's answer was firm, "No fucking way."

"Everything he was, I now possess. He is with me," the remorga boomed, hand up at the retreating back of the Stefano thing, *"And now you shall be as well."*

Several of the nearest demons stepped forward, obviously tasked with herding the team toward the remorga.

"Wait," Lee said, "I need to know something."

"You will know all…with me."

"Indulge me," Lee glanced back at the others and saw Duke and Bobby ready, looking like runners set to dash. Behind them, Dan looked shell-shocked, and Brent was…slowly moving forward, a look of determination on his face.

Lee put his hands up, "Brent, what are you doing?"

He angled his head at Duke, who reached out and grabbed Brent's arm, "Hold on there, boss."

Brent whipped his head around at Duke and a look of confusion passed over his face, "Duke, let me go."

Duke hissed at him, "No fucking way. Just hold on."

Lee was acutely aware of the demons behind him, edging closer. He backed up a step, trying to keep his distance, and spoke up at the remorga, "Just tell me why you need to take minds? For what purpose?"

The orange eyes bored down at him, *"You will understand. Soon, all of your realm will understand."*

The words froze Lee to the spot, *All of our realm?* This thing was going to use their minds, their knowledge, to try and cross over to their world!

He thought about the two men from Endeavor, cooked inside and wandering aimlessly, just like Bill, Frank and now Stefano. He remembered the black smear they'd seen on the rig video and spoke, his voice loud with realization, "You sent…something through the barrier."

The remorga's eyes narrowed, *"An…emissary I sent, a small part of myself. I know that your kind can cross over but know nothing of how or why. You create doorways of your own. It has happened before, but yours is the nearest of those your kind has created. That one,"* its massive head inclined at the grinning Frank thing, *"had much information about this, but I must know more."*

"But you – part of you – were there. You achieved it, you crossed over."

"My...smaller self and my emissaries quickly severed their connection. I cannot communicate across the barrier, but your kind can. I will know how to do this."

Lee tried desperately to seek a way out, "But we use a...a technology to assist us! A technology that also does not function well here, just as your-"

The remorga commanded, *"Enough! Come to me!"* Its voice rattled their bodies.

It reached out toward him with its hand still high in the air and, as scared as he was, Lee suddenly realized something with a shock.

His eyes followed the remorga's body down to where it disappeared into the ground, *It's actually part of the pit! It can't move! It's stuck here, needing to use others to affect the world around it!*

Whether a god itself, or some higher being's servant, it needed others to be its eyes, ears, and legs. Did that mean that it directly controlled everything? Every demon around them? It said it saw and knew everything and it had apparently been able to track their movements, probably by using the flying creatures. It spoke myriad languages, likely gleaned from past victims, but its knowledge was not universal.

It had some strange power to absorb and control other creatures, but maybe it wasn't omnipotent – or immortal.

He felt the hands of a demon push up against his back and his feet slid across the stone toward the remorga. Resisting was useless. It would be like pushing back against a truck. He heard Duke and the others wrestling against the demons pushing them forward as well.

He yanked his bomb off his bag and yelled at Duke, "Now! Everyone down!"

He flashed a look back and saw Duke pushing Bobby down with his bad hand at the same time he was reaching into his bag. Brent and Dan were farther away, and Lee hoped it would be far enough.

He hit the button on his own bomb and counted to three, hoping that Duke had the same timing, then threw the grenade at the base of the remorga. At the same moment, he saw Duke's bomb sail over his shoulder at the body of the creature.

He closed his eyes and threw himself at the floor, wondering what it would feel like to die.

His helmet struck the stone at the same moment that the world turned to noise and heat around them.

Thirty-Two

THE TWIN BLASTS SENT THE team sliding back across the floor. They'd all hit the deck when Duke and Lee threw their grenades, but the concussions were like being hit with sledgehammers.

Most of the blast effects were absorbed by the semi-liquid body of the remorga and the rest went over their heads, burning through the ranks of demons and blowing even the sturdiest of them back. The few next to the remorga were torn apart, their black and yellow body parts pin-wheeling out from the center like heavy shrapnel, causing even more damage to those farther back.

Lee felt like his insides were shattered and he could hear only ringing, but as soon as his equilibrium returned, he pushed himself up to his feet, surprised at being able to do anything at all. The world was pitching and rocking, but he didn't know if it was just him, or if the tower was collapsing.

He saw Duke helping Bobby to his feet. Dan and Brent were picking themselves up farther away, but so were some of the demons close by.

Ears filled with singing cotton, he raised his rifle, flicked the switch to full auto and let loose with a barrage, whipping it back and forth over the team's heads. Every recoil sent a flash of pain through his pummeled body, but he kept his aim sweeping back and forth across the path back to the tunnel access they'd arrived through.

The creatures were all more than a head taller than even Duke, so the team members were safe, while the demons staggered under a hail of bullets to their faces and chests. Those than weren't knocked down immediately were driven back.

Duke and Bobby saw what he was doing and quickly added their own volleys to Lee's and together they began moving as fast as they could toward the exit. Brent appeared dazed and Dan seemed like he'd be little help, as he just stood in shock, staring back behind Lee in the direction of the remorga pit.

Duke grabbed Brent and Bobby ran up to Dan, shouting, "Dan! Help us, for Christ's sake!" He smacked Dan hard in the helmet and spun him around to face the exit.

Lee spared one glance back at the pit and saw through the smoke that the remorga appeared to be gone, though whether it had been vaporized in the blasts or had simply collapsed into the pit again was anybody's guess.

He didn't care at the moment. They'd given themselves a chance and they were going to take it.

Duke and Bobby were keeping the path to the door clear, yelling and firing as they went, with Bobby half-dragging Brent along with him. Lee kept up his own barrage on one side while Dan, who seemed to have recovered from his shock, swept his own rifle back and forth on the other.

The demons were in disarray with many still on the floor, while half the standing ones looked disoriented, not knowing which way to go. Lee hoped it was because their remorga was out of commission, giving them no guidance.

Several of the flying creatures abruptly shot up into the air from closer to the sides of the open space, but they too seemed confused. They didn't attack, but rather made straight for the higher apertures that led to the outside.

Lee saw them leave and he dared to raise his hopes a notch. He still couldn't hear much, but the steady, muted *chuk-chuk-chuk* sound of his own gun and its vibration through his body confirmed for him that he was still alive at least, *We might just do this.*

Then the Frank-thing reared up directly ahead of him. Its ruined eye still dribbled yellow down its pale face, but its black mouth was open impossibly wide in a hungry grin. Its enormous black body lunged forward with taloned hands reaching.

Lee just had time to raise his rifle. His finger clenched on the trigger, and he filled Frank's face with a volley that disintegrated it in a yellow spray. The black body collapsed backward, and Lee sent out a fervent hope that the scientist would be unable to come back again.

The path ahead was now clear, and they made it to the door without further resistance. Lee took a last look back before they exited.

Most of the demons seemed content to stay out of the way for the moment, but there was a mass of the walkers now by the pit. Some were looking down into it, but a few were staring at Lee and the others. The hatred in their orange eyes was palpable even from fifty feet away.

They team ducked through the door and Duke spun back with a bomb in his hand.

He clapped Lee on the shoulder, "Get running! These suits might've gotten us through one blast, but I don't want to test them again!"

He pushed Lee ahead of him, his voice sounding muffled to Lee's ears, "Just a reminder for these freaks not to follow us!"

Lee was going to say that they might need any bombs for later but figured it didn't matter much at this point. He saw Duke press the arming button and prepare to throw it.

"Run faster!" Lee spread his arms and herded the others ahead of him as Duke tossed the bomb back down the path toward the cluster of creatures by the pit.

A few seconds later the bomb went off, but the team were already several yards up the tunnel and the muffled blast merely vibrated the rock underfoot. They lurched and stumbled, but quickly started running full tilt again.

"How many you got left?" Lee asked.

"Only two."

"Better keep them."

"I plan to. If we end up fucked, I can still take us all out."

Duke said it with determination and Lee allowed that final gear of acceptance to turn over and click into place; if they couldn't make it out, they'd at least not end up like the others.

Still, it didn't hurt to run like your ass was on fire in the meantime.

They dashed and limped their way along the inclined tunnel, pushing, pulling, and sometimes dragging each other as best they could. Lee was on point and kept one eye on the path ahead and the other on the frequent gaps that opened onto the interior space they'd just fled.

He desperately wanted to take a look to see what was happening down there, but they couldn't spare even a second and he didn't want to see if the remorga had recovered, or worse, that an army of demons were flowing out the exit after them. He opted to assume the best, rather than witness the worst in this case.

Twenty seconds later they burst onto the landing of the wide tunnel they'd originally entered from. Lee automatically turned left at full speed in order to start down the gradual incline back to the plain outside but skidded to a sudden stop with a spike of adrenaline coursing through his body.

One of the two-headed behemoth demons – perhaps the one they'd originally seen – was blocking the tunnel twenty meters ahead.

It was facing away from them, but as they all clattered to a stop, it turned and saw them. Both mouths opened and it roared in stereo. Its four arms, each as thick as a man's body, spread wide, effectively blocking the entire tunnel, and it started toward them.

At the same moment, Duke opened up behind him, apparently aiming back down the tunnel behind them at pursuers. Lee knew their rifles would be useless against the giant and didn't want to use the remaining bombs – yet.

There was no way to go but up. It would at least buy them some time, though it might ultimately leave them trapped.

The behemoth roared again. As big as it was, it couldn't run even in the wide tunnel, but it was smashing its hands into the walls, clawing out chunks and pulling itself along faster.

Bobby had now joined Duke in firing back down the tunnel behind them, so obviously more demons were in pursuit.

"Come on!" Lee yelled and ran back into the sloped tunnel, heading left and continuing upward.

They all followed him, Duke and Bobby firing over their shoulders as they went.

A few seconds after they re-entered the narrower tunnel, the walls shook as the behemoth apparently ran straight into the tunnel behind them, smashing into the opposite wall. It was too large for the smaller space and couldn't follow them up.

Enraged, it stared flailing at the walls, knocking out boulder-sized pieces of stone, the debris and its own body acting like a plug in a bottleneck and blocking the pursuit of the smaller demons.

Duke was in the rear and saw what was happening, "That'll keep them off our tail for a few minutes!"

They could now shift their attention solely to the apertures that led to the interior space. Any of the flying demons could suddenly swoop in and attack them through any of those.

But they weren't.

Lee could see several of the flying creatures circling around inside, a few of them even at the level they were currently running in, but none seemed to be even interested in the team. They were just flying around erratically, still in a confused state.

He knew it couldn't last long, though. Even without the remorga's guidance, they'd eventually clue in to the location of the interlopers and come after the team.

And if the remorga wasn't out of the game yet…

He banished that thought and plowed ahead.

The tunnel curved slowly around the enormous interior space, slowly spiraling up through the levels. The slope was gentle, but they were basically running on an ever-upward circular ramp with a diameter of over fifty meters. It wasn't long before their exhaustion, injuries and the weight of their weapons had them all gasping and dizzy.

Dan was almost completely supporting Brent now. The CEO was pale and sweating heavily, more stumbling, than running. Lee knew they couldn't last much longer at this pace.

They unexpectedly emerged onto another landing, though this one was just a wide space in the tunnel. There were no passages leading off of it.

Lee made a patting motion with his hand, and they all staggered gratefully to a stop and listened.

The sounds of the demon mob below were gone. Maybe they'd given up. Lee now took the time to glance out of one of the apertures.

The floor level was far below. Surprisingly, they were already quite a distance up. The pit was a black circle the size of a coffee cup from here.

It made him even dizzier, and he leaned back, "I'd say we're halfway up."

Duke stuck his head out and looked up. The ever-present white haze was much closer, its demarcation easier to see against the interior walls of the tower, "Yep, but halfway up to what?"

He glanced down and stiffened, "Fuck me."

Lee jerked forward, "What?"

Duke pointed down, "They're getting their shit figured out."

Everyone moved to the aperture and looked down.

Demons were emerging from the lower openings and beginning to scale the interior walls, using their claws to gouge handholds in the rock. They moved from opening to opening, sticking their heads in for a look. They obviously didn't know where the team was, but they were going to catch up to them soon.

They all ducked their heads back in before they could be spotted.

"Break time's over," Duke hissed, "Move out."

They started limping upward again, now trying to be as quiet as they could.

Lee knew they'd never outrun them. The team took minutes to make one circuit around the tower, which would elevate them by about eight meters, while the demons could scale the same height in seconds if they wanted to. The only thing slowing the demons' progress was their constant stopping to check each opening in the wall.

His mind raced as they stumbled slowly upward, trying to find an option, hoping they'd find a place to hide or an alternate route down, but it seemed this tower was a ramp to nowhere.

The demons were going to overrun them, or they were all going to collapse and die from exhaustion.

It took Bobby half a minute more to figure it out, "Guy, guys," he panted.

"What?" Duke asked.

"We're idiots. We're…getting higher and higher…so the gases are changing…oxygen decreasing…"

Lee realized it too, "Jesus, you're right! Close helmets…and crank O2."

They all snicked their faceplates down and saw their heads-up displays all blinking red.

Lee hit his oxygen and it was like a splash of cool water on his face. It was suddenly easier to breathe, and he felt a jolt of energy enter his limbs.

Duke's voice came over the broadcast channel, "Oh damn, that tastes good."

"Should have realized it," Bobby said, "I feel so stupid."

"We all missed it," Lee said, "It was messing with our judgment. Let's go."

They charged ahead, not exactly feeling refreshed, but with renewed hope.

Another lap around, though, and their enthusiasm started to flag when their suits' external mics now picked up the sounds of claws skittering on stone.

The demons were closing in.

Despite the increased oxygen, they were all moving at barely a walking pace now, legs numb and muscles quivering from exertion.

Lee felt as if his lungs were on fire and wondered how Bobby with his injuries, and Brent with his illness, were managing to keep moving, let alone even stay on their feet.

But they were and that's all the mattered right now.

Until they rounded another curve and almost ran into the figure standing in the middle of the tunnel.

"Lee…Brent…"

The voice was gravelly and distorted, but recognizable.

Angeline.

Thirty-Three

SHE WAS CLAD ONLY IN her skin-tight bodysuit, her armor all stripped away. Her face was pale and slightly shrunken, but she still looked the same.

Until you gazed into the black pools that were her eyes.

Lee felt his heart twist. Until this point, despite what the remorga had said, he still held out hope that Angeline was still with them – still human.

But this travesty before them was as far from human as you could get; an empty husk drained of life, hollowed out.

Just like Bill and Frank.

"Leeeee…" it said again in that gravelly voice and slowly raised a hand to him.

He felt totally defeated. They'd risked everything to find her, and it was too late, probably always had been.

His hands dropped to his side, the muzzle of his rifle resting on the floor, "Angeline."

She smiled, an empty rictus more like a muscle spasm, a memory of what a smile was, *"Come…to me…Lee."*

He couldn't move.

Her brow furrowed slightly, a flicker of confusion crossing her waxen features, *"Lee…Lee…"*

It was the same metronome cadence that Bill had used in the cave, like an echo bouncing around inside the empty shell of her body.

Duke and Bobby had their rifles aimed at her, while Dan was staring at her with a look that could only be described as curiosity mixed with terror. Of all of them, he was having the hardest time dealing with everything, despite his beliefs.

Brent stepped forward between Lee and Duke, "Angeline? Are you in there?"

Her blank eyes didn't move, but everyone felt her attention shift, *"Brent...I am here,"* her head swiveled around to take in the landing, *"I am...with."*

Brent started to move toward her, "Angeline, come with us. You don't belong here. Only I-"

Lee grabbed Brent and stopped him from going further, "Brent, that isn't her. Angeline is gone. That's a...a thing, part of that creature down below."

Brent shook him off and backed up a step, "What do you know, Lee," his voice shook, "That's Angeline. Can't you feel it? She's still in there. If you loved her like I do you'd know it."

Duke put a hand on Brent's shoulder, "That ain't her, boss, any more than that other thing down there was Frank."

Brent smacked Duke's hand away and backed up, eyes wide, "Listen to yourselves! Have you lost your minds?" He pointed at the Angeline thing, "That's her! Look at her!"

The Angeline thing was standing motionless, watching them with the dry smile still stretching the skin of its cheeks, its black eyes glittering.

It shuffled forward a step, *"Brent...be with. You...love me."*

Brent lurched toward her, but Lee and Duke blocked his path.

Lee stared at Brent; *He's lost it. The stress and heat here with his disease.* He put a hand on Brent's chest, "Brent! I loved her too, but that's more of a corpse now than a person. It's a mass of cooked meat!"

Brent pushed away from them and raised his rifle, "Fuck you, Lee! You're insane!"

"Wait!" Lee thrust out a hand at Brent. He turned to the Angeline thing, "Where is your master, the remorga? Gone?"

It blinked slowly, *"Remorga…is here."* It brought up a hand and placed its fingers on its temple, *"Remorga is…with…watching."*

So it wasn't dead after all.

Lee grabbed Brent by both shoulders, his eyes boring into the CEO's, "Look at her. She's a fucking slave to that thing, Brent. Everything that she was is gone, scooped out and replaced with…something else."

The Angeline thing called out softly, *"Brent, be…with,"* it held out its hands, *"Live forever…with."*

Brent whispered into Lee's shoulder, "Yes…forever."

He shuddered and pushed away from Lee, his eyes suddenly clear with a look of determination, "Let me at least go to her. You guys can get away."

Lee had heard Brent's whisper and finally realized something. He gazed at Brent, not wanting to believe what he was thinking, but compelled to say it, "My God. That's it, isn't it? It's not about her at all, not about Angeline. You don't give a shit about her. It's about living forever."

Brent's eyes narrowed, but he at least looked a bit ashamed, "You don't know. I love her."

"I do know, Brent! I know about the MS. I know you're facing a death sentence."

"What?" Duke stared at them, "What MS?"

Dan also looked confused. Apparently, Brent had kept his illness away from everyone except those whom he needed to know.

Brent's shoulders sagged, but he shot a look like daggers at Bobby.

Lee said, "Don't blame Bobby. I noticed your symptoms and forced him to tell me. Bill said as much to me, too."

"What the hell is going on?" Duke demanded.

Lee gave Duke a grim smile, "I was wrong before when I said this whole dig was about the science or fame, Duke. It was really about…what, Brent, immortality? The chance to live forever, or at least long enough that it didn't make a difference?"

Brent suddenly nosed up to him, "Goddamn it, yes!" He spun away, body tight with fury, fists clenched at his sides, "It isn't fair! I worked my whole life – my whole goddamn life – to make myself, and then this company, something that would thrive and endure. And just when I'm on the verge of really achieving it, this happens!"

He spun back and thrust a shaking hand up at Lee's face. The fingers twitched uncontrollably.

Lee spoke more with sadness than anger or disappointment, "How did you..."

"Find out about this place?" Brent laughed, "It was there, on the tapes and documents that Angeline showed me, from the Russians and especially the Japanese. They sent people down – three men – and only one came back. He'd been gone for months, *months* Lee. He'd survived alone and came back barely sane, but he swore he'd only been gone a few hours! And his own chronometer backed him up!"

Brent took a deep breath, "I confess I was confused and disappointed when I first saw the images from down here. You remember, the images from the first cameras we sent down here. The demon we saw was moving around at what looked to be normal speed, not frozen into a slower time frame," his eyes took on a faraway look, "I almost gave up on it then, but Frank assured me there must be a time difference, one that was somehow rectified by the barrier. Some shit about electromagnetics and light speed."

He pointed upward, "Information could transit at normal speed – images and data, but physical objects, or maybe just organic things, were subject to the time difference. And then...and then Stefano told us as much, too."

"Stefano was confused, Brent; barely sane, barely aware of himself, let alone of how much time-"

Brent shook his head, "No, he may not have known how long, but you saw his clothes. You even mentioned it yourself."

He looked down at his own shaking hand, "Months for days, Lee, or even mere *hours*. Time; it's all about the *time*. I figured-"

Lee nodded and spoke in a sad voice, "You figured that, if you could find a way to stay here – to survive here – that you could hole up for what may only be weeks or months for you, while years or even decades passed on our side."

Brent said pleadingly, "We're so close, Lee. So much research has been done recently. It's a certainty that a cure will be found soon. If I stayed up top, I'd have maybe a year at the outside with my version of this fucking disease, but here...I just need-"

"Time," Lee said.

"That's all. Just...time."

Lee felt for the man, but he also felt a surge of anger and disgust, "And what about the rest of us, Brent? Those nine men on the rig, Bill, and Frank," he stabbed a hand back at the figure behind him, "Angeline? How can you think that any of this would be worth it in the end?"

"You don't understand, Lee. It's about living-"

Lee kept his hand aimed at the Angeline thing, his voice raw and hoarse, "You call that *living*, for Christ's sake? That's more of a death sentence than you've got!"

Brent brought up his other hand in a beseeching gesture, "But it wouldn't have to be that way, Lee, don't you see? If a deal could be made, an exchange of technology, culture-"

Duke was incredulous listening to Brent and thundered at him, "A deal? A fucking *deal*? Our friends all dead or turned into zombies because you want to live longer?" He made a fist with his good hand and shook it at the CEO, "God*damn* you to hell, Brent."

Dan stepped forward, "He may, in fact, have already done just that." He angled his head back down the tunnel.

They all listened.

Scrabbling and grunting sounds, very loud.

The demons were on their level now.

Everyone was suddenly in motion, weapons up. They started heading up the tunnel again, moving around the Angeline thing that was still standing in the middle of the landing, seemingly oblivious to everything.

Everyone except Lee and Brent, that is, who were still face-to-face in the middle of the landing.

The others stopped where the landing narrowed at the continuation of the upward tunnel and Bobby hissed back, "Come *on*, guys!"

Lee cast a glance at the Angeline thing. It was still standing like a statue with that stiff smile stretching its face – no, more like a recording unit, no doubt feeding everything it heard and saw straight back to the remorga.

It was watching them through her empty eyes. He could feel it.

He made to grab Brent's arm, "Let's go. There's nothing here."

Brent stepped away from him, his eyes clear and focused with decision, "No. You go on. Like I said, you guys can maybe get away. If the remorga is still here," he nodded at the Angeline thing, "with her, maybe I can negotiate with it."

"Brent! You can't negotiate with something like that. You can't stay here."

Brent gave him a sad smile, "After everything I've done to get here, maybe I have to."

For a fleeting moment, Lee thought of just grabbing Brent and yanking him along. Between him and Duke, they might manage to get their CEO farther up the tunnel, at least away from the Angeline thing.

He saw the determination solidifying in Brent's eyes, though, and gave up, "Brent, I...I don't..."

Brent reached a shaking hand into one of the compartments on the side of his armor. He pulled out a small, blue square of plastic, "Here, take this memory card. I have a copy with me at all times. Originals are on my computer at home."

"What is this?"

"The keys to the kingdom, Lee. You really always were the golden boy, you know; the roving prince."

He put the square in Lee's glove and pressed his hand closed, "Now you get a chance to be king."

He turned away and called out, "Angeline."

The Angeline thing jerked into motion and started toward him, *"Brent... be with,"* its arms came up like an automaton.

Lee stood rooted in confusion, until Duke hissed loudly behind him, "Lee! Let's go!"

He jerked his head around, "Coming."

"No more fucking around. I mean it."

"Right behind you," Lee turned away and looked back at Brent again as Duke and the others started up the tunnel. Their fading footsteps were drowned out by the sound of the approaching horde from the other direction.

Lee put the memory card into his own side compartment and backed away slowly, watching as Brent and Angeline came together on the landing. Behind them, the shadows of many capering figures swarmed over the walls of the tunnel as the demons closed in.

Brent's rifle clattered to the floor. He raised his shaking hands and put them on the sides of Angeline's white face. He pulled her close and Lee saw her lean into his shoulder, turning her pale face into the neck of his suit.

Her black eyes stared straight at Lee for several seconds. Then she opened her mouth impossibly wide, a black mouth filled with teeth that looked too large.

Before Lee could shout a warning, she bit deeply, right above the Kevlar, tearing out a piece of Brent's neck the size of a baseball.

Brent screamed in agony as she yanked her head away, strips of his under-suit fiber and muscle stretching and snapping apart. Blood fountained up to splash the ceiling and walls of the landing. Brent's knees buckled and his voice became an echoing gurgle.

Lee had backed up to the mouth of the tunnel. He jerked his rifle up and fired at them from the hip. Bullets ricocheted off Brent's armor and thunked into his Kevlar, weaving a line up his back to meet Angeline's face.

Dark holes appeared on her where the bullets struck, but she just swallowed what she'd taken and smiled widely at him, a real smile this time.

One that said, *You're next.*

She dropped the spurting body and, even as it slipped to the floor, she reached out to Lee with a dripping hand, *"Lee...be with."*

He spun around and raced after Duke and the others.

He didn't get very far before he heard the noise of the demon horde suddenly get louder behind him, their roars and grunts becoming almost deafening.

He knew they'd entered the landing he'd just left.

He glanced up and saw Duke's back disappearing around the next corner and put everything he had into not looking back and just running.

The others were struggling, and he caught up with them before they were even halfway up the next length of the tunnel.

He pounded up behind Duke, "They're right behind me."

"Thanks for the update."

286

Bobby and Dan were supporting each other, but Bobby was almost down to walking speed now.

Duke said, "Am I going to have to carry you again?"

"Fuck that," Bobby gasped and put on a little more speed.

They were going so slow that Lee could turn around and run backward, keeping an eye on the tunnel behind them.

As he did so, a skittering noise erupted beside him, and he threw himself against the opposite wall just as a long black arm shot through the opening he was passing. The claws scraped his helmet, knocking his head sideways and spoiling his aim as he brought his rifle up reflexively and squeezed the trigger.

Most of the rounds went into the wall next to the opening, but several punched into the chest and face of the attacking demon. It squealed and dropped away.

"Okay," Duke said in a loud voice, "They're all around us now. Circle the wagons."

The team slowed and clustered together. Putting their backs to each other, they kept moving at a walking pace, gasping for breath on shaking legs, rifles pointing outward. Lee and Duke faced back the way they'd come and saw that the tunnel was thick with the scrabbling bodies of demons surging toward them.

Far below, in the depths of the tower, and from the mouths of every demon in it, a deep, grating voice roared, seeming to rattle the foundations of the world, *"You...cannot...escape! All shall be...with me!"*

The remorga was back.

Dan unleashed a short burst at another demon trying to claw through the nearest opening and it fell away. Lee heard him reciting the Lord's Prayer again under the sound of the rifle. One more stuck its snarling head around the corner and Dan fired at it but missed as it ducked.

The mass of demons coming up behind were now only about twenty yards away and Duke muttered, "I think this is-"

Bobby was the only one looking ahead and interrupted him, "Hey, where are we? Is this a dead end?"

"What?" Lee looked ahead over his shoulder.

He couldn't see anything. He was looking at a featureless wall of white that stretched across the roof of the tunnel and cut diagonally down to the floor ahead of them.

A moment of confusion came over him; did they run all this way just to hit the ceiling? Take a wrong turn?

Then he realized the white he was looking at was a pure white, not the sandstone color of everything else. They'd made it right up to the level of the white haze that overhung the entire world they were in.

The tower punched through the haze right here.

Bobby leaned forward and stuck his rifle barrel up into the white. It cut off completely, like an invisible knife had cleaved it.

Just like the cable above them had when they'd arrived.

He pulled it out and examined it. It was whole again.

Duke fired back into the mass of black bodies closing in and frantically looked at Bobby, "What do you think?"

Bobby said, "Either this fog or those assholes," he angled his head at the demons, "I say the fog."

Duke and Lee unleashed a barrage of bullets at the demons, which were now only a few yards away, "Fine, go!"

"What if it doesn't go anywhere?"

"Let's go!" Lee shouted, "It doesn't matter now!"

He and Duke backed toward the white, pushing the others ahead of them while firing.

Suddenly, Dan turned and wrestled with the bag at Duke's side. He grabbed out the two remaining bombs and pushed between Duke and Lee before anyone could stop him.

He stepped beyond their reach and yelled over his shoulder, "Go! I'll hold them off!"

Lee made to go after Dan, but Duke grabbed his shoulder and pulled him back.

Lee yelled, "Dan! Come with us!"

Dan shouted back, "No! I belong here! Maybe you think you don't, but I know I do! We all have a destiny, and this is mine!" he shot a burst one-handed into the approaching horde.

Lee yelled again, "Dan! Don't!"

Dan ignored him. He tossed his rifle away and held both bombs up above his head, fingers on the buttons, "I bring almighty *God* here with me!"

Duke and Bobby had ahold of Lee's arms and dragged him back with them. Lee saw Dan hit the switches on both bombs before they pulled him back into the white with them.

Dan walked forward toward the mass of approaching demons, counting in his head as he spoke out loud,

One – "The Light of God surrounds me,

Two – The Love of God enfolds me,

Three – The Power of God protects me,

Four – The Presence of God watches…"

The closest demons pounced as everything turned to white heat.

He never got to five.

Thirty-Four

LEE TURNED AROUND AS SOON as his head slipped into the white – surprised that everything instantly became black. There was no time to wonder about it, though, as he knew they had only seconds before the bombs went off.

He couldn't see anything, but he could feel Duke's and Bobby's hands on him. He pushed them ahead of him, not knowing if they were safe, or poised on the edge of a precipice in the dark, but he could still feel a surface under his feet. He wasn't sure if his lower half was still in the tunnel or if this was some new surface.

He only knew they had mere seconds and shouted, "Run!"

The three of them dashed into the darkness, seeing nothing and just hearing each other's breath and footsteps. They only got a few steps away before a wave of pressure hit them in the back like a gust of wind, but it wasn't enough to even knock them off their feet and quickly faded as they ran further into the dark.

After a few more seconds it became apparent that the blast, if it even happened, wasn't going to get this far.

Lee called out, "Stop. I think we're okay."

They slowed and bumped against each other coming to a stop. A spear of light shot out from Bobby's suit, arrowing away into the dark.

Duke and Lee hit their lights too, but the only things they illuminated were each other. Everything around them stayed black.

Duke aimed his light downward and its beam showed them nothing, "Can't even see the floor. It's like we're standing on air."

Lee shook his head and tapped the side of his helmet. Their voices sounded strange, as if they were in a confined space like a small closet, though the blackness around them obviously extended quite far into the distance.

He panned his light around, "Feels weirdly like we're inside something."

"The same as when we were in the borehole coming down," Bobby said, "Our lights don't show anything at all, yet it feels bounded somehow."

"What is this place, then," Duke asked, "some kind of limbo or something?"

Lee slowly panned his light around again, watching its beam dwindle into seeming infinity in every direction, "I think it's the actual barrier. We're still inside it."

"I don't feel anything, though," Bobby said, "The first time it felt like my guts were being twisted."

"We're not all the way through it yet," Lee said, "Remember, we hit the shimmer first and that's where we felt shitty."

"Well where the fuck is the shimmer?" Duke asked, "How the hell will we find it in here? Our lights don't show anything," he turned in a circle.

It was impossible to tell which way they'd come from, or which way they were facing. Lee tried to recall if he'd changed direction since arriving, or if he was still basically facing the same way.

He shone his light straight out from his chest, "I think all we can do is head forward and see where we end up. What do you think?"

Bobby shrugged, "As good a plan as any, I guess, as long as we don't end up going back to the tower."

Lee started walking and the others followed, "I don't think we'd be able to get back into it anyway. I saw Dan hit the buttons on the bombs just before you guys pulled me through."

"And then we felt that wind or whatever," Bobby said.

Lee went on, "And in that narrow tunnel, the blast would have probably pulverized everything in it and collapsed the ceiling and walls around the entry point, which is maybe why nothing's come through after us."

"Didn't seem like much of an explosion, though," Duke said, "and we couldn't have been more than a few yards from it."

Lee had a sudden thought; he'd wondered about the same thing, "I think it's the time thing."

"Come again?" Duke said.

"If we exited that frame of time as soon as we crossed over, it's possible that the bombs did go off right next to us, but because of the time difference, we're now moving too fast. The blast is so slowed down relative to us that it's probably still expanding on the other side of the...line or whatever."

Duke murmured, "So Dan may not even be dead yet."

It was a sobering thought that Lee hadn't considered. Even as they spoke, Dan might be in the process of being torn apart – a process that might take hours or even days from their perspective.

They walked on a few steps in silence, their lights spearing out into an otherwise empty universe, then Bobby asked, "Why did he do it?"

Lee shook his head, "I don't know. He seemed convinced that he had to stay, that he was consigned to Hell for reasons known only to him – whoa!"

Bobby was slightly ahead of Duke and Lee and suddenly disappeared in a blinding flash of purplish-white light.

Half a pace behind him, Duke and Lee went through the shimmer without seeing it. Their lights had all been aimed at the invisible ground before them.

Lee felt his insides curl up again and a low rumble started in his ears, climbing rapidly to a high shriek before cutting off abruptly. Vertigo took hold and he stumbled forward, not even aware that he was falling.

Until his hands hit the ground under him and scraped across a pebbly surface. If he hadn't still been wearing gloves, he'd have left skin behind.

He heard retching and realized it was coming from him – and from the others as well. Duke and Bobby's hacking was coming over the suit radio.

He managed to keep his stomach down and rolled over onto his back. His head was throbbing, and his pulse was pounding so hard he expected to feel blood coming from his nose and ears.

Bobby coughed and rasped, "Water...deep breaths."

Duke couldn't hold it down and Lee heard him snap open his helmet at the same time he let loose with a rattling dry heave.

He gasped, "Damn, haven't eaten anything. Only some spit."

Lee looked over and saw Duke on all fours, "You okay?"

Duke waved, "Settling down now."

"Hey," Bobby said in a dry voice, "I can *see* shit!"

Lee realized he could too. Their lights were illuminating dark walls around them. He looked down and saw a stone floor dusted with sand and gravel. He aimed his light up and there was a ceiling only ten feet above them.

He snapped his faceplate open, "We're in a cave or a room of some kind," he said.

"But are we home, though?" Bobby said.

Duke spat again, "Helmet's open and I'm breathing fine. Air is cool."

"We can't be back, "Bobby said, "unless there are rooms like this eight kilometers underground. This isn't the borehole."

Lee got slowly to his feet, "We were at least a mile or two from our borehole. This must be something else. Let's find out."

They helped each other up and looked around. Immediately behind them, there was a perfectly square black opening on the wall about three meters on a side. Their lights played across its surface, showing them silvery ripples, like a pool of oil or water on the floor.

"Well that's the shimmer thing, I guess," Duke said.

Bobby pointed at it, "Wait, that doesn't work."

Lee looked at him, "What do you mean?"

"The geometry doesn't work. Our borehole barrier was horizontal. This one is vertical. If the brane is like a single sheet that cuts through the Earth-"

Duke snorted, "You just walked through a door from one dimension to another after escaping a world full of fucking demons and you're complaining about the *geometry*?"

Bobby shrugged, "It just seems weird, that's all."

Lee glanced back at the pool, "None of this makes any sense to me, but let's worry about it after we get out of here."

They aimed their lights away from the barrier and saw that they were at the end of a long corridor. They shuffled forward, scanning the walls, ceiling, and floor with their lights. It was as black as being inside the barrier, only now the beams flashed across gray stone no matter where they looked.

Lee found it immensely relieving to see the gray. It wasn't the black of the barrier, nor the sandy color of the tower and for that he was grateful.

"Look at the walls," Bobby said.

"Huh?" Lee stepped closer to the wall on his left and peered at it, "What is it?"

Bobby was already examining the wall on his side, "Pictures all over the place. Shine your light at an angle."

Lee turned slightly so his light hit the wall obliquely. Figures seemed to jump out of the stone, shallowly etched so they were the same color and were only visible if the light was at an angle.

The corridor was filled with carvings of figures that would look vaguely human if you didn't examine them too closely. If you looked closer, they'd resemble insects, but Lee and the others knew better.

Demons.

Images of demons mixed with those of strange, distorted skulls – human skulls, but stretched and elongated, with staring empty eyes. The walls were covered with them.

"Holy shit," Duke whispered, "What is this place, their bathroom or something? Are we going to see the equivalent of 'Debbie gives good head' in demon-speak?"

"No, look," Lee said, "The carvings are all at our height – human height - or lower. If demons carved these, there'd be a lot up above us, right?"

"You think…" Bobby started.

"I think we're back home…and in a place where people know about the barrier and the demons."

"Only one way to find out," Duke aimed his light ahead and they all saw stone stairs leading upward.

"Are you kidding me?" Bobby muttered, "We're going to climb *miles* of stairs?"

"Let's hope not," Lee said, "but even if it is, I'll be happy to do it as long as we're home."

"I have broken ribs, don't forget," Bobby complained, "I can hardly breathe as it is."

Duke held his arm up, "And I have a busted wing myself, so I can't carry your whining ass up there. You'll have to do it alone."

Bobby shuffled past him, "Don't say 'wing' at me anymore. After those flying black fucks, I'll certainly never eat buffalo wings again."

Duke started after him, "Don't say 'black fucks' at me either; I might take offense."

They started helping each other up the stairs with Lee behind them.

It turned out they didn't have to go up very far. The stairs switched back and forth seven times and Lee figured they'd gone up only about the equivalent of a few stories when they came to a landing and faced a blank wall.

"Shit, we must have missed a turn or another set of steps or something," Duke groaned. He hit the wall with a fist in frustration and turned away.

Bobby put out a hand to stop him, keeping his light aimed at the wall, "Wait! Look."

They all moved closer and peered at the wall.

Duke had made a crack in it.

Lee said, "This isn't stone. It's even a different color."

Bobby rapped the surface with the armored part of his glove and left a deep scratch in it, "It's like adobe or something!"

Duke turned back, "Well let's have at it, then!" He pounded a fist into the wall and a piece of it the size of his hand fell out.

They used their gloved hands and rifle butts to gouge and hammer at the wall, knocking out chunks that fell to the floor in clouds of dust. The wall wasn't very thick, and they'd carved a man-sized hole in minutes.

Bobby and Lee aimed their lights through the hole, illuminating another space with a stone wall about two meters away, opposite the hole.

Duke stuck his head in and looked around. His voice echoed, "It's another tunnel, but I can see light!"

He leaned back and his face was split with a wide grin, "There's light down that way!" he pointed left.

Bobby flicked a hand at the hole, "What are you waiting for, an invitation? Let's go!"

They each pulled themselves through the hole and looked around the new tunnel. It was gray stone, like the one they'd been in down below, but the walls and floor glistened in their lights and there was definitely a strong light source illuminating the tunnel in one direction.

Lee touched the damp wall, "We must be close to the surface."

"We sure are," Duke said, "Feel that humidity?"

With their helmets open, it was easy to tell that it was quite humid now. The tunnel far below them and the stairs leading up had been cooler and drier, but now that they'd broken through, the air felt clammy on their faces.

They made their way toward the light, unconsciously walking faster as they neared it. The darkness of the barrier and the tunnels was disconcerting, and they were feeling an almost visceral need for light.

They reached the end of the tunnel and found a small room that was open to the outside on one wall. The open side showed them a view of a green hill in the middle distance and what looked like dense jungle beyond.

There was a breeze, but the humidity and heat were high, though it was nowhere near as hot as it had been down below. Lee checked his readout and saw that the atmosphere was exactly what it should be for Earth and that the temperature was thirty-four Centigrade, or about ninety Fahrenheit.

A wooden barrier was halfway across the tunnel exit, and they gingerly stepped over it and opened their suit helmets.

"Smells like a jungle, that's for sure," Duke said, "and I'm getting a hint of…diesel."

"Look at this," Bobby said, pointing back at the low barrier.

Their lights shone on the words, 'Entrada Prohibita.'

"Spanish," Lee murmured. He started for the open side of the room, "Let's find out where we are."

They stepped out into intense sunlight and gazed up at a crystal blue sky.

"Man that looks good," Duke said.

They looked around and saw that they were on the side of a small hill. The room they'd exited from was set into the hill and stone steps led down to ground level where there was a gravel parking lot and an old bus bearing a sign that said 'Cholula Tours'.

"I don't think we're in Africa anymore guys," Bobby said.

They went down the steep stairs, aware that they were attracting attention from the passengers on the bus. A dozen faces were plastered across its windows.

"We probably look like robots in these," Lee said and twisted off his helmet.

Duke and Bobby took theirs off too as they stepped onto the gravel. Duke looked back at the steps and pointed out a sign, "Look."

Bobby read it out loud, "Piramide Tlachihualtepetl, Instituto Nacional de Antrolpologia e Historia. We definitely aren't in Africa. This is Mexico."

"What? How can that be?" Duke asked incredulously, "We started out in Tanzania and never went more than a mile or two the whole time we were down there."

Lee spoke thoughtfully, "I'm guessing that geography and distance are as different there as time is. Frank said the barrier between branes could extend all through the Earth and be of varying depths. I guess the short distance we walked there somehow ended up being a couple thousand miles here and the barrier is only a few meters below the surface."

He took out his smartphone and hit the power. It took a second, but the phone found a signal and locked on, "Look at the date. It's the sixteenth of April. We went through the barrier on the second of March. Almost seven weeks have gone by up here while we were across the barrier for..." he checked his suit chronometer, "only about six hours."

"Jesus Christ," Duke muttered, "Then Stefano may really have been there for decades."

Lee said quietly, "And Brent was right."

They stood in the heat for a few seconds, trying to make sense of the time and distance discrepancies.

Duke gave up first and looked up to the top of the hill above the room they'd exited. Another thirty meters up it ended in what looked like a pyramidal apex. There appeared to be a building surmounted by a cross perched up there.

A Christian church.

He said, "Hey, this is one of those giant Central American pyramids, I bet!"

Lee added, "And it's right over an access point to the barrier. How much you want to bet that's not a coincidence?"

"You're thinking it's not," Bobby said.

Lee shook his head, "I'm betting a lot of places of religious significance are situated near access points. Maybe those towers down there serve as links to this world."

"That would explain a lot," Duke said, "like how so many religions share pretty similar images of demons and Hell. Maybe they all know something about it."

Bobby nudged Duke's elbow, "And thousands of people have kept silent about it through the centuries? Naw, people talk, but I'll bet it's all been forgotten, at least by most."

Lee was quiet for a moment, lost in thought.

Bobby prodded him, "What's on your mind?"

"Just thinking."

Duke put a hand up, "Don't say it. I just want to take a shower and have a beer."

Lee turned to him, "You remember what the remorga said."

"I'm trying not to."

"It said it was a servant to a higher being over there or something like that, so it may not even be the most powerful thing on that side. And it also said it wanted to learn more about us, about our world. It tried to send agents over here."

"Yeah," Duke said slowly, "so you're saying..."

"I'm saying it isn't dead yet and I think it has plans, or its boss does."

"Plans for what?" Bobby asked.

"Maybe plans to move over here...to our side. We can't allow that."

"So you want to..." Bobby trailed off.

Lee nodded, "We have to stop it."

Duke blurted, "How the hell are we going to do that? *Our* boss is dead, everyone at Endeavor probably thinks we are too because we've been gone for seven weeks, we're half a world away from where we started out and even my wallet's on another continent."

Lee reached into his suit compartment and pulled out the small container with the memory card. He held it up and looked at it.

"What's that? Bobby said.

Lee turned the blue case over in his fingers, not really seeing it, thinking about Angeline, Bill, Frank, Dan, Brent, Stefano and who knew how many lost, wandering people down through the centuries.

A mixture of anger and sadness burned inside him. It rumbled behind his eyes, overriding his fears about what he was contemplating. He knew he had to do something, both to avenge all the people who had suffered – and were still suffering - in that other realm. And he also felt they had to do what they could to prevent a looming Armageddon if the remorga followed through with its plan to cross over.

He focused on the blue case and answered Bobby, his jaw set and his eyes narrowed, "I'm not sure yet," he looked at them both, "and I don't want you guys to think I'm dragging you into-"

Duke interrupted him, "Are you kidding? You just get us taped up and showered and we'll be ready to go again, right?" He nodded at Bobby.

Bobby grinned and nodded back, "Just say the word, Boss."

Lee carefully put the card back in his suit compartment, "Thanks guys," he inclined his head at the buses in the parking lot, "Let's at least see if we can bum a ride to the nearest town first. We've got a lot of work ahead of us."

Afterward

SOMETIMES IDEAS FOR STORIES COME to you as a package. You look at something, hear something, get a flash of memory or a dream, and it's enough to start the ball rolling. You say "Aha!" and know where it starts and where it ends, who the characters are peopling it and many of the events that need to unfold to make it come out all right. The fingers on the keyboard are just playing along in time as the story is unspooling in your head.

Other times, you cobble stories together from strips of thought-cloth, laboriously weaving them together, blending the colors and fabrics of ideas into tapestries to tell your tale. You have a storehouse of material lying around just waiting to be used and one day it happens; something shines a light on it all and you can see how this bit folds around that one, this one backs onto that other, and so on.

This story is one of the latter. It coalesced over time from a collection of memories, articles, TV programs and even conversations I've had all jumbled together in my head like the stuff in grandma's steamer trunk in the attic.

The kernel of it was my work four decades ago in Northern Canada as an air-ambulance medic on drilling rigs for a few winters. Those memories are still stark and loom large, mostly because drilling is dangerous work and I saw some awful stuff and had some weird experiences that I've carried with me through the years since. In fact, they figure in another story I started long ago, but have shelved for the time being.

For the science of the story – the deep drilling and the dimensional membrane stuff – one is fact, and the other is theory. The Kola SuperDeep Borehole is a fact. Scientists and engineers did drill a 12.5 km deep hole into the earth on the Russian Kola Peninsula back in the 70s and 80s, stopping only when they encountered the temperature and technical problems mentioned in here. Other various scientific, industrial, or commercial bores have gone down almost as far over the years in a few spots around the world, though none have reported the sorts of problems our guys encountered in here.

Frank Arden's Dimensional Brane stuff is strictly theory and, depending on which physicist you ask, is either valid or bunk. For my purposes it's valid and Frank's explanations of it in this story are the limit of my own understanding as well, so don't go sending me angry emails if I've misrepresented the theory here.

As to the idea of Hell possibly being a physical place that living humans can explore, I kind of owe that to an old friend of mine who is a deep believer in the Catholic vision of Hell. I am not a believer at all, and we've had several debates about religion over the years where I expressed my worry for him about his fears of perhaps spending time there when he 'retires' from the mortal realm. It causes him some anxiety, but if you're Catholic you know what I'm talking about.

In one of our talks he briefly mentioned the idea that perhaps Hell, as well as other versions of reality, resides in one of the multiple dimensions that science conjectures about these days and that thought stayed with me. Add it to the idea of a deep-drill project and membrane theory and suddenly you have a story, at least as far as I'm concerned.

Like most of the stories I write, I started this one years ago, but only wrote the first chapter just to clear it out of my head. I find that if I do that, I can move on to complete other ideas that may be more fully formed and come back to finish it later without having lost the original inspiration.

During the time between then and now, I checked with another old friend in the oil industry about the current state of drilling, since my own meager knowledge is 40 years out of date, and did the rest of the story between the dates you see tagged on at the end. I had just finished the horror novella *Whiteout* and the writing muse was still hunched on my shoulder, so I immediately dove back into this one.

Now that it's done, I need to finish one or two other books I have waiting in grandma's trunk, before hopefully getting back to another installment of my Silk Road adventure series.

My thanks to Henry Bugler and Ken Scott for their arm's-length contributions over the years, Henry for the inspiration and Ken for checking some details. He only ran his eyes over the first chapter to check my suppositions about modern drilling, so everything after that will no doubt be a big surprise to him.

CASTLE BRIDGE MEDIA RECOMMENDS...

If you liked this book, you might also enjoy reading the following titles from Castle Bridge Media available on Amazon or by order at your favorite book store:

Animal Charmer
By Rain Nox

Austinites
By In Churl Yo

Bloodsucker City
By Jim Towns

THE CASTLE OF HORROR
ANTHOLOGY SERIES
Volume 1
Volume 2: *Holiday Horrors*
Volume 3: *Scary Summer*
Stories
Volume 4: *Women Running*
From Houses
Volume 5: *Thinly Veiled:*
The 70s
Volume 6: *Femme Fatales**
Volume 7: *Love Gone Wrong*
Volume 8: *Thinly Veiled:*
The 80s
Volume 9: *Young Adult*
Volume 10: *Thinly Veiled:*
Saturday Mournings
Edited By Jason Henderson
and In Churl Yo
*Edited By P.J. Hoover

Castle of Horror Podcast
Book of Great Horror:
Our Favorites, Top Tens
and Bizarre Pleasures
Edited By Jason Henderson

Dream State
By Martin Ott

Dominic
By Lee Guzman

FRENCH DECEPTION
A Forgery in Paris
By Janice Nagourney
A Forgery in Lyon
By Janice Nagourney

FuturePast Sci-Fi Anthology
Edited by In Churl Yo

GLAZIER'S GAP
Ghosts of the Forbidden
By Leanna Renee Hieber

Hellfall
By Jay Gould

Isonation
By In Churl Yo

JAYU CITY CHRONICLES
The Hermes Protocol
By Chris M. Arnone
Necropolis Alpha
By Chris M. Arnone

Junk Film: Why Bad
Movies Matter
By Katharine Coldiron

MID-LIFE CRISIS THRILLERS
18 Miles From Town
By Jason Henderson
Lost Angel
By Sam Knight
Ties That Kill
By Deven Greene

Nightwalkers:
Gothic Horror Movies
By Bruce Lanier Wright

THE PATH
The Blue-Spangled Blue
By David Bowles
The Deepest Green
By David Bowles

SURF MYSTIC
Night of the Book Man
By Peyton Douglas
Dark of the Curl
By Peyton Douglas

Yesterday's Tomorrows:
The Golden Age of
Science Fiction Movies
By Bruce Lanier Wright

Please remember to leave us your reviews on Amazon and Goodreads!

THANK YOU FOR SUPPORTING INDEPENDENT PUBLISHERS AND AUTHORS!

castlebridgemedia.com

Milton Keynes UK
Ingram Content Group UK Ltd.
UKHW010741080324
438959UK00004B/298